TRIANGLE OF DEATH

Michael Levine

Laura Kavanau

Delacorte Press

Published by
Delacorte Press
Bantam Doubleday Dell Publishing Group, Inc.
1540 Broadway
New York, New York 10036

Library of Congress Cataloging in Publication Data
Levine, Michael.
    Triangle of death / Michael Levine, Laura Kavanau.
        p.   cm.
    ISBN 0-385-31475-2 (hc)
    I. Kavanau-Levine, Laura.   II. Title.
    PS3562.E8979T7   1996
    813'.54—dc20   95-50361
                                                                        CIP

Manufactured in the United States of America
Published simultaneously in Canada
Book design by Susan Maksuta

August 1996

10   9   8   7   6   5   4   3   2   1

BVG

In loving memory of
Sergeant Keith Richard Levine,
New York City Police Department,
killed in the line of duty
11/11/64—12/28/91

ACKNOWLEDGMENTS

A heartfelt thanks to our agent, Kim Witherspoon, for her inspiration and creativity, and to our editor, Steve Ross, for his enthusiasm and X-ray vision.

Thanks to researcher Stacy van Gorder, Paul Winters, and to City Marshal Mel Moser; our friends Richard Stratton and Kim Wozencraft for their generosity, Ellen Winn Wendl, Nancy Harris, Jackie Williams, Sandy Teller, Danny Lehner and In-flight Newspapers, Inc., Kevin Behan and Canine Arts. Thanks to Jeanne Bresciani for her insight into the myth of the hero.

Thanks to the Holocaust Museum Research Center, the Stone Ridge Library, the UCCC Library, the Clove Valley Cafe, and the Egg's Nest.

We would also like to thank our families on both coasts and in Israel for their patience and encouragement.

A special thanks from Michael to the currently serving undercover agents who, at great risk to their careers and pensions, defied the DEA suits' written order against contacting him and made valuable contributions to the writing of this book.

And an extra special thanks to *Sensei* Chuck Merriman, whose life is the essence of Bushido.

TO THE READER

Although this book is a work of fiction, it is inspired by a combination of real cases and events that occurred during Michael Levine's twenty-five-year career as a deep cover agent for DEA (U.S. Drug Enforcement Administration).

Congressional hearings held during April 1992 found that there is among many federal agencies the "appearance of cover-up" for all their misdeeds. Owing to secrecy laws created by these same federal agencies, plus the fact that many of the real criminals involved were on the payroll of covert agencies of various countries (including the CIA) and protected from prosecution, the truth behind many of the events that are the fabric of this book will never be revealed.

Deep Cover *is an undercover assignment in which the operative completely abandons the protection of his official identity and adopts a new one as a criminal, isolating himself in the dominion and complete control of his target. This type of assignment is rare in law enforcement and even rarer in overseas operations, where exposure will almost always be fatal.*
—Drug Enforcement Administration lecture on undercover

If I attack, follow me.
If I flee, kill me
If I die, avenge me.
—*anonymous* sensei, goju *school of karate*

TRIANGLE OF DEATH

DOCUMENT CONTROL NUMBER

DEPARTMENT OF JUSTICE
DRUG ENFORCEMENT ADMINISTRATION

CLASSIFIED MATERIAL

Cover Sheet

- THE CABLE -

XCZM08053 12390314
O 071910X DEC
FM: DEA HQ WASH. D.C.

TO: DEA WORLDWIDE.

TOP SECRET -TSD-TSEC353-0012-0011-NOFORN- NIACT-
IMMEDIATE

ALL EMBASSIES AND AMERCONSULS PASS TO: DEA C/A NIACT
IMMEDIATE

AMEMBASSY BUENOS AIRES PASS TO CA LEVINE - NIACT
IMMEDIATE

REF: DANGEROUS NEW DRUG ALERT (HQCO - S/A
R.STRATTON)

SUBJ: OPERATION: SOURCE "REINA BLANCA" - HQ-TS-1164
1V1-C1

ENTIRE TEXT CLASSIFIED TOP SECRET

1. A NEW DRUG, HAS BEEN APPEARING ON STREETS CONUS,
THUS FAR IN LIMITED QUANTITIES. HQ SCPD HAS RATED AS
"MAJOR THREAT TO NATIONAL SECURITY."

2. STREET NAMES: "LA REINA BLANCA" "WHITE QUEEN" "CUM-
BOMB" "NIRVANA" "WHITE GODDESS" "SUPER O"

3. PHYS EFFECTS: USERS REPORT THAT DRUG SIMULATES IN-
TENSE AND PROLONGED SEXUAL ORGASM, LASTING 10 TO 20
MINUTES. THERE IS, IN SEVERAL REPORTED CASES, IMMEDI-
ATE ADDICTION, AND COMPULSIVE INGESTION UNTIL USER
ODS.

DRUG INHIBITS SEROTONIN PRODUCTION AND/OR RECEP-
TORS, WHICH ARE USUAL INHIBITORS OF VIOLENT BEHAVIOR.
SOME USERS HAVE EXHIBITED EPISODES OF VIOLENT BEHAV-
IOR, ACCOMPANIED BY WHAT HAS BEEN DESCRIBED AS
"SUPER-HUMAN STRENGTH" AND/OR CONVULSIONS. EX-
TREME CAUTION MUST BE EXERCISED IN HANDLING ALL
CASES OF SUSPECTED USE.

(PAGE 1 OF 3)

AUTOPSIES OF OD VICTIMS WITH HISTORY OF SHORT TERM USAGE, HAVE REVEALED INDICATIONS OF ADVANCED ORGAN DAMAGE, OF A TYPE NORMALLY FOUND IN HARDCORE ADDICTS OF MANY YEARS. PRELIMINARY INDICATIONS ARE THAT SHORT TERM USAGE MAY LEAD TO IRREVERSIBLE AND PROGRESSIVE CONDITION. STUDIES THIS AREA ARE CONTINUING . . .

4. LAB TESTS: TESTS THUS FAR INDICATE THAT SUBSTANCE IS UNDETERMINED PERMUTATION OF COCAINE HYDROCHLORIDE, WITH EXTREMELY LOW PURITY. SMALL QUANT RETRIEVED FROM BODY OF USER IN LA INCIDENT INDICATES 5% PURITY.

TOP SECRET - NIACT IMMEDIATE - TOP SECRET

5. STREET TEST: CI REPORTS INDICATE THAT STREET TESTS ALSO SHOW LOW PURITY COCAINE; CRACK ADDICTS USED TO TEST AND VERIFY DURING STREET PURCHASES.

6. SOURCE: UNKNOWN AT THIS TIME. POL R ASSETS INDICATE THAT SOURCE MAY BE MEDELLIN CARTEL. UNCONFIRMED.

7. AVAILABILITY: DRUG HAS APPEARED IN EXTREMELY SMALL QUANTITIES, AND FOR SHORT DURATION, IN MIAMI, LOS ANGELES, NEW YORK, DETROIT, MONTREAL AND PARIS. CI INFORMATION INDICATES THAT NO MORE THAN OZ QUANTITIES SOLD. CURRENT BELIEF IS THAT DUE TO UNKNOWN PRODUCTION DIFFICULTIES DRUG CANNOT BE MASS PRODUCED AT THIS TIME.

8. REQUESTED ACTION:

ALL SACS, RACS, CAS ARE ORDERED TO CONTACT ALL SOURCES OF INFORMATION, ASAP, TO MAKE CAUTIOUS–REPEAT–CAUTIOUS INQUIRIES AS TO AVAILABILITY AND SOURCE OF NEW DRUG, WITHOUT–REPEAT–WITHOUT DIVULGING ANY INFO THIS TELEX.

SOURCES OF INFO, CIS, ETC., ARE TO BE QUESTIONED, IN GENERAL, ABOUT ANY NEW DRUGS ON SCENE. SOURCES SHOULD SUPPLY INFORMATION. EXTREME CAUTION SHOULD BE EXERCISED IN NOT REVEALING CURRENT INFO, AS, ACCORDING TO

SCPD STUDIES, ANY PUBLICITY WILL ONLY ENHANCE AL-
READY GROWING DEMAND, AND ADD IMPETUS TO MASS PRO-
DUCTION.

AREAS WHERE DRUG HAS APPEARED, EVEN FOR PERIODS AS
BRIEF AS SEVERAL DAYS, DRUG RELATED HOMICIDES AND
OTHER DEATHS, COMMERCIAL CRIME, ADDICTION RATES,
ODS, HOSPITAL EMERGENCIES HAVE INCREASED AS MUCH AS
300 PERCENT.

SCPD FORECASTS INDICATE THAT THE CATASTROPHIC EF-
FECTS OF THE INTRODUCTION OF "LA REINA" IN COMMER-
CIAL QUANTITIES, ON CONUS STREETS, CANNOT BE OVER-
STATED. <u>DEA HAS BEEN DIRECTED BY SECURITY COUNCIL,
EXERCISE ANY MEANS NECESSARY IN DETERMINING AND
NEUTRALIZING SOURCE–REPEAT–DEA DIRECTED BY SECU-
RITY COUNCIL, EXERCISE ANY MEANS NECESSARY IN DETER-
MINING AND NEUTRALIZING SOURCE.</u>

INVESTIGATION CONSIDERED, AT THIS TIME, DEA'S HIGHEST
PRIORITY. POL R HAS BEEN DIRECTED TO LEND FULL COOP-
ERATION AND RESOURCES.

TOP SECRET - NIACT IMMEDIATE - TOP SECRET

ALL RACS, SACS, CAS, ALSO REQUESTED TO POLL ALL SPAN-
SPEAKING AGENTS THEIR COMMAND AS TO AVAILABILITY
FOR DEEP COVER AND UC ASSIGNMENTS THIS INV.

BE ADVISED, A DEEP COVER PROBE OF SEVERAL MONTHS IS
ALREADY UNDER WAY IN SA. ALL INFORMATION UNCOVERED
SHOULD BE SENT VIA NIACT IMMEDIATE CABLE, THIS FILE
TITLE, DIRECT TO OFFICE OF ADMINISTRATOR WHITFIELD.

ALL EXPENSES INCURRED ARE TO BE CHARGED TO HEAD-
QUARTERS CASE FILE AND FUND SITE.

ALL QUESTIONS TO BE DIRECTED TO PROJECT COORDINATOR,
S/A/ R. STRATTON, DEA HQ.

(PAGE 3 OF 3)

1

POSITOS, ARGENTINA

THE DAY I GOT SUCKED INTO THE EVENTS CHRONICLED HERE, EVENTS that should have ended civilization as most of us know it, I was in a place the Argentines called Positos—a place I called Hell.

The town of Positos was a scattered sprawl of crumbling adobe and cinder block structures beneath a barren ridge of the Andes on Argentina's northern border with Bolivia. It had one semipaved street, about a block long, in the middle of which sat a decaying combination hotel, bar, restaurant, called La Mujer— the Woman—as a reminder to travelers who knew the place, that there weren't any there. At the end of this street stood the only reason for the town's existence—a decrepit bridge over a dry riverbed that quietly acknowledged the border crossing.

Few maps show Positos. No one goes there out of choice.

Even though I figure that whatever I did to deserve being sent to Positos was my own fault and that the same could be said for all the tragedy that followed, I still feel that my derelict father should bear some of the blame.

My father was an ex-boxer, a very street kind of guy who abandoned my mom, my brother, and me in the South Bronx to pursue a career as a Miami loan shark. Dad—who married and divorced six times—was not too successful at being either a loan shark or a father. But the last time I saw him, when I was thirteen years old, he did leave me with what you might call a legacy.

"Son," he said, "always remember this: If somebody's gonna beat the shit outta you—get their dinner off you—you gotta make sure you get your breakfast. You fucking hurt 'em. Make 'em pay a price. If you don't get your breakfast, they're just gonna keep gettin' their dinner off you. You hurt 'em, they're gonna look to get it off somebody else, somebody who don't fight back. Nobody fucks with a guy who gets his breakfast."

I guess had he told me those words when I was a little older and understood the ways of the world a little better, they might not have affected me as much as they did. My old man had programmed me to fight back even when any sane person would've waved a big white flag. Basically—and I have to admit this—he had created some kind of a kamikaze nut. Not the kind of guy who gets along very well in a government bureaucracy.

I had worked undercover for a couple of years to bust a particularly deadly group of drug dealers. The only problem was that the CIA claimed that their freedom was important to national security. The dopers were released, all charges were dropped—including ones for the murders of a journalist and a half-dozen witnesses—and I was told to just keep my mouth shut, that "our government has other priorities." I didn't like the answer.

I could hear my father's voice: *Hey, these guys just got their dinner off you.* So I decided to fight back. I wrote memos. I complained. I threatened to go to the media. This brought my already plunging popularity with the suits and political hacks who run DEA, to an all-time low.

So the suits decided to show me what an insignificant flea I really was and how easily I could be swatted. In December of the preceding year, after twenty years of working deep cover assignments from Bangkok to Bogotá, they yanked me off active duty and sent me to Positos on an indefinite assignment. Meanwhile, in the States, the shooflies investigated every piece of paper I'd ever signed as a government agent—every expense voucher, every report, every leave slip—to see if there was any reason they could jail or fire me. And while they kept me in Positos there wasn't a thing I could do about it, but wait.

Typical of my life, though, unexpected changes were about to happen.

"Lay-vee-nay. Like the Wild West, no?" said Colonel Adolfo Martenz in English. A hot gusty wind buffeted us as he limped ahead of me, trim and wiry in his olive-green uniform and spit-shined combat boots, toward the middle of what was called the Positos International Bridge.

Adolfo always walked either ahead of me or behind me. Partners cover each other from front and behind. Side-by-side is vulnerable. An intelligence officer who had survived two ambushes—one by political terrorists, the other by Bolivian cocaine traffickers—would think that way.

"Pretty good, Adolfo," I said. It was about the third or fourth time in the five years I'd known him that he'd spoken to me in English.

"You sound a little like Clint Eastwood."

Adolfo didn't crack a smile. As he walked his right hand brushed the handle of his Smith & Wesson Model 460 in its hand-tooled western holster, the only gift he'd ever accepted from a gringo—me. He loved American westerns and hated Americans. Actually, I wasn't sure what he thought of me, other than that he owed me big time and that both of us were uncomfortable with that debt—a debt he took as seriously as the U.S. betrayal of Argentina during the Falklands war in 1982—and that was serious business.

Adolfo was born shortly after the end of World War II, which put him in his early forties—a year or two younger than me. His German family escaped the Nazi hunters by running to Buenos Aires, while mine escaped the death camps by running to the Bronx. There were a lot of kids in Argentina who'd been named Adolfo after Der Führer. I doubted that any of them would want to owe his life to a Jew.

Earlier that day Adolfo had made a seven-hour surprise trip from his office in Buenos Aires, by plane and helicopter, just to have a drink with me. Or so he said. But I knew better. The head of the Covert Intelligence Unit of Argentina's 27,000-man *Gendarmería Nacional*—border police—didn't sweat without a good reason. And as was Adolfo's way, he would let me know what it was when he was good and ready.

Adolfo paused beneath the blowtorch sun, leaned his back on the rail, and considered the procession of grim-faced Indian women in heavy layers of colored skirts and black bowler hats as they slow-shuffled their way across the bridge from Bolivia to Argentina.

"There's the enemy," said Adolfo. "Every one of these women is carrying coca leaf."

"Hey, that's no joke, Adolfo. My report goes right to the North American Congress. I'm going to tell them how you're helping to protect all the kids in the South Bronx from the white death. They might even put your statue in the Bronx Zoo."

The fact was, the Indians were the official reason I was there. Chewing the leaf from which cocaine is made had been in their culture for thousands of years, yet they were counted, in statistical reports to Congress, among America's worst enemies—drug smugglers. The suits claimed they wanted me to make an assessment of how much coca leaf trafficking was going on between Bolivia and Argentina, as if this would really have some effect on kids living in America.

Reality didn't mean shit anymore. After twenty years, I had finally decided I was through fighting. I had two kids in the States to support and alimony to pay, and Keith, my oldest, was a rookie New York City cop. It wouldn't look too great if his dad was fired or prosecuted.

Martenz eyed me with his almost colorless gray eyes.

"Did you ever consider what your bosses might do if they really get fed up with you, Lay-vee-nay?"

"Yeah, send me to Positos."

Martenz shook his head in purse-lipped silence, which was his way of laughing. I'd never even seen him smile. I wondered whether he had always been that way.

Five years earlier he had just been promoted to the position of chief of the Covert Intelligence Division of Argentina's *Gendarmería Nacional*—one of the most powerful military police officials in the country. As DEA's Country Attaché to Argentina, I was assigned to win him over, to put him on an American payroll—by any means possible.

Our having a man of Martenz's position in our pocket meant he would do Black Ops for us: illegal wiretaps, bugging, kidnapping, torture, assassinations—whatever was needed. After all, they were killing off their own people by the thousands for politics; imagine what they would do for money.

Every spy in the American embassy wanted a piece of Martenz—DEA, DIA, FBI, State Department Security, the CIA with a black budget big enough to buy Manhattan Island back from Donald Trump and Leona Helmsley couldn't even get a meeting with him. The CIA station chief, Forrest Gregg, a man who would have sacrificed a thousand Cambodian virgins to put Martenz on his payroll, was astounded when the colonel granted *me*, a "DEA cowboy," a courtesy visit.

"Keeping drugs out of Argentina," Martenz told me on the phone, "is a personal interest of mine."

Gregg—rare for a CIA station chief—was friendly toward me. He let me know that Martenz was recuperating from an auto accident. His wife and two children had been killed, Martenz had been driving. "He's an odd duck," Gregg had said, which to me meant that the Agency had gotten nowhere with him. "Just keep me up-to-date if you make any progress."

There was nothing to report. Martenz was not a man who could be bought or conned in any way. To get a man in your pocket you had to offer him a choice between a hammer over his head or a pocketful of money. *Plata o plomo,* as the Mexican dopers say—silver or lead. Some scared easier than others and some sold out cheaper. But a man who has suffered the loss of his children has no fear of death—his children are already there. And the only thing in heaven or on earth that can buy him—that he would sell his soul for—can be offered by no man.

But I did end up owning Adolfo Martenz. He had made himself my personal guard dog. Not because of any clever undercover manipulation on my part. Rather, because I was just the right guy, at the right place, at the right time. Adolfo owed me big. He knew it, I knew it, and so did everyone else in our nasty little world. It was not a debt I was comfortable with. But it was one that would end up saving my life in a way I would never have expected in a million years.

"I don't understand you or your *jefes, Che,*" he said. "Ever since I know you, you are in trouble. If you were an Argentine, you would have been disappeared a long time ago. That is why I ask if you have no concern about something happening to you."

He was finally getting to the real purpose of his trip. As he spoke his eyes slowly scanned our surroundings. We were in the middle of a bridge, in the middle of nowhere. Whenever he was with me, he worried about electronic listening devices, hidden transmitters and parabolic mikes, and the latest developments: laser- and microwave-powered listening devices. It wasn't so much me that he mistrusted. It was this sense that others were constantly monitoring me, waiting for the perfect opportunity to finish me off.

"To the suits, I'm a flea, Adolfo," I said. "They sign an order, I'm sent here. To them, I'm just as good as dead."

Now he peered directly into my eyes with a look that frightened me.

"Why would gringos in an unmarked helicopter be looking for you?"

"You sure it didn't have a sign, 'Publishers Clearing House Sweepstakes,' on the side?"

He stared at me blankly. All attempts at humor were wasted on him.

"Is that why you're here?" I asked.

"Why would people identify themselves as DEA officers looking for you and not know where Positos is?"

"Maybe because it's not on their map."

He looked incredulous. "They would send you to a place they didn't know?"

The beeping of a horn caught our attention. A cloud of dust billowed in the distance. A military jeep bounced over the rocky terrain toward us, the driver pounding on the horn. The soldier next to him fired his pistol in the air. Martenz calmly watched them.

As the driver hit the bridge with a bounce, the Indians barely moved to avoid getting hit. The jeep skidded to a halt in front of us. The uniformed driver, a *Gendarmería* officer, sweat tracking the dust on his face, saluted Martenz while his partner chattered urgently into a portable radio.

"Ya vienen, mi comandante!"—They're here, sir!

An unmarked Huey helicopter swung over the horizon like an angry black wasp. I saw the flash of field glasses from its side door. It angled sharply and raced toward us.

"Your associates are here," said Martenz. He moved toward the jeep, leaving me in the middle of the bridge, the wind from the chopper churning clouds of dust around him. A soldier handed him a walkie-talkie. He barked an order into the mike.

Suddenly two Cobra gun ships, bearing blue-and-white Argentine flags and the *Gendarmería* emblem, leapt over the horizon bristling with gun turrets and rockets, following close behind the Huey. The unmarked chopper suddenly swung down and landed near the foot of the bridge.

A burly-looking figure in camouflage fatigues jumped out a side door and ran toward me in a smooth, loping combat crouch, passing beneath the rotating blades and straightening. He moved with the ease of an experienced combat soldier, which he was. I recognized him from photos in *The DEA World*, the agency's in-house newsletter. It was Bobby "Bad-to-the-Bone" Stratton, my new boss in DEA headquarters, Washington.

I started forward to meet him halfway.

"Levine, Jesus you're hard to fucking find," he said.

He was a tall, square-jawed black man, built like a professional football player. He had an attaché case cuffed and chained to his wrist. From a distance he looked like a Marine recruiting poster, but up close he had the hard, mean look of a yardbird—a man with a lot of jail time.

"I'm not hiding, Mr. Stratton," I said.

"Cut that Mister shit," he said. "I ever tell you call me Mister, consider yourself on my number ten shitlist."

His true first name was Richard. When he'd first transferred into DEA a redneck border rat called him "Dick" in a tone that Stratton didn't care for. He never said a word. Yardbird mentality is you don't say a word when someone disses you—you just straighten it out. One punch took out all the guy's front teeth. From that day on his name, Richard, somehow became Bobby.

He glanced over at Martenz. Two machine-gun-mounted jeeps had joined the first. Soldiers were poised tensely behind the guns. The *Gendarmería* Cobras continued to hover a couple of hundred yards distant.

"What's all that shit?"

"It's complicated," I said.

"That's the book on you, Levine—nothing simple. Anything we gotta worry about?"

"No. He worries about me."

That was enough for Stratton. He offered me his hand. He had a strong firm grip and looked me in the eye—not typical behavior for a headquarters suit who looked at every undercover as if he'd just ducked out of his wife's bedroom.

DEA was a small, elite agency with only fifteen hundred field agents. Enforcing the drug laws brought us deep into investigations of every kind of crime, from gang rape through murder-for-hire to undercover deals for stolen nuclear weapons technology. We were responsible for almost fifty percent of the federal prison population. In an agency that small and that active eventually everyone gets to know the book on everyone else.

The book on Stratton was that he was a highly decorated Marine combat officer with two hitches in Vietnam, where he was recruited by the CIA. He'd had some kind of problems with the Agency that no one was clear about and transferred into DEA along with about twenty other ex-spooks. Most were never trusted by the street guys. Most were suspected of being spies sent to fuck up drug cases against CIA assets—but not Bobby Stratton.

Stratton had quickly earned himself DEA's highest accolade—a guy you'd go through a door with. A stand-up guy. Bad-to-the-bone fearless. DEA had stationed him in Southeast Asia, where he'd gone to war against his old CIA colleagues by locking up heroin dealers who also happened to be Agency assets. The rumor was that the Agency was applying pressure in Washington to get him transferred and out of their hair. Stratton knew how to play the system. He got the NAACP to back him and he stayed put.

Then tragedy struck.

Stratton's fourteen-year-old son was killed just outside the American embassy in Bangkok when a car bomb exploded. The bomb was generally attributed to one of the many Thai heroin dealers who hated Stratton. His Vietnamese wife divorced him, after which he disappeared for a year or so, on extended sick leave. There were rumors of alcohol and drug problems. When he resurfaced, just months ago, he was transferred to DEA headquarters in Washington and promoted.

"You and René Villarino are tight, aren't you?" he said, his eyes looking through me.

I felt a cold chill. All undercover agents have secrets. Secrets that might make us vulnerable to jail time, death, disgrace, and long sleepless nights. You can't live the undercover life without acquiring them. Secrets you hope to take to your grave. René Villarino and I shared one such secret.

"I know him a long time," I said, my eyes going to the chopper, half expecting shooflies in gray suits to appear, thin-lipped smiles on their faces, mirrored sunglasses, handcuffs in their hands. "Is that why you come to the asshole of South America, Mr. Stratton?"

"Don't get cute with me," he said.

"You're my boss," I said, noticing the death's-head tattoo, a pale blue skull with hash marks, barely visible on the coffee-colored skin of his right forearm. A symbol of a Vietnam secret that Stratton shared with too many. "I don't get cute with bosses. Why don't you just tell me why you're here."

"René Villarino's gone missing," said Stratton flatly.

My heart sank. René was the only man I called friend.

"How? When?"

"You up on your cable traffic? Don't answer—you won't have to lie. Your secretary at the embassy said the telexes piled on your desk go back two months and she hasn't heard word one from you in over a month."

"Well where the fuck have I been?" I said, fighting to control my temper.

He glared at me, lifted a knee to rest the case, snapped it open and shoved a red-jacketed cable at me. It was marked TOP SECRET, which meant national security was involved. I started to read it and felt guilty when I saw that it had been received at my office a week ago.

"Don't bother reading it now," said Stratton. "It's yours. Bottom line is René has been working a deep cover special out of Panama for the past eight months. Forty-eight hours ago he receives a call at his UC residence in Panama. Notifies his contact at HQ. He sounds rushed and excited. Says he's on to the source of this new drug—you'll read about it in the Teletype. They want him to come to Argentina to talk. He says he'll check in the moment he knows something. He arrives at Rio where he's supposed to change planes. He vanishes.

"We track his UC ID. He never passed Brazil Immigration. He either transited to another country using a different ID or boarded a private plane. We've eliminated all but a half-dozen private flights to Argentina and Bolivia. We can't go any further without risk of burning him."

"Why the fuck wasn't I notified about a UC operation in my jurisdiction? I'm still the Country Attaché. I should've been covering him."

Stratton put his big hand up, like a traffic cop.

"Nobody told me squat either. You think I'd put a man out there without backup? This thing's been top secret for eight months. That's why I'm here and this ain't a phone call. I hear you two were close. You got the same fucked-up reputation— hotshot undercovers, loners. You like to do things your own way, don't you?"

I started to speak. The big palm rose again to stop me.

"Sooner or later your luck runs out and somebody got to come out and pick up your fucking pieces."

"Say what you like about me," I said. "I know I'm no fucking hero in headquarters, but René does things by the book. I know him twenty years, he's never blown his cover. The guy's made more Mafia cases on his own than the whole New York FBI. Two days with no word could mean he's living with dopers. We go public we'll blow his cover."

"We're not going public," said Stratton. "And you're right: You're definitely no hero in headquarters. You don't follow rules, you're arrogant, you piss people off. Some people say you're a certifiable fucking loony tunes. Your mouth is usually running long before your brain. But your case record speaks for itself and whoever I talked to on the street all agreed on one thing—if they were jammed up, they'd want Mike Levine coming after them. And I don't mind telling you, a lot of them don't even like you."

"Look, Bobby. The last UC bit I did with René he got stood up at the last minute and asked me to play his bodyguard for one meeting with some Mafia *capo* in New York. A ten-minute meet. I was just supposed to drive and keep my mouth shut, like a good buttonman. Window dressing. An extra.

"René rehearsed me for a week—how I should dress, jewelry, shoes, the kind of cologne I should wear, how I should position myself in the driver's seat. He checked every item I'd be carrying in my wallet and pockets, just in case we were searched. He checked my shirt for identifying laundry marks. For a ten-minute meet? If I didn't love the guy *and* respect the way he did things, I would've told him to go fuck himself. This is a guy who once went to Italy and bought himself a count's title to help bring off a scam. René is an artist, a perfectionist. Two days missing doesn't mean anything."

The big hand came up again. Stratton glanced over at the chopper. The engine blades were still whipping the air. The pilot stared straight ahead, unrecognizable in helmet and dark glasses.

"There's more. René was working with a CI, a Panamanian banker. He was hit this morning."

"How?"

"A fender bender on the street in downtown Panama City. The CI bends to check the damage—the driver of the other car pops him with a twenty-two behind the ear. Broad daylight and a dozen witnesses don't see a thing."

"That might not have anything to do with René," I said, desperately wanting to believe it. "Stool pigeons get offed every day."

Stratton shook his head. "Maybe, maybe not. Until we know he's okay we don't take nuthin' for granted."

"What about tasking NSA and CIA?"

"Done. NSA's programmed tapes of René's voiceprint into the system. He makes a call from anywhere, we'll have him. . . . How do you get along with the head spook in Buenos Aires?"

"Forrest Gregg? Never had any problems with him. You know him?"

"I met him. The guy knows his job. He says he has a lead. When you get back to B.A. check with him first. Then turn your dogs loose—all your CIs, every cop on your payroll, all your counterparts. Get as many eyes out there as you can. I have some surveillance shots of René you can distribute."

"Whoa, whoa, whoa. No photos," I said. "Ninety percent of these Argentine cops are for sale. If I put out photos and they know he's DEA, we'll burn him. Even if he's in trouble, René's a guy that can talk his way out of anything."

"You're right," said Stratton. "I should've thought of that."

For a moment I was taken aback. I'd never heard a DEA boss admit he was wrong about anything.

Stratton removed a manila folder from the attaché case and handed it to me. It contained a typewritten list of names, each with a date of birth beside it and several copies of an eight-by-ten undercover surveillance photo.

The camera had captured the handsome René as he strolled down a crowded street with a man in a dark hat. René wore his black beret, his dark hair fashionably long, curling just above his suit collar. He smiled broadly, his big hands gracefully gesticulating in a typically Italian gesture, as if describing a beautiful woman. Just behind were two heavies in dark glasses—bodyguards. Several stores and a restaurant were visible with signs in Italian.

"He looks a little like that Italian movie actor in this photo," said Stratton. "I forget his name."

"Marcello Mastroianni," I said. "Back in the '60s, when Mastroianni was a big star, people used to stop René on the street and ask for his autograph."

"The other dopers in this photo are dead," said Stratton. "You can distribute it if you think you need to. The list is all the aliases René's been using."

I looked down at the smiling face of my friend in the photo and wondered what he was thinking at that moment. Did he feel the slightest chill of apprehension? I believe that there are key moments in life when we are warned of danger. We must stay alert for them, remain open to vibrations, to premonitions, to primal senses no longer understood—the tiny ripples on a still pond. There are no second chances. No one understood that better than René.

"We've got to say he's some kind of bad guy just wanted for questioning," I said. "I'll put out a reward for information only. If we even hint that his arrest is worth money, these motherfuckers'll bring him in dead."

Stratton's eyes went to Martenz, who was still watching us. The helicopters were gone, but the men and jeeps were still waiting.

"That's the only guy down here I would trust," I said. "He owes me big time and he's got a twenty-seven-thousand-man police force."

Stratton nodded. "I came to the right guy."

"If he's down here, I'll get him back," I said. "And Bobby, I don't want anyone calling up his sons and getting them shook for no reason."

"I'll make sure of it," said Stratton.

"I don't know why, but I have this feeling that we've got to move quickly."

"I've been having the same feeling. I'm hopping over to Colombia to check out some leads. You got a quick way back to Buenos Aires?"

"No sweat," I said.

Stratton paused to study me with his weary soldier's eyes. "What do you go, about six two, two hundred twenty, Mike?"

"Close enough," I said.

"I heard you're a black belt. What style?"

"*Goju.*"

"Okinawan?"

"Japanese," I said, wondering where he was heading.

"Ever compete?"

"I was on the U.S. team that fought in Panama in '74. South

American Caribbean championships. That was the last thing I did of any consequence."

"You still train?"

"I still do *kata*. Kick and punch the shit out of a heavy bag whenever I get near one. It helps keep me sane."

Stratton grinned at me. "You're as dinky-dau as they come, aren't you? You in 'Nam?"

"No. I got lucky. I was in from '59 to '63."

"What unit?"

"Air Force. Sentry dog handler."

He whistled softly and wagged his head. "You *were* lucky. They were some good boys. A lot of them died trying to save their dogs."

"I heard something like that," I said.

He paused and looked off toward the colorless rocky slope of mountain on the other side of the bridge in Bolivia.

"I lost a lot of good men in that miserable fucking country. And from what I can see, this one doesn't look much better."

I nodded. I couldn't think of anything else to say. Stratton started toward the chopper. He stopped and turned.

"I want to know everything you hear, rumors, everything. I don't give a fuck if you think it's irrelevant. *I* want to hear it. You understand, Mike?"

He turned without waiting for an answer. The moment he was in the doorway the chopper lifted off. In moments it was gone as if it had never been there.

2

I STOOD ALONE AT THE EDGE OF AN ISOLATED LANDING STRIP SEARCHING the sky for the *Gendarmería* plane. A deep orange sun was dipping quickly behind the Andes. It had been five hours since I watched Bobby Stratton's chopper take off for Colombia. I had the sense that my friend René Villarino's life was measured in hours, and Adolfo Martenz was three hours late.

He had insisted on personally flying me to Buenos Aires. He wouldn't miss a chance to make payment on the debt. To save time, I gathered my gear while Martenz was flown by chopper to Salta, about 150 miles south, to get a fast plane—at least that's what he told me.

Right about now, I was beginning to wonder how I could have allowed myself to be put in such an exposed and vulnerable position. Death was Argentina's cheapest commodity and I had a quarter-of-a-million-dollar price tag on my head put there by the Bolivian mafia *Cruzeña*, after they found out I was a DEA undercover and not Don Miguel Luis Garcia, Latino drug dealer from Miami.

Martenz was part of one of the deadliest and most corrupt governments in South American history—a government that had turned itself into a mass-murder machine, "disappearing" as many as 25,000 college kids, intellectuals, professors, union leaders, writers, journalists, and anyone else perceived as antigovernment.

I didn't know what role, if any, Adolfo played in all this. In the years I had known him we somehow avoided talking about *La Guerra Sucia*—The Dirty War—as the Argentines called it. What I did know about him was that he was incorruptible and a deeply religious Catholic with a strict sense of honor—which is what made him beholden to me.

It began with a drug bust. I had been undercover in Brazil for a couple of weeks and had conned some Brazilian coke dealers, including a high-ranking Rio cop, into making a delivery of cocaine to me in Buenos Aires. The Brazilian cop rounded up some people with prosthetic legs, hollowed them out, filled them with dope, and then sent them across the border. It was a big case with a lot of sexy media coverage, which, as usual, was followed by a victory party for the *milicos*—as the Argentines called their government agents—who had backed me up and made the arrests. All paid for by Uncle Sam, the world's financier of the drug war. The party was at a chic *confitería* across the street from La Recoleta cemetery where Evita Perón was entombed.

The place was packed with plainclothes cops and secret police. As happens in cop rackets all over the world, before long it was drunk and loud, and everyone in the bar knew the *milicos* were there.

Early in the evening I noticed a big man with salt-and-pepper hair and eyes so full of hate that they seemed to glow white around the pupils, seated with a woman at a table in the corner. The woman watched him, her face taut with fear. Bodies moved and they were gone from view.

I didn't think much more about it. There were a lot of angry-looking people around Argentina. This was right after the civilian government had replaced the military junta. In spite of a great public outcry for *justicia* for the *desaparecidos*, few of those responsible were ever prosecuted or punished in any way. Millions of Argentines were sentenced to a life of looking at every cop and military man they saw and wondering whether it was his hands who tortured and murdered their child. They lived in a constant state of rage with no means of venting it.

I was surprised when I saw Martenz enter the bar, he'd never come to any of the other cop rackets I'd thrown before. The next thing I remember was the rush of a large, powerful body through the crowd, people bouncing off it like bowling pins, coming directly at me. Then came the sudden flash of a butcher knife arc-ing over the crowd in a large hand and the crazed eyes of the man I had glimpsed earlier.

The purpose of a master *karateka*'s seemingly endless repetition of precisely executed punches and kicks is to train the body to react as mindlessly as the blink of an eye to a sudden bright light. A split-second hesitation can mean your life.

I pivoted hard on the ball of my right foot, my left hip and knee raised and swinging inward toward the charging body. I fired the kick like a gun—what the Japanese masters call *yoko geri*, a roundhouse kick—snapping the aluminum-reinforced toe of my boot in a short arc at dead center of the man's face, at the same instant realizing that the knife he had begun to drive downward was not meant for me. It was aimed at Adolfo Martenz, whose back was still turned.

The brute force kick, delivered with the precision of a four-hundred-year-old Japanese art, impacted on the point of the man's nose and upper lip. The force of it caved the front of his face and stopped his forward motion cold. The long triangular-shaped blade had come within a hairbreadth of a spot at the base of Adolfo's neck. He turned just in time to see the knife clatter at his feet and the man writhing on the ground, fighting to breathe, swallowing blood and teeth through a smashed nose and mouth.

The sight of the man's mangled face was such that the room full of *milicos*, who ordinarily would have beat him to death for an attack on one of their own, did nothing but stare in silence.

I was never sure why the guy had singled out Adolfo. I learned later that his wife and son had been among the *desaparecidos* and that he had ended up in a madhouse. He probably had it in mind to kill any cop. Maybe he recognized Martenz from the newspapers, maybe from someplace else.

Whenever I relive the event that had come to define my relationship with Adolfo Martenz, what I realize is that had I known the poor guy's story, I might not have lifted a finger to save Martenz. In any case, it was over and done with and you can't turn back the clock.

The incident was immediately the stuff of legend. There were fifty half-drunk witnesses who within days had told and retold the story so many times that when I heard it again I hardly recognized it. Some claimed to have seen me fly through the air throwing three and four kicks before I landed. Some saw me fight off two knife-wielding attackers, one of whom had escaped into the night. My physical prowess had been described as a cross between Bruce Lee and Muhammad Ali. A rumor even started that I was part Japanese.

The truth was—as any experienced *karateka* would agree—that I might just as well have hit the guy on back of the head with a hammer. I had blindsided him with a haymaker kick that he never saw coming. And the real irony was that Adolfo had not seen a thing. He'd had his back turned the whole time. But there could be no doubt: *Lay-vee-nay the hated American undercover agent, had saved the life of* El Comandante.

From that moment on Martenz was tied to me like a West Virginia coal miner to the company store. And the more I tried to downplay the incident, the more he acted indebted to me—a debt with no number attached. As uncomfortable as I was with this debt, I stored it like a backup gun for use in an emergency. I had never taken advantage of Adolfo's services, that is, not until today.

The landing strip itself was about 1,300 yards of hard-packed dirt on a small mesa surrounded by gullies and rocky gorges full of thick patches of scrub brush. It would soon be dark and there were no landing lights.

The noises had started about a half an hour ago. A periodic rustling of the brush in the gully below. At first I didn't pay much attention, but now the noises seemed to be getting louder and more frequent.

Suddenly I heard what sounded like a short burst of running feet heading toward me from just below the mesa. The adrenaline rush took my breath away. I crouched down on my haunches. I was on the high ground, exposed, a perfect target in the waning sunlight. The nine-millimeter Glock automatic on my hip carried fifteen bullets, which nowadays wasn't enough firepower to get me out of the South Bronx, let alone to protect me against professional assassins hell-bent on collecting a quarter-of-a-million-dollar bounty.

I unzipped my leather carryall. My shaking hand felt for a short, thick hunk of steel buried beneath folded jeans and shirts—my Ingram Model 11, submachine gun. The Ingram—commonly carried by South American drug dealers and hitmen—was not much bigger than a pistol, but it fired 1,200 rounds per minute. I could sweep it around in a quick 360-degree circle with one hand, cutting down anything around me. I had practiced the movement many times. The gun was not authorized DEA equipment, but undercovers who put too much weight on what some bean-counting government attorney authorized didn't usually live to collect their pensions.

It was René who said that a deep cover agent who doesn't practice every technique he may have to use is a fool with a death wish. He was the only UC whose advice I would take to heart. His wise words would save my life more than once.

There was another burst of noise, closer this time. I stayed low, keeping the Ingram in my lap. Night insects had begun to chitter. Next I jerked free the thickest garment in the bag, my Second Chance bulletproof vest, spilling clothing and shaving articles all over the ground. I quickly slipped the vest on over my leather jacket. There were more noises on either side of me.

I slowly raised up to a crouch, leveling the Ingram in the direction of the last noise. It was already too dark to see. I had a powerful four-cell Bianchi flashlight that I was afraid to use—it would make me a target. I was going to put forty rounds, blind, into the next sound. It was then that I heard the distant drone of an engine.

Over the horizon I could make out the lights of a small plane bearing in my direction but slightly off course. I moved to the end of the runway and, staying in a crouch, shone the powerful beam down the center. The plane immediately adjusted course. In minutes a Piper Cherokee with the blue-and-white *Gendarmería Nacional* insignia skimmed in for a perfect landing. The passenger door flew open.

"Lay-vee-nay, let's go," said Adolfo's voice.

As I took a seat beside him, Adolfo reached over and fingered my bulletproof vest. I told him about the noises. He wheeled the plane into a fast takeoff, as if he were driving a Corvette with wings. It was one of those rare times I was happy to be in the air.

"Get ready to fire," said Adolfo as he banked the plane into a sharp turn and then into a shallow dive along one of the gullies that bordered the airstrip. He flicked a switch and a spotlight lit up the ground before us like daylight. Grazing haplessly in the underbrush were several of the Indians' burros laden with bags of coca leaf. I felt the blood rush to my face.

"Like the Wild West, Lay-vee-nay, no?"

It was too dark in the cockpit to see if he was smiling.

I laid my head back as Martenz lifted the nose on a 45-degree angle and began a climb to cruising altitude. A breathtaking blaze of brilliant stars bigger and brighter than I'd ever seen before filled the windscreen. A thought flashed that, at that moment, René was seeing those same stars. My mind suddenly flooded with memories. I had never known anyone more clever, more resourceful, more capable of talking his way in or out of trouble than my friend René. It was hard to believe that we had known each other more than twenty years.

I met René during my first year with the Hard Narcotics Smuggling Division of Customs when I was experimenting with a new UC bit, posing as Mike Pagano, half-Sicilian, half–Puerto Rican drug dealer.

A shady Swiss banker who handled some of the Vatican accounts set up an undercover meet with the *capo di tutti capos* of all Sicilian heroin dealers, Don Pasquale Cologero, alleged to head a heroin ring that used priests and nuns coming from the Vatican to smuggle religious artifacts stuffed with heroin. The banker swore they were real priests.

Actually, busting rabbis, priests, nuns, ministers, monks, yogis, and assorted gurus for smuggling dope had become fairly commonplace during the sixties and seventies, although the stories rarely ever hit the news. There seemed to be some kind of unspoken agreement between the media moguls that a doper in religious uniform got a free pass. But the connection to the Mafia was something very new. There was no way that story would be kept out of the headlines.

The commissioner himself cautioned that we couldn't just stop and search priests and nuns with Vatican ID at the airport, without the media turning the bureau into an empty lot. We had to be a thousand percent sure. I suddenly found myself in a deep cover role with half the government looking over my shoulder. I was given unlimited funds to work a sting operation. Objective: to win the confidence of the Sicilian. Some pretty heady stuff for a kid in his mid-twenties. But I thought I could do it all.

Cologero showed up for the first meeting at an Italian restaurant in lower Manhattan with a caravan of rented cars and a crew of Sicilian Mafiosi that looked like rabid water rats in double-breasted silk suits straight out of the 1930s. The don himself, a dark, brooding guy with a big handlebar mustache, a headful of shaggy gray hair, and a thick knife scar down the side of his face, was like a character right out of *The Godfather*, except for the giant gold crucifix he wore hanging in the middle of his chest. He couldn't speak a word of English. I told him that I was raised in Puerto Rico and spoke only Spanish so the don brought along a Spanish-speaking wiseguy to translate.

The double-edged sword of undercover work is that you've got to make your target like you before he will trust you. To pull that off, I had to find something I could genuinely like about him. And Cologero, who crossed himself and gave thanks to the Virgin Maria at every other sentence, was an extremely likable old-world Sicilian. After our first meeting, a kind of feeling-out session during which the drug business was never referred to, I was certain that I had him on the hook, that he would trust me enough to do at least one deal with me—our first and his last.

But the don was not as easy as I thought. After two months of undercover sparring and haggling with meetings in expensive hotels and restaurants in New York, Miami, and Puerto Rico, he finally invited me to his home, an old mansion in the hills of Palermo, Sicily, surrounded by his vineyards. He personally cooked and served me an incredible meal of local squid, game, and homemade pasta. In between jokes, thanks to the Virgin Maria and the don's quoting Dante, he thoroughly enchanted and interrogated me with an artistry I'd never experienced before or since. With artful silences where I was expected to fill in the blanks, with warm, smiling eyes and a winning openness, he made me—in spite of myself—talk too much.

The bubble burst a few days later when I had to fly to Brooklyn Federal Court to testify. As I passed by one of the adjoining courtrooms the door swung open and I got a glimpse of a man on the witness stand. There was something familiar about the guy. I held the door open a crack and peeked inside.

I was looking at what had to be Don Cologero's son or a close relative. The resemblance was uncanny. The face of the man on the witness stand was identical to Don Cologero's, except that he was clean-shaven, with dark, curly hair, no mustache, and no scars, and appeared to be twenty years younger. And there wasn't a sign of a crucifix. At that moment a prosecutor left the courtroom.

"Who's the guy on the witness stand?" I said.

"René?" he said. "He's FBN. René Villarino."

My stomach dipped right through my balls. The whole thing was so bizarre, it didn't register at first. We must have spent at least a quarter of a million dollars out of our agencies' budgets trying to con each other. I opened the door a little farther to hear his voice. He was speaking in a lightly accented English, but his voice was unmistakable: Don Cologero was René Villarino, an FBN undercover agent.

I slowly entered the court and took a seat. Villarino saw me instantly, turned chalk white, and stopped talking. I laughed. There was a beat, then a moment of recognition and we were both laughing. The judge, fuming, recessed the court to find out what the joke was. That night at dinner in Little Italy, René Villarino and I began a friendship that had endured twenty years. Unheard of in our line of work.

"What is so funny?" said Martenz.

"I was laughing?"

"Like a madman."

"Just a funny thought," I said.

Four hours later we were still flying over the pitch-blackness of the Pampas. Insuring that the search for René became the *Gendarmería*'s immediate priority had been the reason for Adolfo's delay, along with a miscommunication about the plane, leaving him with the slow-moving Cherokee. There was no sensation of movement, only the drone of the engine. Thoughts of what kind of trouble René might be in if his cover was blown plagued me.

"Does this thing go any faster?" I asked.

"No," said Adolfo. *"Tranquilo.* Twenty-seven thousand men have his description."

"It's important that they don't know he's an agent," I said.

For a long moment, the drone of the engine was the only sound. "He must be a good friend," said Adolfo.

"Maybe the only one I ever had," I said.

"You said he speaks Spanish."

"Spanish, French, Italian, English, Corsican—he gets along in a couple of others. He grew up in Corsica and was educated in Italy."

"How did he become an American DEA agent?"

"René married a secretary in the American embassy in Rome. He was going to night school studying economics and had a good job at an Italian bank. They had a son, Marcello, but his wife wanted to go back to the U.S. By the time his wife's transfer came through, she was pregnant with their second boy.

"But in the States things didn't go well. René didn't speak enough English either to continue his education or to get a good job. So he got himself a job as a housepainter . . ."

I paused for a moment, listening to the drone of the engine, wondering what it was that was exploding in my chest, why I was feeling the need to tell René's story. Martenz glanced over at me and I remembered that I was talking to a man who had lost his wife and children. In the orange glow of the instrument panel I could see something more than curiosity in his eyes.

"In Italy, René's wife was the envy of all the gringo women in the embassy—she'd married a movie-star-handsome Corsican university student. But in Washington, D.C., being married to a housepainter who couldn't speak English was something she quickly became ashamed of. So she left him. Broke his heart. René found out that she had moved in with some diplomat who'd been stationed with her in Italy. Maybe she'd been screwing the guy all along."

"¡Chanta perra!" exclaimed Martenz, shaking his head.

"In the meantime," I continued, "René is painting the house of one of the bosses of a special undercover unit of Internal Revenue Intelligence. The man happens to be Italian. So while René's working on the house he becomes chatty with the guy as he does with everyone. He finds out this guy loves to eat. The next thing you know René is cooking lunch for him every day. There aren't too many people who can cook like René. I don't really know that much about it. I spent most of my life happy enough eating glazed donuts and coffee in my car—which used to drive René completely nuts."

I looked over at Martenz and saw what was almost a smile on his face.

"As it turns out this big boss happens to be heading a probe into the Mafia trying to make income tax–evasion cases against the top wiseguys in the country. By the time René finished painting his house, he's got a new job.

"In those days there was special provision for hiring federal law enforcement officers for special jobs, even people who couldn't speak English. They called it Schedule A. So René walked into that house a housepainter and came out a U.S. government undercover agent. It took him almost three years to work his way up the Mafia ladder to become the personal chef of Don Carlo Morello, the New Orleans crime boss. Forty or fifty *capos* ended up indicted for income tax evasion, all on René's testimony."

"So, the Mafia wants to kill him?"

"No, no. They loved René. No Italian I ever knew would kill a man who could cook like that. He did his job. He wasn't crooked. He was just a little smarter than they were. Besides, all that happened more than twenty years ago."

"An exceptional man," said Martenz.

"Too exceptional," I said. "Too good at being bad. That's why I'm worried about your cops getting hold of him."

"Lay-vee-nay, I have followed your instructions to the letter. If *any* action is taken without first notifying me, my men will have severe problems. Believe me, they do not want problems with me. If your friend is anywhere in the Southern Cone we will find him."

3

BUENOS AIRES, ARGENTINA

I GUNNED MY G CAR, A BLACK CHEVY CAMARO WITH DARK-TINTED windows and diplomatic plates, down Avenida del Libertador, an eight-lane boulevard of careening steel that in the morning rush hour became a racetrack from the northern suburbs of Buenos Aires, where I lived, to the downtown area. It was 10:00 a.m. and René had now been missing for more than seventy-two hours.

I jumped three lanes to swerve around slower-moving traffic then stomped on the accelerator, pushing my speed to somewhere above eighty miles an hour. I was flying low when I reached the quick turnoff half a block from the American embassy. I began blinking my headlights.

Ahead a Marine guard recognized my car and swung open the steel-barred security gates. Bouncing through the entrance, I bottomed out with a loud crunch. From the look on the Marine's face I guessed I had broken an embassy speed record. The squeal of my tires echoed loudly off the long gray concrete bunker of a building as I raced to my parking spot in the rear.

The sleek racing-green Jaguar sedan belonging to Forrest Gregg, CIA station chief, was already parked in its spot. It was the only one like it in all of Argentina. No one in the diplomatic community knew how Gregg had managed to get around Argentina's law against diplomats importing luxury cars, but because he was a CIA station chief no one was surprised. Since Gregg was supposed to have some kind of a lead, I decided to go directly to his office before stopping at mine.

December was midsummer in Argentina and the heat was already overpowering the embassy's air conditioners. By the time I was admitted past double sets of steel electronically operated doors and into the long, video-camera-surveilled hallways of one of the CIA's largest field divisions in South America, sweat had soaked through my suit. I strode quickly down the gray-carpeted, windowless hallway beneath a series of red bulbs now brightly illuminated to signify to the spooks that an outsider was on the premises.

Once, joking with one of them, I said, "You know, I think the real reason for those little red bulbs is so you guys don't get caught smoking weed." He didn't think it was funny. Not too many of those guys had a sense of humor, especially when it came to laughing at themselves.

"Michael, old chap," said Gregg, getting to his feet as I entered his office. "I'm sorry about the situation, but I'm glad to see you back."

"I'm still praying there's nothing to be sorry about," I said, moving halfway around the desk to greet him.

His office, furnished with European antiques and Oriental rugs, was one of the largest in the embassy. The windows were covered with wooden venetian blinds that were always closed tight. During the day it was as dark and cavernous as Lefty's Pool Hall of my South Bronx youth and stank as badly of cigarettes.

Gregg seemed to float over the desk toward me in the gloom, like a giant, pale jellyfish. He was a big, soft, ungainly man, at least six feet four, with the fish-belly complexion of a chain-smoker. He had on the horn-rimmed tinted glasses he usually wore. For the six years I'd known him he had fought a losing battle with his weight. The dark-colored suits he had specially tailored in England did little to hide his large pear-shaped body. Although it was common knowledge that his mother was Brazilian and his father a well-known American CIA official from the Midwest, after two years of high school studies in England, he had become more Brit than Sir John Gielgud.

"Not to worry," he said. "I think some of our joes have located your man." He gave me a fleeting handful of fingertips. For a man his size he had unusually small hands and feet, which he was painfully aware of. He sat back, his hands fluttering out of sight beneath the desk. As usual smoke curled up around him from a cigarette left burning in a glass ashtray.

There was another man standing off to one side of the room whom I recognized but decided not to notice.

"I'll feel a lot better when I see him myself," I said.

"A touch of breakfast, some tea? Oh, you're a coffee man, aren't you?"

"There's no time," I said, feeling less patient than usual with Gregg's phony Brit accent laced with the usual condescension most CIA agents have toward DEA.

"You already know *Comandante* Borsalino," said Gregg.

"Yes," I said, finally acknowledging the other man, whom I knew a lot more intimately than I'd ever cared to.

Raúl Borsalino, *Comandante* of the Special Intelligence Unit of the Argentine Federal Police, was a tall, angular man with slicked-back tango dancer's hair and dark beady little eyes. His pencil-thin mustache seemed to accentuate the invisibility of his lips. His eyes looked straight through me. My nickname for him was *Cariculo*—Snakeface. The likeness was unmistakable. He didn't offer me his hand and I was not offended. Any honesty, even honest hostility, is refreshing in an Argentine *milico*.

We both nodded without a word and took seats.

As *Comandante* of one of the most powerful investigative units in the AFP, Borsalino was among those in the business of renting his police unit to any covert agency of any government that was willing to pay for his services. When I took over the Buenos Aires District Office I found that I had inherited the snakefaced son of a bitch. He'd been on the DEA payroll for the past seven years. In defiance of my orders against murdering drug suspects, a common practice of the *milicos,* Snakeface killed a low-level Chilean doper I was investigating, castrating him and leaving the works jammed into his mouth—his way of telling me, Fuck you!

I became the first DEA station chief to fire him.

"Remarkable operative, your man, isn't he?" said Gregg, tapping a cigarette on his thumbnail and lighting it.

"Did you ever meet him?" I asked, bothered that he seemed unconcerned about the time when I could feel in every fiber of my body that we were in a race for René's life.

Gregg stared at me blankly as if he didn't understand the question. "No, I never had the pleasure," he said, leaning away from his desk into the shadows.

"What about this information you have," I said.

"Of course," said Gregg, giving Snakeface his cue.

"Your man was seen in the Arab quarter of Cochabamba," said Snakeface. "He left Cochabamba two days ago with two Colombian drug dealers and flew by private plane into the coca-growing region, the Chapare."

"How do you know it was him?"

Gregg opened the file folder. It was about an inch thick with no name on the index tab. On top was the same photo I had given to Martenz.

I felt like a fool. By now Martenz had to know that Snakeface and the whole fucking AFP also had the photo. *And after all the shit I gave him about being careful with it.* There was as much hatred, mistrust, and competition between the *Gendarmería* and the Argentine Federal Police as there was between DEA and CIA. But the enmity between Martenz and Borsalino transcended politics or interagency rivalry—it was bitter and personal.

"Where did you get that?" I asked, trying to conceal my anger.

"Your administrator Mr. Whitfield," said Gregg. "Vetted through normal channels. Borsalino has already distributed copies to all his contacts."

What else could I expect from a DEA suit?

"He was recognized immediately," said Snakeface.

"Who saw him? How?"

"One of my men," said Snakeface. "Coming out of a bar. El Tejano."

"Who are the Colombians?" I asked.

Snakeface shrugged. "My men could not identify them. When the photos were distributed, your friend had already left."

"I need to speak to your men," I said.

Snakeface looked at Gregg.

"Quite impossible," said Gregg. "They're doing some things for us. Not my decision. If it were up to me you could talk to anyone you wanted."

"If I can't talk to them, what the fuck *can* I do?"

"I spoke to them personally," said Gregg. "It was a positive ID. Villarino is an exceptionally handsome European. In a place like Cochabamba he'd be recognized."

"You must understand, Señor Levine," said Snakeface. "I cannot let the identity of my men be compromised."

Snakeface's message was simple: Take me off your payroll? Go fuck yourself! *If you cut the son of a bitch in two, I swear to God he wouldn't stop wriggling till midnight.*

"How do you know they went to the Chapare?" I asked.

"A *campesino* helped them fuel a small plane," said Snakeface.

"Your agent in Bolivia already has the name," said Gregg.

Snakeface was stroking his mustache and watching Gregg nervously. I knew the sign well. He wanted to leave but he wasn't leaving without money.

"Just give me a minute, Michael," said Gregg, getting to his feet and reaching for a mahogany walking cane.

Borsalino was already standing in the doorway waiting.

"I've got to get to Cochabamba yesterday," I said.

"I won't keep you more than a minute," said Gregg.

"*Ojo, eh,*" said Snakeface, pointing a finger to his eye, an old Argentine gesture that meant, Watch out! "A lot of Arabs and more than a few Germans in Cochabamba. There is still a price on your head, no? If you like I will have some of my people there to cover you."

It was more threat than warning. A good undercover, like a good fighter, never loses his temper. It's all about control, control of body and mind. But at that moment it took every bit of control I had just to keep from punching his mustache down his throat.

"Thanks for the offer," I said. "I'll manage."

Snakeface shrugged and followed Gregg out of the room. There was an envelope full of cash to be transferred. Papers to be signed. Another CIA agent had to witness the exchange. I wondered how much of it was in payment for the information on René.

Alone, my thoughts went to René's sons. Earlier that morning I decided I had better call Marcello, the older of René's two sons, at his mother's home in Connecticut. As I feared, they had already been visited by the suits, who had frightened the hell out of everyone. I tried to calm him.

"Please don't let our dad become a number, Uncle Mike," he said.

"That'll never happen, Marcello," I told him.

Gregg returned and shut the door behind him. I looked at the clock on the wall. I'd been kept waiting ten minutes.

"Some brandy, Michael? I've got some extraordinary, hundred-year-old French. Looks like we can both use a nip."

This was the first time Gregg had ever wanted to speak to me any longer than he had to, not to mention offering me a drink. I started to get to my feet. "I've gotta get moving."

"Please, this is important," he said, taking a seat behind his desk. "I want you to know that I despise that bloody bastard."

"Borsalino? He's just one of thousands."

"I despise every one of them and their miserable *patria*." He sucked on his cigarette. "What are we doing down here, Michael? Here we are, both station chiefs, our daughters used to play together—part of a small diplomatic community—yet what do we really know about each other?"

"With our lives, it's tough to get to know anyone," I offered, wondering where this peculiar conversation was heading. If it didn't get someplace quick, he would be having it with himself.

"A pity, really. Are you sure you won't have a drink?"

"No, I don't handle it too well," I said, glancing at my watch.

"Be careful up there, Michael. You will be putting yourself in terrible danger, you know. And for what? If anything untoward happened to your man, we'd already know about it. Our intel up there is spectacular. Now that he's been spotted, we'll have him located in no time.

"By the way, how is your daughter Nicole doing? You know my Jen is starting university in the fall. She often asks after her."

"Fine," I said, recalling that when Niki and Jennifer were sixth-grade classmates in *Escuela* Lincoln, Niki used to complain that Jen's daddy never remembered her name. And I used to tell her not to feel bad because I didn't think he remembered mine either.

"I've gone on a bit, haven't I?" said Gregg. "I'm afraid I must speak to you for a moment in my official capacity. We cannot offer you protection in Cochabamba.

"Sad about people in our way of life, isn't it? Someone decides to eliminate us and the list of logical suspects would fill a London phone directory." He fixed me with a long, cold stare—the Forrest Gregg I was used to.

"Well, in *my* official capacity, I want to thank your agency for their concern," I said.

"How are you getting there?"

"Adolfo Martenz."

He nodded. "Of course. Be careful. He's no real friend of ours."

"Who down here is?"

Gregg opened the folder again, removed a photo and shoved it across the table to me. I noticed that his small pale hand was trembling.

It was an eight-by-ten black-and-white grainy photo of a group of women standing nude, facing an open trench. Snow drifted around them. The cold was reflected in the strained faces of a group of men in Nazi uniforms cloaked in heavy overcoats, their collars raised against a biting wind. They stood in a semicircle and watched as a black uniformed SS man with no overcoat held a pistol to the back of the head of one of the women.

The camera had caught the precise instant of the gun firing. The woman's face was caught in a twisted death grimace. Her body had begun to jolt forward. The gun barrel was raised slightly from the recoil. Smoke from the discharge clouded the air between the barrel and the woman's head. One of the men in overcoats at the center of the group was circled in red. It was obvious he was a high-ranking officer.

"This was taken during the winter of 1943 at a place sixty-two miles northwest of Warsaw, Poland, called Treblinka," said Gregg. "It was an extermination camp run by an SS officer named Franz Stangl. Have you heard of it?"

"My mother was born in Poland," I heard myself say. I could not take my eyes off the photo.

Gregg continued. "The Nazis tried to erase all traces of this place. They sent all the SS men assigned there on suicide missions. Several of the higher-ranking officers escaped here to Argentina. One of those is the man you see circled in red—Wilhelm Martenz. He was Adolfo's father, Michael."

I gathered all the thoughts that suddenly exploded through my mind and shoved them quickly and firmly into a corner where I stored all the unthinkables in my life. At that moment René's life was measured in hours. Without Martenz my hunt for him was crippled.

"Thanks, Forrest," I said as I got to my feet. "I'll keep it in mind." I turned and headed for the door.

4

I EXPLODED OUT OF FORREST GREGG'S OFFICE AND CHARGED DOWN A back stairway to the second floor. I could see Jackie, my secretary, through a glass door at the far end of a block-long hallway. She looked up from her desk and saw a six-feet-two, two-hundred-and-twenty-pound man sprinting toward her, full tilt.

A sharp pain shot through my right knee—the remnants of two decades of karate injuries and surgery. I fast-limped the rest of the way, trying to peel off my sopping-wet suit jacket.

"My God, *Nene,* not your knee again," said Jackie, rushing to help me pull the jacket off. She was a lanky, freckle-faced Oklahoma girl who'd come to Argentina twelve years earlier, married an Argentine soccer coach, and decided to stay.

"What knee?" I said. "I got no time for a knee. Call Adolfo's office. I need a ride to Cochabamba, like yesterday."

"It's already set," she said. "The Mongoose called. He's been ordered to take you wherever. And to guard you with his life."

The Mongoose was Mauricio Irigoya, one of Adolfo Martenz's most skilled pilots and an ex-lightweight boxing champ. He'd flown me in and out of jungle landing strips as if they were eight-lane concrete highways, chatting casually all the while about his favorite topic—boxing.

"Any messages?" I said, my hand on the doorknob of my office.

"You don't wanna go in there, *Nene,*" she warned.

I opened the door. My sunny corner office looked like the den of a bag lady. Stacks of unread cables and reports covered every surface of the room. The wall behind my desk was covered with Post-it telephone messages.

"I warned you," said Jackie, following me inside.

I started stripping off my drenched shirt and tie. "Anything I gotta do right now?"

"Everything! I've taken care of most of the administrative stuff for last month and forged your name to it. The rest are the quarterlies and annuals, waiting for your signature. I didn't know if you wanted to read them."

"Same fill-in-the-blanks bullshit as the last ones, right?"

"Right."

"Bless you," I said, slipping behind my desk and unlocking the drawer. "Just keep forging away, I got no time."

For a moment I remembered Gregg saying "we're both station chiefs," as if there was some similarity between our jobs. I had to laugh. Technically he was right, our titles and pay grades, GS-14, were the same, but the reality was that from his office, which took up almost a square block, he sent Argentine mercenaries all over South and Central America to do the nasty little business of overthrowing governments, assassinating political leaders, fomenting unrest, and in general playing the role of America's Big Stick in the hemisphere. On the other hand, I was running an almost mom-and-pop operation, with Jackie holding down the store and doing the reams of bureaucratic paperwork while I ran all over the world, changing identities and setting up sting operations.

Yeah, Forrest, we're just a couple of station chiefs, you and me.

I withdrew a small fireproof strongbox from the bottom drawer and removed a stack of about a dozen manila envelopes. Each one had a name, nationality, and job description printed on it. Each contained a passport, driver's license, and business cards. They all had one thing in common: my photo and description. They were the phony IDs I had been using for the past year or two.

I looked up. Jackie was watching me. "Any news about René?"

"Did you know him?" I asked.

"I saw him once," she said. "A long time ago, in headquarters. The secretaries were carrying on so. You'd think Marlon Brando was there. I peeked to see what the fuss was about." She smiled. "He was a fine-looking man."

"Don't say *was*," I said. "I just met with Gregg and Snakeface. René's been spotted in Cochabamba. I'm on the way there now."

Jackie looked worried. *"Nene,* Cochabamba? Is that safe for you?"

"Jackie, after twenty years of this madness, I've run out of safe places." Suddenly I thought of what Snakeface had said about the Arab community in Cochabamba and that I'd heard rumors of PLO terrorist support. It gave me an idea.

"How long will it take to get a call through to Israel?" I asked.

"Ten, fifteen minutes."

I scribbled a phone number and name down on a Post-it and handed it to her. "Then call Thibadeaux in Cochabamba. I'll need him to pick me up at the airport at about five this evening."

While Jackie made the calls I selected an Argentine diplomatic passport that described me as Bernardo Viola, member of the Argentine delegation to the UN in New York. The stamps and visas were up-to-date. There was an international driver's license and phony calling cards that went with it. I'd make undercover inquiries at first. If I needed muscle, DEA would supply it.

Jackie's voice came over the intercom: "The call to Israel."

I punched the blinking light on my phone.

"Shalom, Michael," said a soft, familiar voice.

"Avi. I need a favor. A big one."

"I'm glad to hear you're well, Michaela. Maybe you're a little curious how your family is doing?"

"I'm sorry, Cousin," I said, feeling too rushed and harried to feel guilty.

Avi Abramovich, my first cousin, was also an agent of the Mossad, the Israeli spy agency that is pound-for-pound the most efficient in the world. He had never actually told me of his work. In fact, I had never even heard him use the word. In Israel the Mossad does not officially exist. But events in our professional lives had overlapped and Avi showed himself capable of making miracles happen in places far-flung from tiny Israel.

"Just so you shouldn't wonder—we're all fine. I'm only happy to see you haven't changed, Michael. So what can I do for you?"

"I'm looking for someone," I said, conscious of thousands of miles of telephone lines and hundreds of listening ears. "Do you have any friends I could talk to in Bolivia? Cochabamba?"

My reasoning was that wherever in the world there was a large Arab community, especially one able to tap into the world's two largest economies—guns and drugs—there would be a Mossad presence. "Friends" to the Mossad, who had no friends, meant informers.

"I haven't spoken to him in a while," he said cagily. "I have to check that his address is current. How do I get the information to you—in person?"

"Get it to a man named Thibadeaux in the American consulate, Cochabamba." I spelled the name for him.

"So how is the family?" said Avi. "How is my favorite aunt Carolina?"

"Please forgive me, Avi. This is serious. I'm in a rush."

"For you, my cousin, it will be there within the hour. When will you come to visit?"

"I wish I knew. Thanks, Avi."

I hung up and hustled across the office to the room-size vault where I stored weapons, electronic listening devices, special cameras, and other investigative equipment. I selected a Sony minirecorder about half the size of a pack of cigarettes and a small leather packet that contained lock-picking equipment, and shoved them into my leather carryall. Then I remembered the one tool without which there would be no such thing as undercover work. I had to open another safe to get at it.

The metal box contained fifty one-hundred-dollar bills—all the cash in the Buenos Aires District Office. It was to be used for payments to informants and undercover expenses. If more than $5,000 was needed, a special request had to be made to headquarters to justify it. I counted out fifty hundreds and marked the ledger for the amount taken. Jackie would file a voucher while I was gone, so that—according to DEA regs—the money would be automatically replenished. I would have to stop at the embassy cashier to break two of the hundreds down to singles. A stack of hundreds wrapped around a stack of singles made a much more impressive bankroll.

"Mongoose is at Aeroparque, ready to go," said Jackie on the intercom.

"Tell him I'm on my way," I yelled.

It was 11:30 a.m. If Mongoose had the twin-engine Piper Cheyenne he usually flew, we'd be in Cochabamba by 5:30 p.m.

I took a last look around the office. A small framed photo on the ego wall, almost lost in the rows of photos, awards, and plaques, caught my eye. I had almost forgotten it. It was a photo of René, me, and our sons taken at Victor's Cafe in New York almost eight years ago during a father-son dinner that had become a custom with us.

The photo brought with it a memory, a memory that began with lonely and terrifying days in Bangkok, Thailand. It was during the Vietnam War and the night streets of Bangkok flowed with wild-eyed, stoned combat soldiers on R&R. My son, Keith, then eight years old and living with his mother in the States, was in a bad way. I had been in-country for almost three months living in deep cover with Chinese drug dealers.

René and I shared the anguish of trying to be good fathers. Only to each other could we admit that a deep cover operative by definition was a scumbag as father. Anyone who's been there would say you have to give up one or the other. We loved our kids, but we were as addicted to the undercover life as a junkie to his needle. My own father had abandoned me when I was eight and I knew what it felt like growing up feeling that he was alive and well someplace and didn't give a fuck if I was alive or dead. I could never find a way to explain to my son, in a way that would take the hurt from his eyes, why he didn't always have a daddy there like other boys.

Just before I left for Thailand I was notified that I would have to testify in an upcoming trial in Miami for my last case—a gift from God. DEA would have to bring me back to the States for at least a week of trial. I'd stretch it to three or four with my son. We'd go fishing, race go-carts, and hang out together. I had Keith sent to his grandma's house in Delray Beach, Florida, to wait for me so he'd know it wasn't more bullshit followed by another disappointment.

Anticipating the trip was what kept me going through the assignment. I had this deep sense that being with my son at this moment in his life was critical; that he was at some kind of crossroads from which his little life could take off in any direction, depending on the way the push went.

Weeks slowly turned to months. There were two trial delays. I risked late-night trips, checking myself for tails, cutting through back alleys, changing cabs, to call my mom's house. I'll be there, I promised my boy, just have patience.

Finally, a definite trial date was set in two weeks. After I told

Keith when I was coming, I got on the phone with my mother. She told me he had lit up like a lightbulb. I left the booth crying and laughing at the same time, as I made my way along a dark, isolated klong in Bangkok, probably under surveillance by people who'd off me at the slightest hint that I was betraying them.

The dopers were running an operation out of Chiang Mai, in northern Thailand, transporting heavy amounts of pure heroin down to Bangkok, where it was turned over to American GIs working in the Graves Registration Section of the army. This was the unit that transshipped the bodies of GIs killed in Vietnam back to the U.S. for burial. A couple of these ghouls were hiding plastic sacks full of dope in the corpses of our boys to be picked up by their partners waiting to process the bodies on arrival in the States. I was a hair from learning their main connection.

The Bangkok faction had invited me to the "factory" itself, somewhere north of Chiang Mai. They were only waiting for the approval of the main man running the operation. To cover for my absence, I told the dopers that I had to meet with my criminal organization in the States and would return in a month.

On the eve of my trip to Miami, I received a coded call at my hotel room that meant I was to go immediately to the rear entrance of the American embassy. A note was handed to me through the fence that said *Trial postponed indefinitely*.

What I didn't know at that moment was that a suit in Washington had decided the case was too important to let me go to Miami and had not only engineered all the trial delays, but days later would also make it official that no one was to tell me that my son was missing. If it weren't for René Villarino, only God knew what might have happened.

When my mom told Keith I wasn't coming, he'd run out the door and had been missing for more than two days. I never got a chance to tell him I was going to buy a ticket anyway and be there by the end of the week—trial or no trial. With no way of reaching me in Thailand, my mom panicked and reported it to DEA, where the information sat in a desk drawer.

There was a message waiting for me in my suite at the Siam Intercontinental with a phone number in Miami: *Urgente! Llame a Sr Pasquale Cologero*. I recognized René's cover name immediately. A wild, twenty-minute cab ride across downtown Bangkok and I was telephoning the U.S. from the lobby of the Nana Hotel, a small, pimp-and-hooker-infested dive. I looked at my watch. It would be 4:00 a.m. in Miami.

René Villarino answered after the first ring. *"Mighe,"* he said. "Your boy, Keith, he is safe now. He's a good kid. He stays with me and my boys. I wanted you to know this before you hear anything else."

"What the hell is going on?" I shouted. "What do you mean *safe?*"

René had as many informants in Washington as he had in the underworld. He'd heard the buzz about Keith being missing and that no one was telling me. He dropped what he was doing, ignored the edict from the suits, and got a BNDD pilot to fly him to Fort Lauderdale from New York, where he performed the kind of magic only a guy like René could do. Through the local FLEOA representative he got more than a hundred agents from Customs, BNDD, FBI, and ATF to scour the streets from Fort Lauderdale to Miami Beach on their own time and without alerting the press. Within hours, Keith was found wandering the Miami beachfront.

I will never forget that moment, my insides twisting between relief, rage, and gratitude, words choking in my throat. I held the phone away from me. I didn't want him to know I was crying.

"I can never thank you enough, my friend."

"Not to thank me," he said. "I count on you to do the same for me if my boys need me and I can't be there for them."

"Dad, it's neat here," said Keith, his voice hushed and excited, the most spirited I'd heard him in months. My insides swelled. "Mr. Villarino said he is my uncle . . . Marcello and Paolo are my cousins. Is that true?"

"Yeah, Son. It's true."

I had never really looked at the photo closely before. It showed the five of us facing the camera, arms over each other's shoulders. I noticed that René's head was on a slight angle. He was looking at me with a sad smile.

And then I thought of Marita Salazar, René's longtime girlfriend. If anyone in the world knew where René was at any time, it was she. If I couldn't bring René back by tomorrow, I would have to track her down. A last resort. René and I shared a secret with Marita that could destroy us all and I didn't want to dredge up the past if I didn't have to. I pushed her from my mind. I couldn't blow my cool and lead the shooflies to her.

Suddenly I remembered that some time ago René had asked me to make him a copy of the photo—it had slipped my mind. I took it off the wall and put it in my carryall.

When I saw him, I would give him mine.

5

COCHABAMBA, BOLIVIA

"SO YOU DON'T THINK TYSON COULD HAVE BEATEN ALI?" SAID THE Mongoose as he pitched the nose of the twin-engine Piper Cheyenne sharply downward into a steep dive. My stomach slammed back against my spine, my intestines tying themselves into squishy little knots.

"No," I managed through locked jaws.

"There's the shithole, down there," said the Mongoose.

Below I could see our target—the narrow strip of white that was Cochabamba International Airport. I closed my eyes and reminded myself that the Mongoose had won his nickname for his lightning reflexes in the ring, that handling five tons of steel hurtling at half the speed of sound was second nature to him, that Adolfo called him the best of the best.

"*Dios,* what I wouldn't give to see that fight. I'd put my money on Tyson—the man is inhuman, like a tank. The size of his arms. *U-fa! . . .*"

The Mongoose was still talking when the plane bounced in for a landing. I opened my eyes. My shirt was drenched with cold sweat. We sped toward a small terminal building.

Special Agent Roscoe Thibadeaux, DEA's man in Bolivia—a tall, hard-looking mulatto from Louisiana—was waiting for me at the terminal. His face was covered with three days of black stubble, his eyes blood-red from booze and lack of sleep. He handed me a sealed envelope and began walking quickly, leading the way through the derelict little building that served as the main air terminal for Bolivia's third largest city. Lots of dark sullen eyes followed us. No one moved. It was impossible here to distinguish the watchers from the curious, or those with the usual hatred of *los Yanquis*.

"Some guy left that for you at the office," he said, moving a stride ahead of me. He was about six four with legs like a giraffe. "Ah got every muthafuckin' CI on the books out beating the bushes for Villarino. Zero."

"What about the bar, El Tejano—the Agency's info?" I said as I tore open the envelope. Once again I was amazed at the long reach of the Mossad. Inside was a slip of paper that read:

> SZION ABAN, RESTAURANTE CRUZEÑO, 278. AVENIDA 27 DE AGOSTO. KNOWLEDGEABLE OF LOCAL EVENTS. EXPENSIVE. ASK BUT DON'T TELL. SAY: "LOOKING FOR NASIR."

"I talked to fifty people who spend half their life hustling that place," said Thibadeaux. *"Nada!* Them muthafuckin' tango dancers ain't lettin' me near their guy."

We reached Thibadeaux's car, a battered late-model Chevrolet with bullet holes in the trunk and rear window. I tossed my leather carryall onto the rear seat and got in. I thought I heard a car engine kick over right behind us and twisted in my seat to look. Nothing.

"Nervous, Cuz?" said Thibadeaux, slipping into the driver's seat. He raced the engine and jammed the accelerator to the floor. We roared out of the dusty little airport parking lot and up a steep hill.

"You better close your window," he said.

Before I could roll it up the stench of human excrement hit us. "Welcome to Cochabamba," laughed Thibadeaux.

We shot past row after row of ramshackle tin-and-cardboard huts. A cop carrying a .45-caliber grease gun, his military cap peaked front and rear with the kind of grommet the fifty-mission pilots wore during World War II, paused to watch us whiz by with flat black eyes. Two Indians crouched on either side of him defecating in the morning sunlight.

We swerved through another ramshackle street, Indians scattering like chickens. "Man you can't hit these muthafuckas if you try," said Thibadeaux. "I dunno, Cuz. Where you wanna go? We can go back and kill some more time at El Tejano. But if you want my opinion, the info is bull-fucking-shit."

"You think the Argentines lied to the spooks?" I asked.

Thibadeaux snorted. "Sheeeit. You wanna know what I think? I think the spooks know exactly where he is. Villarino's jus' pullin' the same super-secret undercover shit he always does. Hey, this ain't the first time he disappeared. He's probably workin' *for* them and they're coverin' for his ass."

We hit a street lined with shops. Traffic was stopped dead. Horns blew all around us. "This here is the business section of town," Thibadeaux explained.

Cochabamba was one of the wealthiest cities in Bolivia, allegedly from farming and light industry. If you count harvesting coca leaves as farming, this was true. Wealthy or not, the city was old and shabby-looking. Posters advertised ten-year-old Chuck Norris movies and early Madonna records. There were beauty parlors on every block and kids wearing the latest in oversize sneakers attempted a John Travolta New York bop walk.

"You know this address?" I showed him the slip of paper, folding it over to hide the name and message.

"Main drag. We're on it. 'Bout six, seven blocks straight ahead."

"Drop me about a block from it."

Thibadeaux shook his head. "Do me a fucking favor, Levine."

"What's that?"

"René pulled his tightrope deep cover act one time too many. Know what I'm sayin'?"

"No, what are you saying?"

"I'm saying, if you gonna do UC with no backup, this is the last muthafuckin' place you wanna do it. Look out there, man. Everything you see bought with dope money. You go missing too, the suits are on *my* ass."

"It's a comforting thought to know I got a guy like you backing me up, Roscoe," I said. I grabbed my leather carryall from the backseat and slipped out of the car, leaving him stuck in traffic. I heard Thibadeaux curse and punch the steering wheel. I didn't look back.

I had waded about three blocks along narrow sidewalks crowded with dark people who came up to my shoulder, when it happened. I sensed the danger before I saw it.

The man was a block ahead of me on the other side of the

street and peering into a store window. I'm not sure what it was that attracted my attention, all I knew was that I couldn't take my eyes off him. He was a bit taller than the average on the street, a bit fairer-skinned, perhaps European. He wore a loose-fitting guayabera shirt that went to his hips, common enough dress in South America, also great for concealing a gun. Observing people through window reflections was a technique commonly used by spies and agents, but the street was full of people window-shopping.

As I watched he moved away from the window and dodged through the jam of cars, crossing over to my side of the street. He seemed to swim toward me, his head lowered, concealing himself in the pedestrian flow. As the gap narrowed our eyes met for a brief instant. It was as if a bolt of electricity cracked between us. All doubt vanished. *He's coming for me.*

I slowed. Too many people. Too close. It could be a two- or three-man trap—its jaws already closing. I had only identified one. A narrow alley between buildings to my left. I would reach it a few seconds before him. It would help me cull friend from foe. I needed those seconds.

I remembered my friend and karate *sensei* Chuck Merriman's words: *An edge of a hundredth of a second can be the difference between life and death.*

I veered across the short pavement toward the alley. I thought of going for the gun, but what if I was wrong? The last thing in the world I needed was to have to identify myself to the local cops, or get into a shoot-out with them. I'd be worthless here looking for my friend.

The alley stank from an accumulation of two hundred years of human excrement. *My luck has really turned to shit this time.* The man was reaching under his shirt as he turned in behind me. My body was already in mindless motion with my thoughts a beat behind it. His eyes opened wide as he realized I was striding straight toward him, smiling broadly. The gun was already in his hand, but the surprise bought me another eighth of a second.

A *mae geri*—a forward-thrusting kick—can be as devastating as a cannon blast, even more so when your target is walking toward you. I took a quick giant stride, like a football player kicking off, and speared the reinforced toe of my boot into a spot below the navel and above the groin, a spot where the soft bladder is unprotected by muscle or bone.

Fear is good, Sensei *used to say. It delivers the maximum energy a man is capable of. It can give a man the strength to lift a truck with his bare hands. The trick is to harness and focus its energy in a technique, a kick or blow.*

I had enough adrenaline racing through me at that moment to light up Hoboken, New Jersey—every ounce of it was in that kick. My toe didn't stop until it hit somewhere near his spine.

The gun's muzzle blast seared my ear. It bounced off my shoulder and clattered on the ground behind me. The man was on his knees in front of me, his forehead on the ground, his body heaving for air.

A crowd watched from the mouth of the alley. There were screams and shouts, but no one else followed. A lone assassin? Perhaps. I stepped over him and moved quickly toward the crowd. People hustled to get out of my way. At moments of extreme violence witnesses are most susceptible to suggestion.

"Llame la policía!" I said. "He tried to kill some guy. He's got a gun." I pushed through the crowd, repeating this. Wild-eyed cops waving guns came charging from different directions. "Careful, he's got a gun," I shouted. They hurtled past me into the alley.

As I had hoped, no one in the crowd volunteered any information. There were one or two confused glances my way, but Bolivia was a place where only a complete fool got involved in police business.

Car traffic remained at a standstill. I watched from the edge of the crowd as the police dragged the man from the alley clubbing and kicking him. He was unconscious and in far worse shape than when I left him. I'd have to get Thibadeaux to follow up. At the moment I didn't even want to think about who the guy was and what this was about. It would throw me off my course. I walked away.

The address Avi had sent me was a Middle Eastern restaurant advertising falafel sandwiches in the window. A sign in the door said *Cerrado*—closed. I peered inside. It was a neat little place with seven or eight Formica tables and a bar. On the wall behind the bar was a yellowed photo of Yasir Arafat. I tried the door. It opened with a jangle of bells.

A fat woman with frizzy black hair wearing a red muumuu the size of a circus tent appeared from a door behind the bar. Before I could say a word she disappeared. The door opened again and a man appeared—obese with a thick, wild thatch of jet-black hair. His eyes worked me up and down as he waddled slowly around the bar. He wheezed loudly as he moved.

"We are closed," he said in Spanish with a heavy Middle Eastern accent.

"You didn't have to come all the way out here to tell me that," I said. "You're Señor Aban?"

"Who's asking?"

"I'm looking for Nasir."

It was as if I had pushed a personality-change button. He seemed to duck his head. His eyes darted to the street.

"You are the Argentine?"

"Yes. Friends gave me your name and address."

He studied me closely. His eyes were two black olives half swallowed in mounds of swollen flesh. "You're not a Jew," he said.

"And you are," I said.

His hand raised. A diamond glittered from its entombment in the folds of a sausage finger. "Only my cursed father. But I don't ask any questions."

"Fine with me."

"What is it you want?"

"A man came to Cochabamba two or three days ago. He was with two Colombians. He may have flown into the Chapare. I need to find him."

"Coca?"

"Probably."

"You speak English?" he asked.

"Not well."

"You're not a cop?"

"If I was a cop, would I come to you?"

He studied my face. I had great confidence in my face getting me over. Many have described it as an evil face, a face that belonged wrapped around a criminal mind. In the two decades of my undercover career so many truly evil people have trusted me that I believe it must be true. He smiled in affirmation. Both his incisors were bright yellow gold. "Only if you were smart," he said. "But I don't ask any questions."

"Can you help me or not?"

"Maybe, maybe not. I get a thousand-dollar retainer, up front.

Two thousand more if I find him for you. I only accept American dollars."

I took the roll of hundreds wrapped around a hundred singles from my bag and counted out a thousand. He was impressed. His thick hand moved, the diamond winked at me, the money disappeared. When I returned the roll to the bag I let him glimpse my Argentine diplomatic passport.

"You are a diplomat," he said.

"Yes."

"Sit," he said, pulling a chair out from one of the tables. He sat across from me. He had to slide his chair about four feet back from the table to fit. Over the next ten minutes I described René—height, weight, the languages he spoke, the kinds of clothes he wore, where he was seen. Finally I showed him a copy of the photo.

"A man like this traveling with Colombians here would be like a fireworks display. He would leave tracks. And if there are tracks, Szion Aban will find them."

"How much time do you need?" I asked.

"Where can I call you?"

"I will call you. Write your number down on something."

"Fine," said Aban. "I don't ask questions."

He heaved his bulk sideways and produced a wallet. He withdrew several business cards and selected one. The shiny olive eyes narrowed. The expression on his face lacked only an illuminated lightbulb over his head.

"You're an Argentine diplomat. Maybe you have some government connections?"

"Possibly."

"You know anything about the oil business?"

"Nothing."

"Even better. What if I tell you, with the right connections in your country, you could make a quick couple of million. Cash. American dollars."

"I would listen very carefully."

"Legal," he added.

"Of course."

"I have a friend in Morocco." He indicated the business card in his hand. "He has access to a significant quantity of oil that is for sale at well below the OPEC price. I don't ask too many questions."

"Of course not."

"I have heard that there are some Argentine brokers who would be willing to handle this."

"Why tell me?"

Again he studied my face. The gold canine teeth flashed.

"The deal would need someone with government influence. I believe it is a matter of hiding the country of origin of the shipment. Nothing illegal, mind you. But you must understand that, let's say one of the OPEC countries wanted to sell oil cheaper than the others, it would be in that country's best interest to hide the transaction. Obviously."

"Obviously."

"And the commission could be as much as a dollar or two per barrel. We are talking about millions of barrels." He paused to study my face again. He saw interest and greed. It was curiosity.

My life has always been full of strange events that have turned out to be unexpected doors of opportunity. As long as René was missing I was going to open any door that presented itself and at least take a peek.

He turned the card over and scribbled a phone number on the back. "Call me in four or five hours for news." He passed me the card. "My friend in Morocco."

I glanced at the front of the card. There was a name and address in Casablanca, printed in both Arabic and English. I put it in my leather bag.

"If you think you can do something," said Aban, "call him and tell him I gave you the number, or call me. Day or night."

I walked out into the bright sunlight. I took a breath of thick oily air and started walking. A car horn beeped. Thibadeaux was parked at the curb waiting for me. He was on his cellular phone.

"In the Guajira?" he said as I got into the car beside him. "They sure it's him?—right—okay, he's right here. Yeah, I'll tell him—yeah. Yeah. Gotcha!" The phone beeped as he broke the connection.

"Like I told you, Levine." He laughed. "False fucking alarm. We got him. He's okay."

I felt my insides swell with relief and realized that I was more afraid than I had wanted to admit. "Where is he?"

"In the Guajira with two Colombian dopers."

"In Colombia?"

"I just got off the phone with Bogotá. *Our* boys got him located."

"They're sure it's him?"

"Orders are to *back* the fuck off. He's on a special right outta the administrator's office. They don't want him burned. Case closed. You, by the way, been ordered back to Argentina."

"In other words he's still out there with no backup?"

"All they told me is everybody's bein' told to drop the search."

The cellular phone began beeping loudly from its cradle below the dashboard. "You got a problem with that," he said reaching for it, "take it up with the man on the fifteenth floor."

"Thibadeaux," he said into the phone. His eyes shifted to mine. "Yeah he's right here. Go 'head patch it through." He passed me the phone. "Call comin' through the embassy switchboard for you."

"Lay-vee-nay." It was Adolfo. The line crackled with static. It sounded as if he was using one of his military field phones.

"Yes."

"You must return, at once. Mongoose has orders where to take you."

"What's going on?"

There was a long static-filled silence. For a moment I thought the connection was broken.

"Listen to me, Miguel . . ." *Some Argentines called me that name. It was the first time Adolfo had ever used it.* "Drop what you are doing. Come. Now!"

6

THE PAMPAS

"IT'S NOT MUCH FURTHER," SAYS MONGOOSE AS HE STEERS THE *Gendarmería* jeep over the rutted road. It's the fourth time he's said those words in the last three hours. The long ride is a welcome rest for me after the panic of the last few days and besides, I'm not looking forward to returning to Positos any faster than I have to. We're about four driving hours west of the town of Santa Rosa, somewhere in the vast expanse of the Argentine Pampas.

The Pampas are rolling, grassy plains dotted by lonely *estancias*—cattle ranches. Every couple of miles we pass herds of cattle driven by hard-faced men on horseback who ride like they were born in a saddle. They wear baggy pants, fancy silver belts, and flat-crowned hats. They are gauchos—Argentine cowboys. Their history is mythical in Argentina and reads every bit as romantic and nasty as that of their American cowboy cousins, including a war that wiped out the local Indians.

We come over a small rise and slow to a crawl as a herd of cattle crosses our path in the fading sunlight. They seem wild and barely under control. Mongoose is unconcerned. Two gauchos loom a mile above us on horseback, their faces expressionless as they watch the government jeep crawl by. Mongoose smiles and salutes them. They don't respond. He shrugs, "Hardheaded bastards."

The sun is barely an ember when Mongoose says, "We're here."

Ahead I can see a helicopter and several military vehicles

parked around a one-story ranch house. I hear the sound of a generator. Shadow figures move in all the windows.

Mongoose pulls up near the front of the house and edges between two military trucks. I'm out of the jeep almost before it stops and striding toward the house. Two *Gendarmaría* officers in the doorway recognize me and step out of the way. They look beyond me unable to meet my gaze.

The instant I open the door the smell slams me in the face. The pungent odor of rotting flesh. I feel my stomach turn and cover my mouth to keep from retching.

Men move about the room with handkerchiefs covering their faces. Some wear hospital surgical masks. Wires crisscross the room bringing electricity inside from the generator. A man in uniform measures the room. A half-dozen men are carefully dusting for fingerprints. The house looks abandoned. There are a few broken and discarded pieces of furniture. The wood interior walls are rotting. I can see stars through a hole in the roof. A man films the scene with a video camera. He points it at me.

All this is going on as the room buzzes with big black flies.

On the floor beneath my feet is what at first looks like a thick black stripe, only it is alive and moving. An army of maggots coming from the next room marches in formation toward a rotting hole in the wall behind me. I have seen enough death to know what this signifies. My mind seizes on facts as if they were handholds at the edge of a yawning black pit.

Flies are attracted to the odor of rotting flesh. They lay their eggs in the open orifices of the corpse. The eggs hatch to form larvae. The larvae feed on the corpse until they reach a certain size and it is time to pupate. Some species of maggot will march off like armies in search of safe places to hatch. By studying the life cycle of maggots one can actually determine the time and place of death. . . .

Someone calls out, "*Comandante, ya llegó Lay-vee-nay.*"

I am in the doorway of the next room, although I don't remember taking any steps to get there. Silent men, their faces masked, watch me. I notice camera equipment and movie lights.

In their midst as if holding court for this masked audience is a grotesque thing that seems to be moving and pulsating. The thing itself, I see, is not moving at all. The movement comes from a black, writhing mass of maggots instinctively living out their life cycles. The thing, I see, has my friend René Villarino's black curly hair with flecks of gray on the side.

I don't remember leaving that room. My next memory is of being on my hands and knees in high grass and darkness vomiting my guts out, until my insides felt like they were being shredded. I sat up. Someone was beside me. A bottle was placed in my hands.

"Take a drink," said Adolfo's voice.

I took a big swallow that burned its way down my raw throat, and then another. The third drink no longer burned. The bottle was gently removed from my hand.

"What happened?" I asked.

"Do you want to talk now, or wait until—"

"Now!" The word exploded out of me.

"Some passing gauchos heard cries coming from the house."

"When?"

"Two days ago."

"Two days," I heard myself repeat, my mind groping for where I was two days ago.

"They thought the house was abandoned. They saw a plane land nearby. The cries stopped, so they did nothing. Out here you mind your own business. Yesterday one of our mounted patrols happened upon them and one of them mentioned the incident. They investigated and called me immediately. They touched nothing. When we arrived we found an Italian passport nearby in the name of Fabrizio Calvi—one of the names on your list. Nothing has been moved. That is exactly as we found him."

I had a hard time focusing my thoughts. All I could think of was that two days ago, while my friend was fighting for his life, I was running around in fucking circles. *I just wasn't smart enough. I missed something. René would have caught it. I had failed him. I had failed his children.*

"Exactly when and how?" I asked.

"Our pathologist estimates that he has been dead between forty-eight hours and seventy-two hours."

"While I was sitting around the fucking embassy."

"We don't have to talk now," said Adolfo. "My investigators are preparing a complete package for you."

"I need to know, now."

"Your friend died very hard. He was tortured. Medical measures were taken to keep him alive."

"How long?"

"Twenty-four hours, maybe more. They must have wanted to

know something very badly . . . or they were trying to make a point."

I felt numb, the world had gone dreamlike. Something that would happen to me during the most terror-filled moments of my life. I became an observer. None of this was real. As an outside observer I could make cold, calculating decisions. Judge what steps needed to be taken immediately and what could be delayed. There was one measure that could not be postponed.

"I need a favor, Adolfo," I said.

He was silent, waiting for the rest. I could not see his face clearly, only his silhouette in the light coming from the house.

"No matter what happens, no matter who they send down here from my country to investigate, no matter what kind of pressure is put on you—whatever information you learn, you tell me first."

Adolfo then did something he rarely did. He lit up a cigarette, took a deep, satisfying drag and exhaled.

"I thought you wanted a favor," he said.

I looked past him at the house, eerily lit in the blackness of the Pampas. Before I left I was going to go back inside and take a long look at what they did to my friend. I wanted to burn it into my brain—to open a wound that wouldn't heal.

7

A HALF HEMISPHERE AWAY FROM ARGENTINA, A BLACK MERCEDES sedan carrying three DEA undercover agents raced through the rain-deluged streets of downtown L.A., a blue emergency light attached to its roof flashing frenetically. They were on an emergency run that was about to suck them into what had just become my worst nightmare.

"Lima Alpha Base to those units en route 21075 La Cienega," squawked the radio voice from a hidden speaker beneath the front seat.

"Thirty-three-zero-one to Lima Alpha Base," said DEA Special Agent Tito "Monguin" Garza. He had the mike cord stretched as far as it would go into the backseat, where he always rode when he was in charge. "Zero-one, eight and nine are ten-eight, en route that twenty."

"Ten-four, Zero-one, what is your ETA?"

"Zero-five," said Vinnie "Black Boy" O'Brien at the wheel, his broad Irish face with its boxer's mashed nose spread into a wide grin. His wide shoulders and big hands wheeled the heavy sedan into a turn with an effortless grace. He mashed the accelerator to the floor. "We flyin' low, like Jock-coe-moe."

"Zero-five," repeated Garza into the mike.

"Be advised, headquarters is on land line," said Lima Base. *"LAPD report meets White Queen Profile. They want confirmation ASAP."*

"That's ten-four," said Garza. "Gimme the latest status at destination." He released the mike button. "Fuck headquarters where they breathe."

The radio hissed and crackled with static.

"LAPD radio indicates several injuries and fatalities," said Base. *"Subject described as under influence of undetermined substance. LAPD responding with EMT and fire department. No further at this time."*

"Get it down, Georgie, word for word," snapped Garza at the man in the passenger seat.

"I got it," said Special Agent Jorge "Georgie" Mendoza, a dark, clean-cut Chicano in horn-rimmed glasses, suit, and tie, as he scribbled frantically into a notebook.

"Pendejo desk jockeys are watching us," said Garza. "We got to cover our asses with asbestos." He pressed the mike button again: "Thirty-three-zero-one, Lima Base, we need backup. ASAP."

The radio crackled again. *"Lima Base, Ten-four. Break. Lima Base any units in vicinity of downtown?"*

Garza listened intently as other units responded to the call for backup. O'Brien wheeled the Mercedes around a corner. "Damn, will you look at that!"

A hundred yards ahead, every type of emergency vehicle in the Los Angeles County fleet was scattered all over the street. Pulsating red, blue, and amber emergency lights lit up the front of the converted warehouse that housed the Snakepit, L.A.'s hot nightclub of the moment. A dozen officers in plainclothes and uniforms carefully searched the street, seemingly oblivious to the driving rain. Paramedics carrying stretchers and gear rushed toward the club, passing others on the way out with loaded stretchers.

Off to one side a body lay covered with a black plastic tarp. A commotion erupted in the crowd around it.

"There!" ordered Garza, "Near the front! Get as close as you can."

"You got it!" O'Brien tapped the siren button, people scattered as he drove the Mercedes up onto the curb.

Garza was out of the car before it stopped, striding quickly across the sidewalk. Cops turned to gawk curiously at the dark Latino. The full-length leather coat, diamond earring, and slick black hair tied in a short ponytail seemed incongruous with the gold DEA badge hanging from his neck.

"Get your fucking hands off me!" screeched a woman in a drenched black cocktail dress that clung to her by a miracle. Her face was a black running mask of mascara. She plunked herself down on the ground near the head of the covered body. A huge, red-faced LAPD sergeant gripped her forearms over her head from behind and was trying to drag her to her feet.

"DEA," said Garza, cornering a young, wide-eyed cop in a rookie uniform. "What's the deal here?"

"Guy went berserk inside. Must've been on something heavy," said the cop, staring at the badge around Garza's neck. "I seen people dusted before, this hadda be more than angel dust."

"Why you say that?"

"Take a look inside," said the cop. "He drove a broken beer bottle halfway into one guy's head. One of our guys inside tried to stop him. The perp took four nine-millimeter slugs in the chest, stabbed the cop with a wineglass, took two more slugs in the back and then made it out here before he went ten-seven." He nodded toward the body. "A waitress saw him and his girlfriend snorting white powder. Whatever it was it turned him into a moon rocket."

"Who's the *mamita*?" said Garza, cocking his head at the struggling girl.

"The perp's girlfriend."

A group of cops surrounded the three DEA agents, eyeing them suspiciously. Garza grabbed Mendoza's collar. "Get on the radio," he ordered, switching to Spanish. "Tell base it's confirmed, *La Reina Blanca*. And find out where the fuck our backup is."

Mendoza ran for the car. Garza turned on his heel and pushed through the crowd toward the struggling girl with O'Brien at his shoulder.

The dead weight of the girl had proved too much for the sergeant, whose profuse gut and veined, bulbous nose spoke of a lot more hours spent lifting beer bottles than weights.

"You! Gimme a hand," he said to a short black patrolman with a shaved head.

The cop grabbed the struggling girl in a behind-the-neck choke hold, lifted her and bent her over backwards.

"That's it," said the sergeant, gripping her buttocks and letting his hands linger as he slid them down her thighs toward her kicking legs, holding them fast against his gut. "Okay, let's get the bitch into the cruiser."

They started across the sidewalk.

Garza blocked their path. "Can I talk to you, Sarge?"

"What the fuck kinda kiddie badge is that?" said the sergeant. The black cop tightened his grip on the girl's neck.

"Special Agent Tito Garza, Department of Justice, DEA. I gotta talk to her."

"Get the fuck outta my way *Tit-ohh,* or whatever ya name is. Fuckin' feds. Ya wanna talk to her, call LAPD headquarters. Okay *Tit*-ohh?"

Garza didn't move. O'Brien, still grinning, had positioned himself a pace behind.

"That yer muscle, Tit-ooh?" laughed the sergeant, nodding at O'Brien. "He here to protect ya, so nobody kicks yer greasy little butt an' takes yer pretty gold badge away?"

A Chevy sedan roared to the curb behind them, blue light spinning on its roof. Three men in street clothes, gold DEA badges hanging from chains around their necks, jumped out quickly, leaving the car doors open. They moved through the circle of cops surrounding Garza and the sergeant.

Mendoza, wild-eyed with excitement, pushed through to Garza's side. "They want you to take it over," he said into Garza's ear. "National security authority!"

Garza didn't seem to be listening. He and the sergeant were locked in a stare-down contest.

"I—am—a—fucking—federal—agent," said Garza, enunciating each word. "You know what that means, *pendejo?* It means *I'm* taking the bitch, an' *you* can call *my* headquarters. You stop me, I'm gonna lock your fat, *maricón* ass up for interfering with a federal officer." Garza's handsome face contorted and trembled with the effort to hide his rage.

There was a stir among the cops around them. Some covered grins. Others didn't bother. A berserk druggie butchering people was routine, but a fed confronting a sergeant was entertainment.

The sergeant glared down at the slimy little greaser blocking his way. Didn't even come up to his shoulder. Typical of the scum they were giving federal jobs nowadays. Every bit of resentment he'd ever felt about spics, feds, Head Start programs, school taxes, government giveaways, illegal aliens on welfare, niggers and spics who'd been promoted over him just because they were niggers and spics, exploded in his head.

He dropped the girl's legs and moved close to Garza, his massive gut brushing the shorter man's chest. "Now you listen ta' me ya little spic," he hissed, jostling Garza back with his gut. "I don't give a flyin' fuck who ya' are—"

At that moment there was only one human being Tito Garza hated more than that *hijo de puta* Fidel Castro—it was the fat *hijo de puta* in front of him.

All four of Tito's punches landed in less than a measured second. A hard right uppercut to the sergeant's gut drove his overloaded bladder back to the spine, causing the instantaneous release of a recently finished quart of beer. Two bullet-like left hooks, delivered as if Garza's shoulder were a ball joint, smashed the sergeant's already misshapen nose into a blood-gushing pulp. The coup de grâce was a hard right uppercut deep into the solar plexus that Garza leaned into with all of his 157 pounds. For an instant his balled fist was buried to the wrist in rolls of fat.

"Ooof," a dozen male voices gasped in unison.

The sergeant went *splat* on his huge butt, vomiting, bleeding, and urinating at the same time.

"That's a motherfuckin' bias crime," said Garza, standing over him. "Racist motherfucker. I oughta lock you up."

"Yo, bro'," said Vinnie O'Brien, gently taking the girl from the hands of the black cop. "You heard it. He dissed my partner."

The cop looked at the battered Irish face. "I heard what I heard," he said.

"Sure you did," said O'Brien as he started walking the stunned girl toward the Mercedes.

But Garza hadn't had enough. "You fat motherfucker, *tu madre es más puta que* Heidi Fleiss!" he raged over the gasping sergeant. "Why don't you call me a spic now?" He cocked his leg back to kick and was grabbed by Georgie Mendoza, who wrestled him away.

"¡Basta ya! You won, *Monguín*."

Garza jerked away from him. "Don't you *ever* call me that!"

Mendoza raised his hands in surrender. "I'm your partner *ese*. The guy's not doing anything. You got him—"

Garza jabbed his finger into Mendoza's chest. "Then be my partner, but don't *ever* call me that again."

"Hey I don't even know what it means. I thought that's what they called you in New York. *No soy tu enemigo*, Tito."

"Never motherfucking mind what it means! And talk English! You ain't in Guadalajara."

"You were just speaking to me in Spanish!"

"That's *Newyoriquen*, fucko." Garza's face suddenly broke into a wide grin. "Maybe some day I'll teach you hicks about *La Gran Manzana*. Meanwhile, I need you and the other guys to get inside and get the story. Find out who sold that shit to Mr. Deadmeat wrapped in that doggy-bag over there. Witnesses, the fucking works. Any cop tries to get in your way, it's national, fucking security. Let 'em call Washington."

"You got it, *ese*."

"Okay, move!"

Mendoza disappeared into the club along with two other DEA agents.

Garza got into the Mercedes. O'Brien was at the wheel. The girl was handcuffed to a special steel loop on the floor of the backseat. Garza twisted in his seat to look at her. She peered back at him, her eyes wide, her lips quivering. The makeup had washed away. She looked like a lost kid who had sleepwalked into a nightmare.

"Look at you, *mamita*," he said softly. "So young, so pretty."

O'Brien shot Garza a sideward glance.

The girl started to sob.

"Don't cry, baby," said Garza reaching back and taking her hand. "Tito's here. Tito's gonna make everything all right."

A few minutes later Mendoza appeared outside the car, leaned into the window and saw Garza holding the girl's hand. He and O'Brien exchanged quick looks.

"Two dead inside," said Mendoza. "Two might not make it and four more injured. It's not pretty, *ese*. Witnesses say the guy had the strength of a gorilla. Almost tore one guy's head off with a broken bottle."

"It's that White Queen shit," said Garza. "Where'd he get it?"

Georgie nodded toward the girl and switched to Spanish. "She had it when they came in. A waitress said she took it out of her bra. She thought it was coke. The perp inhaled it with a straw."

"You get the vial?" said Garza.

"There's about a thousand of 'em all over the floor, *ese*."

"Get back in there. Get 'em all. Get everything."

Mendoza started toward the club.

"And get photos," yelled Garza. "Nasty ones."

Mendoza paused. "Nasty photos?"

"Yeah! The nastier the better. Blood, guts, *toda la mierda*. Meet me at HQ with them."

O'Brien backed off the curb carefully negotiating the chaos of emergency vehicles and people. Tito Garza leaned over the seat and took the girl's hand in both of his.

"What's your name, *mamita*?"

She didn't answer. Her head was bowed, her hair hanging over her eyes.

"That's okay, baby," he said, stroking her arm. "You don't have to say nuthin'. Three people dead, 'cause you gave your boyfriend some blow. But you don't have to say nuthin'."

She raised her head. "I didn't know," she pleaded. "I thought it was just regular coke."

"What a shame, baby," he cooed, stroking further up her arm. "I wish we met before all this, *mamita*. You and me could have had some fun. What do you think—we coulda had some fun, right?"

"Yeah, maybe," she murmured, unable to look at him.

"See now, baby, if I let that fat cop take you, you'd be charged with accessory to homicide, possession, distribution. Right now you'd be in a dark, metal room, with a couple of bull dykes fightin' each other for who got to do you first."

"Oooh," said O'Brien.

The girl began to sob. Garza glanced over at O'Brien and winked. O'Brien just wagged his head.

"Tell me your name, *mamita*."

"Ch-Cheryl," she sobbed.

"You a Catholic girl, sweetheart?"

She looked at him through teary eyes and nodded.

"Me too," said Garza. "You got a lotta confessing to do, Cheryl."

———

At 10:00 a.m. O'Brien guided the Mercedes slowly along a high adobe wall that was the outer perimeter of producer Jerry Mishkin's Beverly Hills home.

"You know who this guy is?" said O'Brien.

"A dirtbag, piece of shit," said Garza from the rear seat.

"The dude's last movie grossed something like a quarter of a billion dollars, that's all," said O'Brien.

"I'm not impressed," said Garza.

"That's 'cause you just like yo mama," said Vinnie.

"I'm warning you, Vinnie," said Garza. "I'm not in the mood. You wanna be a black man—do it on somebody else's fucking time."

"Everybody from New York so uptight?" said O'Brien. "Lighten up, dude, you're in California." Georgie shot him a warning look. Garza had been their senior partner for three months. O'Brien ought to know better.

"Don't fucking remind me!" snapped Garza. "Shut up and lemme think."

Twenty minutes later the three agents were seated on a white overstuffed couch in a living room that Garza estimated was the size of DEA's New York auditorium. The place was carpeted in a luxurious shag in a black-and-white diamond pattern that seemed to extend into infinity. Across an amoeba-shaped glass table sat thirty-five-year-old millionaire film producer Jerry Mishkin, in linen slacks, ostrich skin loafers, and no socks. Beside him sat the dapper Harold Safirstein, Esquire, attorney to the stars.

Garza took his time studying Mishkin's carefully sculpted shoulder-length hair, the wafer-thin gold watch, and the manicured fingernails. He saw money, arrogance, and power. He also saw fear. And he saw something else. Mishkin was strung out. There were deep hollows around his eyes, his hands shook. A druggie, thought Garza.

There was a certain balance of power that money still couldn't buy. At that moment Tito Garza, a Cuban immigrant from Brooklyn, could bring this millionaire motherfucking druggie to his knees. He could flip him the way he did Cheryl, but it had to be played cool.

"You know why we're here, Mr. Mishkin?" said Garza.

Mishkin looked at his attorney.

"No, Mr. Garza," said Safirstein. "My client hasn't the slightest idea of the purpose of your visit."

Garza paused, letting the tension build. He snapped open an attaché case, removed a Sony mini-recorder and set it on the glass table with a clang that made Georgie wince. He fixed Mishkin with a baleful stare then slowly and dramatically pressed the

Play button. Garza's voice suddenly echoed across the wide room from the tiny speaker.

"This is Special Agent Tito E. Garza, Drug Enforcement Administration. The following phone call is being monitored with the consent of Cooperating Individual, Cheryl Rachel Hall. The call is being made to area code 213, telephone 555-0084, an unlisted telephone number registered to a Mr. Jerry Mishkin, president of Mishkin and Moser Productions."

The sound of Touch-Tone dialing followed. The phone rang seven times before it was answered. Garza watched Mishkin, whose eyes were fixed on his attorney.

"Yeah?" croaked the sleepy voice of Mishkin.

"Jerry . . . It's Cheryl," said Cheryl Hall's frightened voice.

"Cheryl? Jesus, what time is it? Why are you calling so early?"

"That gram of White Queen you gave me . . ."

"What about it?" His voice was suddenly wide-awake.

"Something horrible happened . . ."

"W-why the fuck are you calling me at home?"

". . . I gave it to my friend. He went crazy . . . People died, Jerry—"

Click!

"Jerry? Jerry? . . . I think he's hung up."

Garza turned off the recorder. "Smart move—I mean hanging up like that, Jerry," said Garza. "Too bad you talked so fucking much."

"What's that supposed to mean?" said Safirstein.

Garza reached into the attaché case and fished out a stack of black-and-white photos. He tossed them onto the glass table. The top photo was of a dead man's face with the broken stem of a wineglass jammed into his eye. The rest were equally gory depictions of the nightclub massacre.

"This is what I'm gonna charge your client with," said Garza.

"Now wait a second, Agent. That phone call was a setup. My client was clearly awakened out of a sound sleep. No jury—"

"That photo's gonna be on page one of the L.A. *Times,* this afternoon," interrupted Garza, "when we charge your client with possession, distribution, conspiracy, accessory to homicide. By tonight the news'll be all over the fucking world."

"No jury in the land is going to convict him of anything."

"Maybe," said Garza. "Maybe not. Either way, his ass is mine. He goes from here right to jail without even passing fucking Go.

And I'm gonna make sure his trial makes the O.J. trial look like fucking traffic court. You don't have to be a fortune-teller to predict what his next year's gonna be like or what's gonna happen to his business no matter what a jury says—do you, Counselor?"

The room was quiet.

"I presume," said Safirstein, "that we're talking because you have an alternative to suggest."

"You presumed right. I *suggest* that your client tells me every fucking thing he knows. He either puts me into the source of the White Queen or I put him where the only deals he makes are gonna be for fucking cigarettes.

"And that's the only alternative," said Garza, tossing a pair of handcuffs onto the glass table, with a clang.

Safirstein requested a moment alone with his client. They were out of the room for more than a half hour. When they returned it was as Garza thought it would be—complete surrender. He could smell the glory—or so he thought.

After an hour of interrogating Mishkin, Garza learned that the producer knew nothing about the source of *La Reina Blanca*.

Mishkin's story was that a Frenchman by the name of Jean had showed up at his office three days earlier, unannounced, carrying a couple of one-gram vials of White Queen. Mishkin, who admitted that he had a cocaine problem, had put the word out to all his dealer friends that he would pay top price for the new cocaine, so he wasn't surprised by the visit.

"It blew me away," said Mishkin. "I heard about it but I wasn't ready for it. It was like an orgasm that just keeps going and going until you scream for it to stop, and when it does, you want more. It's mad-dog vicious."

"So what happened?" asked Garza.

"The Frenchman only had three grams. I paid around fifteen thousand—I don't remember exactly. About fifty times the price of regular coke."

"And what did you do with it?"

"I took two grams and gave the chick a gram."

"You *gave* away a gram of White Queen?"

Mishkin shrugged. "I wanted to get into her pants. Only Cheryl didn't take it—she gave it to somebody else."

"How do you contact this Frenchman?"

"He's a weird guy," said Mishkin. "He said when he had something he would come to me, in person."

"Then I guess you can't help me, can you?" said Garza.

"I told you everything I know."

"Too bad, it's not enough." Garza rose to his feet. "You're under arrest."

"Now you wait just a second," said Safirstein, jumping to his feet.

"Hold on, Harold," said Mishkin. "Maybe Agent Garza would consider a different trade."

"I'm listening," said Garza.

"What if I told you that I can give you something even bigger."

"What would that be?"

"*El Búfalo*," said Mishkin.

The three agents looked at each other. *El Búfalo* was one of the most powerful and elusive drug traffickers in DEA history. While people like Pablo Escobar and Carlos Lehder occupied the front pages of American newspapers, *El Búfalo* quietly murdered his way up the ladder from being a contract hit man to a top *capo* in the Colombian cartels—some believed *the* top man. Garza had been hunting him for a decade but could never even get close.

"You can give me *El Búfalo*—Felix Restrepo?" said Garza.

"I have his private numbers in Colombia. I can call him right now."

"How do you know him?"

"The Colombian cartels invested in a couple of our movies," said Mishkin. "Everything was handled personally, through him. I can get anything I want."

Garza's head buzzed with anticipation. The headline he was seeing in his mind was one he had spent his career dreaming about—the Attorney General's Award, the Octavio Gonzalez Award, maybe a presidential citation. Tito's photo taken with the president on the front page of *The New York Times. The agent who busted* El Búfalo. For a millisecond he considered going a little easier on Mishkin—after all, there would eventually be a Hollywood deal.

"You can set me up to make a direct buy from *El Búfalo?*"

"Not exactly," said Mishkin. "If you know anything about him, you know that the moment he even thinks I introduced him to an undercover agent, he won't just kill me. He'll go for my family first—I've got two kids."

Garza stared at Mishkin, trying hard not to show any emotion.

Doing *El Búfalo* was like a baseball player's hitting more home runs than Babe Ruth.

"Okay," said Garza. "Lemme think for a minute. . . . Suppose you introduce me as a guy you once bought some coke from—a Marielito Cuban. I meet him in Miami. I tell him I got a Mafia customer from New York and I want to middle the deal for a commission. A big-time Mafia guy shows up, *he* makes the buy. *El Búfalo* gets busted for making a deal with the mob guy—he'll never know I was an agent. You're two people and a whole fucking country removed."

A tremor had begun in Mishkin's face. Garza knew he'd probably sell one of his kids to freebase some blow about now.

Mishkin pointed at the photos. "I never get charged with this?"

"You got a deal," said Garza.

An hour later the Mercedes, O'Brien at the wheel, was speeding down Coldwater Canyon Drive, toward downtown L.A. A rapper's voice, over a Latin beat, kept intoning the line *Just another brother in lockdown,* over and over. O'Brien was moving his head with the beat, trying to make rap noises with his mouth. Garza, in the rear, beat out the rhythm on the seat behind Georgie's head.

"How are you going to handle headquarters?" asked Georgie. "Our orders say Operation White Queen only."

"Stop whining," snapped Garza. "This is major headlines for headquarters. I'm gonna make your fucking career for you. I'm the senior agent here. All you gotta worry about is doing what I tell you to do."

"Where to?" said O'Brien.

"Let's get to a phone. I gotta find Levine."

"Mike Levine?" said O'Brien.

"You know him?" said Garza.

"Yeah, I hear the guy draws a lotta heat," said O'Brien.

"Right," said Garza. "And heat is exactly what we need to get *El Búfalo*."

8

"DEA UNDERCOVER AGENT FOUND TORTURED TO DEATH IN ARGEN-
tina!" echoed from the television as a black-bordered photo of
René filled the screen. The same photo was being shown on every
channel: the official one taken for credentials and ID cards, the
flat deadpan mug shot that is flashed when you say, *You're under
arrest.*

I sat up most of the night in my hotel room in the downtown
Marriott with a terrible sick pain inside me, unable to sleep while
outside the first heavy snowfall of winter was burying our nation's capital.

All the DEA Country Attachés from more than a hundred offices around the world had been summoned to headquarters for
an emergency meeting. The Teletype said that it was to "coordinate the hunt for the murderers of Special Agent René Villarino."
The last time anything like this had happened was when Special
Agent Enrique "Kiki" Camarena had been tortured to death by
Mexican cops working for dope dealers in Guadalajara, Mexico.

About half of the station chiefs were in the hotel bar drinking
the night away, but I hadn't seen one of them. I just couldn't pull
myself away from the television set. The media story was the
customary factoids: a father of two sons, born in Corsica, divorced, a twenty-year highly decorated undercover agent murdered under mysterious circumstances. There were rumors of a
Medellín cartel involvement and a super-drug. One report men-

tioned the possible involvement of the Colombian government. DEA had no comment. The investigation was ongoing.

I kept hoping to see a news flash announcing that René had been found alive; that the whole thing had been just another one of his elaborate scams to fool some doper into believing he was dead. But that news flash never came and I was left with the image of his rotting corpse in that house on the Pampas.

DEA Headquarters, War Room 10:00 A.M.

"Goddammit! I want this evil drug off the streets," said Hubbel Whitfield, the administrator of the Drug Enforcement Administration. Profanity did not roll naturally off the tongue of the dour-faced, bushy-headed, ex–university president whose political aspirations kept the DEA press staff working overtime to keep him in the public eye.

Historically, the people chosen to run DEA—like the drug czars—have no background in narcotic enforcement. They are political appointees with connections in whatever party happens to be sitting in the White House. No DEA administrator in the agency's history could have qualified as a drug expert on a federal witness stand. Professor Hubbel Whitfield was no exception.

The Whitfield family name was among the wealthiest and the most politically powerful in the country. His appointment to head the lead agency in the drug war was, as the press put it, "an accommodation." Two other key appointees for cabinet positions had been rejected by the Senate so Whitfield's nomination was allowed to sail through. He was the latest flag run up the drug war flagpole and we had to salute him.

From the moment of his appointment he never missed a photo op or a media shot. *Larry King Live* and Ted Koppel's *Nightline* had him on as their resident international drug "expert." He exuded confidence from every pore. His television image was powerful and authoritative. When Hubbel Whitfield faced the television cameras and said, "This scourge will end!" the voters could just picture hordes of frightened drug dealers packing up and scurrying back to Colombia. *Who could stand up to that?* His approval and recognition ratings soared. His political future was bright. It wouldn't occur to anyone that the dopers didn't watch *Larry King Live.*

All of this would ordinarily be just another of the many jokes the government plays on the taxpayers. Most appointees understood that even though they had been given the keys to the jumbo jet, they really didn't know how to fly. They would leave the actual running of the drug war to the men on the street and content themselves with accepting the credit on the evening news. But whenever a guy came along like Whitfield, who took his press notices seriously, good men would end up dying.

"From this moment on DEA shall do nothing else until this White Queen is purged from the face of the earth," bellowed Whitfield, pointing his index finger toward the heavens like a televangelist. "I've given the White House my personal guarantee."

Whitfield was seated at the head of a large oval table around which about a hundred DEA station chiefs were jammed into seats from the edge of the table to the walls. Behind Whitfield stood his four-man squad of dark-suited personal bodyguards, their backs against a huge map of the world festooned with little red markers representing DEA's 110 overseas offices. Flanking him on the right sat the gaunt-faced chief of Internal Security, Myles Bydon—the man who for the preceding five years had been directing the investigation of my alleged wrongdoings. On Whitfield's left sat Bobby Stratton.

I sat directly opposite Whitfield at the other end of the long table, restless and barely listening. I had come to this meeting expecting that DEA would aim and fire me like a gun at René's killers. So far the fucking suit had barely even mentioned René's murder.

"Before I go any further," said Whitfield, "you've all had time to review the file before you. It contains a synopsis of Special Agent René Villarino's assignment to find the source of the White Queen. Everything discussed here today is classified top secret. If word leaks to the press—or anywhere else—I will have every man in this room polygraphed. The leak will be fired and prosecuted. Do I make myself clear?"

When Whitfield got emotional his oversize, rubbery, and mismatched lips quivered and flapped like stretched-out galoshes. René used to say that he spoke like a badly dubbed Russian screen actor. I started to laugh as if René had just said the words. Then I saw Bydon watching me and turned it into a cough. But no doubt about it, had René had been sitting across the room we both would have had to duck under the table. I was going to miss him terribly.

"Are there any questions thus far?" said Whitfield.

A hand went up. It was Francis "Buddy" LaGrange, the Country Attaché assigned to Chile. His face twitched and grimaced with the rigors of sobriety. It was the first time I'd ever seen him completely sober.

"Uh, when's René's funeral gonna be?"

"The body is being returned to his family in Corsica for burial," said the robotic voice of Myles Bydon. "There's a memorial ceremony at St. Patrick's Cathedral in New York, the day after tomorrow."

In a seated crowd, unless Bydon stood, you had to look twice to see where his voice was coming from. His eyes never blinked, his lips barely moved, and in the ten years I'd known him, I'd never seen his face change expression. The only time anyone ever reported seeing the Ventriloquist smile was when an agent whom he was interrogating for padding his expense voucher by a couple of hundred dollars jumped out a tenth-floor window.

"Is it mandatory that we gotta attend?" persisted LaGrange. "There's an embassy Christmas party." There was a low murmur around the room. LaGrange continued: "I gotta be outta here by tonight."

"No one's *gotta* be anywhere," snapped Bobby Stratton. "There's less than fifteen hundred street agents in the world. One of us was just tortured to death. You have something else to do, fucking do it! Nobody's taking attendance."

LaGrange looked as if he was about to speak again, thought better of it and studied his hands.

I remembered *Sensei's* words: *If you ever want to understand just how necessary each of us really is in this life, just stick your finger in a bucket of water, pull it out and watch how fast the hole fills.*

"If there are no questions . . ." Whitfield began.

I raised my hand, and Whitfield nodded at me. I wanted to scream out that the contents of the thin red folder before me purporting to be the details of René's eight-month deep cover investigation were a fucking lie and a disgrace. Instead, fighting to control my temper, I said, "The synopsis here says that René was last seen with Colombians in Cochabamba. Have we verified that and how? And how the hell did he get from Cochabamba to the Pampas of Argentina?"

Stratton shot me a warning look.

"I'll answer that," said Ed Hernandez, the Country Attaché in charge of Bolivian operations—Roscoe Thibadeaux's boss. "The spooks gave us that information," he said, addressing Whitfield as if I didn't exist. "Thibadeaux located someone in Cochabamba last night who corroborated it—a hooker who spent the night with René. And it's impossible to verify these clandestine flights between Bolivia and Argentina—Levine oughtta know that."

"A hooker?" I said. "I knew René twenty years. He never went to a hooker in his life."

"No one can know what a man is really like," said the Ventriloquist.

I knew that Marita Salazar had been the only woman in René's life for the past eighteen years, but even the mention of her name would open a can of worms that could send me to prison.

"And what about this positive ID that he was in the fucking Colombian Guajira?" I said. "Where'd that bullshit come from?"

Whitfield slammed his fist down on the table. "Profanity is not necessary, Agent Levine," he said, his face crimson. "It's all in the file in front of you. An Italian drug dealer was mistaken for René. It could have been his double."

"Yeah, well who is the guy? Where is he now? There's nothing in this file," I said. "Where's René's reports? The taped conversations? A year of deep cover work and there's nothing here but expense vouchers and a bullshit synopsis. What happened? Where are the leads?"

Whitfield lowered his head like a bull about to charge.

"Read the synopsis, Levine. His assignment was classified top secret. René's contact with headquarters was limited to me and only when *he* felt it was completely safe to make such contact. This was by *his* choice. I'm surprised I have to explain this to you."

What qualified you to be René's lifeline, you son of a bitch?

"Wasn't there some kind of emergency notification setup? I mean, what was he supposed to do if he needed help and you weren't available?"

"Just what are you inferring?" interrupted the Ventriloquist, swiveling toward me.

"He had to have notes. René always kept notes and diaries."

"There was a safe in his Panama office," said Whitfield. "We found it empty."

"It's not mentioned in the synopsis," I said.

Whitfield glowered at me. I was doing the unthinkable for a street agent—questioning the administrator's performance. I was telling the emperor he was butt naked.

"There was nothing in the safe so there was nothing to report," said the Ventriloquist.

"So why are we so sure Colombians are behind this?"

"Should I read the synopsis out loud for you, Levine?" said Whitfield. "He left a message on my machine that he finally had a big break in the case. Next he's seen with Colombians. Next he's dead. Do you need me to tell you that the Colombian cartels control the world cocaine supply? Do you need me to tell you that their laboratories and scientists are constantly seeking to improve quality, profit, and the addictiveness of their product? What do you think is behind this drug, Agent Levine, extraterrestrials?"

There was a burst of nervous laughter around me. Whitfield smiled.

"Unless Levine has any other questions, I'd like to give the floor to Dr. Wharton."

A small man in a white lab coat, seated alongside the Ventriloquist, adjusted his Coke-bottle glasses and read from his notes: "The drug we refer to as *La Reina Blanca* or the White Queen first makes an appearance in Miami about a year ago. In a month's time the addiction rate, overdose deaths, and drug-related-violence statistics elevate almost three hundred percent. At this time we obtained our first sample. Tests indicated cocaine hydrochloride at an extremely low purity—an average of from four to five percent.

"For reasons we still do not understand, the drug has a direct and intense effect on the sexual centers of the brain, causing a sensation that simulates sexual orgasm, a sensation that reportedly lasts as long as ten to twenty minutes."

There were some titters around the table. A low whistle.

Buddy LaGrange had his hand in the air. "Perfesser. I got a question. Where can ah get me some o' this stuff?"

More nervous laughter.

Stratton catapulted to his feet. "Are you a fucking idiot?" The cords in his thick neck stood out. LaGrange's face flamed. His head did its best to sink into his body. Bydon leaned over and whispered something to Whitfield.

"I'm sorry, Doctor," said Bydon. "Please continue."

"Addiction to this form of cocaine is immediate," continued Wharton. "The compulsion is overpowering, often leading to overdose and death. There is another by-product that seems to happen in a high percentage of users—episodes of extreme violence accompanied by superhuman strength.

"But the most troubling finding of all is the evidence of extensive, irreversible organ damage found in short-term users. Even those who use the drug for as little as three or four weeks may sentence themselves to a terminal condition—the slow deterioration of the heart, liver, and kidneys. Our computer projections indicate that certain death, in the majority of these cases, will follow in three to five years. I cannot stress the importance of stopping this drug before it reaches mass production. It will be catastrophic. An Armageddon, gentlemen."

"Why the secrecy?" asked a voice from the side of the room. "Why don't we go public, get the media involved and scare the piss outta these people?"

"That seems like common sense," said Dr. Wharton. "Unfortunately, common sense and the psychology of the drug user are two different things. We have found, for example, that hard-core heroin addicts will actively seek out for the potency those street brands known to have caused overdose deaths. News of overdose deaths actually act to stimulate the heroin market.

"The fact that it is now well known that sex and intravenous drug use are the primary causes behind the spread of AIDS has done nothing to diminish either sexual activity or intravenous drug use.

"This new drug, the White Queen, we must remember, is primarily a sexual experience. We believe that publicizing it would drive up demand, along with the impetus for it to reach mass production. Just the rumors have already driven up price and demand. And the news of its potentially devastating effect on our economy could cause chaos in the financial sector."

"Got to protect that stock market," mumbled a voice.

"There's already rumors on the news," said another.

"And we're going to find the source of those rumors," said Bydon, glaring around the table, his eyes coming to rest on me.

"If the press learns the true nature of this drug, gentlemen," said Whitfield, "the American people will demand an answer. And we had better be ready with one."

"What about CIA, the FBI, and the Pentagon?"

"Every covert agency in the government has been alerted," said Whitfield. "The White House is looking at us first. We're supposed to be the drug experts."

"Shit sounds like fuckin' chemical warfare to me," mumbled LaGrange. "We sure the Chinese commies or some ragheads ain't behind this?"

There was some sporadic laughter.

"That's no joke," said Whitfield. "I've had several meetings with the president's security advisors and that is exactly what some of them have theorized. According to the evidence we have thus far, everything is pointing at Colombia and the cartels. CIA, by the way, is in full agreement with us."

I could no longer contain myself.

"What about René?" I said. "I thought we were here to coordinate a hunt for his killers. All I hear is this *motherfucking* drug."

There was a stunned silence.

"Have you been paying attention to this meeting, Agent Levine?" said Bydon. "Villarino's killers and the Colombian source are one and the same."

"We don't know that," I protested. "Maybe that's what someone wants us to think. We're gonna walk out of here with the whole fucking government looking for the source of this dope and no one looking for René's killers."

"You have a better idea?" asked Whitfield.

"I think that all our resources, all our informants and assets, should be concentrated on René's murder. We've got to re-create a day-by-day picture of all his movements and contacts for the past year; identify every human being he had anything whatsoever to do with and interview them, polygraph them if we have to. And that's just for starters."

"All that, of course, will be taken care of," said Whitfield.

"We can't wait," I insisted. "We can't move fast enough. We can't let the trail get cold the way we did Kiki Camarena's. We've got to put everything we've got into it, right now, sir."

"Do you have anything else, Agent Levine?" said Whitfield coolly.

"Yes sir, I'd like to get a copy of all René's and his informant's phone tolls for the past year so that I can begin running down their calls to Argentina."

"I already told you that would be taken care of," said Whitfield. "We get the source of this drug we'll have René's killers. Isn't that clear enough for you, Agent?"

"It can't wait," I insisted. "I need the information now."

Whitfield turned away from me in disgust and looked at Bydon.

"You have your marching orders," said the Ventriloquist. "You have a problem with them?"

"Watch how fast the hole fills," I said, getting to my feet, gathering up the files in front of me. My hands were trembling with rage. If I stayed a second longer I was going to lose it and someone was going to get hurt. I headed for the door.

I barged out into the hallway almost knocking over Bobby Stratton's secretary. "Mr. Levine, I was just coming to get you. Your secretary is on the phone from Argentina. She says it's urgent."

I moved past her down the hallway to Stratton's office. I had always disliked being in headquarters, but now I despised the very smell of the place. I picked up the phone and punched the blinking button.

"Oh Mike," said Jackie.

"What's up, honey?" I said.

"I didn't know whether to bother you, but I thought I better. Someone named Garza has been calling from a Miami hotel," said Jackie. "He must've called about twenty times. He says he's an agent. That you know him."

"Obnoxious. Fast-talking. Chip on his shoulder. Called you *mamita*. Tried to put the make on you over the phone?"

"You do know him," she said.

"Tito Garza—my partner for three years in New York," I said. "It was like we did twenty years hard time together."

"That bad?"

"We were lucky to survive each other. It's complicated."

"He said it's an emergency. Should I tell him where you are?"

"Tito's hard to take on a good day, Jackie. Not today. I just couldn't handle him."

After I hung up, I headed out to the elevator bank. Stratton caught up with me just as the elevator doors opened. "Don't say a fucking thing," he said, shoving me ahead of him.

"You know this is bullshit," I said when the doors shut.

He put his fingers across his lips to shut me up.

Outside DEA headquarters he steered me across 14th Street

into a park that was a meeting place for mental patients, home-less vagrants, junkies, winos, street hookers, and government employees taking coffee breaks. It was a sunny winter's day and the overnight snowfall was rapidly melting into a brown goo. A crowd had gathered to watch some black kids singing a cappella.

"I stuck my fucking neck way out to get you involved in this and look what you do to me," said Stratton.

"What am I supposed to do? René was my best friend. These motherfuckers turned him into a road kill."

"Why you think I wanted you on this?" snapped Stratton. He suddenly slammed his open palms into my chest. I stumbled backward. He was amazingly quick and strong. He'd taken me completely by surprise. Street people turned to look, some already smiling in anticipation of a fight.

"Why'd you do that?"

"People in that fucking room would love to do a lot worse to you. You're a lot dumber than I thought. You wanna go after René's killers, so do I. But you and your fucking big mouth and temper just got yourself tossed off the assignment. Now what are you gonna do, Mr. Undercover?"

"I'll go on annual leave. I'll do it on my own," I said, feeling like a fool.

"How in God's name you gonna do that when Whitfield just told me he wants you out of Argentina by the end of the week?"

"Let him fire me then," I said, feeling more foolish every time I opened my mouth.

"He'll be more than happy to. How's that help you find René's killers?"

I looked around us. The street people had already lost interest.

"What do I have to do, Bobby?" I said.

My pager began to beep. I pressed the button. A Miami phone number appeared on the tiny screen followed by the numbers 911. It was Tito Garza using our old code for an emergency. When we were partners I would have dropped everything and run, but I didn't owe him a fucking thing now. If he had an emergency, it was his emergency—not mine.

"Something you have to take care of now?"

"It'll wait," I said. "You're my boss. Tell me, what am I supposed to do?"

"This is your last chance, Mike," he said, looking me squarely in the eyes. "I'm gonna tell Whitfield that you were overwrought but that you're gonna follow orders. Bydon is livid—he wants you out of Argentina and off the job, so I'm gonna bypass him. By the way, LaGrange just got his P&G orders for opening his mouth. He's got till the end of the week to move out of Chile."

"I always told him he should stay drunk," I said. "First time I see him sober and he's in trouble."

Stratton laughed. "Yeah, when I left he was trying to decide whether offering the Ventriloquist a blow job would do any good."

"Thanks, Bobby," I said.

"I can't guarantee anything," said Stratton. "But if I get him to go along with you, I gotta know everything you're doing, Mike. I'll cover for you, but you can't back-door me."

"You've got my word," I said. "I guess I should tell you right now. From here I'm going to Corsica to the funeral."

"I figured that," he said. "Just stay in touch."

———

I could hear a phone ringing as I got off the elevator at the Marriott. It grew steadily louder as I walked the length of the long hallway. Someone was in a real panic, I thought. By the time I reached my room and realized that it was my phone it must have rung twenty times.

"*Judío!* Don't hang up on me. You don't know what the fuck I went through to find you."

I recognized Tito Garza's voice instantly. With it came the same sensation of annoyance his telephone voice always provoked. The only thing more abrasive was his in-person voice.

"Is this business, Tito? I'm in a bad way."

"Hey look, I'm sorry about René."

"You don't make condolence calls, Tito. Get to the point."

"I need my old Money Man, Levine."

The phrase evoked the memory of hundreds of undercover deals Garza and I had done from the Bronx to Bogotá, a thousand nights in Latin bars listening to El Gran Combo de Puerto Rico and Tito Puente on the jukebox, Garza playing imaginary conga drums on the bar, waiting for dope connections. Garza played the role of the hustling Cuban street dealer looking for the big connection. I played his half–Puerto Rican, half-Sicilian, Mafia money man.

The roles came naturally to us. I grew up in the South Bronx in a mostly Puerto Rican neighborhood and went to school in Little Italy. It was a tough, violent neighborhood that scared the hell out of me. My remedy was to become tougher and more violent than anyone around me. With a father who was already a loan shark, the role of Mafia money man was one that—had it not been for a few lucky twists of fate—might have been my real one in life. Garza, born in Cuba and brought up on the mean streets of South Brooklyn, was equally intimate with his role. Together we came across as the real thing. No dopers, no matter how paranoid or experienced, ever made us as undercovers.

In one year, using the Street Hustler–Money Man scam, Garza and I had made more than three hundred major arrests. As partners, we held DEA's records for arrests, seizures, and awards. And they weren't all dopers either. We would work any kind of case—murderers, armed robbers, rapists, muggers—all of it was in one way or another dope-connected anyway. We were like two hunting hounds with too much prey drive. Both of us were divorced, both of us alimony-and-child-support poor, and both of us addicted to adrenaline.

In the three years we were partners Garza and I lived through the kinds of heart-stopping events that should forge deep and undying friendships and even love. But that never happened with us. We just never got along. Our personalities were like two chemicals that when mixed formed a caustic, nauseating substance. When the three years ended with an incident that we survived only by suicidally risking our lives to save one another, we separated like two people who'd been on a bad date.

"Tito, that's impossible!" I said.

"You're gonna want a piece of this one, Levine," said Garza. As usual he was on his own track speeding to wherever it was he wanted to go. "When I tell you what I got you're gonna wanna tongue-kiss with me."

"Just get to the point."

"Your ex-*socio* is about to make fucking history . . . and make you famous too. I got *El Búfalo* set up. I need you to play Money Man."

For a moment he had me. The name *El Búfalo* conjured up the image of two small bodies—a ten-year-old girl and an eight-year-old boy—hanging from meathooks in Long Island City. The children of one of our CIs. Both kids had been sexually molested and tortured before they were murdered. Just some gratuitous pain for their father, who would take his own life within months. The image was ten years old but as fresh as a minute ago. The message to the whole drug world was: *Fuck with the cartel and no one in your family is safe*. Everyone on the street knew that the job had been done by a group of cartel enforcers headed by Felix *"El Búfalo"* Restrepo.

Garza and I had worked around the clock for months trying to put a case together on *El Búfalo*. The man's strength was in the fear that surrounded him like a noxious cloud. In the superstitious South American drug world, heavily populated with believers in voodoo, Santería, and macumba, Restrepo was believed to be a *santero*—a Santería high priest. His appearance—a huge head, with eyes set so far apart that they appeared on the sides like those of a buffalo, and an immensely thick Botero-like body—added to fears of him having supernatural powers. No one we talked to—no matter how big a hammer we held over their heads—would say a word about him. *El Búfalo* was the biggest piece of unfinished business the Levine–Garza partnership had left when we split.

"It's our old scam, man," said Garza. "A fucking classic Garza–Levine buy/bust. *El Búfalo* is gonna be there himself. I am a fucking genius, I told his people that you, Señor Money Man, were coming direct from the *capo di tutti frutti* himself, Gentleman John Gianotti. He thinks he's gonna be the first Colombian doper to open up the Italian mob connection."

"I can't do anything now," I said.

"And for the cream, I ain't even mentioned yet. If there's two guys in the world that can parlay busting this Buffalo head muthafucka into finding out where *La Reina Blanca* is really coming from—it's Garza and fucking Levine."

"You're not listening to me, Tito. The only thing I'm doing now is going after the motherfuckers that did René."

"¡Coño! *Judío*, you think there's anything going on down there that *El Búfalo*'s not on top of? We get that *cabezón* motherfucker, he'll know everything. We'll get credit for that too! Besides, you got any other leads?"

"You think the suits are gonna authorize me playing Money Man, Tito? They still have me under investigation."

"Is this the Mike Levine I know?" said Garza. "The Jew-Rican? Or is this a wrong fucking number?"

"You're not even listening to me, Tito—"

"Or is this some headquarters suit muthafucka with no *cojones*? You gonna turn your old partner down?"

"I could never talk to you when we were partners, I still can't talk to you."

"I saved your fucking ass, Levine!"

"Because I was trying to save yours!"

The line went quiet.

"Look Tito," I said. "Try and understand—"

"I don't wanna talk anymore. I'm gonna say some shit I might be sorry for. There'll be tickets waitin' for Luis Miguel Garcia at Washington National. That's who I expect to get off the plane tomorrow night in Miami."

He slammed the phone down in my ear.

9

MIAMI INTERNATIONAL AIRPORT

I STEPPED FROM THE AIR-CONDITIONED COOL OF THE AIRPORT TERMINAL into the steamy Miami night. I had to admit, Garza was right for once. If anybody in the South American dope world knew about René's death it would be *El Búfalo*. But getting next to him would be a lot easier said than done.

A tall, broad-shouldered guy with a boxer's mashed nose, decked out Mafiosi style in an Italian silk suit, was watching me, his hand on the back door of a Lincoln stretch limo parked at the curb.

"Mike?"

I nodded.

"Special Agent Vinnie O'Brien," he said, opening the door for me. "They're waitin' for you at the Omni, man. We got to smoke a trail."

"Where's Garza?" I asked.

"With the Buffalo's people. Just waitin' for *you*, Mr. Money Man."

I slipped into the backseat. O'Brien rode shotgun. The driver, a clean-cut Latino, slammed the accelerator down. The engine roared. The half-block-long limo chirped rubber and leapt out into traffic. He handled it like a sports car.

"You said 'his people'—what about *El Búfalo*?" I asked. O'Brien twisted his powerful frame to talk to me.

"They keep calling someone local for instructions. We think it's him."

"So no one's seen him yet?"

"You got that right."

"Anyone from headquarters fly down?"

"Man you can't even find a place to take a dump without runnin' into one of Whitfield's press people. The man himself is here for the big bust. He wants the world to see the *Búfalo*'s big head on the little screen tonight. There's more TV crews out there now than fucking agents. Give the news guys some guns instead of cameras, we win the drug war. Ain't that right, brother Georgie?"

The Latino, his eyes fixed on the road, nodded absently.

"The suits know I'm playing Money Man?" I asked.

O'Brien laughed. "You gonna be the big surprise."

The Latino swerved into an open lane and accelerated.

"You look just like Garza said, bro'," said O'Brien.

"How's that?"

"A heavy dude, man. Serious business. This, by the way, is Georgie Mendoza."

The Latino glanced at me through the rearview. He looked tense.

"We your New York family tonight. The flash be in the suit-cases," said O'Brien.

There were two large American Tourister suitcases on the floor beside me. I flipped one open. It was stuffed with packets of hundred-dollar bills.

"Hot from the Federal Ree-serve. Two million in Franklin."

"How's it broken down?" I asked.

"Two hundred packets—a hundred C notes in each."

I selected a rubber band–wrapped packet of bills at random and began counting, the way I knew *El Búfalo* would. I also checked the serial numbers to make sure they weren't in sequence. A Federal Reserve clerk in New York once gave DEA a million in brand-new bills for a flash roll with the serial numbers in perfect sequence, just the way they were printed. The under-cover, twenty-seven years old and just out of the academy, never checked it—the doper did. The undercover got a bullet in the brain for not doing the basics.

"What about the White Queen?" I asked. "Any mention of it?"

"You don't find that stuff. *It* find you."

I finished counting and shoved the packet back into the valise. "I don't want you talking like that on the set," I said.

"Like what?" said, O'Brien.

Georgie laughed. "You know like what, Vinnie."

"No way, man," said O'Brien. "Tonight I am *undercover*."

"In case you haven't noticed, Vinnie's the only Irish guy who thinks he's a black man trapped in a white body," said Georgie, eyeing me in the rearview.

"Georgie, is it true people be dressin' up like yo' momma for Halloween?"

Georgie threw a punch at O'Brien's shoulder. O'Brien blocked it laughing.

"Cut the fucking grab-ass!" I snapped. "Before I kick the two of you through the fucking windshield."

O'Brien and Georgie glanced at each other then stared silently ahead. For a long moment the only sound was the whirr of the tires on the pavement.

Fine! I'm not here to play and if they didn't know it when I got off the plane, they know it now.

"Look," said Georgie, "I think we got off on the wrong foot. Vinnie and I are really sorry about Villarino. It's like we didn't know what to say."

"There's nothing you can say. Let's just do the job. What's the game plan?"

Suddenly I was feeling bad. Maybe I was too short with them. Being on an undercover set with dope and adrenaline-charged Colombians is about as dangerous as it gets. And right after an undercover is killed on the job, when everyone is feeling even more afraid than usual, guys can act pretty stupid. It's all nerves. You have to give them some leeway.

"Tito figures it like this," said O'Brien, barely able to meet my gaze. "The Buffalo's around here somewhere with a hundred keys. His people want to check you out. You pass the test, he meets you to do a hand-to-hand and talk about long-term business with *La Famiglia*. The moment he hands you the dope, you give the signal. We got the bust of the century. Tito gets the AG Award. And me and Georgie get a break."

"Better check out the rip-off pen," said Georgie.

"I almost forgot," said O'Brien, handing me what looked like an ordinary ballpoint pen. I pressed the button. A loud beeping noise erupted from the car radio. A red light flashed on the dashboard. I pressed it again. The noise stopped.

"There's about two hundred SWAT guys out there," said

O'Brien. "The minute you push that thing, they'll be coming in doors and fucking windows like Batman. If I were you, I'd just dive for cover."

O'Brien reached into the glove compartment, flicked a switch and grabbed a mike. A tiny red bulb illuminated. "Eight to Command Post One, Uncle Money Man picked up. Ten-eight en route to set. Rip pen functional."

"Ten-four," squawked a voice.

"Status?" asked O'Brien.

"No change. Uncle Number One still in room with Badguys, numbers two, three, and four. Crackhead is still moving around room, checking closets. Definite gun in belt. Poppa guy seems cool. Twenty of Bravo guy still unknown."

"Ten-four," said O'Brien, turning off the radio. "You get that?"

"I take it the room is wired," I said.

"Like Candid fucking Camera."

"What's this about a crackhead and a gun?"

"One of them's smoking *basuca*," said Georgie, watching me in the rearview. "Camera picked up a gun on his belt."

"Basuquero with a gun on an undercover set," I said. "Real nice."

No sense worrying. It's time to start thinking about my role. In a few minutes I have to be Money Man.

"You mind if we ask you something?" said O'Brien, glancing at Georgie.

"Go ahead."

"How long ago were you and Tito partners?"

"They split us up eight years ago."

"Was he always such an asshole?"

"You a fighter, O'Brien?" I asked.

"My nose?" He laughed. "Nah, I'm just not too good at ducking."

"You don't call Tito an asshole to his face, do you?"

Georgie blinked nervously in the rearview. O'Brien was silent.

"Tito ever tell you about our last UC deal together?"

"No," said O'Brien.

"We were doing the same routine we're doing tonight with East Harlem smack dealers. Tito goes up to a fifth-floor tenement apartment with three of them to check the dope. I'm the Money Man sitting in a car downstairs with a fifty-thousand-dollar flash roll in a camera bag waiting to hear the word that everything was right. The dopers had lookouts all over the street. We had three backup cars, about a dozen agents parked two blocks away. Both me and Tito were carrying rip-off pens just like this one. We show the badguys the money, they bring us the dope, we press the button, they go to jail—a classic buy/bust, just like tonight, right?

"Wrong! Whatever can go wrong usually does in this life.

"Tito's wearing a bug. I can hear everything. All of a sudden the voices change, they're nasty, frightened. I realize they've got guns on Tito, they're searching him. Tito's carrying a little five-shot revolver on his ankle. They miss it, and the mike. They order him to go to the window and tell me to come upstairs with the money. Tito's choice is to die right away or go to the window.

"I press the rip-off pen and wait for our backup. Nothing happens. I get on the radio and call a Ten-one-thousand. No fucking answer."

"Jesus," said Georgie.

"Next thing I see Tito's head is out the window. He's waving for me to come upstairs. Because I'm taking too long I hear one of them get hysterical. He wants to just kill Tito on the spot.

"I'm not even thinking at this point. The next thing I know, I'm out of the car moving up the stairway, scared shitless. In the hallway I take my nine-millimeter out and stick it in the bag. By the time I reach the top floor, my heart feels like it's gonna explode out my chest."

"Jesus, Mary, and Joseph," said Georgie.

"I start down the hallway, my hand inside the money bag on my gun. The door opens. One of the badguys is there looking at me, smiling his ass off. Now I *know* I'm dead. I'm gonna walk past him and start shooting, I think. But I've got to make sure I don't hit Tito.

"The second I'm in the doorway, what do I see? All three of them have guns pointed at me and my gun isn't even out yet. But they made one big mistake. They took their eyes off Tito.

"Tito's gun was out and blazing before I could move. I just dove for the ground. I got my gun out but I never got off a shot. I didn't have to.

"There were two dead motherfuckers almost on top of me and the third, brain-shot, a vegetable for the rest of his life. And there's me and Tito, not a scratch. He had five bullets in that gun, he made every one of them count. Our backup never did show up.

"Whatever you think of Tito Garza, there aren't too many people in this life who you can really count on when you're up against it. I never met you guys before. You got something bad to say about Tito, don't say it in front of me, okay?"

"We didn't mean anything by it, *ese*," said Georgie. "We're just trying to get along with the guy."

"No problem."

"What about this *Monguín* stuff?" said O'Brien. "A guy from New York calls up and asks for him by that name. Georgie uses it and Tito goes schizoid."

"What about it?" I asked.

"What's it mean? We checked it out—it ain't even Spanish."

There was no point explaining—it would only cause more problems. "If he doesn't like it, just don't use it."

Ten minutes later we zipped into the underground garage of the Omni. Undercover agents appeared from behind pillars and out of doorways. One slipped behind the wheel. The three of us headed toward the elevators. My heart was beating at about 160. I have always, at rest, been able to meditate it down to the mid-fifties. Nothing was working.

"The flash," said O'Brien. "We forgot the money."

"There's no deal yet," I said. "The only guy who's gonna see that money is *El Búfalo*. Leave it in the car."

In the elevator O'Brien closed his eyes, took a deep breath, and said, "Let's do it."

I nodded, unable to speak, fighting butterflies, trying to orient myself. *Soy Miguel "Mike" Pagano, padre Siciliano, madre puertorriqueña. Soy Miguel . . .* It is a great pleasure to make your acquaintance, *Señores. Mucho gusto.* Business and more business. The most important thing in life is business. One must have confidence in his people. *Confianza.*

Georgie pressed a button and the elevator surged. We burst out of the underground in a glass-encased bullet racing through a tiered lobby of restaurants, lounges, couches, potted plants, and glitter. Below us I saw quickly shrinking people, walking, sitting at tables, carrying luggage. A blonde in a red dress glanced up from a martini and seemed to watch us.

I touched the rip-off pen in my jacket pocket and imagined what would happen if I pushed the button at that moment. Men rappelling down the side of the building and crashing through wall-size windows. Stun grenades exploding. Combat-rolling

Rambos in black outfits emptying Uzi submachine guns at shadows.

"I wear my Glock on my ankle, what are you packing?" I asked.

"A 469 on my ankle," said Georgie.

"A Beretta in the middle of my back," said O'Brien. "Safety's off."

Lesson from a Combat Shooting course: "In a shootout know where your partners' guns are carried, in case they're down and you need a gun."

The elevator stopped.

We moved rapidly down the hallway toward the double doors of the luxury suites. Bang! A door at the end of the hallway opened. A short, dark man with black Indian hair and chiseled features was watching our approach. His body was half hidden in the doorway. The angle told me he was packing. His pupils were wildly dilated—crackhead.

I moved past Crackhead trying to show no sign of fear, perfectly calm, business as usual.

The atmosphere of an undercover set is usually so charged that the slightest emotional change of one is felt by all in the room. It's bluff poker and everyone is betting his life. The moment of first impressions for an undercover agent is like a quick dash through a minefield.

"You're late," said Tito Garza in machine-gun Cuban Spanish. He was sprawled on a couch across the room from me, a drink in hand. I marveled at how relaxed and natural he looked. He was born for this work.

"Blame the airlines," I said.

Beside Garza, a bushy-haired Colombian got to his feet.

I recognized Gonzalo "Papo" Perez—one of *El Búfalo*'s top aides—from his photos. We shook hands. He didn't bother introducing his two *pistoleros*. No time was wasted on niceties. Likewise, I didn't introduce Georgie and O'Brien. O'Brien was the only one in the room who spoke no Spanish, which was an advantage in his job of reading body language.

"Hey, Miguel," said Garza. "You know what Papo here's telling me? That when you hang a guy, he gets a hard-on and comes."

Immediately I was confronted with vintage Garza doing his

crazy jig at the edge of the cliff—playing chicken with me. Years vanished. I fell into my role.

"Sure," I said. "That's why they call jerking-off 'choking the chicken.' Didn't you know that, *pendejito?*"

Now *Monguín,* the Wise One, the all-knowing Garza, stared at me blankly, uncertain if I was pulling his chain. I was reminded of how he got the nickname that plagued him for all the years he was stationed in New York.

Even Papo, the prototypic Colombian doper-killer—who knew nothing but dope dealing and murder—was smiling. He thought he'd just learned some new and interesting fact about chickens.

Crackhead slipped behind me. The other *pistolero,* tall, gaunt, and sporting a ponytail, leaned against the wall near the door. He wore dark little sunglasses with lenses the size of quarters. His right hand was unabashedly inside his jacket.

O'Brien and Georgie had taken up spots on either side of the window, for a good reason. When the SWAT team crashed through, they would be out of the line of fire.

I got down to business.

As the Mafia representative from New York—the Money Man—I came with the authorization of the "family" to bargain for the best price. When I learned that Tito had already offered $1.8 million for the hundred kilos, I exploded.

"You fucking *cabrón,*" I said, deciding to come on stronger than usual. "Who the fuck authorized you to go that high?"

Garza was taken aback. We hadn't done the act in eight years. He really had to fight to control his hair-trigger temper and show me the kind of respect that Papo expected to see. The act had the ring of authenticity that I wanted.

"This is a first transaction," I told Papo. "The family wants the same price you would give us if we were buying a ton."

"That is impossible," said Papo.

"I'm not asking for the delivery price in Colombia. What would the price be for a ton delivered right here in Miami? That is the price I will pay."

"Out of the question," said Papo. He was upset, but the last thing in the world he would imagine was that he was dealing with undercover agents.

"If it's out of the question, then we're wasting each other's time. I didn't come here to do one transaction—I came to open up a business relationship between my family and yours. You can't give us a better price, we go elsewhere."

"You're making me look like a bullshitter," said Garza, his face flushed. "I made a fucking offer."

"If your offer was $1.8 million you *are* a bullshitter. If you were authorized to go that high, I wouldn't have had to come all the way from New York. Now I'm here, so you just keep your fucking mouth shut!"

"*Suave,*" said Papo, playing peacemaker between Garza and me. "No need to get upset. These things happen." Now everyone in the room looked upset, but it was all business and that was okay.

"What do you consider a fair price?" asked Papo.

I answered quickly. "Thirteen thousand a kilo, $1.3 million cash. I have it with me. *Dando y dando.*"

Papo couldn't possibly be authorized to agree to that low a price, yet it was not a totally unreasonable offer. I was trying to corner him into reaching out to *El Búfalo* for instructions. If I didn't force his appearance, he was liable to let Papo handle the whole thing.

Papo shook his bushy head. "Impossible," he said. Behind him Crackhead was also shaking his head.

"Is it impossible if I guarantee that after this transaction we'll take a minimum of two thousand kilos a month and keep a balance of twenty million on account from then on?"

Now he took a long thoughtful look at me. I had just offered him, probably, the biggest deal he'd ever seen—a third of a billion dollars in business for the coming year including a $20 million cash-down payment.

"I have to make a phone call," said Papo getting to his feet. He headed toward the door with his men following.

"What the fuck you pulling, Levine?" said Garza the moment the door closed. He was pacing the floor, rotating his head like a boxer—signs that he was hopping mad. "I had the fucking deal done. All you had to do was agree to a fucking price—any price. *El Búfalo* is sitting out there somewhere with a hundred fucking keys."

"Where can we talk?" I asked.

The room was bugged and everything we were saying was

being transmitted halfway around the world. Garza stormed into the bathroom. I followed and closed the door behind me.

"How do you know he's here?" I said.

"Because *he* said he'd fucking be here! He woulda been on the way to the hotel with the dope by now. Done! Fucking AG's Award. But no, you had to go do your mind games. Now they're burned."

"And you think *El Búfalo's* just gonna walk in here with a hundred kilos of coke because he wants to make a couple of lousy million? Even you can't be that dumb. He's here for one thing—he thinks he's gonna be the first Colombian to make a connection to the New York mob. These guys just wanted to see if I was the real thing and the real thing would bargain his ass off. Only undercovers agree to pay too fucking much."

The phone in the bathroom rang. Garza grabbed it.

"I know they're out. Don't you fucking think I know they left the room?—They said they gotta make a phone call—What the fuck you want from me?—He's here 'cause I asked him!" He slammed the phone down.

"My boss. You're gonna jam me up, *Judío*!" said Garza, pacing the small room. "This thing was supposed to go like clockwork."

"If *El Búfalo* shows," I said, "I want to go through with the buy."

Garza's jaw dropped open. "Are you off your fucking noodle? Whitfield's already here for the press conference. He dropped *everything* for this. You ain't even supposed to fucking be here."

"You called *me*—remember?"

"Don't fucking remind me." He slapped himself on the forehead. "When will I learn? Levine, every fucking time I got jammed up on this job it was because of you. You ain't draggin' me down with you this time."

He stopped and stared at me suspiciously.

"You ain't gonna pull another Stan Getz on me, are you?"

Garza had once spotted the great jazz saxophonist in a brand-new Cadillac convertible, buying heroin near the Paris Hotel in New York. If we took him for possession we had headlines and an award, and the car was ours. But I had learned to play the saxophone listening to Stan Getz records. How could I bust the man who brought that magnificent sound into the world for having a little dope habit? I pulled the G car to the curb with Garza screaming in my ear and let him go free. Tito added the incident to the long list of things he would never forgive me for.

"Tito, just calm down and listen to me," I said. "It doesn't make any sense to arrest him now. There's no way we're going to flip him. If we make the buy, we've got credibility. We're *El Búfalo*'s business partners. You're the guy who told me that if anyone in the world knows what happened to René *and* can get the White Queen, it's him. A little patience and we get both. We can bust him any time. We bust him now, we get nothing but a headline for Whitfield."

"No, no, no," said Tito, shaking his head, pacing. "No fucking way."

The sound of radio voices came from the other room. Garza charged through the door, I was right behind him. Vinnie and Georgie had a DEA portable.

"Badguy One still on the phone," said a whispered radio voice that sounded like a UC talking on a lapel mike and probably standing right near the Colombians in the lobby.

"Where's Two and Three?" said another voice.

"Checking out the lobby," said a third.

"He looks like he's having one hell of a conversation, anybody hear anything?"

"Hold it! Hold it! He's off the phone. He's looking around," said a voice.

"Back off. Back off!" whispered another. *"Okay, okay, Two and Three are joining him. They're talking. . . . Okay, okay, they're heading back to the elevator. Repeat: Badguys One, Two and Three proceeding to elevators."*

"They're comin' back," said Garza. "Get that fucking thing outta here!"

Georgie grabbed the portable and rushed out of the room to hide it. The room was quiet. We listened to the sounds in the hallway. Finally we heard the sound of the elevator door opening followed by footsteps.

There was a light tap at the door. O'Brien opened it and Papo entered alone. He moved straight toward me. He was nodding, a wry smile on his lips.

"I understand now why your people call you Money Man. The person I am responsible to said that the final price is $1.5 million—you can take it or leave it. He is very interested in doing regular business with your people. In consideration of that, he has decided to give you a discount—but if it is always this difficult, it is not worth the trouble."

"I understand completely," I said. "I just want to know how flexible you people are, or it isn't worth it to us either."

He smiled. He understood drug world logic.

"So, we are in agreement?" said Papo.

"I didn't come all this way to talk," I said.

"There is a problem. My men have spotted people in the lobby. Maybe police." He paused, watching me closely for a reaction.

"Watching you?" I asked, showing appropriate concern.

"Maybe. You know where the private hangars are in Lauderdale International Airport?"

"Yes."

"Drive there with the money. Alone. Flash your lights twice."

Papo watched me, waiting for a response. It could be a test. An undercover agent going alone to an isolated spot with $1.5 million is a violation of every regulation the government has. The Colombian knew it. All dopers knew it. Any hesitation, I sensed, would blow the deal.

"I'll be there."

Papo slipped out of the room without looking back.

Garza was wild-eyed. "I'll ride in the fucking trunk."

"Suppose they put a bullet in the trunk, like they did with Marty Bello," said O'Brien.

Bello had tried to cover a buy/bust operation from the trunk of a car and had his spine severed by a bullet from a Dominican drug dealer who noticed that Bello's partner, a rookie agent, kept looking at the trunk. Bello was paralyzed from the shoulders down and his partner later committed suicide.

"At that hangar you can see people coming from a mile off," said Georgie.

"That's the general idea," I said. "There's one big problem we've got right now. They're already hinky. If I take too long getting there—they're in the fucking wind. It's over."

The phone rang. Garza grabbed it.

"Yeah!—Well you fucking heard it. We got no choice." Garza's face reddened. "He's here 'cause I asked him to come. It ain't his fucking fault! You heard the son of a bitch. He made *your* people in the lobby. Fucking amateurs!—You heard me, I said *fucking amateurs!* Want me to waste time explaining now and blow the fucking case?" He slammed the phone down.

"Levine," said Garza, fixing me with a murderous stare. "The minute you see *El Búfalo* you better push that button. Fuck me now and I swear on the Virgin, I'm gonna put a bullet in you."

10

Fifteen minutes later I was at the wheel of a Lincoln Town Car rocketing northbound on I-95 toward Fort Lauderdale International Airport. I had $1.5 million in two suitcases in the trunk.

A portable radio that someone had left under the seat crackled with calls as an army of undercover agents raced ahead of me to the area, along with an even bigger army of press and media. I heard my progress marked by helicopters. I was hitting a hundred on the speedometer when I saw headlights in the rearview gaining on me as if I was standing still. I reached for my gun. A news van marked LIVE ACTION NEWS whizzed past me.

The press and government agents were ordered to set up their ambush a quarter of a mile away from the airport so that counter-surveillance by the Colombians would not detect them. A repeat of the performance in the hotel and I was a dead man.

The moment I saw drugs, I was to press the rip button—the cameras would roll and the armies would charge. Every news network in the U.S. was waiting jaws agape like starving vultures for their video feeding. *El Búfalo* was to be this week's main course.

As I drove through the industrial area surrounding the rear entrance to the airport, I tried to spot something out of the ordinary. Everything looked clean. The television war on drugs had made the newsies better than the government at surveillance and camouflage.

At exactly 11:30 p.m. I pulled up to the rear gate. The private hangars appeared dark and deserted. I got out of the car. The gate had been left unlocked. I swung it open, noticing movement in the shadows around a Learjet parked just beyond a series of small hangar buildings. The ground shook with the deafening roar of a jumbo jet taking off just a few hundred feet away. I got back into the car and made sure the portable radio was hidden well under the seat.

As I edged the car slowly forward I flashed my lights on and off twice. Headlights in the darkness answered. I headed toward them. A stretch limo was parked almost beneath the wing of the Learjet. A light was on in the cockpit and two heads silhouetted inside. The plane was being made ready for takeoff.

I pulled up alongside the stretch. I could see only deep blackness and the reflection of distant lights in its tinted windows. A rear window slid down. I eased the Lincoln forward until I was alongside.

Staring out at me was the man himself: *El Búfalo*. His photos never did him justice. They didn't capture the sheer size of the head and the frightening effect of eyes set so wide apart that they seemed to peer at you from the sides.

"You know who I am," he said, his voice surprisingly soft.

"That's why I'm here," I said.

"Then there's no need to play games."

A door of the limo swung open. I took a deep breath, left my car and stepped inside. The interior light was switched on. I was seated across from *El Búfalo* himself. His sheer size was extraordinary; not obese so much as thick and full of energy like his namesake. Alongside him was Crackhead with a nine-millimeter automatic pointed at my head. Papo was seated beside me.

The tension I saw in their eyes almost set me off. I had to stifle a sudden impulse to go right for the rip-off pen—the movement alone would have made him pull the trigger.

"Undress," said Papo. "We've been seeing too many people, first in the hotel, now out on the street—something's wrong."

"I hope you will understand," said *El Búfalo* apologetically.

"I understand perfectly," I said.

I removed all my clothing and handed it to Papo who examined each item. The huge man inches away and breathing loudly through his nostrils studied me closely. For a terrifying moment Papo fingered the rip-off pen. Instead of pushing the button he unscrewed it and found nothing unusual.

As I dressed, Crackhead leaned over the rear seat and pulled two large suitcases out and lay them on the floor between us. He flipped one open. It was filled with brick-sized packages wrapped in duct tape.

"Do you want to check it?" asked *El Búfalo*.

I pulled the pen from my pocket and selected a package. My finger was on the rip button. The whole deal was right there in front of me—one hundred kilos of cocaine and one of the world's most wanted men. A push of the button and every news show in the world would be featuring the story for the next couple of months.

Using the tip of the pen I punched a tiny hole in the plastic package. The chemical smell of freshly crystallized cocaine is like no other smell in the world. It reached deep into my nostrils. I had been buying cocaine for so many years, I could smell the purity.

"No," I said. "For a lousy hundred kilos I don't have to check anything. I'm only here because the family is interested in doing real business with you. I won't insult you the way you just insulted me. You'll find the money, a million and a half, in my trunk."

"Ramón," said *El Búfalo*.

The driver flashed the headlights. I heard the jet engines start up.

El Búfalo ordered Papo to put the cocaine in my car and to return with the money. The ground thundered with the takeoff of another jumbo jet as Papo and Crackhead slipped outside to carry out the order. For a moment the area behind the car lit up in the red glow of brake lights. I glimpsed two men carrying submachine guns cradled in their arms, peering off into the darkness.

"All I can do is offer my apologies," said *El Búfalo*. "I came all the way here to open up a line with you people, but there's too much going on around here to feel safe."

I could see the gleam of the whites of his eyes, feel his tension. There were *pistoleros* all around me. If I hit the rip button at that moment, I was a trigger-pull away from dead. The moment I saw headlights, I'd have to take a dive into the darkness and keep running.

Crackhead and Papo returned with the money. Grunting under the weight, they laid the two suitcases on the floor between us and opened them. Packets of hundreds toppled out onto the floor.

"How is the money packed?" asked *El Búfalo.*

"A hundred-fifty packets, ten thousand in each," I said. "All hundreds."

El Búfalo selected three stacks, handed one each to Crackhead and Papo, then undid the third himself. While the other two counted he carefully checked for signs of counterfeit or serial numbers that ran in sequence. The car was silent except for Crackhead, who counted out loud, *"sesenta, sesenta y uno, sesenta y dos . . ."*

"So how is Señor Gianotti?" said *El Búfalo.*

"Anxious to do business," I answered. "With honorable people," I added.

"Todo correcto," said Papo.

"Check another stack?" said Crackhead.

"No," said *El Búfalo.* "Get it on the plane. Move. We don't have much time. I got a bad feeling here."

He checked his watch, a diamond-studded Rolex. At midnight no more takeoffs and landings would be permitted. In a few minutes I wouldn't even have to press the rip button. He'd be stuck here.

Papo, Crackhead, and another *pistolero* lugged the money from the limo to the plane.

El Búfalo lowered his window to watch them. "Papo tells me you want to do some serious business with us," he said, his eyes roving the darkness.

"Yes."

He reached into an inside pocket and withdrew a business card. "Call me, personally, when Señor Gianotti is ready. Next time, come to me directly."

On his pinky finger, which was about the width of a hot dog, was an enormous jade and gold serpent ring with two large emerald eyes—his fabled *iman.* The word in the drug world was that *El Búfalo* believed the ring to be the key to his invulnerability.

"Mr. Gianotti's a little nervous about us going down south, especially now, after that agent from *la DEA* was killed," I said, putting my finger back on the rip pen. My heart was going like a machine gun, but I had to give it a shot, I had to hear his reaction.

He took a long, hard look at me. I met his gaze.

"Bad for business," he said simply.

"What about *La Reina Blanca*?" I asked.

He looked startled. "What do you know about her?"

"We want her," I said.

"So do a lot of people."

"No one will pay more. Name your price."

He laughed and the whole limo seemed to shake. "You couldn't prove it with this transaction."

"Then you don't have her," I said.

"Soon," he said. "I will have the White Queen soon."

"That's when we'll come to you," I said.

A moment later *El Búfalo* lumbered up the short stairway into the Learjet, his bulk barely fit through the doorway. The plane was moving before the door was shut, taxiing quickly toward the runway.

Back in the driver's seat of the Lincoln, I flipped on the portable radio and begin to unscrew the top of the rip-off pen.

"Confirmation from tower," said a voice. *"They're taking off right now."*

"We gotta fucking stop em!" said Garza's voice.

"Belay that," said a voice that I guessed was Garza's division leader. *"We don't know who's taking off. There's still two cars there! We don't know what happened. You just cool your damned heels. Anybody got an eyeball?"*

"I think Uncle's back in the UC car," said another voice. *"Too dark to tell for sure."*

"I think there's still people inside the stretch," said another.

Once the top was unscrewed and the pen shaft removed, the innards slid out in one piece. I bent two tiny metal tab contact points away from each other just far enough to disable the transmitter. My fingers were shaking. I wiped the tabs carefully with the edge of a handkerchief. The suits would try to get a partial fingerprint, but I didn't want to wipe too much and remove Papo's prints.

As I started to screw the rip-off pen back together the Lear roared down the runway and into the night sky, heading at first westward, then banking slightly and turning south. A million and a half U.S. dollars and one of the most wanted men in the world were safely on the way back to Colombia.

Angry frantic voices chattered back and forth on the portable. I turned it off and slid it back under my seat. I started the Lincoln and rolled slowly toward the gate.

11

I DROVE SLOWLY OUT THE AIRPORT GATE INTO DARK, SILENT STREETS lined with small industrial buildings. Blinding headlights suddenly roared at me from every angle. A car streaked wildly out of nowhere, skidding sideways to block my path. I slammed down my brakes. My car spun. Tires screeched. Feet pounded pavement. There were shouts. Silhouettes moved crazily through light and shadow. I threw my hands up onto the windshield, the classic sign of surrender in the street wars—the pose that says: *Shoot me and everyone will know I was unarmed.*

The door opposite me jerked open. A wild-eyed Tito Garza peered inside, the barrel of his gun pointed at me. His eyes went to the suitcases full of cocaine on the backseat and then to me.

"You always have to fucking do it your way, don't you?" he hissed.

The driver's side door was jerked open, I felt myself grabbed from behind the collar and jerked backward. My head cracked hard against the pavement. My last memory was a blinding flash of light and pain.

DEA Headquarters, Washington, D.C.

"You understand that anything you say may be used against you in a court of law," said Myles Bydon, chief of Internal Security. "Would you like to consult with an attorney?"

I peered at the faces seated around me at the large rectangular conference table in Whitfield's office and tried not to think about the pain behind my eyes. The emergency room doctor in Miami had said "minor concussion," but there was nothing minor about the pain.

"Can I ask what I'm being charged with?" I said.

The son of a bitch knew I wouldn't ask for a lawyer. To ask for a lawyer, or to refuse to answer questions, would give the suits grounds to immediately suspend me. And then what could I do?

"We'll get to that," said Bydon, sliding a stapled packet of neatly typed legal-size pages toward me, each of which bore my signature—my version of the events leading up to El Búfalo's "escape."

"You understand that if you lied on this statement"—Bydon tapped three times on the stack of papers with his bony finger to emphasize the point—"you've committed a felony violation of Title 18, Section 1001, punishable by up to ten years in federal prison."

"This man has shamed the agency," said Whitfield, his lips flapping together like frightened fish. He got to his feet. "I'm not going to sit here and listen to any more of his lies. I don't want him leaving this room with his job."

Stratton, in a suit jacket that strained at his thick biceps, couldn't look at me.

"Where's the lie, Mr. Whitfield?" I said.

"The tech people say that *someone* bent the contact points on the rip-off pen," said Bydon, his thin lips barely moving, giving me his baddest I-gotcha look with his gray bureaucrat's eyes. "Agents O'Brien and Mendoza have signed statements indicating that you tested the pen in their car and that it functioned perfectly. We have a tape recording of you in the hotel bathroom telling Agent Garza that a buy *should* be made—in spite of headquarters' instructions. *Your* statement is that one of the Colombians took apart the rip-off device to examine it, then you saw the drugs, then you pushed the rip button and it simply did not work."

So much for the bathroom being a safe place to speak.

"That's correct, sir," I said. "I thought a buy *should* be made. It gives me credibility with El Búfalo as a Mafia money mover, the chance to go deep cover into the Colombian cartels, the best shot we have of finding the source of the White Queen *and* René Villarino's killers."

"So you're admitting that you prevaricated the story about the pen?" said Bydon.

"No sir, I didn't plan it that way," I said. "It was simply my opinion."

I reached into my pocket and tossed the card *El Búfalo* had given me onto the table. "That's his home phone. I made a hand-to-hand buy from him. A hundred kilos. My testimony puts him away for two lifetimes. I'm the only witness against him. You fire me, you prosecute me—you lose him for good. I become the headline instead of *El Búfalo*—does that make sense?"

They looked around the room at each other. There was no pretense left. If the suits could get away with it, they'd put a bullet in me. I had them by the balls. And the sudden worried look on Whitfield's face told me that my reference to "headline" had hit the nerve I was aiming for.

"I say we should go for it," said Stratton, speaking for the first time. "It makes sense. No use cryin' over spilled milk."

All eyes shifted to him now. Other than me, he was the lowest-ranking man in the room. But he was widely respected and his background with CIA seemed to put him in a special category.

Whitfield paced the room for a moment. His bodyguards shifted uneasily. Stratton had offered him an honorable exit and he was no fool.

"He's in your division," said Whitfield. "You'll assume full responsibility for his actions?"

"Of course," said Stratton.

"Be advised," said Bydon, "that as far as Internal Security is concerned, this matter is far from closed."

"That's none of my business," said Stratton. "I'm only concerned about Levine's actions under *my* command. You get something on him, I'll put the cuffs on him myself." Stratton fixed me with a long gaze that said he meant every word.

Moments later it was over. I had gone in the door with the Ventriloquist reading me my Miranda warnings and come out with permission—under the close supervision of Desk Officer Bobby Stratton—to proceed with an undercover investigation into the source of *La Reina Blanca*. It was a victory, yet I felt only weariness and the ache in my head.

As I got to my feet Stratton said, "I want to see you in my office."

I knew that was coming.

———

"Great fucking performance," said Stratton the moment the door had shut behind us. "Your bullshit's about as subtle as a New Orleans funeral."

Stratton's office was military neat. Reports and cables stacked in the In and Out boxes. The brown veneer of his desk, highly polished. On the walls were rows of awards, plaques and framed photos, most of which showed Stratton in jungle settings with groups of men in combat gear and camouflage paint on their faces. On a wall behind a couch was a tattered Viet Cong flag.

Stratton took off his suit jacket and slumped onto the couch. "Sit," he said, motioning for me to take a seat across from him.

"Levine, you *ever* try to jerk me around the way you did those assholes, there's gonna be a fucking fight."

He wore a short-sleeved shirt that barely contained his torso. Even relaxed the heavily veined and corded arms seemed to be flexed. I found myself staring at the blue death's-head tattoo on his right forearm. Beneath it were four vertical lines slashed diagonally through with a fifth that I hadn't noticed before. I'd heard that the tattoo signified a special CIA-run sniper operation during the Vietnam War called Operation Phoenix whose main objective was to kill specially selected targets.

"You talk like I was trying to get away with some kinda crime," I said.

"You're lucky you fell on your fucking head. I swear to Jesus I think it saved you from a bullet. You know how many people you pissed off?"

I shrugged.

Stratton suddenly slammed his fist down hard on the table. "I stuck my neck out for you and you fucked me."

"I never lied."

"Don't play with me, Levine. I'm not one of those fucking bank tellers you just conned. You broke your word!"

"If I asked for your permission, would you have given it?"

"So you just break your fucking word? What kinda man are you?"

"How far would you have gone if René was your best friend?

99

Did you get a look at what they did to him? How many buddies of yours were written off by the suits?"

"I'm not talking about anything but you and me here. Fuck me again, I'm coming after you."

We locked eyes. I looked away, shaking my head. He slumped back in his seat.

"You think I'm dirty, Bobby?"

"If I did, you'd be in a cage waiting for your indictment."

"Then give me some room to maneuver. We both want René's killers. We both know that the people who run this agency couldn't give a shit."

"What exactly is that supposed to mean—'give me some room to maneuver'?"

"You don't have to know everything I do. I'm going after the motherfuckers who killed one of ours."

"What you got up your sleeve, Levine?"

"A couple of ideas. Just let me do what I gotta do."

I met Stratton's gaze and held it. This time I caught a fleeting glimpse of a deep pain in his eyes, the kind of pain I was feeling, the kind of pain that I could not imagine anyone with an assassin's insignia on his arm being capable of experiencing. His face suddenly cracked in a wry smile.

"So you're offering me plausible deniability—that about it?"

"Exactly," I said.

Stratton nodded his head slowly. His tattoo was an emblem of plausible deniability.

"How you going to finance whatever it is you've got in mind?"

"I've got the five thousand petty cash fund in the safe and some undercover credit cards in different names. I'll put it all under Operation White Queen. That's the theory anyway, isn't it? René was going for the source."

Stratton fixed me with that crazed combat look of his.

"You're on your own, Levine. Cover your Government Issue ass well, my friend. A lot of people are praying for the chance to do you."

"The trip to Corsica for the funeral—still authorized?"

"That's as far as I go," said Stratton.

"Thanks, Bobby," I said, getting to my feet.

"Don't thank me. After the funeral I'm ordering you back to

Argentina to go to work on the White Queen. You choose to do something else, you're on your own."

By the time the cab picked me up at the Marriott I had already made flight reservations to Corsica. My first stab at finding out what *El Búfalo* knew wasn't a home run, but it did get me to first base. Getting back into him would take planning and enough time for Garza to cool off so that we could be in the same room together. My problem at the moment was that I didn't have a clue as to who killed René. I couldn't face his family without having *something* to tell them. They would count on me for that.

Someone had gone to a lot of trouble to erase René's deep cover tracks. He was murdered because he got too close to something big and well protected. Maybe it was the White Queen, maybe it wasn't. I had run out of alternatives. No matter what the consequences, I was going to have to risk tracking down the one person who knew René better than anyone—Marita Salazar.

12

"PASSENGERS WILL PLEASE RETURN TO THEIR SEATS AND FASTEN THEIR seat belts. We are beginning our descent into Montevideo," the stewardess said over the loudspeaker.

Usually when I fly, I never leave my seat or unbuckle my seat belt, in the firm belief that without my total concentration, the plane, weighing roughly the same as seven New York garbage trucks, would plummet straight to the ground. Yet on this flight my mind kept drifting back through twenty years of memories.

The Jews believe that if a person lives in your memory, he lives. This is one of the reasons for so many commemoration ceremonies and prayers for the dead. I had enough vivid memories of René to keep him alive for as long as I lived—some I would have just as soon forgotten.

René, his dark, handsome face solemn, appears in the doorway of my office. He closes the door behind him. As usual, he is immaculate in a custom-tailored blue suit, a gleaming white shirt, and a silk tie of swirls of muted blue and gold. The perfection of his appearance highlights the harried look I see in his eyes.

"Mighe, do you call me friend?"

"That's a funny question, René."

I wait for him to continue. He doesn't. His eyes are scouring the office as if he were on an undercover set looking for a bug or a booby trap. He takes a folded slip of paper from his pocket and opens it in front of me. Written in block letters is the name MARITA SALAZAR.

"Do you know her?"

Marita Salazar was a name that figured prominently in the piles of reports on my desk. "You know I'm about to indict her, don't you?" I say.

René puts a finger to his lips and motions toward the door. I follow him. He doesn't speak again until we're a block from the office on West 57th Street near the Hudson River.

"Marita is a special friend, Mighe. *She never touched drugs in her life," says René.*

Now I'm nervous. Agents secretly working for Internal Security had tried to set me up before. But René? The man who'd risked his job to find my boy? That didn't seem possible.

"I don't have her for drugs, René. She's being charged with murder."

He scans the street around us. "Mighe. Have I ever lied to you?"

"What do you want, René?"

"Forget her name."

The thump of the plane making contact jerked me out of my reverie of a moment lived almost two decades earlier. I double-checked the documents in my attaché case and the case itself for any signs of my true identity. My passport and credit cards said my name is Pedro Casso, Argentine businessman.

The Customs inspector in Montevideo leafed through my passport, which showed extensive travel between the U.S. and South America. Then he opened and carefully examined my attaché case for false bottoms and sides. He peered at me suspiciously. "No baggage?"

"I'm only here for the day, maybe the night."

"No change of clothes? No toilet articles?"

"If I need it, I'll buy it."

He fished his hand deep into the file flap and came up with my palm-size seven-by-fifteen field glasses. "What are these for?"

"Oh those," I said, keeping a perfectly straight face. "When you put them to your eyes they make distant objects seem as if they are up close."

He stared at me for a long moment, unblinking. Without a word he tossed the glasses into the case, closed it and shoved it toward me.

"Next in line," he said, looking past me.

Outside the Customs control area I went to the storage lockers. In locker number 106 I found a small, compact package wrapped in brown paper, exactly as I had left it two years earlier. I hefted its reassuring weight for a moment. The five .38 caliber bullets in the chamber weighed almost as much as the gun itself. It was a Smith & Wesson revolver with a shrouded hammer, made with an especially light alloy, aptly named "the Bodyguard." It fit easily in my pants pocket, the shrouded hammer making it easy to slip in and out without catching on the material.

Mighe, *an undercover who doesn't practice, practice, practice, with all the tools of his trade, will one day die with his hands empty and his holster full.* I had another just like it at home in Buenos Aires that I would practice quick-draw with. It would be my only companion, my only protection for whatever was about to come my way.

A twenty-minute cab ride later and I was on Calle Río Negro in downtown Montevideo, feeling as if I had stepped back in time to the 1940s. The street sloped downhill toward the Río de la Plata and was lined with grimy old buildings, none higher than six stories. Most had long since seen their fiftieth birthday. Many of the cars chugging by would have been collector's items in the U.S., but in Uruguay, where Model A Fords were still used to deliver milk, they were just more signs of poverty.

The London Palace Hotel was on the 1200 block of Río Bravo and directly across the street from the Ritz, a cabaret-style whorehouse. It was 3:00 p.m. The place wouldn't open until five. I was right on schedule.

Two years earlier the Ritz had been owned by an informant of mine, Moritz, a Polish Jew who had fled to Uruguay just before the war to escape the Nazis. His prostitutes, he boasted, were the youngest and most beautiful in South America. He even had a kind of delivery service. For select customers he would send girls—for a night, a weekend, or sometimes longer—to La Costa del Sol, Buenos Aires, and as far away as Rio.

The girls made incredible informants. Every international criminal who came through Montevideo stopped at the Ritz. And it was just as my loan shark father once told me: *When the little head gets hard, the big head really does get soft.*

When these guys were in the rooms upstairs with nothing but a naked woman and a bag full of white powder, they would talk and talk and talk. They would usually talk themselves into a long stay in a Uruguayan prison, sometimes a permanent one on the bottom of the Río de la Plata. And the girls, who despised the johns, loved the work. They'd make more U.S. taxpayer dollars per doper's body than selling their own and DEA's protection thrown in as a bonus.

Two years ago Moritz had called me at the embassy in Buenos Aires to tell me he was selling the place and retiring. He had wanted to know if I knew anything about the buyer, a cabaret singer named Marita Salazar. I told him I didn't know her.

My room in the London Palace would have been considered, at best, unacceptable and, at worst, unbearable in the U.S. By Montevideo standards it was considered a little above average. It was about the size of the average broom closet in any Marriott and a little smaller than the jail cells on Riker's Island. But it had what I needed: a window facing the entrance to the Ritz.

I set up an OP by the window, lowering a yellowed shade until the window was covered. I cracked it on the side and peeked out. There were eighteen windows in the three stories above the Ritz, each a separate bedroom. All had shades that were fully drawn.

I took the field glasses from the attaché case and hung them around my neck. Then I removed a manila envelope. Inside was a folded poster from a São Paulo nightclub announcing a Christmas show featuring a singer named MARITA. The poster had withered and yellowed with age. I had had to reinforce its folds with Scotch tape. I opened it carefully. It featured a full-length photo of the singer in a black low-cut evening gown. It was the only photo I had of Marita Salazar, the only way I had of recognizing her. I had investigated her for two years, yet I had never seen her in person.

I carefully pasted the poster up alongside the window and studied the photo for features that wouldn't change with age. Marita had shoulder-length dark hair and a voluptuous figure. There were hard lines around the eyes and cheeks. Of all her features, the eyes were the most striking.

They were light brown according to available records yet they photographed almost gray. They were soulful eyes, intelligent eyes, warm, liquid eyes that caught your attention, made you want to know what gave them that little extra light.

"Marita Salazar is tied up with the Triangle of Death—Nazis, drug dealers, the Cosa Nostra. She worked directly for Auguste Ricord. She's a fucking hooker and a madam—What are you doing with her, René?"

René suddenly grips my tie and collar. The button pops. His jaw is gnashing. The veins in his forehead bulge. "You don't talk about her. You don't know anything about her."

My hands are over my head palms open. People cruising up 57th Street twist in their seats to watch this typical New York scene, but no one stops. I've known René a long time and have never seen him even close to losing it. He is the consummate, unflappable pro. And he is my best friend.

"What's happened to you?" I say. "Are you in trouble?"

He relaxes his grip. "She saved my life."

He straightens awkwardly. He looks dazed, panicked. He starts to walk again. I follow.

"She knew I was an undercover and kept her mouth shut for two years. How you think we learn the routes of drugs and money? How you think we learned there even was a Triangle of Death? Look at those reports on your desk. Source 23 is me, Mighe. If Marita talks, Source 23 is dead and there is no Auguste Ricord case and the Triangle of Death lives forever."

We are both checking the street around us now.

René continues: "Who stops them—the U.S. government? Don't make me laugh. And you want to indict her for murder?"

"What else do you call it, René? She makes a date with a Moroccan dissident named Ben Barka in Paris. He shows up—she doesn't—he's murdered. Testimony of two of her girls corroborates that she made the date. Ben Barka's son says his father had left to meet her. I have the testimony of Claude Pastou, one of Ricord's dope couriers, that Auguste Ricord himself had set up the hit."

"The girls they are nothing but little whores—and don't look at me like that—Marita is no putan. You prove different. And without Pastou you have no case."

"Why are we arguing, René? What choice you think I have here? The whole world is watching this thing. President Nixon himself is threatening the president of Paraguay to give up Ricord. What can I do?"

"Forget Marita's name, Mighe. These squifozo politicians and bureaucrats won't miss her. They have Ricord, an ex-Nazi, a dozen Mafiosi from all over the world. They can tell the Americans how they break the back of the Triangle of Death. They give each other a couple of medals, everyone is happy. No one will miss one little cabaret singer."

"How do I live with myself, René? She set a man up to die. And you're asking me to commit a felony. If anybody finds out, you and I can get twenty years."

I lifted the field glasses. Across the street a dark skinned, heavyset man and woman had stopped at the front door of the Ritz. The man fidgeted with keys in the locks. It was growing dark, but I could see clearly enough to know that the woman was too young to be Marita. They went inside. Within minutes a large neon sign over the facade flickered and lit. The Ritz was open for business.

Over the next two hours I watched fifteen women arrive in evening dresses. It soon became too dark to see clearly with the binoculars. Now men started to straggle in, first one at a time, then in groups of three and four. Upstairs, the lights flicked on in one of the rooms. Shadows moved across the drawn shades.

Time to move.

I shoved the little gun in my pocket and headed for the door.

The inside of the Ritz had changed little. The room was dingy and dark, and dominated by a circular bar. Shadowy booths lined the walls. An ideal place for anonymity. An old Sly & the Family Stone song, "Dance to the Music," blasted from the jukebox as I entered and moved along the perimeter of the room. It was crowded and reeked of cheap perfume and stale beer. The women were hard at work pressing their bodies, stroking, groping, sitting on laps, their smiles painted on with lipstick.

The heavyset dark man who had opened the place watched me from a seat at the rear of the bar. I slid into a dark booth at the far corner of the room. Out of habit, I had chosen the same booth where Moritz and I used to talk business.

"*Hola,*" she said, smiling down at me, her breasts exposed to the dark edges of aureolas. She looked no more than eighteen years old. Her eyes were ageless and cold.

"*Hola,*" I answered.

She slid into the booth next to me, moving close, her thigh resting on mine. These girls worked on a time clock. Time was money and this girl wasn't wasting any.

"Buy me a drink?"

"You're Cuban?"

"Yeah, I am," she said, her hand moving up my inner thigh. "You like my company?"

"A man would have to be made of stone not to like your company," I said.

She smiled. A gold tooth flashed. Visions of us happy together in suburbia vanished.

"Buy me a drink," she said, her hand now where under biblical law she would be described as having "carnal knowledge" of me.

"Sure I'll buy you a drink. . . . Where is Marita?"

The smile vanished. "You're a cop."

I laughed. "No, no, no. Actually, I'm a friend of hers."

"Oh? How come I don't know you?"

She looked toward the dark man who was watching us. An unspoken signal. He started toward us. She removed her hand from its friendly welcome.

"Because we've never been introduced," I said.

The gold tooth flashed again. This time the smile matched the eyes. "I don't like you," she said. She got quickly to her feet.

The big man was by the table looking down at me. She whispered in his ear. His eyes studied me as she spoke. She disappeared toward the bar and he sat slowly across from me, not taking his eyes off me.

"Parlez français?"

"Not well," I answered in Spanish, thinking it odd that he would speak to me in French. "Why don't we speak Spanish?"

"I have a gun aimed just above your groin right now," he said in Spanish, with a thick Brazilian accent. "It has a silencer on it. I pull the trigger six times and no one here will even flinch. You will be just another fucking drunk carried out of here."

"Why?" I asked, cursing myself. Both my hands were on the table, both of his below it. If this guy killed me now, nobody would even come looking for him. I was in Montevideo with phony ID and a gun in violation of Uruguayan law, U.S. law, and every DEA reg in the book. As far as the suits were concerned I was already a rogue agent. My family wouldn't even get my death benefits.

"Dance to the Music," sang Sly & The Family Stone. An alto sax riffed sharply down the scale, the drumbeat shook the walls, couples groped in the darkness. He didn't need a silencer.

"You're looking for Marita," he said. "You have a gun in your pocket. I already told your fucking people I don't know where she is. I warned you about coming back here."

Metal detector on the door. The guy is as tense as bridge cable. How many other eyes are watching me in the darkness? Making a move at his gun now is crazy. A move for mine—suicide.

"Why don't you ask me *why* I carry a gun before you mess your booth up with my blood?"

"Talk," he said. "Fast."

I raised my hands up off the table. I gingerly reached into the breast pocket of my sport jacket with two fingers and extracted a Pedro Casso business card. I slid it across to him. His left hand reached for it. He held it up so that he could watch me and read the card at the same time.

"So that's who you say you are," he said.

"Do you know Moritz, the guy who sold Marita this place?"

"Why?"

"I had a deal with him. I'd take a couple of girls for business parties at a special price. All I wanted was the same deal from Marita."

"How do you know Marita owns this place?"

"I told you. Moritz is an old friend of mine."

He raised his hand over his head without taking his eyes off me. A woman appeared out of the gloom—the young one who had opened up with him. She leaned over so that he could watch me as he spoke into her ear. Facing me she had looked pretty, but her profile was parrot-like. She nodded once and disappeared toward the back rooms.

"If you're lying you are a dead man."

"Look, I'm just a businessman," I said, forcing my voice to remain steady, remembering *Sensei*'s words: *Show fear, you act like prey. Act like prey and you will be prey.* "All I wanted was a couple of girls. I'm not involved in any of this."

"Any of what?" His head was hunched over, both his hands were under the table. He looked at me out of the tops of his eyes.

"Whatever it is that has you pointing a gun at me."

"Oh but you are involved now, Señor"—he looked at the card"—Casso. And what is the gun for?"

"A few years ago I was robbed when I left here. This place is a target."

A woman with straight blond hair came out of the back. As she neared the table she was already nodding with recognition. She looked familiar but Moritz could go through a hundred girls in a year. She leaned across the table and spoke into the Brazilian's ear then hurriedly left.

He leveled his eyes at me. "You piece of shit," he hissed. "I don't know what your game is and I don't care who you really are. I feel like killing you on general principles. But this time I would rather you spread the message to the others: Marita is gone. No one here knows where she is. The place is mine. The next time you motherfuckers come here and slap around my girls—"

"But you've mistaken me—"

MICHAEL LEVINE AND LAURA KAVANAU

"Shut up! Get on your feet, slowly."

René killed. Marita suddenly on the run with French-speaking people after her. She had to know something. But asking anyone in this place to help me find her was too risky.

With my hands raised so that he could see them clearly, I slid out of the booth and got to my feet. He moved with me. I glimpsed the gun as he slipped it beneath his jacket. An automatic with a blunt silencer attached. I felt the palm of his hand pushing me firmly all the way to the door.

"You tell your people that if it is a war they want, they will have it. I am not alone. Whatever business you have with Marita, it is none of mine."

The door slammed behind me. My heartbeat slowed to normal.

I stood outside the Ritz for a moment. A soft, misty rain was falling. There are few places in the world more dark and depressing than downtown Montevideo in the rain. I was still nowhere. In a couple of hours I would be on a plane to Corsica to face René's family.

13

CALVI, CORSICA

As I climbed the steep hill, high above a dirt track where a taxi had just dropped me, I could hear an eerie chant, the voices growing louder as I approached the top. On the final rise, I paused in my tracks, stunned.

Illuminated by the crimson rays of the setting sun, a chorus of women, black shawls covering their heads, stood in a swaying semicircle around an ebony coffin, their backs a few scant feet from the edge of a cliff. Their chant rose and fell with the crashing of the waves on jagged rocks at least a hundred-fifty feet below them. Rows of mourners, hundreds of them, faced the chorus. The men wore black head- and armbands. And there was the intoxicating smell of the macchia flowers that grew wild only on Corsica. The world's most famous Corsican, Napoléon, during his exile had said that with his eyes closed he would know his beloved homeland by its smell. And now I understood.

The weariness of sixteen hours of travel from Montevideo suddenly vanished. I had arrived just in time. It was the last night of René's wake. He would be buried on this spot in the morning.

"Uncle Mike." René's oldest son, Marcello, his face red and swollen with tears, came running toward me, his arms open wide. I dropped my bag and embraced him. Behind him stood a big man wearing a black headband, whose face was an older, rougher version of René's.

"This is my uncle Paolo," said Marcello.

"René always spoke about his brother Paolo, the police inspector," I said, extending my hand.

The big man put his arms around me.

"*Mighe*," he said. "We finally meet." He kissed me on both cheeks. "I am talking to a brother." He stood back and looked at me, "René said you looked like a Sicilian fisherman. He was right. Come." He led the way toward two benches only feet from the coffin. "We want you to sit with the close family."

A space was cleared for us next to an old woman who sat bowed with grief, her head covered in black. She looked up at me and it was like looking into René's eyes.

"This is our *nonna*," said Marcello, "our grandmother."

Marcello and Paolo both spoke a few words in Corsican. I heard René's name for me, *Mighe*. Tears filled her faded, dark eyes. Her arms reached for me. Gnarled hands pulled me down into a crouch beside her. She held me tightly for a long time, murmuring in Corsican. Suddenly she pulled back and looked deeply into my eyes. She spoke slowly in French.

"*Mighe*, you were the only one from over there that my son spoke of with love and respect." She bowed her head and began to sob. I held her, feeling lost.

This shouldn't have happened.

The wailing of the chorus started up again, this time picked up by the crowd of mourners surrounding us. A sudden commotion erupted around the coffin. There were screams and shouts. A woman's voice shrilled insanely. I couldn't believe my eyes.

The lid of the coffin had been opened. One of the women was leaning inside cutting at something with a large knife. Another woman collapsed writhing on the ground. The crowd of mourners pushed forward shouting. Benches were toppled.

The woman rose out of the open coffin holding a dark piece of cloth over her head. "*Vendetta!*" she shrieked.

The coffin started to topple. Men fought to steady it. A man peered inside and paled. The lid was replaced.

The woman strode toward us holding the cloth and knife over her head. The crowd parted before her. Her eyes were on Marcello as her voice wailed an incantation in Corsican. I heard the word *vendetta* repeated over and over again.

"It's tradition," said Paolo. "A piece of my brother's clothing dipped in his blood is given to his eldest son. It is our family duty to carry out *vendetta*."

Several men moved out of the crowd and closed around us. The woman extended the cloth toward Marcello. Before he could accept it, Paolo shoved forward. He grabbed the cloth and knife away from her. Men surrounded him with their hands extended chanting *Vendetta!* Paolo sliced pieces off the cloth and handed them out.

I stuck my hand out. Paolo stared at me.

"You understand what this means, *Mighe*?"

"Yes," I said, believing I did.

He handed me a strip of the dark, stained material. I wrapped it in my handkerchief and put it in my pants pocket.

When it was over, Paolo pulled me aside.

"Come. There is something I want you to hear."

———

"Please, let me die," whispered Gabriela, René Villarino's youngest sister.

She was curled up on the floor in a corner of a sparsely furnished room, bruised, shoeless, and trembling like a frightened dog. Her black dress was torn and soiled. Her bed was untouched. The two women relatives assigned to watch her had moved aside when Paolo and I entered the room. They were on suicide watch. Some of the Villarino clan was afraid she would commit suicide, others had urged her to do it.

"Gabriela," said Paolo, crouching over her, his hand on her shoulder. "*Mighe* has come a long way. He wants to find these people."

"You did nothing wrong," I said. "They would have fooled anyone."

Her head came up. Her eyes were glistening black olives. "Please," she said, her voice almost a whisper. "Don't lie to me."

"I'm not lying. I loved your brother."

She looked like a madwoman. But after living through what she had, who wouldn't go mad.

"They were professionals, Gabriela," I said. "They fool highly trained spies. You thought you were protecting René. They already suspected him or they would never have come."

"*Nonna* is right," she sobbed. "A Corsican who speaks to police about their family, for any reason, should die."

"But your brother was a special kind of policeman," I said. "That makes it different. You're the only one who saw them."

113

"Yes, I saw them," she said. Her body began to tremble violently. "The *imbuscata*."

Nonna had told her that René's spirit had put the *imbuscata* on her—the evil with which the dead can curse the living, the ancient spell which all Corsicans live in mortal fear of.

"René wants to protect you," I said. "You can help me. What did they look like? What did they say? I need to know, Gabriela. René is watching us right now."

She reacted as if jolted by a cattle prod, sitting up straight, her eyes roving around the room.

"They wore business suits," she said, her eyes fixed on me now. Her bottom jaw had begun to tremble. "They spoke Parisian French. They said they come from the government."

"Did they show you identification?"

"DGSE," she said.

"The French Secret Service," said Paolo.

I put my hand on his arm. "Tell me exactly what you remember, Gabriela."

"They say they are looking for René. I am alone, working in the garden. They come out of the macchia, walking."

"They knew René's true name?"

"No, they have a picture. The kind that they take of prisoners."

"What did they say?"

"That René murdered a policeman. Unless I helped them other police would catch him first and kill him."

"And what did you tell them?" I said, pushing as gently as I could.

"I tell them they are mistaken. The one who does all the talking is tall, with dark hair. He shouts at me. He wants to know where René is. The other stays back and says nothing. He watches all around. I should have known. . . . They had documents with the photo that say René is a criminal, only they say a different name."

"Did the documents look official?"

"Yes," she wailed.

"Do you remember the name?" I said.

"No, no, maybe if I hear it."

"Was it Fabrizio Calvi?"

"Think, Gabriela," pleaded Paolo.

"I . . . I . . . I can't be sure," she sobbed. "They said my brother was a murderer and a drug dealer. They would shoot him on sight, unless I helped."

She began to rock back and forth.

"What did you say, Gabriela?" I asked.

Her head bowed suddenly. "May God kill me," she murmured.

"Gabriela, it's important," said Paolo.

"That René is American now—that he works for their government and that the records are false to protect him."

"And then what did they say?" I asked.

"They look at each other, then they leave very fast," she said, her voice suddenly a dull monotone. "I know something is wrong. I try to telephone René. But there is only a recording machine."

"The boys were both away at university," said Paolo.

"I was afraid," said Gabriela. "I did not want to cause trouble for my brother. I telephoned a number in Washington that René left for emergency."

"What was the number—can you remember?"

She reached into the pocket of her dress and handed me a folded piece of paper. On it was printed a phone number that I recognized immediately. It was the main number to DEA headquarters in Washington.

"I ask for my brother. A man tells me it is impossible to talk to him. I should tell him why I am calling. He will tell René. So I tell him."

"Do you remember his name?" I asked.

"He did not tell me."

"Did you ask his name?"

"Yes, but he did not answer me."

Later, Paolo and I stood outside in the darkness listening to Gabriela sobbing. He lit a cigarette and sat down on a rock overlooking the harbor. I sat beside him. It was a moonless night. For a few minutes we watched the lights of small boats slowly crossing in the darkness.

"What does your government know, *Mighe*?" he said, his voice tight.

"Nothing," I said. "The only potential lead is what happened with Gabriela."

"Half of our family are police. We can find them."

"Not yet. If they're really French Secret Service they're expecting an inquiry. If they aren't, it won't make a difference, they're long gone. Besides, it may have nothing to do with the murder."

"What do you mean?"

"René had a lot of enemies. He spent twenty years getting dangerous and powerful people to trust him and then putting them behind bars. Destroying them."

"He was very good, wasn't he, *Mighe*?"

"The best," I said, remembering that Paolo was the oldest. Their father had died a few years after the war from wounds suffered as a member of the French underground and young Paolo had assumed the role of the man of the house. There was love and respect between the brothers but little closeness. Paolo resented his brother for abandoning the island.

"I could never imagine that little *squifozo* becoming a cop," said Paolo, and for the first time his voice broke. I was glad I couldn't see his face in the darkness.

After a moment Paolo continued: "He was always in trouble. When he was fourteen he used to go into this shop in Bastia that catered to tourists . . . mostly Germans. They had this prize parrot from Africa. Very expensive. René was in there every day playing with that thing. I thought he must love it.

"Then one day I'm here with our mother and two of our uncles. The owner, a Parisian, comes storming up the hill carrying the parrot in a cage. He's breathing fire."

Suddenly Paolo was laughing so hard that at first I thought he was crying.

"What happened?"

When Paolo could catch his breath he said, "It seems my little brother taught the bird to say 'Your mother is a whore' in German. And the guy insists . . . we buy the bird."

Now I was laughing with him.

"And while we're standing there, *Mighe*," said Paolo, gasping for breath, "I swear to you . . . the damned bird squawks 'Heil Hitler.' "

When we finally stopped laughing, Paolo said, "So I grab my little brother and start beating him on the head. René claims he's positive the guy was a spy for the Germans during the war. Who knows if it was true, but anyway, René just had to get even. Can you imagine a kid like this becoming a cop?"

"Are you kidding me?" I laughed. "He was perfect. If there was anything wrong with René being a cop, it was that he had too much heart. It got him in lots of trouble.

"One night I get a phone call from him, about midnight. 'Come into the office,' he tells me. 'Don't ask questions, just come.' And I think, 'Oh my God, what now?'

"When I get there I see this guy with orange hair sitting behind the boss's desk. It's one of René's informers, a gay Cuban we used to call *Mariposa Colorada*—the Red Butterfly. A great stool pigeon, but a guy you wouldn't trust with your dirty underwear. And there's this little old white-haired couple sitting with him sipping coffee, acting like they run the place.

" 'What the fuck is going on here, René?'

"He pulls me aside. 'You gotta go along with me,' he tells me. 'The son of a bitch told his poor mother and father that he's a secret agent working for the American government. He's their only son, *Mighe*.'

"René is pleading with me to pretend I *work* for this stool pigeon. You don't trust *any* informer, no less this lowlife. But your brother begs me. 'It would break the old people's hearts to know what he really is. They're going back to Miami in the morning. Who knows if they'll ever see their boy again. Just go along with it for a couple of hours, *Mighe*.'

"So for the rest of the night this guy is ordering me and René around like a little dictator. I'm driving them all over town on a sightseeing trip with him screaming at me. Then he tells me: 'You! My father wants Cuban coffee. Get the hell out there and don't come back till you find some!'

"I wouldn't take that kind of talk from a *real* boss, no less some guy whose head reminds me of a dog's dick."

Paolo and I were both laughing.

"Only for René. So what do you think happens next? The stool pigeon wants to take the boss's car to drive his parents to the airport. He wants to be *alone* with them. René gives him the keys to the boss's Mercedes. We never saw that car again."

"I don't believe this," said Paolo, doubled over with laughter.

"Believe it," I said. "To this day I don't know how René talked us out of going to jail. The guy could talk his way out of anything."

We were both suddenly quiet. The only sounds were Gabriela's sobs and the ocean breeze. Paolo lit another cigarette. "You have a plan, *Mighe*?" he asked.

"Ideas," I said. "I don't know enough to have a plan yet."

"I want to help."

"The best help you can give me, right now, is to make sure your family doesn't make too much official noise. Not yet. And to protect Gabriela."

"*Vendetta* is a way of life here, *Mighe*," said Paolo. "Many thousands have died to satisfy *vendetta*. The code hasn't changed for more than six hundred years. It is very strict and has more power here than any religion. From the time I was a boy almost every story ever told to me about our family had to do with *vendetta*. And the *imbuscata*. You notice that my brother is not being buried in a cemetery?"

"Yes."

"The family knows that he is crying out for *vendetta*. Some even claim to have heard him. So they put him at the edge of the ocean, facing west where it happened so that he can send the *imbuscata* where it belongs. Today there were some who said they heard him curse Gabriela."

"Paolo," I said. "Come on. Just the fact that they knew to come here to look for René's true identity tells me that no matter what she said, his fate was sealed. Protect your sister. Your family has suffered enough."

I was the only one here who could have saved René. If anyone should suffer the imbuscata *it was me.*

14

THE WAVES EXPLODED AGAINST JAGGED ROCKS FAR BENEATH WHERE THE mourners were gathered. The bitter sea-wind gusted sharply inland as four powerful men lowered René's casket into the ground, hand over hand with ropes. Winter was the season of the *maestrale*—the winds that English-speaking sailors called "the mistrals." "Beware the mistrals" was the nautical warning that everyone around me seemed to be ignoring.

A woman, veiled and dressed in black, had caught my attention earlier when she edged close to touch the coffin and then drifted behind the crowd to stand alone. What I noticed was her subtle shifting from spot to spot whenever it appeared that someone might speak to her. As the coffin was lowered she moved to the opposite side of the grave from me. The wind suddenly gusted and the veil flew from her face. She snatched it back in place. I had not seen her long enough to be certain, but she looked like Marita Salazar.

I moved through the tightly packed crowd as quickly as I could, trying not to attract attention. She had already started down the steep hill.

Suddenly there was a horrific scream. A woman's figure cloaked in black hurtled toward the cliff's edge. The crowd of mourners rushed up the hill pulling me with them. I lost sight of Marita. I pushed against a throng of people and spotted her again. She was halfway down the hill and moving quickly.

"Marita!" I called.

She kicked her shoes off and ran. I chased her. A car was waiting at the bottom of the hill. The driver, leaning against the fender, saw her coming, opened the rear door then slipped into the driver's seat. His jacket flapped open and I saw a gun handle in his belt. I heard the engine start.

I had taken my eyes off the rocky ground in front of me an instant too long. I tripped. For a terrifying moment I was air-borne, going head over heels downhill, then I crashed down hard on my back and butt, skidding along the ground. Pain knifed up through my bad knee. I lay there dazed trying to gather my senses. Finally, I pulled myself up to a sitting position in time to see the car, a black Peugeot sedan, race off and disappear.

Behind me I heard someone scream that Gabriela had jumped to her death.

———

The road snaked crazily. The high beams didn't quite reach the curves waiting in ambush in the blackness ahead of us. We flew through every one of them skidding on two wheels while I leaned hard against the curve to keep us from flipping into the inky blackness.

Paolo was grim-faced at the wheel. I was in the passenger seat, groping for the seat belt. It was a dozen Motrin pills later and I was still trying to gather my senses. He said he knew the serpen-tine, roller coaster of a road like the palm of his hand, but I wasn't convinced.

Paolo had located three women who seemed to match Marita's description. The closest was in a hotel in the city of Ajaccio, some 70 miles to the south, registered under the name M. Saldano. There were two other similar women in the town of Bastia, on the other side of Corsica, about a 150-mile drive.

As we swung into another wild series of heart-stopping curves, it occurred to me that the whole thing might be crazy and that crazy is why a lot of people die. But I had this sense of urgency about speaking to Marita. Paolo knew almost nothing about her. I realized that he knew little of his brother's private life away from Corsica. He asked no questions. His only brother had been butchered in a faroff land, his sister was dead at the bottom of a cliff; his need to do *something* could only be taken out on his Renault, and on my heart.

"Before you arrived I made some inquiries," said Paolo, his

eyes fixed on the road ahead. "The Secret Service denies looking for my brother. What do you think?"

I wanted to tell him that I think he'd made a mistake by contacting them but the damage was already done. "Does the French Secret Service investigate murder?"

"They are not police, they are spies."

"So the whole thing sounds phony."

"Maybe. But I am not so certain."

My thoughts went to Gabriela's suicide. It seemed to come as a relief to the family; more an inevitable extension of René's funeral proceedings than her own death. For Paolo, the hunt for this unknown woman was most important now.

Nonna and a few other women in the clan had cried, but most had been stone-faced in their acceptance. Gabriela had broken a centuries-old code of silence and shamed the family. Her very life would have been a constant and painful reminder of René's horrible death and nothing anyone said or did would ever change that. Gabriela's death was nothing less than *vendetta*. The only honorable thing to do. If she hadn't taken her own life, sooner or later, one of her relatives would have taken it for her. It came as no surprise to me when Paolo told me that more than 36,000 people, on this island with a population of only 250,000, had been killed in *vendettas*.

We roared into Ajaccio, Corsica's largest city, at about 3:00 a.m. We screeched to a halt a few feet from the entrance to the Hotel Fesch, a small neat place with about eighty rooms, just off the Boulevard Sampiero on the waterfront. The streets were deserted.

Paolo reached under his seat and brought out a large automatic pistol. "Take this," he said, handing it to me. I held the gun in my hand. It was sleek and deadly-looking. Paolo knew that I was unarmed, that an American DEA agent cannot legally carry a gun in France and that I would not take the chance of trying to smuggle my own through Customs.

"It is an MAB-15. France's best," said Paolo. "We want you to have it."

"René's?"

He nodded. "It is loaded with fifteen rounds—nine-millimeter, hollow points. There's a round in the chamber. Are you sure you want to go up alone?"

I shoved the gun into my belt beneath my jacket.

"If it's really Marita, we need her help."

The lights in the small, neat lobby were dimmed to a magnesium green. The front desk was deserted. I hurried through a door marked *Escalier* into a narrow vestibule and a staircase. I moved quickly up to the third floor hallway. The woman was registered in Room 35.

I moved down the hallway on tiptoes. The wood floors creaked under my weight. I crouched in front of the door to Room 35 and listened. My right ear makes a ringing sound that no doctor has been able to diagnose other than to say it probably came from being too close to gunfire. In the silence it sounded like my head was inside a whistling teakettle.

The lock was a common tumbler-wafer type. From the inside flap of my wallet I removed a tension bar and a rake that I kept there for these special occasions. I carefully inserted the tension bar into the bottom of the keyhole and began to exert a steady clockwise pressure on the cylinder. With my other hand I inserted the rake along the top of the key hole and began a slow, careful raking back-and-forth motion. As each wafer fell into place, the cylinder turned with a faint metallic click. The lock finally opened with a dull scraping noise. I pushed gently and the door opened slowly inward.

The room was dark. I could just make out the shape of a body beneath the bed covers. I gently closed the door behind me. Keeping my eyes on the bed, I slipped my hand along the wall locating a light switch. Two bedside lamps came on. My heart sank.

The bed was empty. Pillows had been used to shape the form of a sleeping body.

"There is a gun inches from your head," said a whispered voice in Spanish, the accent Argentine. "I am afraid and my hand is shaking. The slightest move and I shoot."

I raised my hands slowly. "You have nothing to be afraid of."

A hand patted me down. I felt the gun removed from my belt. I smelled a woman's perfume.

"Turn around," she said. "Slowly. Very slowly."

I turned to find the barrel of my new gun aimed squarely at my face, in a hand that was trembling violently. The woman holding it was in a full-length Oriental silk robe. Behind the gun were cat-shaped amber eyes similar to Marita's in the poster— but I still couldn't be sure.

"I'm not here to hurt you," I said, raising my arms over my head.

"How did you find me?"

"Find you—do you know who I am?"

"What difference does it make—the Triangle sent you."

"The Triangle of Death? You *are* Marita."

"On your knees," she ordered, jerking the gun up and down. I dropped to my knees. "You know me, Marita."

She backed up without taking her eyes off me and peeked out at the street. The gun hand was shaking more than ever.

"I'm René's old friend, Mike Levine. It was me at the funeral."

She stared at me. There was a sudden glimmer of recognition. Then her face softened into a wan, tired smile. *"Mighe, is it really you?"*

"Yes, it's me."

"Now I remember. The photo. Your hair is thinner. You've aged."

"This is not an easy life." My heart started beating again.

Marita lowered the gun. Suddenly she slumped onto the bed. Her body began to quake. I moved across the room and sat beside her, gently taking the gun from her hand. She fell into my arms, sobbing.

"Mighe, the famous *Mighe.* Please forgive me."

"There's nothing to forgive."

"He came to me for help and I helped him kill himself." She sobbed.

"Please talk to me, Marita."

She cried for a long time in my arms as if it was the most natural thing in the world.

"She was set up, Mighe," *says René, his voice rising above the roar of the West Side Highway. "The Triangle put her in the middle. All Ricord tells her is to have him come to a meeting. He is a terrorist who kills women and children. He is to be arrested by the government."*

"What government?" I say.

"What difference does it make? Everyone wanted him dead—the French Secret Service, the CIA, the Moroccans—everyone. He was a terrorist."

"You telling me that the Triangle was setting up people for the CIA?"

"I don't ask you to believe anything except that Marita never knew he was to die."

"Why her, René?"

"Ben Barka travels with a dozen bodyguards. You never know where he is. He has only one weakness."

"Marita."

"No, Mighe," he says wearily. "It's not like that. His weakness was all women. He calls Marita because he trusts her. Everyone trusts her. That is why Ricord used her to manage his clubs. He knew that if she even suspected that Ben Barka was to die, she would never do it. She would kill herself first. If you knew her you would know, Mighe. She betrays no one . . . not even an undercover agent who could have destroyed her.

"Forget her name."

"All those years," she murmured in my ear. "And you were the only one who knew about me, *Mighe.*" She laughed through her tears and then sighed. "Look how I even call you *Mighe*, the way he did. I always knew that in the end there would be only pain. I savored every moment with him. But for all the years we had together, I owe you a debt that I can never repay."

"But you can."

She looked up at me. I was conscious of her open robe, her soft white skin, her luminous cat's eyes. Her face suddenly paled. I felt her go rigid.

"How did you find me?"

"René's brother Paolo found you."

"He is here?"

"Outside, waiting for me."

"Who else knows I am here?"

"No one."

"How did he find me, here, in this hotel?"

"He's a policeman. There aren't many hotels here and not too many women register by themselves."

"God, I am a fool! He made the calls himself?"

"Yes, but he doesn't know who you are. I only told him you were a friend who might be able to help. He's René's brother!"

She pondered this a moment and sighed.

"I am already dead. If *you* found me the Triangle must be close."

"The Triangle was destroyed in 1973, along with Auguste Ricord," I said.

"You really believe that? Yes, I'm sure you do. I tried to warn René and he didn't believe me, why should you?"

"Are you saying it's the Triangle that killed René?"

"The Triangle never kills—it produces death. It directs it the way a stage director choreographs action, without ever taking part in it. Whenever, wherever death is necessary for its protection, it happens. If children must be tortured to hurt the father, it is done. If a plane with hundreds of passengers must be blown out of the sky to kill one, it is done."

"We destroyed it," I said. "Fifty of its directors in seven countries are now spending their lives in American jails."

She stared at me in weariness and disbelief.

"The Triangle is stronger than ever. It is everywhere and nowhere, like shadows. René didn't believe me either."

"I want to find out how this happened to him. I need to know everything."

"Then you're going to die too, *Mighe*. The moment they are even aware of you, you won't have to look for them. They will look for you."

"No one gets out of this life alive, Marita. René had no choice, neither do I. Help me."

"It began when René asked me to introduce him to Mario Razouk, a man who used to manage gambling houses for Ricord."

"When?"

"About ten months ago."

"Who is Razouk?"

"An Arab, a Lebanese. He came from Europe with Ricord and the Germans. He provided oil for the Nazis in North Africa. He was one of the original group."

"Why don't I know his name?"

Her laugh was short and bitter. "There were many names you Americans never knew. Some, perhaps, you didn't want to know."

"Why did René want this particular introduction?"

"He knew Razouk was looking for contacts to launder drug money."

"So you introduced them?"

"No, no. René would never expose me that way. He arranged a chance meeting."

"How?"

"I lost contact with Mario Razouk years ago but I knew that he came to Buenos Aires to play blackjack in the Club Arabesque on

125

Nueve de Julio. So René and I would go the club, but never together. If I saw Razouk, I was to call René's pager. If René saw him he was to call me. I knew both men, so the natural thing would be an introduction. We rehearsed it many times—the precise words I was to use, the tone of my voice. He drove me crazy with this stuff. Over and over until he was satisfied." She suddenly paused. "Why are you smiling?"

"I was just remembering how he was."

It was suddenly quiet again. Marita stared blankly at nothing with tear-filled eyes. Outside I heard a car engine idling.

"Then what happened?"

"Three weeks went by and we did not see him," she said. "I was starting to have bad feelings. I tried to talk René out of continuing. 'Maybe Razouk doesn't come here anymore, maybe he is dead,' I told him. But you know how René is. He was obsessed. So I kept going.

"A few nights later I arrived at the Arabesque and Razouk was already there at the the blackjack table. He plays very high stakes. It is his addiction. I telephoned René's pager and then positioned myself so that Razouk will notice me. It was important to René that Razouk initiate *every* move. By the time René appeared, the plan was working perfectly—Razouk had already bought me a drink and asked me to sit by him.

"I notice René at the dice table. We nod at each other and smile, as we rehearsed. Razouk reacts just as predicted—he asks me about René. 'A customer,' I tell him, 'an Italian banker from Panama.' I pretend not to remember his name. 'A banker?' Razouk says. 'Introduce us.' 'Fine,' I say."

"Let me guess: René takes over from there—you disappear."

Marita smiled. "He could charm anyone. They spoke in Italian. In minutes Razouk is laughing. It is as though I was invisible. Razouk invites us to dinner. I tell him I have an appointment and leave."

"Razouk speaks Italian?"

"He speaks many languages. He did business with both the Italians and Germans during the war."

"Did you hear any of the conversation?"

"A little. I speak only a little Italian. Razouk asks René about his business. Whatever René said caught his interest."

"What name did René use?"

"Fabrizio . . . Fabrizio Calvi. He had business cards with an address in Panama. The banking business."

"What happens next?"

"I never saw René again. He called me a few times. He never spoke openly on the telephone."

"He didn't say anything at all about what he was doing?"

"Only that business had gone much better than he had expected. That he would not be able to see me for a while . . .

"There is something else, *Mighe.* A woman."

"A woman?"

"It was rare that a month would go by that I wouldn't see him; wherever he was, whatever he was doing, my sweet *nenito* would find a way to spend a night in my arms. . . . Did you know that he loved to cook for me?" She seemed to drift in thought. "He would always come with baskets of my favorite foods, I wasn't allowed two steps into the kitchen."

"But you think he was involved with a woman?" I persisted.

She stared at me blankly for a moment. "There was something I heard in his voice, a tinge of guilt. I knew him so well. I asked him about it and I was immediately sorry. He told me the truth. Yes, he said, there was someone . . . someone very special."

"You weren't angry, jealous?"

"More afraid than jealous, afraid that I would lose him forever. And now there is nothing—not even a photo of us together. And . . ."

"And what?"

"And you are looking at a dead woman."

"Marita, you're going to be fine. There's no way they can know anything."

"They know everything. They have people to whom torture is an art form."

"You don't know that."

"It is not necessary to talk to me as if I were a hysterical woman. I have accepted whatever happens to me from the day I protected him from the Triangle."

I reached out a hand and caressed her cheek. Her hand held mine.

There was a sudden, low rapping sound. Marita paled. I moved behind the door.

"It's Paolo," said a voice in a harsh whisper. "Open, quickly."

I opened the door and Paolo rushed into the room.

"A car with three men inside was watching the building," he said. "They showed me Secret Service credentials. I don't like the look or smell of them. Something is wrong. They drove off but they were in no hurry."

"We have to get her out of here, right now," I said, noticing that Marita was already getting dressed.

Paolo handed me his car keys. "The car is parked three blocks in the direction we came from. The corner of Rue des Trois Maria. Use the window and fire escape at the end of the hall. Stay off the main street. I will stand out front in case they return."

———

Ten minutes later I was driving over the coastal road with Marita beside me. She directed me to a road that snaked through heavy brush country. My heart was racing, but Marita was amazingly cool. I remembered that she had finessed me out of my gun.

"Do you know where we are?"

"Yes—the macchia. Our little insurance policy. We have a cottage here. Corsicans have been hiding from *vendettas* in the macchia for six hundred years. René told me that during the war there was one Nazi soldier on this island for every two Corsicans, but even they couldn't find the resistance fighters in the dense brush. It was so legendary that all French resistance fighters became known as *Maquis*. It was the only place in the world that he felt safe. And now the only place left for me." Her voice broke.

For a long time the only sound was the hum of the engine. Ahead all I could see was blackness and a winding road engulfed in dense brush.

The lights of a village appeared in the distance.

"Villanova," said Marita. "We're here."

I drove slowly through the dark main street of a tiny village. At the outskirts on the far side of town was a lone phone booth.

"Stop here," she said.

I waited while she made a phone call, watching her, vulnerable under the light. I kept checking the rearview, expecting to see lights behind us. It was nearly five in the morning, but someone was on the phone with her. In a moment she was back in the car.

"This is where we say good-bye. I have friends who will take me into the macchia. I'll be safe, for a while." Her arms were suddenly around me. And I held her, feeling my heart sink.

"God, I miss him," she breathed.

She was suddenly out of the car. She took her bag off the rear seat and quietly pushed the passenger-side door shut until it clicked. She leaned into the window.

"I will tell you what I should have told René: You are just a man, *Mighe*—not a god. And life is not a Hollywood movie. Many years ago I could have destroyed René; tonight I could have killed you—and I am nothing but a lone, frightened woman. You can't bring René back. *Vendetta* against the Triangle is a war against mirrors and shadows—it is everywhere and nowhere, and breathes death. And what would you prove? You will only follow in René's footsteps."

As I drove back toward Ajaccio I kept hearing Marita's last words—*You will only follow in René's footsteps*—repeated over and over in my head. Something clicked. There *was* only one way I would ever find René's killers—and it was the last thing they would expect.

Yes, I would follow in his footsteps.

15

"Do you remember the Auguste Ricord–Triangle of Death investigation?" I said, the moment I heard Jackie's voice. I was out of breath from my sprint to the telephone center, just off the main concourse. It was Sunday morning and I had telephoned her at home in Buenos Aires from the Campo dell'Oro Airport, where I had just arrived.

"Do you know what time it is, Mike? It is four o'clock in the morning. *Sunday* morning."

"God." I banged my head on the phone. "Please forgive me."

"Mike, if I had to forgive you every time you did this, that's all I'd be doing. Yes, I know the case."

"Perfect! Get on the computer. Run every name from the original case file for currently-actives. Then I need to locate one of the attorneys who prosecuted the case—André Rosen. I'm sorry, Jackie. No time to explain, gotta catch a flight. I change planes in Paris. I'll call you from there."

"Mike, do I know you long enough to give you some advice?"

"Sure," I said. "But hurry."

"Get a life!"

Her words were immediately lost on me. Minutes later I was in my seat waiting for takeoff. I lay my head back, closed my eyes and my mind drifted back to one of the most memorable nights of my career.

It was 1:00 a.m., December 20, 1972. At a given signal thousands of law enforcement officers were about to launch simultaneous raids, making 335 arrests in fourteen countries and eight time zones. Nothing this big and complicated had ever been done before. For law enforcement it was the equivalent of a moon landing. And I had played a tiny part in making it happen.

Code-named Operation Springboard, it was to be the death blow to the Triangle of Death, a huge, multinational drug smuggling and murder-for-hire organization run from Paraguay by a mysterious Frenchman named Auguste Ricord, an escaped Nazi collaborator responsible for the torture deaths of hundreds of French resistance fighters, a man whom France had sentenced to death in absentia.

A moment later an agent picked up a telephone in Washington, D.C., and said "Go" and the word was rocket-relayed around the world in a dozen different languages. Raiding officers crashed through doors in New York, Paris, Palermo, Bogotá, Buenos Aires, and only God knew how many other places. The world was told that what might have been the deadliest and most powerful criminal organization in the history of man had been crushed.

The world believed it. And so did I.

"There's nothing active on the Triangle of Death," said Jackie. It was hours later and I was calling her from Orly Airport in Paris. "Every one of the original group is either dead, in jail or whereabouts unknown."

"Run the list of whereabouts-unknowns for a Mario Razouk, a Lebanese. I need everything available on him. Photos, the works."

"Check."

"What about the prosecutor, Rosen?" I asked.

"Now there's a story for you. His latest address is the state prison in Dannemora, in upstate New York."

"What! How?"

Rosen, a French Jew whose family had been gassed at Auschwitz, had emigrated to the U.S. as a child, was a Harvard Law School graduate and one of the most respected prosecutors in New York's Southern District Federal Court.

"I don't know, *Nene*. Whatever it is, there's no record on the computer. I called Main Justice and red flags went up. They want to know *why* I want to know. I figured I'd better drop it until I spoke to you."

"Good move," I said, my mind racing. Secrecy over what

should be a simple records check is the smoke signaling a smoldering fire.

"You want someone to pick you up at Ezeiza?" asked Jackie.

"No," I said. "I've had a change of plan. I'm heading to the States. Last item: make sure the five thousand bucks in petty cash is replenished."

"Mike . . ." she began wearily.

"I know: Get a life!"

Washington, D.C.

I had been watching the front door of DEA headquarters from a coffee shop at the corner of 15th and Eye for more than two hours when Bobby Stratton came out the front door and headed toward the corner walking quickly. He was coatless in the thirty-degree weather and carrying a gym bag.

I threw a couple of bucks on the counter and followed, lagging behind him on the opposite side of the street. After about a block and a half he did a sudden about-face and trotted across the street, dodging traffic, coming straight at me.

"What is it with you, Levine? You're as dinky-dau as they say."

"I was waiting for you to get a little distance from the office," I said. "I didn't want anyone to know I'm here."

"Some fucking plausible deniability this is."

He raised his hand for a passing taxi. A half-hour later we were seated in the rear of a coffee shop in Georgetown.

"This better be good," said Stratton. "I ordered you back on post."

"Remember the Triangle of Death case?"

"Who doesn't. I caught part of it in Bangkok. The best this government's ever gonna do in this drug war. What about it?"

"You remember André Rosen?"

"Yeah, he was one of the prosecutors."

"I just heard he's in Dannemora. You know anything about it?"

Stratton's eyes narrowed. "Why?"

"You're supposed to be giving me space," I said.

He laughed. "This is rich—who came looking for who?"

"If I tell you what I got in mind, there may be a problem."

Stratton thought about this for a moment.

"He stole dope and money from a federal court evidence safe. He was living with a hooker, freebasing coke. Shit happens in this business. Maybe the white man's guilt got to be too much for him."

"How come it wasn't in the papers?"

"You know how that goes. He knew a lot that could've jeopardized ongoing cases, people's lives at stake. High-level informers. They cut a deal. He got twenty-to-life instead of life with no parole. Does his time in a state prison. Keeps his mouth shut. At least that's what they say."

"What's that mean?"

Stratton glanced around us. The place was small and on a side street. We were the only two customers.

"The Company had an interest. Who knows what the truth is."

"I need a favor, Bobby. I have to speak to him."

"You're a DEA agent. Go up there and knock on the front gate."

"I don't want my name on any visitors lists."

Stratton wagged his head. "Some fucking plausible deniability." He pulled bills from his pocket and tossed them on the table between us.

I waited.

"How was the funeral?"

"A nightmare," I said.

He nodded his head. He'd been to enough young men's funerals to know.

"Okay, where are you staying?"

"At the Marriott."

Stratton got to his feet. He studied me thoughtfully, his lips pursed. "There'll be a message waiting for you."

He walked out the door.

———

The state prison in Dannemora, called the Siberia of the New York State prison system, sits smack in the middle of a moldy little town on the New York side of the Canadian border. Dannemora is one of the most depressing places in the universe. I imagine they sell more Prozac than milk in Dannemora. I had been there enough times to know that I couldn't handle spending the weekend in the local Holiday Inn, no less doing serious time in the prison.

They were expecting me when I arrived at the main gate. I was escorted across a yard of chain link fences topped with razor wire, toward the prison block. The temperature was hitting ten below, which was typical for Dannemora. The incessant pandemonium of noise that is the same in every prison in America reached out to greet me.

"Hey muthafucka," boomed a foghorn voice over the din. "You comin' in here, you gonna get fucked! You hear me? I'm talkin' to you! First you gonna get bitch-slapped. Then you gonna get fucked right in your ass!"

Whoever you are, my friend, you've got a lot in common with the suits.

Minutes later I was alone in a bare room with a rectangular metal table and six chairs around it—"the warden's special conference room," the guard told me. The muffled racket seeped in through the walls. A door opened with a crash. A stone-faced guard led a prisoner into the room. His hands were cuffed and connected by about two feet of chain to a belt encircling his waist; leg irons were fastened to each of his ankles separating them by about two and a half feet of chain, leaving him enough room to shuffle but not enough to walk. Prison always changed a man, but I wasn't prepared for what it had done to Rosen.

The André Rosen I remembered was a soft-spoken, studious man with a full head of brown curly hair, who wore horn-rimmed glasses and dressed like a forgetful young college professor in ill-fitting tweed suits. The man taking a seat across the table from me was all bulk and muscle straining against a faded orange jumpsuit. His head was bald in a way that made it appear as if it had swollen and burst out of his hair. He glared at me through wire-rim glasses with lenses so thick, they made his eyes look like giant oysters.

"I'm Mike Levine," I said.

He turned his back on me to watch the guard back out of the room. When he turned to face me, I said: "I was one of the agents who worked on the Auguste Ricord case. I debriefed Claude Pastou, one of his couriers."

"You got a cigarette?" he said. Even his voice had changed to what I called a prison rasp, sounding as if his vocal cords had hardened into hacksaw blades.

"Sure."

I had three packs of Marlboros and a couple of books of matches that I always brought on prison visits. I slid them across the table. I watched him manipulate his cuffed hands with practiced ease. He opened a pack, lit a cigarette, took a long, deep drag and focused on me again.

"What do you want, motherfucker?" he rasped. There was still a hint of a French accent.

"Do you remember me?"

He nodded slightly rocking back and forth, dragging on his cigarette and blowing the smoke at me. "I'm jerked out of population. Brought to the warden's private little rat room. All I know is, you're a government hack. What do you want?"

"I came to talk to you about the Triangle of Death."

His face broke into a slow, mean grin. His teeth were yellowed and rotting, his gums receded to black little ridges. "That means nothing to me."

"But you were a prosecutor," I said. "I worked the case."

He suddenly leaned his torso over the table toward me, stretching his hands to the end of his chain, showing me that I was within his reach. I started to recoil, but controlled it. We were face-to-face, inches apart.

"Aren't you listening, *motherfucker*?" he said, spraying my face with spittle. "I said it means nothing! *You* mean nothing!" He spit in my face, leaving his face jutting into mine, begging me to smash him.

Suddenly I was back in the South Bronx. My fist was flying almost before the spit hit my face. I somehow stopped a punch that should have driven his glasses into his eyeballs.

"Go ahead, government *motherfucker*!" he shouted, jerking his head forward, his forehead and nose brushing mine. "Smash my fucking face!" He was trembling with rage, his eyes so bugged, they looked ready to pop through the lenses.

"Look, *fucko*!" I said, wiping the spittle off my face with the back of my sleeve. I stayed nose-to-nose with him. "I didn't know you too well when you were a lawyer, but whatever put you in here, *I* didn't do it. I just came here to talk. A private citizen. Too much for you, Counselor?"

"You, too much?" He laughed. "What you think you can do to me that hasn't already been done?"

"Did you know that René Villarino was tortured to death in Argentina?"

He leaned back slowly. The softening of his expression was barely perceptible. "I heard some noise about a fed. People in here celebrate that shit, but I didn't know it was him. Too bad it had to be a good guy."

"René was my best friend. He went deep cover in Panama posing as a money launderer and ended up dead in Argentina. DEA's trying to bury the case. That's why I'm here on my own. Someone who should know told me he was mixed up with a member of the old Triangle of Death."

He took a long, deep drag on his cigarette. "Okay, you got my attention."

"Is there any chance the Triangle could still exist?"

Rosen suddenly slammed his fists down on the table. The cigarette showered both of us with sparks. "Ask your fucking bosses! It existed then! It exists now! When Ricord disappeared from the headlines you DEA scumbags went on to better things. You didn't come to me *then* to ask me anything, did you?"

"I'm here now."

"I tried to tell them and they cut my fucking tongue out."

"How did they do that?"

"They knew the Triangle was still strong. They didn't want anyone else to know."

"Who?"

"Main Justice, the Congress, DEA, the press," he rattled off. "Everyone."

It was as if Federal Prosecutor Rosen had suddenly made an appearance. I tried to hold on to him. "But there was no proof."

"Proof?" Rosen shook his head in disgust. "The Triangle owned Paraguay. Nixon had to threaten Stroessner with a *fucking* military invasion of his country before he would extradite that motherfucking Nazi. *That's* proof!

"The Triangle worked for every spy agency in the world— assassinations, kidnappings, black bag jobs. You want somebody dead in Paris—it's done. They had the French Secret Service in their pocket. You get the picture?"

"The French Secret Service?" I said. "I heard rumors, but we never moved on them."

"Ricord was convicted right after the war as a fucking Nazi collaborator. He murdered French freedom fighters. The French sentenced him to death in absentia, yet when we got him, they didn't want him back—a little odd, no?

"I was a fucking idiot," he said, the veins in his head and neck swelling. "It never occurred to me that they might have *our* government in their pocket too."

"What happened?" I said.

"I stepped right into their trap. After we got Ricord, I asked Main Justice and Congress for a task force—FBI, DEA, CIA, the military. I wanted to go for the rest of them. I had names of hundreds of suspects on three continents, half of them ex-Nazis.

"They bring me to Washington. A closed-door session with Congress. Executive session. Everything classified. I lay out the facts and suddenly it's *me* on trial. Some good-ole-boy senator says that I'm misusing my office to be a Nazi hunter. They want me to resign and go to work for the Wiesenthal Foundation. They had me by the balls, all the facts were classified. But even that wasn't enough for them. They wanted to make sure nobody'd ever listen to me again."

"They set you up?"

Rosen stared down at his hands. They were bleeding. His nails had been chewed down to the nubs. There were thick scars on his wrists. Suddenly tears welled in his eyes.

"How'd they do it?" I asked.

He looked away, lowering his head and raising his chained wrists to wipe at his nose and cheeks. "I was sitting in a bar, fucked up about the whole thing. It was the night before I was to meet with a *New York Times* reporter to tell him everything.

"Then a lady shows up. A real looker. She sits next to me. She smells so fucking good." He shook his head rocking from side to side for a moment. "Soon we're talking. I don't remember how it begins. I'm fool enough and drunk enough to believe she's really interested in me. She takes me home with her. She says she likes to do some blow when she fucks. I should try it. It took us three years to destroy Ricord. It took them only three weeks to destroy me. I haven't seen my daughter now in ten years."

"I'm sorry," I said.

"The whole fucking world is gonna be sorry. Ricord was just the tip of the iceberg. A horde of escaped Nazis and their children scattered throughout the world are the glue for the Triangle. After guns and bombs, the drug business is the biggest on earth.

Whoever controls it has the power of God and the Triangle's out there getting more powerful every day."

"You think they're untouchable?"

"What I think now doesn't mean a fucking thing."

"I need your help."

"No you don't. René Villarino already figured it out for you."

"What do you mean?"

"Drugs generate rivers of money. You have to do something with it. Whatever you do—investments, real estate, purchases, bank accounts—there's a record. A name. A signature. Evidence. It's the classic weakness of drug crime. It's how I proved the case against Ricord.

"René was a very clever man. It's no mistake that he posed as a money launderer. He must have offered them some ingenious way to hide money. The door opened wide enough for him to step inside. But he wasn't ready for the size of the monster waiting for him in the darkness, was he?" He paused for a moment. "And neither was I."

"What would you say if I told you I wanted to go after them for René's murder?"

He leaned across the table as close to me as he could get and whispered. "I would say you had better be careful who you say that to." He abruptly got to his feet. "Guard! Get me out of here!"

I watched André Rosen shuffle out of the room, his chains dragging between his legs.

People accuse me of being like a bull in a china shop when I'm on a case; that I'm cold, callous, and focused on what I'm doing to the exclusion of everything and anyone around me. It's not true.

If anything, too much affected me too deeply. If I wanted to stay sane I had to be careful where I expended emotion and energy. There was only a limited supply. And at the moment the only energy I wanted to expend was in hunting René's killers.

The essence of karate training with its Bushido philosophy was practicality. You exploit any weaknesses in your opponent's defenses. René was on to the only weakness in the Triangle of Death—the money trail. He had used it to slip inside. To find his killers, I was going to have to exploit that same weakness.

16

BUENOS AIRES

"I HAD TO READ ABOUT RENÉ IN THE NEWSPAPERS, DAD?" SAID MY angry son's voice over the phone. "You should have called me!"

I had just landed at Ezeiza Airport and come straight to the embassy, where my office phone was ringing off the hook. It was 10:00 p.m.

"It's all I've been working on since it happened. I'm sorry, Son."

"He wasn't just *your* friend, you know."

"You're right, Keith," I said. "I just wasn't thinking."

"Tell me something new. I feel sick about this, Dad. Big time. Who did it? The papers say it was the Colombians."

Just a few short years on the NYPD and my young son had already picked up some of the cop nuance in his speech. For a moment I remembered the little boy I used to take in my G car with me on surveillance and wondered what he might have been had I played baseball with him like other fathers. I worried that I had somehow programmed him to live his life in harm's way.

"You're on the job long enough to know about believing what you read in the papers," I said.

"That's why I called my father."

"I wish I knew, Keithy. I'm lost. How'd you know I was here?"

My son laughed. "Hey, I grew up learning from guys like you, and Uncle René, remember? You left D.C. under your own name.

It didn't take Sherlock Holmes to figure you'd go straight to the embassy. Look, I feel like I've got to do something."

"Like what?"

"I could ask around. There's as many Colombian dopers and stools here in New York as there are in Bogotá. I've got friends in Queens Narcotics."

"If you want to mess me up, go ahead and start asking questions in Little Bogotá," I said. "Son, there's about seven thousand miles of telephone wire between us . . ." He knew the rest.

The line was quiet.

"You wanna do something?" I said. "Call Marcello. He asked about you. And Son, make sure you wear your vest."

My office was as chaotic as when I left it. A spot had been cleared in the middle of my desk where a lone manila file folder lay. Jackie had come through again. It was the dossier on Mario Razouk—the last person known to have seen René alive. The contents of the file were sparse. A computer printout:

RESTRICTED OFFICIAL USE ONLY

SUSPECT: RAZOUK, MARIO, MNU–NADDIS 09794535

DOB: 090219 HT: 5'10" WT: 235 EYES: BRN

POB: LEBANON ADD: UNKN PHONE: UNKN

NAT: PARAGUAY

REMARKS: SUBJECT ID'D AS BUS. ASSOC. AUGUSTE RICORD ORGAN. ALLEGED TO HAVE SOLD OIL & PETROL TO NAZI FORCES N. AFRICA, WWII. LISTED AS UNINDICTED COCON-SPIRATOR, AND MANAGER OF VARIOUS RICORD LEGITIMATE ENTERPRISES. AS OF 11 AUG, BELIEVED TO BE OWNER VARI-OUS BARS, NIGHTCLUBS BS. AIRES, ASUNCION, SAO PAULO

CRIMINAL ACTIVITY: UNKNOWN

RESTRICTED OFFICIAL USE ONLY

There was also a photo of Razouk and a woman at a table in a nightclub, which looked like it had been taken in the late 1960s.

I took the file home to *La Lucila,* about a half-hour north of Buenos Aires. My house, a two-story concrete bunker on Avenida Enrique Sinclair, was set back from the street and hidden by a high hedge. I loved the place because it was full of memories of my kids. But after they had gone back to the States it had never been the same.

It was a steamy hot night. I stripped down to my underwear, laying the contents of my pockets and my leather carryall on the low dresser across from my bed—the Razouk file, my credentials, my passport, my gun, a book of GTRs that enabled me to write myself an airline ticket for anywhere in the world, various business cards, and a jumble of American, French, and Argentine money. And finally, the photo of René, me, and our sons. I laid it facedown on the dresser.

I studied the tools of my trade. I was stuck. I knew what I had to do but I didn't know how to go about it. Then I noticed a business card with writing in Arabic. I picked it up and examined it.

It was a Moroccan oil broker's card with the name Hassan Belkassami printed in English and Arabic, along with a phone number and address in Casablanca. I turned it over; it had Szion Aban's name and phone number in Cochabamba written on it. My recollection of the meeting with this "friend" of the Mossad brought with it an idea. An incredible idea. An exciting idea. The ultimate in scams. A deal that not even the Triangle of Death could refuse.

My hand shook as I reread the printout on Razouk. I dressed quickly.

Minutes later I was heading downtown in heavy late night traffic. Sometime after midnight I parked about a hundred yards from the entrance to the Club Arabesque just as a group of people were exiting.

I raised a pair of night-vision binoculars to my eyes. I could see their faces clearly. The man was fat, about the size Razouk should be and about the same age—late sixties, early seventies. But it wasn't him. No such luck.

My plan hinged on the chance that Razouk, like all gamblers, was a slave to habit and superstition, that he still gambled in the same place. What I had in mind was so way-out and would require so much preparation, that it did not make any sense to start unless I knew he was there.

I spent a week surveilling the Arabesque, from midnight until dawn, staying away from the embassy, not answering phone calls, avoiding all contact with DEA. I was afraid that the suits would find some reason to take me out of Argentina before I could make my move.

It was close to dawn on a Sunday morning when I saw the first stretch limo I had ever seen in Buenos Aires pull up to the front door of the Arabesque.

"No way," I murmured to myself, picking up the night glasses. The car had Paraguayan plates. *Razouk has Paraguayan citizenship.*

Two men, acting like a Secret Service protective detail, leapt out of the car before it had fully stopped and opened the rear door. A big man got out of the car. I could see his wide girth clearly from behind. His hair was thick and black under the bright lights of the marquee. It couldn't be a man as old as Razouk. Then he turned. Maybe the photo was more recent than I thought, or perhaps he just hadn't aged much, but there was no doubt. It was Mario Razouk.

I watched him pass through the bright lights of the entrance flanked by his bodyguards. I was looking at René's last footstep in this world, his last human contact. I could feel it. There was nothing left to think about. I had gone over the plan a thousand times.

I was home in twenty minutes. My first call was to the airlines. I made reservations to Tel Aviv for a flight leaving in a few hours. Then I dialed the Argentine operator and placed an emergency call to the three numbers I had for my cousin Avi, the Mossad agent.

The call finally came through an hour before my flight was to leave. The moment I heard Avi's voice I said, "How fast can your friends in the desert turn a Jew from the Bronx into a shady Arab oil dealer?"

Avi laughed.

"I don't think I recognize the voice, but the personality, I know it well. From anyone else I would think this is a joke—"

"I can't talk," I said. "I'll miss my flight. I'll see you tonight."

17

TEL AVIV, ISRAEL

"So what is it you think I can do, Michael?" said Avi Abramovich. My first cousin and I sat facing each other drinking grainy black coffee at a sidewalk table in front of a small Arab quarter cafe, a few kilometers north of Tel Aviv.

"I want to make them an offer they can't refuse. A trade: oil for cocaine. Instant, undetectable, untraceable money laundering."

Avi and I were one year apart in age. Many said we could pass for brothers. My mother, Carolina, and Avi's father, Kalmon, were brother and sister who, like many fleeing the Nazi murder machine, kissed each other good-bye as children in Derezchna, Poland, and ended up growing up in different parts of the world. I thought of us as being prototypic of most of the men in our family—dark-skinned, swarthy Mediterranean types who probably survived thousands of years of repeated attempts to liquidate us because we passed for anything from Hispanic and Arabic to mulatto and Pakistani—natural undercover agents.

Avi's eyes kept surveying our surroundings, only half listening, his fingers drumming the table, chain-smoking as I told him about René's murder and the Triangle of Death. I had to remind myself that I was talking to a professional soldier and spy who had served in front-line combat in four bloody conventional wars and spent the rest of his life in silent back-alley hand-to-hand global combat with fanatical terrorists to whom life was only an inconvenience. But the world had changed in the last two decades. His war and mine now overlapped—drug traffickers and terrorists had become one and the same.

When I finished, my cousin glanced impatiently at his watch. "Interesting idea," he said.

"I need a cover identity. Someone with enough contacts in the Middle East to make that kind of an offer—a shady Arab criminal type."

"To make it short," said Avi, "you need an identity, *and* you want us to train you to fit that identity. Arabic language, culture, the oil business."

"Yes, and a history and documents that will hold up to a thorough background investigation."

He looked at me for a long moment, shook his head, and said, "And this you want us to do without your country's knowledge?"

"I don't have a choice."

"This is a problem. U.S.–Israeli relations, especially since the Jonathan Pollard affair—"

"I'm not a spy," I interrupted. "This is about murder—the murder of my best friend."

He nodded thoughtfully.

"I can't promise. I will talk to some people. Perhaps we can arrange something, but you will have to spend a year here. Isolated. No contact with the outside. Extremely difficult conditions, Michael."

"Impossible, I only have four weeks. Five at the most."

Avi's expression went from amusement to disquiet.

"I'm happy to see you again, Michaela. I'm sorry you came all this way for nothing. I speak to you as a cousin: If I could convince my people to help you, I would only be helping you to get yourself killed."

I was ready for rejection. I knew enough of the Mossad's history to know that unless I had something to offer Israel, they would take no gambles with me. I reached into my jacket pocket and handed Avi a cable marked TOP SECRET—the White Queen cable.

As he read, he transformed before my eyes.

When I was stationed in New York one of my side duties was as DEA's liaison with Israel's National Police. I used to meet periodically with an officer who worked out of the Israeli consulate to share information about traffickers who traveled back and forth between the U.S. and the Middle East.

"Israel," he once told me, "is a tiny country, surrounded by two hundred million Arabs who want to push us into the sea. We cannot afford an American-style drug problem. Our young people are our only defense."

I knew that a drug like the White Queen would represent to the Mossad as grave a threat to their security as any conventional war. It was my ace in the hole.

When Avi finished reading, he hustled over to his car to use his car phone. In a minute he was back with a pad to take notes.

For the next hour or so my cousin was no longer my cousin, he had become an interrogator. Looking into his dark, almost Oriental eyes, my family's eyes, from this new perspective was an odd sensation.

"What do you know about the oil business?" asked Avi.

"Nothing. But I don't need to know much. Just enough to make sense. Enough to convince both the oil dealers and the dope dealers, separately, that it's a good idea—and, most important, that I'm someone who can make it happen."

"You want to pose as an Arab who doesn't speak Arabic? It will take you at least a year of deep immersion to become fluent. You don't even speak Hebrew."

"Lots of Jews don't speak Hebrew, lots of Arabs don't speak Arabic—they grew up in the U.S. or South America. I just need enough to pass as an Arab who grew up in another country, preferably a Spanish-speaking country. I need to know about as much Arabic as I know Yiddish. *Bubi* spoke to me in Yiddish when I was a kid and I would answer her in English. I don't remember much but what I do remember is natural, authentic. I just need to be believable, Avi."

"Michaela, Michaela, Michaela," said my cousin, mimicking *Bubi*, our grandma, shaking his head in bemusement. "You just don't know."

"Don't know what?"

"What a position you put me in. I speak to you as both a cousin and as an agent of my government. As an agent I would use you. If you die . . ." He shrugged. "You're a professional. As your cousin, I tell you this is much more complicated and dangerous than you think."

"Avi. I'm going to do it, with or without your help."

We sat staring at each other. There was nothing left to be said. Avi shut his notebook.

"My colleagues are waiting to meet with me. I will have your answer tonight."

———

Before dawn two Israeli soldiers came to my room at the Tel Aviv Sheraton. "Leave your things," said one who spoke English with a Russian accent. "Where you are going you don't need them."

I had my answer.

"Not to worry, someone comes to take care of the bill and your belongings."

We left through a basement exit. They didn't want to be seen with me. I was taken to a covered jeep, a hood was placed over my head, and I was driven for about two hours over rough terrain. When they removed the hood I was inside a small encampment in the desert—a chain link fence topped by concertina wire around three prefab huts.

This was where I would spend the next five weeks of my life going through an espionage assembly line dedicated to transforming me completely. They were turning a Ford into what looked and sounded enough like a Mitsubishi to fool a mechanic.

I guessed that I was south of Tel Aviv in the Negev. I had been ordered not to stray more than a few paces from my hut by a dark, bearded man with pale blue eyes called Mordechai, who I assumed was the head of the program. He told me that I was in a high-security area that was sometimes crossed by terrorists. If I strayed too far, I might be mistaken for one—that would be my own responsibility. The isolation and complete lack of any kind of distraction were supposed to be conducive to total focus and complete concentration . . . along with high anxiety and deep depression.

I spent my first full day being completely debriefed by a series of men and women who spoke to me in either English or Spanish, then in Arabic once I started language training. Each was a specialist in different areas of espionage and intelligence operations. Each asked specific questions about my plan as well as the kind of identity I *thought* I would need. They asked endless questions about the White Queen, the Triangle of Death, Auguste

Ricord, and Mario Razouk. They also wanted to know everything I knew and suspected about René and his last days.

By late that night, I lay back on my cot feeling that my brain had been wrung dry.

Whatever the Mossad intelligence machine found must have impressed them. In the coming days I could feel their machine working on me with increased intensity. No joking around. No extraneous conversation. All business. My instructors, introduced with only one name, often a nickname, took turns at me for sixteen hours every day, with an average of five to eight different instructors daily. The principal focus was the oil business . . . and terrorism. The oil business in the Middle East, as I was reminded over and over, is inextricably linked to terrorist groups.

At the end of my first week in the desert, Mordechai, the bearded, sullen man in charge, appeared. His manner as usual was brusque, almost rude. He took his place across the wooden table from me and motioned for me to sit. He never wasted a word. He opened a file.

"We have your new identity."

My name, as of that moment, was to be Omar Legassi. I was born in Tangiers, Morocco forty years earlier. My father and mother, nonpracticing Sunni Muslims, emigrated to Argentina when I was six years old. I was orphaned at age eleven when my parents and my baby sister, Salimah, were killed in a car–truck head-on collision that I survived. At age eighteen, after leaving an orphanage in Mendoza, I became involved with Colombian cocaine traffickers. I had a reputation for being a smart, trustworthy loner who could keep his mouth shut. I began my own smuggling operation at age twenty-two. At age twenty-four I was arrested in the U.S. and served four years in Fort Leavenworth Federal Penitentiary. At age thirty-four I began a career in arms trafficking. The Mossad first noticed me when they learned I was selling arms to the PLO. A half-dozen attempts were made on my life—cleverness and luck kept me alive. At age thirty-seven I was wounded in the leg in a Caracas shoot-out and walked with a slight limp. At age thirty-eight, two years ago, I disappeared from the face of the earth.

"What do you think?" asked Mordechai when he had finished.

"The Triangle can find anyone it wants to find," I said. "What happens if they start to check me out and find *him*?"

"They won't," he said with finality. "However, our intelligence has learned that this organization has access to police files in many countries; perhaps even Interpol."

"It doesn't surprise me."

"What this means is that we must alter as many of Omar Legassi's records on files and in computers as possible. Replace his fingerprints and official photos with yours. A process that we must begin immediately so that by the time you leave here, you can instantly assume the identity."

"Can you do that?"

"This is an expensive and risky proposition for my country. . . ." He paused and stared at me.

"What do you want me to say—thank you?" I said.

"There is a more serious problem with this identity. Omar Legassi was a man with many enemies. Some we know about, but there must be others. When word surfaces that you have appeared, people will hunt you, PLO terrorists among them. Our friend Omar failed to deliver a shipment and kept the money."

I waited for him to continue.

"Do you understand this and accept this risk?"

"Yes."

"There is more. Some things on his records may be impossible to change. Physical things."

"Like what? Don't tell me he wore a nose ring."

"Close enough," said Mordechai without cracking a smile. "He was quite slim, never more than a hundred and eighty pounds—you are at least forty pounds too heavy. He walked with a permanent limp. Your hair is salt-and-pepper—his, black. He smoked Gauloises and always used a cigarette holder—you don't smoke."

"No problem," I said. "In five weeks I'll be a skinny, limping, Gauloises-smoking, black-haired Moroccan."

Humor was wasted on Mordechai.

"He also had a large tattoo of an Oriental dragon that covered from just below his right shoulder to his elbow."

"Fine," I said. "Let's do it."

That evening, working from a photo of a tattooed arm, which I assumed was the real arm of Omar Legassi, a tattoo artist turned my right arm into a piece of Oriental art. After the jeep drove away I took the bandage off and looked in the mirror. According to rabbinical law, tattooed Jews cannot be buried in a Jewish cemetery. Mordechai and I never even discussed that. We both understood that I had crossed a mental point of no return that satisfied the Mossad.

Days later, Mordechai and a soldier put a hood over my head and drove me to what looked like a high-tech film studio. A half-dozen people were waiting. They flew into action speaking rapid Hebrew among themselves.

I was seated before a mirror, where a small blond woman began applying makeup as Mordechai directed her. My hair, salt-and-pepper, was sprayed with something that turned it as black as it had been in my twenties. My mustache was also skillfully colored and a goatee carefully pasted on my chin. She worked carefully on the lines of my face until, like magic, they disappeared. In the soft lighting of the mirror, I looked at least fifteen or twenty years younger.

I was then brought across the room—dressed in a T-shirt that would show the tattoo—onto some kind of theatrical set with a variety of furniture, props, and set decorations of all sorts. Stacks of different background sets were piled against a wall.

I was instructed to sit in a chair behind which was a plain gray-colored screen. A chain and plaque were brought out and hung from my neck. The plaque said *Policía Federal Argentina*—Argentine Federal Police—followed by a date some twenty years ago and a serial number. It was the first of fifty or sixty arrest photos that I would pose for over the next three hours; each set of mug shots taken with a different background and neck plaque; each with the makeup artist's using wigs, beards, and makeup, like a magician to gradually age me. Each set represented a different arrest, a different date, and a different country.

"These will be substituted for Omar Legassi's real arrest photos in police files in Argentina, Venezuela, Brazil, the U.S., and Interpol. Others will be placed in Intelligence files, as undercover surveillance photos," added Mordechai.

When the photo sessions were finished I was brought into a small room, where a fingerprint specialist, working like a machine, rolled about sixty or seventy sets of my fingerprints on the official fingerprint cards of half a dozen different countries. I signed each one with Omar Legassi's new signature.

"These will be substituted for the real fingerprint cards at the same time as the photos," said Mordechai. "Our handwriting people will add the signatures of the actual police personnel."

Then I was measured for clothing. Omar Legassi had expensive, flashy taste. Laundry and dry-cleaning marks had to be forged. The clothing had to be aged. I had already begun starving myself, but allowance had to be made for the loss of at least another thirty pounds.

I had no sense of the passage of time. There were no windows, no clocks. People worked on me, over me, and around me, efficiently processing me. There were myriad forms to be signed with the new Omar Legassi signature. Dental X rays and X rays of my right knee, operated on five years earlier, were taken to be substituted in prison hospital records.

The days and weeks that followed—spent in two rooms of isolation in the middle of the desert, facing a nameless procession of mechanics dedicated to hammering and reshaping Michael Levine into Omar Legassi—seemed like years. The only thing that kept me sane was *kata*.

After I was left alone at night I would go out into the cold desert under a thick blanket of stars, shirtless, and practice *kata*. I would lose myself in the martial arts dance that required me to imagine myself in physical combat with three and four opponents, moving, ducking, parrying their attacks, counterattacking with precision kicks and blows, fine-tuning the body as a combat machine, keeping my responses automatic and mindless. An hour of *kata* gave my mind the rest and my body the workout I needed to survive not only the grueling routine, but the crushing loneliness.

———

After a short lunch of *harira*, a thick, spicy Moroccan soup brought to me by unsmiling, silent men in military uniforms, Shoshanna, my religion-and-culture tutor, appeared carrying a rolled-up carpet under her arm.

As usual her appearance had a theatrical flair about it. She seemed to flow and swirl rather than walk, with bright bits of silver glinting from her wrists, neck, and ears: a vision out of *The Arabian Nights.* She was thin for an Israeli woman, almost boyish, with a Semitic profile, but she had a special something, a kind of inner glow. She was darker-skinned than me—which is very dark—with raven-black hair, a dazzling white smile, and coal-black eyes whose whites flashed when she looked at me. My favorite instructor, actually the only person I'd met in the past five weeks who seemed to care whether I lived or died. I was certain that her true name was not Shoshanna, but as far as I was concerned, it didn't matter, the name fit perfectly—it meant Rose.

"*Asmeetek?*" she asked, sitting across from me, her eyes direct and curious.

She spoke pure Moroccan dialect. Her face and hands bore exotic tattoos that intrigued me. I always assumed that all my tutors were Jews, although most looked as if they'd appeared in answer to a casting call for Arab terrorists. But tattoos on a Jew were unusual, and primitive tattoos on a dark-skinned, exotic woman seemed somehow both blatantly irreligious and exciting.

"Omar Legassi," I answered using the name I had been reborn with. We were both sweating. It was early morning and the desert heat was already overcoming the struggling generator-powered air conditioner.

"*Min wayn hadirtak?*" she demanded.

"*Haalan? Ana min,* New York," I said.

"*Hal tatakallam Ingliizi?*"

"*Eeyeh,*" I answered, "*qaliilan.*"

"Your accent, for five weeks, is quite good. You do understand, however, that you are messing up," she added.

"How?"

"You've managed to mix classic Arabic with Moroccan."

"I was only born in Morocco," I said. "I grew up speaking Spanish."

"It certainly sounds like a plausible explanation to me," she said with thinly veiled sarcasm. "But then again, you don't really have to convince me of anything, do you?"

"What would you suggest?" I asked, controlling my temper.

"Since I *am* Moroccan by birth," she said, "I would suggest that you stick to Moroccan Arabic, as, essentially, that would have been what your parents spoke in the home, and living in a Spanish-speaking country you would have had little opportunity to use the classic form, other than in reading the Koran—something Omar Legassi was not likely to do."

"And if I slip and use both forms—isn't that something that could normally happen?" I asked, feeling combative.

"Oh, it might not be noticed at all," she said blithely, "but the optimum, I expect, would be that you don't slip—wouldn't it?"

"*Beexai lHamdoo llah,*" I answered. "*Kee dayra? Ddraree labas?*"

She laughed, a beautiful laugh; too open and direct for a spy, which probably made her an incredibly good spy. "How do you know that I have children?"

"How could you not? I'll bet you have to use an Uzi to keep your husband off you."

"Don't be a naughty one, Omar," she said, using my undercover name with a natural ease. "Now we speak English because it is very important that you comprehend the information. Omar was not a religious man, but he would have absorbed the basics. It won't be bad that you learn a little more than you need.

"Now we speak of your duties as a Muslim. There are five: *shahadah*, your profession of your faith that Allah is the only God and that Mohammed is his prophet; *salah*, that you pray every day; *zakat*, that you are charitable; *sawm*, that you fast during Ramadan; and *hajj*, that at least once during your lifetime you make a pilgrimage to Mecca."

"All religions sound so well intended, so peaceful, why do you think we end up killing each other because of them?" I said, studying the intricate geometric designs tattooed on her right hand, which at the moment was resting on the table between us. The workmanship was so exquisite in its detail that until you looked closely, it appeared as if her hand was half covered by a fine black lace sleeve. Her face was also tattooed with fine, dark blue lines that seemed to trace the whiskers of a cat.

I picked up her hand and examined it. She tensed for an instant and then relaxed.

"It is never really about religion," she said, slowly pulling her hand from mine. "Religion is a pretext—it is always about territory."

"What do the tattoos signify?"

She was silent a moment. I thought she was going to ignore the question, as she usually did if I got too personal. "In Morocco it used to identify your tribe and symbolize important events, the passages of life. In recent years it has become only for decoration."

"You could probably tell me quite a story about your operations in Morocco, couldn't you?"

"The Berbers have a saying: 'Life is a loom, whose threads are the days. God decides when to cut the threads, even though the work is unfinished.'"

Her eyes bore into mine as if trying to determine whether I understood the meaning of those words or the purpose of her telling me them. I was never sure whether she was referring to herself or to me, or something else—I said nothing.

She got to her feet and unrolled the carpet on the ground. She knelt on it and said, "A Muslim must pray five times a day, Omar. He kneels like this, facing east toward Mecca, responding to the call from the mosques—*Allah o akbar*, God is great. He recites prayers from the Koran as he prostrates himself before almighty God, Allah."

She bent forward, gracefully, her hands describing inward arcs toward her head, her forehead touching the ground, reciting prayers in Arabic. "The prayers always begin with the words 'In the name of God, the Merciful, the Compassionate.' It will take you too long to learn the prayers, but, in most cases, I think it can be simulated quite easily. Just learn the motion." She repeated it again and then turned to look at me.

"*In sha' Allah*, Michael," she said pronouncing each syllable clearly and distinctly. I thought that her switch to my true name was no accident. "When you use this expression you must always take care to pronounce each syllable."

"What does it mean?"

"It is a very useful expression; perhaps one of the most useful. It can mean many things, depending on your intonation. It can mean 'if God wills it,' or 'possibly,' 'perhaps,' or 'maybe.' It means that you accept without question that your fate is in the hands of God and that there is nothing any man can do to change that."

When she left I was conscious of the deep loneliness that was my life. I had the feeling I would never see her again.

"*In sha' Allah*," I said.

Late that night Mordechai appeared. "I have something for you." He laid a manila envelope on the table. I sat opposite him. "Open it and study it," he said.

Inside the envelope I found an Argentine passport for Omar Legassi. I opened it and found my photo staring back at me. I thumbed through the pages of the worn-looking passport. It was a masterpiece, as good or better than the CIA's work. The pages were stamped with dated entries and exits into and out of various countries in South America, the Middle East, and the United States.

"Happy Birthday, Mr. Legassi," said Mordechai.

18

THREE JEEPS MOVED SLOWLY ACROSS THE DESERT NAVIGATING UNDER THE light of a full moon, each packed with hooded men and bristling with arms. The engines were specially muffled and made little noise, or in the quiet desert night I think I might have heard them. I often wondered how differently things would have turned out had I heard them. But I didn't.

The jeeps stopped. Harsh commands were whispered in guttural Arabic. Hooded men leapt to the sand lying flat on their stomachs. Another command was whispered and they raced forward running low to the ground, hugging their weapons close to their bodies. Fifty yards ahead, over rough, undulating terrain on a flat stretch of sand was a tent, vulnerable and solitary.

Inside that tent, wrapped in a sleeping bag that might as well have been a straitjacket, I was in a deep sleep.

Earlier that evening Israeli soldiers had hurriedly moved me to the tent, telling me that the encampment was no longer safe. There was information about a large-scale terrorist infiltration. The tent, they said, was in a safer, heavier patrolled zone.

I awoke to the sound of furtive movement and whispers. My first thought was that I had no gun. I started to unzip my sleeping bag. A flashlight blinded me. I was slammed hard on the head from behind. Stunned, I lay still, my head aching. Hands pressed me down. There was quick movement around me. The voices spoke in Palestinian Arabic that I could barely understand.

I was smacked hard in the face. I rolled into a fetal position. I was kicked hard in the back and ribs.

I offered no resistance. What frightened me most was that *they* were frightened, I could hear it in their quick, uneven breathing. If they wanted to kill me they would have done it already, but fear might make them act irrationally.

A voice speaking in Hebrew ordered me to my feet.

"Mafhemtsh"—I don't understand—I answered in Arabic.

Hands grabbed me. A hood was placed over my head, a rope tied tightly around my neck sealing it shut. The sleeping bag was jerked from around me. I was pulled to my feet, choking, by the rope. My hands were cuffed behind my back and I was led stumbling by the neck like an animal, shirtless and barefoot, out into the cold desert night. Finally I was shoved into the back of a jeep. I felt bodies close and cold steel against my skin. Muffled engines kicked to life and we were moving.

For what seemed like hours we drove slowly through the desert. Suddenly we stopped. My head was forced forward. I stayed silent and completely yielding.

In my mind's eye I saw *Sensei* pacing the floor of the *dojo* lecturing his black belts on Bushido—the Way of the Warrior. *When there is a choice between life and death, a* true *warrior will always choose death.* I had heard the lecture many times, I had always wanted to ask: *How does that Japanese feudal warrior philosophy translate to a gun at your head while you're unarmed?* But like the rest of us, I kept my respectful silence and dipped my head. *"Oos!"*

In the distance a truck engine grew louder and then faded. My captors became frantic. I understood that an Israeli army patrol had just passed.

"Kill him now," said a deep, raspy voice in Arabic. "We can't take the chance."

"Shut up!" said another.

We were moving again, bouncing and swerving. Abruptly we hit level ground and began moving faster. I felt my captors relax. About a half-hour later we stopped. I was jerked roughly from the jeep, dragged and kicked through a door.

My handcuffs were removed. I was forced onto my back on top of what felt like a metal examination table. Hands worked at me quickly fastening thick leather restraints to my biceps, forearms, thighs, and shins, pulling them tight until I barely had circulation. The hood was torn from my head. A bright light shone in my eyes.

"Who are you?" demanded a voice in Arabic.

"My name is Omar Legassi."

"You are a Jew!"

"No, I'm an Arab. Born in Morocco raised in Argentina."

I was slammed on the head by something that felt like a heavy book. Bright lights flashed. My ear rang louder than ever.

"Liar! You are a Jew," said Raspy Voice.

"No."

"What were your mother's and father's names?"

"Hussein and Lalla," I answered, using the names I was given.

"What are you doing in the Negev?"

"I don't know . . ." I hesitated, unable to express myself in Arabic.

Slam! I was hit on the head again.

"What do you mean you don't know?"

"Please," I said in Spanish. "I rarely use Arabic since my childhood."

"Go ahead!" said a voice in Spanish.

"I came here from New York . . ."

"Where is here?"

"Tel Aviv . . . I'm taken off the plane, arrested, and interrogated, and brought out to the desert. First the Israelis beat me . . . accuse me of being a terrorist—now you . . ."

There was an animated discussion. All I could understand was that they weren't buying my story. My eyes were blinded by the bright light.

"I have your passport in front of me, Señor Legassi," said Spanish Voice. "It shows no departure from New York."

"They don't stamp passports when you leave the U.S.," I answered.

"There is no arrival stamp in the U.S. either," he said.

"Because . . . I didn't enter legally," I said.

SLAM! I was pounded on the head again, then smacked across the mouth. I tasted blood.

"*Why* did you enter illegally?"

"A drug deal."

There was a sudden flurry of conversation around me.

"Why did you come to Israel?" asked Spanish Voice.

"To meet a man, a Canadian Israeli. He was going to introduce me to a Lebanese connection for hashish."

"Filthy drug dealer," said Raspy Voice. My head was rocked with another slap. "Names, you piece of shit!"

"Maurice Ashkenazi . . . is the Canadian," I said, sticking as close to the truth as possible. Ashkenazi was a real drug dealer currently smuggling from Lebanon to the U.S. and Canada. "The Lebanese, I don't know . . ." SMACK! I tasted more blood. "He was Ashkenazi's connection—how could I know him?"

SLAM! I was bashed on the top of the head again. It was Raspy Voice. "I don't believe you. How did you contact this Jew?"

"He has a club in Montreal, called the Kit Cat Club," I said.

There is no way they can check the story. Ashkenazi never talks on the telephone unless the caller knows the appropriate codes.

"Kill him and dump him back with the Jews," said Raspy Voice.

"Do you speak English?" asked someone in English.

"No mucho," I answered.

"What was your mother's maiden name?" This time the question was in Arabic.

"Lalla Shaheen."

"Where are your parents?" asked Spanish Voice.

"Died . . . in a car accident in Argentina."

"Liar!"

I was hit on the head and smacked in the face simultaneously. Blood trickled into my nose and mouth.

It went on for what seemed like hours. Questions about my background, what I was doing in Israel, my family, what languages I spoke—over and over, repeated dozens of times in different languages. Attempts to trick me punctuated by a thump on my head or a smack in the face. I used what I had been told about the real Omar Legassi. What I didn't know I blamed on memory.

In the midst of it all, I tried to remember the thousands of interrogations I had conducted in little rooms with bare chairs and tables, where *I* had all the trump cards and some poor, handcuffed guy terrified for his life had to answer *my* questions. *Where did you get the stuff? Who paid you? Who were you going to give it to? How many times have you dealt drugs?* No physical force was necessary or ever used. My hammer was a forty-years-to-life sentence. Many would rather die.

I tried to remember attitudes that appealed to me, that made me go a little easier. Begging did not. Neither did anger, machismo, rebelliousness, or confrontation. In real life the John Waynes and the Clint Eastwoods don't last long, only their deaths are slow.

There was, however, a way about some guys that would affect me. I'd ease back, I'd give them a break. It was a certain kind of cooperation, cooperation out of cool, calculating choice, not out of fear. That's what I had to try for.

"To run is no shame," Sensei used to say, *"as long as you run out of confidence and not fear."*

For a long moment it was quiet. Then Spanish Voice said, "There is a stamp in your passport signifying a legal entry into the United States a year ago, on April fifteenth. What was the purpose of this trip?"

I tried to visualize the passport—its pages stamped with entries and exits from countries all over South America, the Middle East, and the U.S., but the image was vague. I had been told to memorize it. I didn't. I couldn't hesitate too long—it would be a red flag.

"To meet with Ashkenazi," I answered.

There was a long silence. The lights went out. *Not a good sign.*

When the lights came on again Mordechai was standing over me. Avi was beside him.

"Jesus," I said. "I don't believe this."

"If this were real, you would now be dead," said Mordechai. "There was no entry in your passport for April fifteenth. It was a bluff. You're not ready. My recommendation is to terminate the mission."

I looked around me, dazed, my head still ringing from the blows.

"The people who beat you are gone," said Mordechai. "You will never see them again." Then he turned to Avi. "The last thing Israel needs is the Americans blaming us for him."

Mordechai stormed out of the room. Avi began removing my restraints.

"Are you all right, Michael?"

"Avi, that guy has a problem with me personally. He was going to find a flaw if it took him all night."

"I'm sorry about this, Michael. It had to be done."

"I could have talked my way out of it. He didn't give me a chance."

"I'm sorry, Michael. I want you to go back to your hotel and rest. There is going to be a meeting about the whole affair tonight."

———

Two hours later I was alone in a hotel room, looking at my battered, bruised, and humiliated self in a mirror. Omar Legassi peered back at me. I'd been tattooed, I had grown a goatee, I had lost almost forty pounds, my hair had been died jet black, one of my eye teeth had been capped in gold, I had become addicted to cigarettes for the second time in my life, and I had spent so much time practicing a limp that it had become my natural gait. And now I was supposed to just put on the brakes, go home and forget about it? Well, fuck the Mossad. I didn't need them. They'd already given me more than enough.

Avi came to my room early to wake me. The moment I saw the somber way his eyes studied me, I knew something was up.

"Get dressed and packed," he said. "There's been a change."

"What kind of change?"

"We'll talk on the way."

"Where?"

"You'll see."

Twenty minutes later Avi was at the wheel of a BMW, a cigarette in his lips, driving ferociously through downtown Tel Aviv.

"We have decided to back you," he said simply.

"What? I can't believe it. After all the shit Mordechai gave me?"

"Mordechai was *in favor* of helping you. He had a change of heart. What does he care what happens to you? There were others against it—not because they care if you live or die—they don't want to risk embarrassing Israel. They, too, decided to back you."

"And you, Avi?"

"I am family, Michael. I was the only one against it."

"I don't get it—what happened?"

"Your drug, your White Queen, has made an appearance here. The son of one of our diplomats—an air force pilot—went berserk in a hotel. He killed two security men. The police had to shoot him. You won't see it in the papers. We thought it was a simple psychotic episode brought on by heavy cocaine use—rare, but it happens. But with the information you gave us, we took another look—everything matches this drug."

Avi stopped on a busy street and pointed to a nondescript six-story office building. "Someone will be waiting in the lobby."

"You're not coming?"

"No," he said looking out at the traffic. "It is better that I don't."

"Why?"

He turned away. "It's just better this way. Hurry, they are waiting and you have much to do."

"Am I going to see you again?"

"Not this trip," he said.

I stepped out of the car and leaned in the window. "Hey, Cuz!" He turned. "Don't sit shiva for me yet, okay? Give Aunt Miriam my love."

He pressed the accelerator. The tires chirped and I watched him roar into traffic, cutting off two cars and taking a corner on two wheels.

————

A young man was waiting for me in a narrow hallway dominated by a desk and a uniformed security guard. "This way, sir," he said, his accent Israeli British. He led me briskly past the security guard and into an elevator. We descended for about twenty seconds—there was no floor indicator. The door opened and he led me through a series of doors with coded locks.

Mordechai and an elderly man with a shaved head and watery blue eyes were seated at a table in a small, bare room, waiting for me. Mordechai motioned for me to take a seat opposite them. The bald man had his forearms resting on the table with his calling card exposed—a concentration camp tattoo.

"Michael Levine must leave here today and disappear," said Mordechai, as if nothing had happened last night. "There can be no record of your ever having been here. We have made travel arrangements. You travel to Morocco through Spain under your Michael Levine diplomatic passport. You will be met in Tangiers where you will be furnished with your Legassi identity, your new wardrobe, and all the latest intelligence on your first target—Mr. Hassan Belkassami, the oil dealer in Casablanca. You will then leave all your identification documents and clothing with our people and surface as Omar Legassi."

He turned to the other man, who was studying me with a detached air, and said something in rapid Hebrew. The man produced a weathered leather billfold and handed it to me.

I examined it. Other than feeling a little stiff, it seemed quite ordinary. "What is this for?"

"Is state of the art mini-recorder," the other man said in Russian-accented English. "Components are in wallet lining, not thicker than credit card. Most of movable parts are plastic, can't be detected by metal detectors. Has capacity to record on a filament wire, forty hours of conversation. Battery is special nickel cadmium construction."

"How do you use it?"

Tattoo Arm took it from me.

"They take it away, search it . . ." He opened it and pulled the flaps out. "They find nothing. You want to record conversation—you zip shut." He closed the zippered part of the billfold. "Is now recording. In quiet room can pick up conversation to twenty or thirty meters. Is best to carry in inside jacket pocket, or front pocket of trousers. Never in rear pocket."

"Then what am I supposed to do with it?" I asked.

"We are going to considerable trouble and risk," said Mordechai. "All we ask in return is that you keep us abreast of everything you learn. If you record everything—all conversations, all your activities—and give us the tapes, it will eliminate the necessity for too much contact with us—which would be exceedingly dangerous. Periodically you will be requested to turn the wallet over to an intermediary, who will furnish you with an exact duplicate as a replacement."

So the Mossad wants insurance that they get bang for their buck, whether I live or die. So what else is new?

Tattoo Arm handed me back the billfold.

"Practice using it," said Mordechai. "Keeping your business cards in the zipper section might be a good idea."

"What about telephone conversations?" I asked.

"Hold top part of billfold against earpiece," said Tattoo Arm. "It will record both sides of conversation."

"Can I play it back to see if it's working?" I said.

"Don't worry. It will work. You must have special equipment to listen. Only we have it."

"I'll need copies of the tapes," I said. "It will be important evidence for prosecution in America."

Tattoo Arm looked at Mordechai.

"You'll have them," said Mordechai. "When the operation is complete."

"How do I find my contact in Morocco?" I asked.

"Omar Legassi doesn't look for contacts," said Mordechai. "Follow your instructions and we will find you."

19

TANGIERS, MOROCCO

STANDING AT THE PROW OF THE SLEEK WHITE FERRY AS IT CROSSED THE Straits of Gibraltar from Spain to North Africa, my first sight of the ancient city of Tangiers was the towering minarets and dark, crenellated walls of the Kasbah.

I flashed back to my childhood in the South Bronx, playing hooky from school, taking the Seventh Avenue Express southbound and standing at the front car window, watching the winding tracks streak beneath me, filled with a sense of speed, adventure, and danger. Then, just beyond the Jackson Avenue station, plunging deep into the dark, twisting tunnels of underground New York, going deeper and faster passing beneath the Harlem River, feeling a rush of adrenaline that would carry me all the way to Bowling Green, the end of the Island of Manhattan—for me the end of my known world.

And here I was, more than three decades later, once again at the end of my known world, once again riding a wave of adrenaline, only this time there was no joy in the journey.

Suddenly I imagined the armadas of soldiers and spies, fighting wars over thousands of years, who had crossed these same straits and watched the almost identical sight as they approached the city. It occurred to me that for many of them it would turn out to be a one-way trip. They, like me, came far from the safety of home for what each no doubt believed was a cause worth dying for. Except, unlike them, I no longer knew where my home was. I was adrift. The only flag I was fighting for was the one I carried in my pocket, the stained piece of cloth hacked from René's burial suit.

The Mossad had done all it could to conceal my stay in Israel. They had arranged a midnight flight to Bilbao, Spain, on a private jet belonging to an Israeli construction company. No witnesses. It was as if Michael Levine had suddenly vanished on the way to Israel and reappeared six weeks later in Bilbao, Spain. In Bilbao I had rented a car and driven the length of Spain to Algeciras, where I booked passage on the ferry to Tangiers.

The port of Tangiers was a swarm of tourists from all over Europe lining up for Immigration and Customs checks, lugging baggage, speaking a half-dozen different languages, fighting off young, hungry-eyed pretty-boy hustlers. Some not fighting them off.

The Immigration officer spoke fluent Spanish to me when he saw that my American diplomatic passport was accredited by Argentina and Uruguay. As Mordechai had said, an American with a diplomatic passport needed no visa in Morocco; a little polite conversation and he waved me by with a smile.

In another moment I was moving with the crowd spilling onto the waterfront streets of Tangiers. I was walking at a normal pace, trying not to attract attention, acting as if I knew where I was going.

The streets teemed with all sorts of people, from Moroccan peasant women in big straw hats that reminded me of Mexican sombreros and men in stark white turbans and robes with veiled faces, to European woman in sandals and string bikinis barely covered by thin beach jackets. It was a combination of Times Square and Miami Beach—a hustler's paradise. The perfect place to blend in unnoticed.

Rue de Portugal wound uphill alongside the walls of the Kasbah; I followed it slowly as I had been instructed, passing street vendors, beggars, hustlers, and male prostitutes.

By the time I had reached the corner of Rue de la Plage I was aware of three dark young Moroccans dogging me—one behind me, the other two paralleling me on the other side of the street. I was so intent on them that I almost walked into a hooded and veiled woman wrapped in an indigo blue cloth that had an incandescent shine to it. She held a white straw basket clutched to her breast in a tattooed hand. Her eyes shone into mine. It was Shoshanna.

She glanced at one of the men following me—a lightning exchange of recognition—and turned onto Rue de Portugal, where we stood side by side waiting for the traffic light at the corner. The three men had stopped behind us. When the light changed and we crossed the street, they stayed where they were.

I let Shoshanna walk ahead of me uphill and then onto a main thoroughfare called Boulevard Pasteur, where there were a lot of banks, luxury shops, and well-kept old European-style residences. She turned up a narrow street and entered a three-story white stucco apartment building. She was waiting for me in the cool darkness of the hallway. Her veil was off. She put a finger to her lips and motioned for me to follow.

We moved past an ancient elevator to a steep, spiraling wrought-iron staircase. I watched her slender hips move with the lithe grace of a dancer as she led the way, her sandaled feet barely making a sound. She unlocked the only door at the top of the staircase and led me into a sunlit apartment with French doors opening onto a balcony and a panoramic view of the bay.

"Please, be comfortable," she said, unwrapping her hood and veil and dropping it casually over the back of a chair. Beneath it her body was covered by a complicated wrap that formed pantaloons. She moved quickly to the French doors and drew shut a diaphanous curtain that whipped and swayed in the breeze.

I dropped my suitcase and looked around the simply furnished apartment. The furniture was Swedish modern. There were prints and framed photos on the walls, but nothing personal, nothing that would indicate that the place was anything more than a safe house.

"Something to drink?" asked Shoshanna in Arabic. "Beer, wine, something to eat, perhaps?"

"Omar would ask for red wine," I said.

She smiled. In a moment she brought out a bottle of red wine and two glasses on a tray. She set it down on a coffee table at my knees and took a seat opposite me.

"We have much to talk about," she said as she poured the wine. "You are to leave this apartment as Omar Legassi. All traces of Michael Levine will be left with me."

I looked at her expecting a smile, a sign of humor—there was none.

"Your belongings will be delivered to your home in Buenos Aires."

"I'm sure they will," I said. "I assume you know the men following us."

"Of course." She downed the wine, checked her watch, and poured herself another. "They are to ensure that there is no countersurveillance. Our relations with the Moroccan government have always been exceptional. We cannot afford any problems."

"I wouldn't want to cause any."

She checked her watch again. "Come!" she said, getting to her feet. "There is not much time."

She led the way into the bedroom. The king-size bed looked inviting. The room also had a balcony and a view of the bay.

"Omar Legassi's wardrobe," she said, indicating two Samsonite suitcases and a leather attaché case on the floor. "Try the clothing, now." She moved around the room closing curtains. "There must be no surprises."

"Fine," I said, standing at the foot of the big bed, feeling awkward.

"The attaché case contains your identification," she said, standing before me, her dark eyes boring into mine. There was no longer even a hint of the playfulness that I saw there during our training.

"Your passport, birth certificate, Argentine driver's license and an American Express card in the name of Omar Legassi. You will notice business cards in your name with an import-export company in Buenos Aires. The office exists and the phone number is already in place."

"Already in place—what does that mean?" I was afraid of the Mossad's taking too many liberties with my cover without first consulting me.

"I will explain everything," she said, moving toward the door, picking up her veil and hood. "Right now, just try the clothing and familiarize yourself with the documents. I will be back later."

She was out the door before I could say another word.

It was many hours later when I heard the key in the door. The room was in darkness. I was sitting in the open doorway to the balcony. I had opened the curtains to look out at the spectacular night view of the bay and was enjoying the sounds and smells of yet another new world.

"Omar," she whispered, her voice tense. She was a shadow in the doorway.

"Should I turn the lights on?"

"No, wait," she said. She moved across the room toward the window. The dizzying scent of her filled my brain. She quickly drew the curtains. The lights came on and I saw that she was carrying a small gun in her hand. It looked like a twenty-two. The discharge would make less noise than a small firecracker. Not a gun for self-defense but a hit man's gun. Or a hit woman's.

"That for me?"

She ignored the remark. "You have tried the clothing?"

"Perfect fit," I said.

She went to the refrigerator and took out a tray of ice, putting some in a glass, taking one cube and rubbing it slowly over her lips and then down the back of her neck. I sat on the couch and watched her. In a moment she was across from me with another glass of wine in her hand. She took a drink and sighed. She seemed exhausted.

"Life is treating you hard?" I asked in Arabic.

Her eyebrows arched in surprise.

"Your accent is very good," she said.

"Thank you."

"Did you go over the documents?"

"Yes."

"Omar Legassi's passport shows an arrival in Morocco two days ago from Argentina on tickets bought through Aerolíneas Argentina. You have an open return ticket."

"You seem to have thought of everything."

I picked up one of my new business cards. It read AGUIRRE S.A. *Omar Legassi, Representative.* "What about these arrangements in Buenos Aires?"

"They are friends with an import-export business. You have a desk there, a secretary and an answering service. The American Express bill, when you use the card, will be sent there. You, of course, will be responsible for the payment."

"Of course," I said, wondering how long my five-thousand-dollar DEA petty cash fund would last.

"You will find a watch, a Rolex Cellini, and an antique twenty-two-carat-gold cigarette holder in your case. They were Omar's. The cigarette holder belonged to Omar's father. They are valued at twenty-two thousand dollars. You will be expected to return them at the conclusion of the operation."

"Fine," I said. *If all else fails I can pawn the watch.* "What do the people in the import-export business know about me?"

"That you are working for us."

"How reliable are they?"

"They helped us in the Eichmann affair."

"What else are we supposed to go over?" I said.

"You are angry?"

"No. Just tired. I've been gone so long I almost forgot what it was that got me here in the first place. I want to get it on already."

"Get it on?"

"Yes . . . just *do* what I came to do."

"We need to go over your plan."

"Simple," I said. "First I convince our oil baron, Hassan Belkassami, to trade oil for cocaine. He'll give me proof that I have access to a significant quantity of oil. Then I'll approach the drug dealer, Mario Razouk, in Buenos Aires—the last man who saw my friend alive—with the same offer. From there I don't know what will happen."

"I understand," she said. "Now we must plan your initial contact."

"Shoshanna. I don't need any help in planning anything. Just tell me what you know about the man—I'll take it from there."

"You think you are just going to walk in to Belkassami's office—a stranger—and he will accept your offer?" She laughed, which annoyed me.

"I've been doing this for twenty years," I said. "I don't have to explain this to you."

She shrugged. "Your ego may be a bigger enemy than your target. But have it your own way.

"Mr. Belkassami is, as you Americans say, the genuine article. Our Intelligence tells us that he has access to Libyan oil, which he trades below OPEC prices. He is a known financial supporter of terrorist activities, in return for which he is protected."

"What about his personal life?"

"He has had a long and bitter feud with his only brother, Nasir. The brother is a competitor in both business and for the affections of his wife. The woman's name is Fatima. She lives with his brother—an absolute outrage in his culture. This is all we have been able to learn without risk of him learning of our inquiries."

"What else?"

"The codes and phone numbers you must use to reach us are on a slip of paper in your passport. Memorize and destroy it."

"Why would I contact you?"

"You may find information that is vital for us, or we may have information that is vital for you. You must go to a safe phone and follow the instructions. You have already agreed to this."

"That's the agreement," I said.

"And your pager—we have made an adjustment to it."

"I guess you guys just do whatever the hell you feel like, don't you?"

She ignored this.

"When it is set at the middle setting it will transmit a signal that we can track anywhere in the world."

"Why the hell would you want to track me?"

"If we signal three ones on your pager it is an emergency," she said impatiently. "The only way we can page you is if we have an approximate location. If you choose not to call, well, that is your choice, isn't it?"

I was tired, frustrated, and afraid. I had managed to alienate her. I was sorry, but, well, you say things. *Shit happens, and there's no going back.*

"I'm sorry if I sound uptight . . ."

"I do my job," she said, looking at her watch. "There is a reservation for Omar Legassi at the Hyatt in Casablanca, for to-morrow—it is the kind of place Omar would stay." She got to her feet. "You can spend the night here. Do not forget to leave all Michael Levine's things. From now on you can, as you say, 'get it on.' "

Without a word she wrapped herself in her hood and veil. The gun disappeared in a fold of cloth somewhere about her middle. At the door she paused, those dark eyes burning into mine.

"Good luck, Michael. *Shalom!*"

"Wait." I was on my feet. "Please forgive me."

"There is nothing to forgive."

"Yes, there is. You've worked hard for me. I was rude."

"I work for my country."

"I've been alone, for a long time . . . I just forgot how to act."

She sighed. "Alone . . . is something I know very well."

We both smiled.

"Friends?" I said, leaning toward her. I kissed her mouth, at first softly, and then it was as if my twenty years of loneliness swallowed us both. She moved into my arms, her body molding to mine. I felt a deep, sinking sensation that wouldn't stop.

She pulled away from me, her eyes wide. "I'm sorry, Michael." She turned and started down the stairway.

"Shoshanna, please, don't go."

She never looked back.

———

The Hyatt Regency in Casablanca was a Western-style luxury hotel with a piano bar that featured original posters of Humphrey Bogart and Ingrid Bergman and other memorabilia from the movie *Casablanca*. The bar was my first stop after checking in. Before I called Belkassami's office, I had to establish a high-roller reputation.

I had a couple of glasses of red wine, smoked a few cigarettes with Omar Legassi's antique gold cigarette holder, and chatted with the bartender telling him a little of my background, being intentionally vague and mysterious. Then, to make sure I made the appropriate impression, I took a long look at the magnificent, wafer-thin, eighteen-carat-gold Rolex on my wrist and left him a fifty-dollar tip.

Before dialing Hassan Belkassami's office from my room, I zipped shut the Mossad wallet activating the recorder and held it to the earpiece.

"Belkassami," said a man's voice.

"Nasir? Nasir Belkassami?"

The line was silent a moment. "Who is this?"

"Is this the number for Nasir Belkassami?"

"He is my brother—who is this?"

"Allah be praised," I said, laughing. "He never even told me he had a brother. I lost his phone number. Information gave me this one—my prayers were answered."

"Nasir is not here—is there a message?"

"He was waiting anxiously to hear from me. I just arrived from Argentina. Is there a number I can call him?"

"This is business?"

"Urgent business."

"He is out of town," said Belkassami.

"Oh this can't be," I said, sounding upset. "He was expecting me. Is there a way to contact him? If we delay we lose the opportunity of a lifetime. They will find another broker."

A moment of silence.

"We are in the same business," said Belkassami. "Maybe I can help."

I paused for a long moment.

"Did Nasir tell you about the business with South America?"

"I . . . Yes, I think he mentioned something."

I waited another long moment before answering. I could hear heavy, nasal breathing at the other end.

"No, I don't think so," I said. "Is there any way to reach him—perhaps through Fatima?"

"You know *Fatima*?"

"We met only once, but who could forget such a beauty."

There was another silence. I thought I heard a gurgling sound.

"Yes," said Belkassami, his voice strained. "He will call here for messages. Where can he call you?"

I had delayed identifying myself, keeping open the possibility of a second approach if this one seemed doomed to failure. But the venom I heard in his voice for his brother told me I was dead on target.

"I'm staying at the Hyatt. I'm not going to move until I hear from him. Omar is my name. Omar Legassi."

Three hours later I was at the bar again, chatting with my new friend the bartender, when my pager began to vibrate. The little screen read three ones—the Mossad's signal.

I used a booth in a nearby telephone company office and dialed a pager number in Tel Aviv. I punched in my code and the phone number I was calling from, and hung up. The phone rang within minutes.

"Omar?" said a voice in English.

"Yes."

"You have made contact with that party in Casablanca?"

"Yes."

"Be advised that inquiries have been already made about you with the Moroccan police."

"What kind of inquiries? By whom?"

"We have no further information."

The line went dead.

20

THE MOMENT I ENTERED THE LOBBY OF THE HYATT I KNEW SOMETHING was up. The desk clerk looked at me and dropped his eyes too quickly. As I entered the piano bar lounge I noticed a quick exchange of looks between the bartender and a short man with a big toupee that seemed to rest on a pair of oversize ears, seated with his back toward me at the bar.

Dark, scruffy-looking men with scraggly beards wearing wraparound sunglasses and loose-fitting shirts kind of stand out in a place which normally caters to wealthy American and European tourists. There were about a half-dozen of these bozos scattered around the room watching me.

I crossed the room and took a seat two stools away from the man at the bar. The bartender's hand shook as he poured my red wine. I could feel the eyes of the man on me as I took out my con man's bankroll—three hundred-dollar bills wrapped around a three-inch stack of tens and twenties—and lay a Franklin on the bar. A Moroccan piano player was playing "As Time Goes By." He did a barely recognizable imitation of Louis Armstrong. I put a twenty in his glass and checked Mr. Toupee out with a glance.

He was a stocky, dark-skinned man in his mid-forties, with a pencil-thin mustache. The oversize toupee made him about three inches taller, and he was still short. He smiled and nodded, flashing a gold tooth.

"*Assalaamu alaykum*," I said, bowing slightly.

"*Wa alaykum assalaam,*" he said, sliding over to sit next to me. "You are Mr. Legassi?"

"I'm sorry," I said. "You must be mistaken. I don't know you."

"You do," he said. "We spoke on the phone."

I took a long look at him and smiled.

"Ahh, of course . . . I see the resemblance now—Nasir's brother."

I shook his hand enthusiastically. My enthusiasm was real. This odd little man, who looked like a character in a Three Stooges movie but who also happened to control enough Libyan oil to light the world for the next decade, was my first hurdle in what promised to be a long race. I needed him to provide me with the oil for my oil-for-cocaine trade—the offer of instant, untraceable money-laundering that I had planned to use as my entrée into the Triangle.

"I have bad news for you," said Belkassami. "My brother has left the country for a few months."

I noticed a twitch in his right eye when he mentioned his brother. In conjunction with the twitch, his toupee rode forward slightly.

"This is terrible," I said. "I can't believe he wouldn't notify me."

"How well do you know my brother?" he asked, his eye twitching a little more noticeably.

I invented a story of a meeting in Paris with Nasir and his stunning woman, Fatima. I told him of the wonderful time we all had at the home of friends of mine. Every time I mentioned Fatima, his eyes would bug out like a Maori warrior's, his forehead would wrinkle, and again the toupee would ride forward about an inch. The only thing missing was steam hissing out of his oversize ears. I also realized by the liberties I was incrementally taking with the truth, that he had been completely out of touch with his brother for years.

I spoke vaguely of a big and complicated deal his brother Nasir and I had worked out involving the shipment of oil. I told him that some very powerful people were now waiting for confirmation that it could be done.

"I cannot believe Nasir would just disappear," I said. "He knew I was working on this. He must have lost my phone number."

"I am going to tell you the truth," whispered Belkassami, leaning toward me, the front edge of his toupee pointed in my face and moving as if it were alive. "It pains me to say this, but you are lucky he is gone. My dear brother is a thief and a scoundrel. And if he told you he had access to oil, at anything less than OPEC prices, he is a lying dog."

I went into deep, theatrical shock.

"How could he do this? What could he gain? Many millions of dollars are involved—why would he lie to me?"

"To draw you in," said Belkassami. "Then he would raise the price when you had committed yourself."

"How despicable," I said. "How could such a magnificent woman like Fatima love this man so much?"

I looked away and sipped my wine, concentrating on fitting a cigarette into the gold holder. I was afraid his eyes were still bugged out and maybe his toupee on sideways by now, and I would not be able to contain myself.

Finally Belkassami took the bait. He wanted to know what the deal was.

"You seem like a gentleman, Hassan, but I don't really know you. For all I know you may be some undercover policeman," I said, dropping my voice to a conspiratorial whisper, letting him know that the deal was illegal.

This seemed no surprise to him; if anything it incited him further, confirming that he had seen Omar Legassi's criminal record. He insisted that we move to a private booth where we could speak more freely. I followed him, noticing that he was wearing shoes with two-inch heels. The tip of his toupee still only reached just below my shoulder.

In the booth he pulled out his wallet and gave me the same business card that I'd been given by Szion Aban in Cochabamba. He showed me his driver's license and identity card to prove he was, in fact, Nasir's brother. Now I had the son of a bitch hooked. All I had to do was reel him in.

By the next morning Belkassami had guaranteed me as much Libyan oil as I could handle. The trade would be cocaine base, valued at about $2,000 a kilo, for high-grade Libyan oil at a trade price of $15.00 per barrel. The current OPEC price was $18.53.

I would convert the cocaine base to pure cocaine myself and guarantee Belkassami a minimum of $20,000 a kilo when it was sold in Europe, which meant he would be grossing roughly eight times the OPEC oil price. I also guaranteed that the first shipment would be a minimum of a million barrels of oil for 7,500 kilos of cocaine base, which would convert to 7,500 kilos of pure cocaine, which, in turn, translated to a gross of $150 million. My commission would be $2.00 a barrel plus ten percent of everything above OPEC profits—roughly $15 million.

Belkassami was ecstatic with the knowledge that while Nasir was screwing Fatima, he would at least screw Nasir out of more than $100 million.

I was now ready to follow René's trail, as Omar Legassi.

21

BUENOS AIRES

"Do you wish to place a bet, Señor Legassi?" asked Alfonso, my favorite dealer at the Club Arabesque.

"I'm going to sit out a few hands, Alfonso," I said.

"Certainly, Señor," said the short, slim *porteño*. He shot cards to the players around me with scarcely a flick of the wrist.

I twisted in my seat, my eyes searching the plush, dimly lit gambling casino, praying for the appearance of Mario Razouk, the last person René had been seen with before his mutilated body was found on the Pampas. It had been more than two months since the night I had first spotted him emerging from his limo. A lot can happen in two months.

I had ten blue chips in front of me, each worth a hundred U.S. dollars—all the money I had left in the world. I had already gone through the DEA $5,000 petty cash fund, plus the last $753 of my own money.

Actually I had been pretty lucky. After eight nights of playing high-stakes blackjack while waiting for Razouk's appearance, to be down only $4,700 and still have managed to tip every dealer and cocktail waitress in the club with hundred-dollar blue chips, meant that I'd been holding my own. It also assured me that should someone ask any of the club's employees about Señor Legassi, the ominous-looking Arab in the black silk Armani suit, they would most likely say that he was some kind of high-rolling Arab gangster.

Money wasn't my only problem—I was also running out of time.

Belkassami was waiting to hear from me. The longer the delay, the greater my fear that Fatima would turn up on her knees at his doorstep. Women are a hell of a lot less predictable than men. But I had no choice. Mario Razouk's addiction to blackjack was the only button I had left to push.

I had returned to Buenos Aires eleven days ago and moved into a furnished undercover apartment on the fashionable Avenida del Libertador that I had rented ten months earlier for an undercover deal that had gone sour. A breeder of Thoroughbred racehorses was smuggling dope into the U.S. from Argentina by forcing rubber condoms filled with cocaine up the horses' rectums. The guy was kicked to death before our first meeting, by a horse who refused to be a "mule." A year's rent had been paid in advance and the place never used.

I spent the next two days showing my face around the neighborhood. I tipped the concierge and doorman a hundred bucks each to "take good care of me," which meant they would let me know if anyone came around asking questions. I called my new office at Aguirre Imports and asked for myself in Arabic. A man told me that Omar Legassi was out of the country.

The stage was set, the only actor missing was Mario Razouk. And now, on the eleventh night, still no sign of him.

In an authorized DEA deep cover operation the U.S. government would have picked up the whole tab. My Government Form 1012, Expense Voucher, would have read: *Tips and other related expenses to establish deep cover reputation and role as wealthy upper-echelon criminal type.* I would have filed the form through Stratton and asked for thirty or forty thousand a month as a budget for as long as the case lasted. I would have also been furnished a team of about twenty undercover agents to cover me, to film and record all my meetings, to play the roles of my bodyguards and drivers, to conduct last-minute inquiries about prospective targets that might be needed to insure my survival. Both Michael Levine *and* Omar Legassi had deadly enemies throughout South America—I couldn't afford to run into the wrong person as either one.

But this was no ordinary case. As far as DEA's Internal Security was concerned—should they find out what I was doing—I had stolen the money and used it to gamble and live the high life.

As a so-called corrupt agent I would be sentenced to about thirty years in prison and some Americans would feel safer in their beds, knowing that their government was out there protecting them from people like me.

Spinning plates, I thought, *I'm spinning plates again.* Undercover work had always reminded me of the circus act where a guy spins a whole bunch of plates on the end of long flexible sticks, running frantically up and down the row as each one totters, giving it another spin so that it doesn't fall. If one falls, it can knock the whole row down. *Phony ID, language, act, cover business, backup documentation and records, phony reputation, secret codes, contacts and agreements, money-money-money, government bureaucracies, Internal Security, murderous gangsters, family, bills, mental and physical health, watch your back, money-money-money—plates to keep spinning, spinning, spinning.*

How long could it last?

Like gambling casinos everywhere, there was an air of quiet desperation and danger about the Club Arabesque. Big, grim-faced men in tuxedos were scattered about the room with ear mikes that looked like hearing aids. Two-way mirrors and surveillance cameras were everywhere. Players were either wide-eyed and flushed with excitement or as pale and somber as undertakers. It took an enormous effort to hide my own growing feeling of desperation. If Mario Razouk didn't show up soon, I'd have to hock Omar's Rolex just to keep playing.

A few feet to my right stood the dice table where Marita had introduced René to Razouk. My mind drifted. I was focused on a black spot on the rug that looked like shoe dye. René always wore highly polished black shoes. I imagined the spot as his last footprint. That was the moment I heard words that snapped me out of my reverie.

"Good evening, Señor Razouk," said the dealer, "I haven't seen you in a while."

I turned casually and tried not to look directly at the heavyset man in the white tuxedo taking a seat across from me. Razouk was supposed to be in his late sixties; in the flesh he looked at least ten years younger. His complexion was as dark as mine, his hair full, wiry, and coal black. He was smoking an ornately carved ivory pipe. The sweet scent of an exotic tobacco enveloped the table. What was recognizable were his bushy eyebrows and dark eyes that had the same look of amusement as in his photo.

"Man's costliest expenditure is time, Alfonso," Razouk said with a heavy Middle Eastern accent. "How have you been spending yours?"

Razouk settled into his chair and neatly stacked three piles of chips before him—bronze rectangles worth a thousand dollars each. I estimated about $20,000 on the table in front of him.

"As you see, Señor," said Alfonso, shuffling the thick stacks of cards, without looking, doing a slick one-handed cut and then pausing to do remarkable little finger calisthenics, "lots of exercise."

Razouk laughed a deep baritone, reached into his pocket and flipped the dealer a blue hundred-dollar chip for the performance.

"Thank you, Señor," said the dealer, raising the chip for the surveillance cameras, then slipping it into a cup beneath the table.

Razouk's eyes inventoried the table, now full with seven players, pausing momentarily on me. My heart was racing. Everything came down to this moment.

"Place your bets please," said Alfonso.

Razouk tossed a thousand-dollar chip onto the table.

Alfonso looked at me. I placed five of my ten remaining blue chips on the bet line. Razouk, his back turned, hadn't even noticed. He was speaking to a couple of dark-suited men in sunglasses, apparently his bodyguards.

Alfonso shot cards around the table, giving himself a king. I had a six and a five. My hands started to tremble, I put them in my lap and crossed my legs. Alfonso worked his way through two players—it was Razouk's turn. He was still talking to his goons.

"Señor?" said Alfonso.

Razouk turned briefly and puffing on his pipe glanced at his cards. He tapped the table to indicate he wanted another card.

Alfonso turned over a queen of hearts.

"The card of love," said Razouk. "Only me, she doesn't love." He tossed his cards in. He'd gone bust with twenty-three. He placed two chips on the bet line, doubling his bet to $2,000 and resumed his off-table conversation.

"Señor?" said the dealer—it was my turn.

I looked at my cards—a six and a five. Eleven. I was in trouble.

With eleven points you have the choice of turning your cards up and doubling your bet on the turn of one card. If I doubled and lost, I would lose everything.

Eleven always doubles—the bet a true gambler *had* to make.

If Razouk was at all aware of me and I didn't, he'd know instantly that I was either not a gambler or didn't have the money to be at a high-stakes table.

"Double." I turned up my cards and put the rest of my chips on the line.

"Good luck," said Alfonso as he slipped me a down card.

"In sha' Allah," I said.

Razouk turned back to face the table. Peripherally I could see him studying me.

I watched the dealer work his way through the next two players. Mike Levine dreaded taking a peek at the hole card. But Omar Legassi had to casually take a look and show no emotion. I lifted the edge of my card concentrating on keeping my hand from trembling. A four. I had a total of fifteen points. The dealer had a king showing, which meant that if he drew anything higher than a six, I was done for.

The dealer's hands flashed. He turned a five, then another king—twenty-five. The house had gone bust.

My pile of chips was doubled—twenty blues. Two thousand dollars.

Razouk was watching me openly now, a curious look on his face.

I left the $2,000 on the bet line.

The next hand I was dealt was an ace and a king—black jack!

Mike Levine would have screamed for joy; Omar Legassi coolly inserted a cigarette into the four inches of gleaming yellow gold and smiled, making sure to show his gold tooth. My pile of chips now totaled $5,000. The dealer had replaced the blues with five bronze rectangles worth a thousand each.

Razouk had also won his bet. He glanced at my chips and left the two bronze chips on the bet line, then added three more.

We both had $5,000 on the line.

Razouk smiled and winked across the table at me. *"Hazz,"* he said, wishing me luck.

"Shôkran," I answered, thanking him with the Moroccan phrase.

I was dealt a second blackjack and a cheer went up around me. A small crowd had gathered around the table. The dealer quickly went bust. Razouk also won.

"*Tbarka llah leek,*" I said, congratulating him.

"May Allah bless you," he answered in Arabic—the traditional response.

The dealer piled chips worth $12,500 in front of me. I was suddenly aware of the scent of an unusual spice perfume. An Oriental woman stood behind me in a red gown. An amber amulet gleamed at her throat. Her face reminded me of one I'd seen on a statue in a Buddhist temple in Thailand. I was suddenly certain, beyond all rationality, that this woman was the omen of luck responsible for my winning.

I left all my chips on the bet line.

"I'm sorry, Señor Legassi," said the dealer. "I must get approval from the manager for any bets over ten thousand dollars." He motioned toward an ashen-faced man with a completely bald head, watching us from the edge of the crowd.

"May I ask why?" interrupted Razouk.

The manager squeezed through the growing crowd and entered the dealer's space. The two put their heads together. I could see the dealer's lips moving frantically, his eyes on Razouk.

"Señor Razouk," said the manager. "We were not aware that this gentleman was your friend," he said. There was a fear in his eyes that transcended the mere offending of a good customer.

"Why has this rule not been applied to me?" said Razouk. "I might have saved myself quite a bit of money." The question was pointed but still had an edge of humor to it. Razouk winked at me.

The manager looked flustered. "I'm sorry, but it *is* a house rule, Señor."

"It wouldn't have anything to do with the fact that my friend Señor Legassi is an Arab, would it?" Razouk was still smiling, but the humor was gone. He laid his pipe down in front of him.

He remembered my name.

"Certainly not, Señor," said the manager, almost choking on his words. "Alfonso, no limit for these gentlemen." He gave a quick nod at the dealer.

Razouk watched the manager move off to one side and then looked across the table at me.

"What is your first name, brother?" he asked in Arabic.

"Omar," I said.

"How much is my friend Omar betting?"

"Twelve thousand five hundred," said the dealer.

"I will match the bet." Razouk pushed a pile of chips across the table. "I have a feeling that my brother and I are going to break this son of a bitch bank tonight."

Razouk winked again and, in Arabic, said, "I hate these Argentine bastards, Omar."

"The pleasure is all mine," I said as I watched the dealer shoot cards around the table.

The house showed a queen of hearts. I drew a nine and a three. The dealer played around the table. Two players went bust. Razouk stayed pat. It was my turn. Razouk was watching me, his eyes aglow.

If I took a hit and went bust, I was broke. I would walk away a loser with no way to explain to Razouk why I didn't throw another $20,000 on the table.

I glanced over my shoulder. The Oriental woman still stood behind me. I waved my hand over my cards indicating that I would stay pat.

The dealer's hands became a blur of motion. He turned over a three, for a total of thirteen. House rules were that anything under seventeen points meant he had to take a hit. He flipped another card. There was an audible gasp from the crowd—another three. He turned another card—an even louder gasp. He had gone bust with a six, just one point over twenty-one.

My pile of chips grew to $25,000.

Razouk flipped his cards over. He had also stayed pat, with twelve. He looked at my cards and laughed. "Well done, my friend," he said as chips were piled in front of him. "Let's make these bastards really sweat."

"I would like to bet twenty-five thousand on this card," he said, looking across at the manager.

The manager nodded. Alfonso checked the other players for bets—one by one each dropped out. It was my turn. I glanced behind me. The Oriental woman was moving away. Without thinking, I grabbed her hand. She turned and glared at me.

"Please," I said. "Could you stay a moment longer? I think you bring luck to anyone around you."

She looked at her man, a tall, distinguished-looking gray-haired Argentine in a tuxedo.

"Let her stay, *Che*," said a voice in the crowd. There was a chorus of agreement. The man flushed and reluctantly nodded his assent. The woman smiled demurely, pleased with the attention.

"Thank you," I said, drawing her closer by the hand until she was pressing against the back of my chair.

"I'll join Señor Razouk. Bet it all."

"Bravo, Omar. To my friends I am Mario."

"*In sha' Allah*," I said.

"*In sha' Allah*," he echoed, rubbing his hands together.

A look passed between the manager and the dealer that I did not like. Razouk also caught it. Alfonso was poised to deal. He'd had more than enough time with attention away from him to stack the deck with a blackjack for the house.

"I'd like a new deck please," I said.

"Excellent idea," said Razouk.

The crowd around us was silent as new decks of cards were handed to the dealer, who made a show of breaking the seals one at a time and deftly mixing and shuffling.

"I'm in the mood for some champagne," said Razouk. "How about you, Omar? Is this not a moment to savor?"

"Sure."

The manager snapped his fingers and a tuxedoed waiter appeared with chilled bottles of Piper Heidsieck.

Alfonso placed the deck before Razouk to cut.

"No, give it to my new friend, Omar."

The deck was placed before me.

"Let her cut," I said, bringing the woman in red forward.

Again the dealer looked at the manager. He nodded. The woman smiled into my eyes as she cut the cards. The deck disappeared in a blur of hands into the card dispenser.

"I'm superstitious too, Omar," said Razouk. "Drink with me."

Still holding on to the woman with one hand, I picked up a full champagne glass with the other. Razouk and I downed the glasses in one gulp.

"Deal," said Razouk, and the dealer shot cards at us.

I looked at my first card. It was a black queen. I looked at the second and almost fainted. Ace of spades. I wanted to scream. I had blackjack.

I had just won $62,500—more money by far than I had ever won in my life. Over a year's salary. Mike Levine wanted to jump up and down and hug everyone. But to Omar Legassi, drug dealer and arms trafficker, this was nothing more than an enjoyable evening.

I casually turned my cards over. A shout went up. Hands pounded me on the back.

It was Razouk's turn. The dealer had nine on board.

Razouk, grinning like a Cheshire, turned over a seven and a four. *"Doble,"* he said, doubling his bet to $50,000. "Put the balance on my credit line." He held up his glass. It was immediately filled, as was mine.

The manager stepped forward and he and the dealer tallied Razouk's chips. Razouk raised his glass to me and downed the contents in one gulp. So did Omar Legassi.

"Fantástico," breathed the Oriental woman in my ear, squeezing my hand. Once she spoke I felt the spell had been broken. I felt the cold chill of a loss coming. *Superstition? Absolutely.*

Another man appeared with a tuxedo and clipboard. Razouk signed for the amount of credit he was granted. The crowd hushed as the dealer slid a card facedown toward Razouk. He looked at it and smiled. The dealer's hand went *flick, flick,* and the house had gone bust again. A cheer went up around us. The crowd around the table was now ten deep.

The dealer had changed our chips to the gold rectangles that signified $5,000 each. Razouk did not hesitate. He shoved $100,000 onto the bet line.

"Bet it all," he said, and looked across at me.

I reached down inside myself somewhere and found the smile of Omar Legassi, Moroccan Argentine hustler. I pushed all my chips forward.

"In sha' Allah," I said, for the third time that night, pronouncing each syllable clearly and distinctly, the way Shoshanna had taught me.

At that moment several of the undercover plates I was spinning started to topple. The Oriental woman's hand was wrested from mine. I turned to see her being pulled away from me through the crowd. I glimpsed a face watching me that I recognized. An Argentine cop that Mike Levine, DEA Country Attaché, had seen in the embassy with Snakeface. I turned away.

Another commotion had begun across the table from me— Razouk was at the center of it. He was on his feet facing the manager. Flanking Razouk, their eyes invisible behind dark glasses, were four broad-shouldered men in dark suits and ties.

The manager had tried to bring in another dealer. My guess was that the new dealer was a magician, a specialist whose magic was to make winning hands appear when and where he was directed. Razouk must have had the same suspicion.

"This is not my choice, Señor," pleaded the frightened manager. "It is Mr. Grimaldi's orders."

"Where is that *chanta* sonofabitch? Bring him here right now."

In Buenos Aires calling a man a *chanta* is roughly the equivalent of calling him a sleazy con man. To a man like Humberto Grimaldi, the owner of the Arabesque and a known Mafioso, this was an insult to kill for. If Razouk was nervous about this, he certainly hid it well.

"I can't, Señor. The order was given on the telephone. Believe me, Señor Razouk, it is a house prerogative anywhere in the world."

"Unfortunately for you, *gusano*, this isn't anywhere in the world." He jabbed a finger into the man's chest. "I hold you responsible for calling him in the first place, *pedazo de mierda*."

The manager blanched, his mouth moving and no words coming out. You could have put his photo in the dictionary next to *scared shitless*.

Razouk turned his back on him and winked at me. "If I were you I wouldn't play any longer, my brother. Come let's have breakfast together."

I started to gather my chips.

"Let my men do that for you," he said, putting a thick arm over my shoulder.

Two of Razouk's men led the way through the crowd while the other two gathered our chips. Ahead the Argentine cop was standing in our path watching me. A few months ago he had briefly met a clean-shaven Mike Levine who was forty pounds heavier with graying hair. I made sure my limp was pronounced and looked him straight in the eye.

I prayed that he thought he was mistaken.

22

"*Fi sahitak*," said Razouk, raising a full glass of champagne and touching it to mine.

"And may God give you health," I responded. He tipped his head back and the liquid disappeared as if he'd inhaled it. I gulped mine down and peered out the window at the dark streets drifting by.

We were sweeping along the vast predawn emptiness of Nueve de Julio, the widest city street on earth, in Razouk's stretch limo, two of his professionals in the front seat and two in the jump seat behind us. The one called Bruno now riding shotgun had our winnings in two attaché cases "donated" by the Arabesque. He had a broad Russian face, dark skin and brown, Mongol eyes.

Razouk poured us another champagne from a wet bar. I was getting dizzy. I had forgotten to zip the wallet shut to activate the Mossad recorder and decided to leave it off. I could not take the chance of even this seemingly insignificant move in such tight quarters.

"Omar," he said. "Be frank with me. You were playing the system, weren't you?"

I smiled enigmatically and took my time answering—Omar Legassi was a cautious man, a man with secrets.

"An acquaintance of mine played the system," I said. "He had a photographic memory—counted cards, remembered every card thrown and calculated the odds. All done in his head. At the end of thirty hours of play he never had less than two hundred thousand in winnings. Within a couple of months the Las Vegas casinos caught on, photographed him, distributed the photos to every casino in the world. Now he can't get far enough past the door of a gambling club to have a heart attack."

Razouk laughed and downed his glass.

"The moment I saw you, I knew you were a son of a bitch camel trader—so you *do* use a system."

I shrugged. "I don't have the patience."

"I know you, Omar Legassi. Camel traders never tell their secrets."

"And there are those who have the truth within them, but they tell it not in words," I said, remembering one of a half-dozen lines I had memorized from *The Collected Works of Kahlil Gibran*. Among the things Marita had remembered about Razouk was his passion for the Lebanese poet-philosopher. The opening seemed perfect.

"Son of a bitch!" Razouk gaped in surprise. "I've read everything that Lebanese *hijo de puta* wrote, a thousand times, and cried each time. You are full of surprises, Omar—you are Moroccan, no?"

I gave him the short version of my background. He listened intently. When I finished he said, "Why have I never seen you at the club before?"

"My business keeps me traveling," I said, throwing out the bait.

My timing was bad. At that moment the limo stopped at the front door of a nightclub in the old Boca district, La Cumparcita, one of the few remaining genuine tango clubs in Buenos Aires.

A big man rushed from the club to open the door for Razouk. "Your private room is ready, Señor," the man assured him with a bow.

We moved through the packed room to the music of a full tango orchestra behind a singer doing an imitation of Carlos Gardel's "Mi Noche Triste." A three-man wedge of bodyguards led the way while Bruno protected our rear.

Razouk paused to watch the small dance floor where two women, in sleek black dresses slit to the top of their thighs, swirled together in a body-hugging, leg-flying Argentine tango. One had platinum blond hair, the other jet black, both worn in short bobs. Both wore heavy makeup and bright red lipstick—

they might have been twins. They saw Razouk, smiled, and performed a slow, sensual grind for him running their hands down each other's body, ending with their tongues touching.

The audience exploded in shouts and applause. Razouk sent one of his men to stuff hundred-dollar bills into the garter of each. More applause and shouts. Razouk grinned and waved as we were led to a garish private dining room with walls featuring large gilt-framed portraits of Argentine historical figures on horseback in turn-of-the-century military uniforms. A dark mahogany dining table was ornately set for two.

Razouk gave orders as if he owned either the club or its owner.

Waiters served us plates of *lomo a caballo*, the traditional Argentine meal of thick cuts of lean, tender steak called *lomo*, covered with melted cheese and easy-fried eggs. There were more bottles of champagne. The moment he was served Razouk began to wolf his food down followed by healthy swigs of champagne. The waiters quietly backed out of the room, closing the door. We were alone.

We ate silently with Razouk savoring every mouthful, sometimes with his eyes closed. When he finished a second portion and another half bottle of champagne, he sat back in his black leather-upholstered chair, burped and farted loudly, and then sighed contentedly.

In the silence my mind drifted to the thought that Razouk had either murdered René or led him to his death. I brushed the thought away. To think about it would show in my eyes, in my voice—Razouk was much too sharp to miss it. I had to *like* this man. To an undercover agent *like* is synonymous with *trust*. Once I had his trust he was mine. I would involve him with me in a criminal plot; he would confide in me the way partners in crime almost always do. And I would learn the truth.

"Tell me about yourself, Omar. What exactly do you do?"

I took my time answering. Only con men or undercover agents come prepared with quick answers.

"I've been doing some exporting," I said vaguely.

"What sort of merchandise?"

"Basically, anything that turns a profit," I said. "Up until recently I was involved in the weapons business with some Belgians."

"The Middle East?"

"You can trust no one over there."

He shook his head sadly.

"That thing has destroyed the city of my birth, brother Omar. The jewel of the Middle East. The city of Gibran. There is a hole in my heart where my beautiful Beirut used to be."

"Yes," I agreed. "I was there in the '70s."

"It is something I will never understand. What the hell is the difference between us and the Jews? We're kissing cousins. Sons of Abraham—it's in the Koran and the Old Testament. We should be in business together, not war. The Middle East would be a paradise, not this disaster. Terrible for business."

"Yes," I said noncommittally.

"Do you have a business card?"

"Certainly." I took out the Mossad wallet, fished out an AGUIRRE S.A. business card and zipped the wallet shut, activating the recorder. I wrote down the phone number at the undercover apartment. "My private phone," I said, passing it to him.

Razouk examined both sides of the card briefly and slipped it carefully into an inner jacket pocket.

"I read people very well, Omar. It is my business. You are a man with something on your mind, something troubling you," he said, pouring us both champagne.

Razouk downed the glass in a gulp. I took a sip. I was already feeling tipsy and I had not had a quarter of what this old man had drunk. Timing in an undercover scam is critical. Too soon creates suspicion, but in another couple of minutes Razouk might be too drunk. There might not be a second chance.

"You're amazing, Mario," I said. "You're exactly correct. I'm at what you might describe as a crossroads in my business. It's not exactly a problem. It's more an opportunity that requires a partner. What has me worried is that if I even approach the wrong person it could be disastrous."

His bushy eyebrows raised. "That bad?"

"Well . . . problems with the law. And other problems. I should warn you, my friend, that what I do is not exactly legal."

Razouk exploded in wheezing laughter. "Anything else from you would have surprised me and bored the life out of me. Be specific, my brother, perhaps I can help you."

"I went into business with some Colombians," I began.

"Cocaine of course."

"Of course," I said. "The first transaction turned out very well."

"What kind of numbers did this . . . transaction involve?"

"My investment was a million and a half U.S. dollars, which I managed to turn into three million with some Spaniards in Tangiers," I said, sticking to the exact details of my transaction with *El Búfalo*. If Razouk happened to know him, at least half the story would check out.

"In how much time?"

"About six weeks."

"A one hundred percent return in six weeks—what is the problem?"

"It's complicated."

"Somehow that doesn't surprise me about you, Omar."

"I moved some Colombian powder from Morocco into Spain. In Morocco I met people with access to large quantities of oil at below OPEC prices. I suggested a possible barter deal and they were in agreement."

Razouk's olive-black eyes gleamed as if electrified. "Oil for weapons?"

"This is where it gets interesting," I said. "It's like blackjack: you're dealt two aces—do you go for double the money or don't you? I showed them how—by trading oil for cocaine base, and furnishing me with a laboratory to crystallize the base into cocaine—they could make several times the money they would ordinarily expect per barrel."

"Ahhh. Black gold for white. Very clever, Omar. Where would your profit come from?"

I saw no suspicion, only growing interest. I plunged ahead.

"My oil people will pay me on a per-barrel basis. Two dollars a barrel, plus ten percent of all profits above OPEC prices."

"How much oil are we talking about?"

"A guaranteed minimum of a million barrels for the first transaction."

"The first?"

"They have access to unlimited amounts—why not continue?"

Razouk whistled softly. The barbed hook was slowly sinking in.

"Where would the cocaine base come from?" asked Razouk.

"*That* is my problem. My only source is the Colombians. They are crude and uneducated. Every major Colombian dealer sooner or later is caught by the gringos—how? The money trail. Yet they don't change their methods.

"I don't think they would understand that trading for oil at a discount, and then reselling it at OPEC prices both gives them additional profit and instantly launders the money.

"And to suggest that retrading the oil for arms and then selling the arms back to the the same people with the oil would double and even triple their profits—and, of course, mine too— would be too complicated for them. They have no imagination. All they know is silver, powder, and lead."

"Exactly," said Razouk, his gaze on me intense, as if discovering me for the first time.

"But the real trouble is, if they refuse they become a danger. They are jealous, they have no loyalty. They will be afraid that one of their competitors will accept and will do everything they can to destroy the deal . . . and me."

Razouk's head nodded slowly.

"Brother Omar, I had a feeling about you from the moment I saw you. You *are* a camel-trading son of a bitch. No offense."

"None taken," I said.

"I ask you a hypothetical question," said Razouk. "If I asked you tomorrow to prove that you had access to this oil, could you?"

"Of course."

"How rushed are you to do this . . . business?"

"The Moroccans are pressuring me—I don't want to lose them."

"Yes," he said thoughtfully.

The door burst open. The two tango dancers pranced into the room, looking like bookends. Razouk beamed and got to his feet.

"Hola, papito," they said almost in unison. They both moved into his arms. Their hands went inside his shirt, their lips left red splashes of color on his face. He grinned like a schoolboy.

The blonde had a silver box in her hand. She opened it and scooped cocaine into a tiny gold spoon that dangled from a long chain around her neck. She held it to Razouk's nostril. He inhaled sharply. The powder vanished up his nose. He laughed and looked at me with watery eyes.

"This is my friend Omar," he said.

The other got to her knees and started to unzip his fly.

"No, no, no," he said, laughing. "Not here."

The blonde slithered at me with a heaping spoonful of powder. She held it under my nostril.

"No, thanks," I said, backing off and forcing a laugh. "I sell the stuff—I don't use it."

Razouk was watching me with a look of surprise.

Maybe I should have taken a blow, I thought, but the moment was over. I had known many drug dealers in my life; most of the biggest never touched the stuff. *You don't get high on your own supply*, was the saying. *Razouk had to know that*.

Taking dope for an undercover agent opens the door to all kinds of problems, not the least of which is that you are violating the law you are enforcing. I had known undercover agents who had been fired and jailed when they tested positive for drug use. The only official exception to this rule was *if* you *believed* that your life was in danger and you *had* to take drugs in order not to blow your cover. Even with that limited permission, there were cases on record of undercover agents in deadly situations who— rather than face the shooflies and suits and explain their actions—refused to take drugs and paid with their lives. Paranoid drug dealers hip to the rules killed them on the spot.

"*¿Como es tu nombre?*" said the woman, snuggling up to me, one hand inside my shirt, the other probing beneath my belt, rubbing in larger and larger circles.

Was she looking for a wire, a weapon, or Wonderboy?

"Omar," I said, fighting to keep a relaxed smile on my face.

Up close, her makeup was a coat of paint not quite thick enough to hide the corrosion; her cheap perfume so pungent that I had to fight nausea.

"*¿Arabe, no?*" she said, her thick tongue wet-licking my earlobe.

"Come, Omar," said Razouk, "I have a private suite in the rear. That one can suck the peel off a banana. It's already paid for."

His arm was around the other twin's neck. Her hand was inside his pants. The two moved together toward the door as if they were in a three-legged race.

"Thank you, my friend," I said, disentangling myself from the banana sucker as gently as I could. "I just don't feel in the mood."

"Omar, you disappoint me," said Razouk, giving me a cool look. He shrugged. "Suit yourself."

The trio—both women now busily groping Razouk—managed to get through the door.

I was alone. My mind was full of *could haves* and *should haves*—but it was too late. There are no second chances in this business. The Mossad tape recorder was rolling. If my plan worked, Razouk was going to end up in an American court on trial for his fucking life. And according to the DEA regs, an undercover agent who pops some banana sucker ends up with his own ass on trial. A good defense attorney would make me look like Son of Sam with a banana instead of a gun, and Bydon would add Section 6012, (b) (6), Moral Turpitude, to the rest of the charges against me.

Two of Razouk's men suddenly appeared in the doorway. The one called Bruno had the attaché case with my winnings.

"Come with us," he said curtly.

23

"Señor Razouk asked that I escort you to your apartment, Señor Legassi," said Bruno, opening the rear door. He spoke with a mixed French and Italian accent. We had just arrived in Razouk's limo at the front of my building, a relatively new high-rise not far from El Museo de Bellas Artes and the American embassy.

"Not necessary," I said.

I grabbed the case and limped quickly across the sidewalk. Inside the hallway I picked up a morning copy of *Clarín*, the daily newspaper, from a pile on the concierge's desk. As I waited for the elevator door to close I saw that the limo was still out front. Bruno was watching me through the glass doorway.

The newspaper headlines hit me like a punch in the face: DEA AGENT MURDERED BY COLOMBIAN DRUG TRAFFICKERS.

The name René Villarino leaped out at me. By the time I reached the apartment on the fifteenth floor I had read the whole thing. The story quoted an Associated Press report:

DEA Administrator Hubbel Whitfield Jr. announced today in a nationally televised news conference that an intensive undercover investigation has revealed that the Medellín cocaine cartel was responsible for the torture murder of undercover agent René Villarino, and that high-level Colombian government officials may be involved in a cover-up. A multi-agency task force of law enforcement officers, under the direction of

Whitfield, is to focus on the cartel in what promises to be one of the biggest manhunts in South American history since the hunt for Butch Cassidy and the Sundance Kid in Bolivia.

Whitfield denied rumors of Villarino's death having anything to do with an alleged new killer cocaine called "the White Queen" . . .

The rest of the story was about outraged Colombian government denials and interviews with all the usual media drug experts.

That son of a bitch suit had made another media play.

You don't know who did it, so blame it on the Medellín cartel—the world's Bogey Man. Who could doubt that?

René died right after meeting Razouk. I could feel his presence in Razouk's private dining room. I could sense it in the way Razouk looked at me. There was no link to Colombians or Razouk would have said something when I laid my Colombian story out for him.

I grabbed the phone and dialed the operator. There was still no direct dialing from Buenos Aires, except from the embassy. I slammed the phone down. *Shit! I needed the secure phone.*

I opened the attaché case. My money, in packets of hundred-dollar bills, was neatly stacked. I took ten thousand and shoved it into my jacket pocket. I found the French nine-millimeter automatic Paolo had given me and slipped it into my belt covering it with my sport jacket.

I left the building through a rear hallway door that led to a series of backyards. I moved through the deserted early morning streets to where I had parked the black Camaro with diplomatic plates—on Avenida Ocampo, about three blocks distant. I was in big trouble if Razouk's people saw me, but I had to get into the embassy quickly—no stopping at gates.

The engine roared to life. I raced through back streets keeping my eyes on the rearview.

The Marine on desk duty at the embassy was a good ole boy from Mobile, Alabama. He had seen me in many disguises before, but this time demanded to see my identification.

"That you in theah, Mr. Lee-vine? That's yo best getup yet."

Within minutes I was in my office. My desk was piled with messages and mountains of reports. I touched nothing. I grabbed the secure phone and telephoned Stratton's home in Virginia. It was about five in the morning there. Stratton answered on the second ring.

"Yeah." He sounded wide-awake.

"I just read the story in the news."

"Where the fuck are you?" His voice was controlled fury.

"Following René's tracks."

"Who the hell you think you are disappearing for two fucking months?"

"Bobby, you know what I'm trying to do. Believe me, it was totally out of my hands . . ."

"It's out of your hands now—I'm officially ordering you off the case and back to Washington."

"Whitfield's statement *can't* be true."

"If I were you, Levine, I'd forget about this case and hire myself a lawyer. You knew how bad they wanted to do you—you just laid your head on the chopping block—AWOL, funds missing from the safe."

"The funds are back."

"Too fucking late. Inspectors already inventoried your office."

"How does Whitfield know the cartel did it?"

"If you'd been where the fuck you were supposed to be you'd know. Forrest Gregg's informants have come up with positive evidence."

"What kind of informants? Did you talk to them?"

"DEA talk to a *CIA* asset? Besides you better fucking pray that Forrest is right. The only reason they haven't officially charged you with theft, AWOL, and—from what I hear—a whole bunch of other shit, is that they think *El Búfalo* ordered René's death, and they need *you* to testify against him on the drug charge."

"Bullshit! I don't believe it. *El Búfalo* is after the White Queen just like René was."

"Maybe that's why he had him killed."

"Wrong, Bobby! That's not the man's style. *El Búfalo* would've walked into his office and blown him away, or blown up his whole fucking building. It's all too pat, too easy to blame the Medellín cartel. Every fucking politician who ever ran for office claims the Medellín cartel has a hit contract on him; every dope bust—from Podunk, Iowa, to Eldorado, Oklahoma, is linked to the Medellín cartel. It's bullshit!"

"That's what headquarters believes, that's our marching orders. And as long as you're DEA, it's *your* marching orders."

"Oh no, Bobby—not you too. And what about the White Queen?"

"It's all coming out of Colombia."

"The spooks tell us that too? I'm only surprised they didn't blame it on Castro."

"You're not listening to me, are you? As far as headquarters is concerned—case fucking closed! We know *who* done it, we just gotta make 'em pay."

"The whole thing stinks."

The line was quiet for a long moment.

"Levine, I am tired. I gave you a direct order."

"What happens if we never had this conversation?"

"Then I'll be ordered to send a man down there to take charge of your office. Your records will be seized. DEA will prosecute you."

"And what happens if I don't do it?"

"Insubordination. Failure to obey a direct order. You're history."

The line went silent. I looked around the walls of my office, unable to think of anything to say. There was a photo of me and Vice-President George Bush when I worked for him on the South Florida task force, next to it was a photo of a group of deep cover agents receiving awards—eight of us. I was wearing a beat-up leather jacket and had a shaggy black beard. Next to me stood René, as impeccably dressed as ever, a thin, knowing smile on his lips, his arm over my shoulder.

"I stuck my neck out for you, Levine, level with me—what exactly are you doing?"

"I built a cover story," I blurted. "I met the people René was with, just before he disappeared. I don't know where it's taking me."

"Talk to me, Mike, you're not telling me anything. Give me something—names, dates, places. Not this vague undercover bullshit. If I agree, I'll go to the wall for you."

"You've been around as long as I have. You know this whole thing is a cover-up. René told no one but Whitfield what he was doing and his cover got blown."

"What are you saying?"

"That's exactly what happened—right or wrong?"

Stratton was silent.

"I trust you, Bobby, but there's no way you can keep quiet and back me at the same time, or they end up targeting you too. When I'm inside and have proof they can't deny, and the trap is set—you'll be the first to know."

"You're committing suicide," he said. "Are you thinking about your kids?"

"I gotta go now," I said. I didn't want to hear his words.

I hung up.

I replaced the five-thousand-dollar petty cash fund in the safe and was in my car and rolling toward the security gate before 8:00 a.m. As the Marine guard wheeled open the heavy steel gate, he signaled me with his white-gloved hand to stop so that another car could enter.

CIA Station Chief Forrest Gregg's Jaguar rolled through the gate. It slowed as it approached. The tinted black window of the rear passenger seat started to lower. I pressed the accelerator, whipping past him and out the gate. I sped around the small park across the street and into the early morning traffic on Avenida del Libertador. A maniac driver, spinning rubber and skidding through traffic is nothing out of the ordinary for Buenos Aires.

I parked the car a half mile from my apartment and walked, actually limped, home. There was nothing left to do but wait. The next move was Razouk's.

———

I awoke with a start, my pager beeping on the nightstand beside my bed. The doors to my balcony were wide open, showing a murky night sky. The digital clock radio showed ten past midnight. The pager had the capacity to store twelve phone calls. I pressed the message button. The screen showed five urgent messages to call Israel, the first coming at 7:00 p.m. I had slept through all of them.

The first signs of dawn were lighting the sky when the Mossad returned my call.

"Omar," said the voice. "It is extremely urgent that you check into your Buenos Aires office."

The connection was broken. If Razouk had the line *chupada*—tapped—which I had to assume he did, he would know nothing.

At 10:50 a.m. I entered Aguirre S.A., a small business office on the third floor of a high-rise office building on Avenida Córdoba.

I had limped the crowded streets for an hour before entering the building and noticed nothing out of the ordinary.

I opened the door to room number 333 and found myself in a reception area. A receptionist behind thick glass said, "Good morning, Mr. Legassi," as if she knew me well. She opened the door to a carpeted hallway with several closed doors. "Your office is at the end. There's a message waiting for you."

I opened my office door. In a trim gray business suit, behind a desk, sat Shoshanna. Her face was as taut as piano wire, there were dark circles under her eyes. The venetian blinds on two large windows had been drawn shut. A grimy recessed ceiling light cast the room in a harsh glare.

"Shoshanna," I said, moving toward her.

"No. Claudia Cezanni."

Her cold professional voice stopped me in my tracks.

"Okay, Claudia."

"You *must* respond to messages, Omar."

"You going to say hello?"

"This is not child's play," she snapped. "Someone has made extraordinary worldwide efforts in the last twenty-four hours to obtain everything available on Omar Legassi. Police reports have been pulled, all the photos and fingerprints copied. Inquiries are being made in every country that Omar Legassi had ever set foot in. We've never seen this kind of clandestine power before. We are certain that your phone is tapped and that you are under twenty-four-hour surveillance. Have you noticed anything?"

"No," I said, feeling foolish.

The phone on the desk rang. She answered it.

"*Aguirre. Buenos días—Cómo no. ¿De parte de quién?—Sí Señor, se lo digo.*" The fluency of her Spanish reminded me of how little I knew about this woman.

She covered the phone.

"A Señor Razouk for you."

I activated the Mossad recorder wallet and held it to the phone.

"Hello, my brother," I said, aware of Shoshanna studying me.

"Omar, my favorite camel trader," said Razouk. "I was afraid that you might be a little upset with my rudeness. Please forgive me. I'm not so young anymore, and I'm afraid I spoil myself when it comes to taking advantage of the moment."

"Perfection is not for the pure of soul . . ." I said, quoting Gibran again. "No apology necessary."

" 'There may be virtue in sin' is the rest of the quote," said Razouk, laughing.

"I hope so," I said.

"Listen, my friend, some business associates have expressed interest in your project. Why don't I send a car for you to your office at one p.m. My plane is already at Aeroparque."

"Plane?"

"We'll dine at El Cerro in Montevideo. It's a short flight."

"Fine," I said, "but let's make it at my apartment building. Your driver knows it."

"By the way—the woman who answered the phone?"

"Yes?"

"Her accent is Middle East, no?"

"You never cease to amaze me, Mario."

"*Ttreq ssalama,*" he said.

"*Bessalama,*" I answered, and it occurred to me as I hung up that he had used a phrase that one says to someone leaving on a long journey.

I hung up and repeated the conversation to Shoshanna.

"I only have a few minutes," I said. "Am I going to see you?"

"Of course, Señor Legassi, I'm your secretary."

"No, I mean tonight," I said, trying to see the woman of the soft, hungry kiss and seeing only the cold hard eyes of a professional spy.

"Omar," she said, her expression softening. "Focus on what you are doing. Come back safe, and we'll see."

24

TEN MINUTES AFTER TAKEOFF I REALIZED THAT SOMETHING WAS WRONG. Montevideo was less than a half-hour flight eastbound over water. I glanced out the window and realized that we were over jungle and heading north.

I tried the cockpit door. It was locked. I banged on it.

A voice over the speaker said, "Señor Legassi, please return to your seat. The location of the meeting has been changed. Señor Razouk sends his apologies."

I sat back in my seat and fought a rising feeling of panic. René had boarded a private plane in Brazil and then vanished without a trace. I quickly activated the Mossad recorder, leaving it in my inside jacket pocket, then set the pager to emit the signal that the Mossad claimed they could track anywhere in the world. I leaned forward in my seat and, speaking into my jacket, dictated the time of takeoff, our approximate direction, and the model of the airplane—a Gates Learjet.

Once again, as had happened more times than I cared to remember, Oliver Hardy's line to Stan Laurel flashed: *A fine kettle of fish you've gotten us into now, Stanley.*

Two hours earlier, Bruno had picked me up outside my apartment building and taken me to Aeroparque for my flight to Montevideo. Two Argentine pilots were finishing their preflight as I was deposited at the gangway. Bruno showed me to my seat and then left me alone in the plane. The pilots sealed themselves off in the cockpit without ever saying a word to me. At the time, my only thought had been that Razouk ran a tight operation. Now the whole picture looked ominously different and out of my control.

At 3:25 p.m. I felt us begin our descent. We had been flying for approximately an hour and twenty-five minutes. The Gates Learjet had a top speed of a little more than 500 miles per hour, which put us about seven to eight hundred miles north-north-west of Buenos Aires—somewhere in the Matto Grosso jungle, in either Paraguay or Brazil.

The plane touched down smoothly. Dense jungle foliage whipped by.

"I'm on a runway," I muttered into the recorder. "Jungle growth almost to edge of the concrete. Rolls of green camouflage piled alongside. Probably used to conceal the runway."

The plane taxied to a stop. A Range Rover with two men in khakis, one armed with an AK-47 slung over his shoulder, the other with a holstered automatic on his hip, were waiting. I flicked the switch on the pager, shutting off the tracking signal. Criminals were as high-tech as the governments hunting them: sophisticated electronic devices that could detect the signal were common.

The engines died. The fuselage door slid open and the jungle heat clobbered me. It was like stepping into a steam bath.

"Welcome, Señor Legassi," said the man with the automatic. "I am Henri." He was tanned a deep bronze, with dirty blond hair tied in a ponytail. The man with the AK-47 had dark skin and flat Indian features that were just visible beneath the brim of his bush hat. He made a quick study of me.

"Please," said Henri, leading the way toward the Range Rover.

"Can you tell me where I am?" I asked, conscious of Mr. AK-47 behind me.

"Señor Razouk will tell you everything you need to know."

During the drive I sat in the front passenger seat. We followed a road of hard-packed red clay that wound through deep jungle beneath a heavy canopy of vegetation, at times completely blocking out the sun, at times becoming a fern pattern that looked like light gleaming through a finely patterned linen fabric. The car windows were up, the air conditioner was running, and a cassette played classical guitar music. I had the feeling that I had entered another world.

After a few minutes I heard the drone of turbine engines. I caught a glimpse of huge generators. Enough to light a small city.

Minutes later the road curved sharply and we burst into a large clearing. The sight stunned me. Ahead lay a compound completely enclosed by a heavily camouflaged wall topped with a mishmash of concertina wire and jungle vines. A man peered down at us with field glasses from a guard tower. A heavy steel gate painted a dark green was opened electronically and we drove inside.

The size of the compound was staggering. In the near distance there was a series of long, low buildings around which were caged areas where an array of animals roamed. Some, like the black-and-gold-spotted jaguars and the large rodent capybara, I recognized, others were like nothing I'd ever seen before. Men loaded a caged jaguar onto a large flatbed truck.

In the far distance I could see what looked like a sprawling modern glass building.

"Here we are," said Henri. He parked in front of a small square building a dozen yards past the gate. "Come with me."

I followed him inside. Mr. AK-47 followed close behind, his hand resting on the gun's housing.

The inside of the building was air-conditioned. A bald man in a khaki uniform seated at a desk looked up from a computer screen.

"Señor Legassi," he said, his eyes coolly appraising me. "Welcome. Please remove everything from your pockets. All your jewelry, and anything else you might have in your possession."

"May I ask why?"

"Your things, Señor, please," he insisted.

Omar Legassi was in no position to protest. I was searched and every item in my possession carefully examined. I thought my heart would stop while Baldie handled the Mossad wallet and pager. Finally I was fingerprinted and photographed.

A half-hour later, trying to make sense of what was happening, I was driven farther into what seemed to be an animal sanctuary of some sort, except that it was heavily patrolled by armed guards.

I took the dark-stained cloth from my pocket and clutched it in my hand as a reminder of what the hell I was doing here in the first place.

Finally we reached one of two glittering glass buildings reflecting the rich green jungle. At one end, an immense glass dome towered above the rest of the structure. Beyond it I could see an ultramodern building that resembled a large oyster shell, something like the old Pan American Airlines terminal at JFK Airport in New York.

Henri led me along a long, tiled hallway that led through the building and into the glass dome. It was as if a giant bowl had been lowered over a corner of jungle creating a jungle within a jungle.

The place teemed with cackling, chattering wildlife. Brightly colored birds fluttered back and forth. Large white furry monkeys with flaming red faces peered down at me from the trees, some of which reached to the top of a dome that seemed two hundred feet high. Water cascaded into a large reflecting pool from a fifty-feet-high waterfall constructed of volcanic rock.

What the hell can this place have to do with the Triangle of Death?

"Wait here," said Henri. "Señor Razouk will be with you shortly." He turned before I could say a word and left me there alone.

The place seemed hotter and more humid than the jungle outside. Sweat drenched my black linen shirt. I peered around me. A trail of red clay curved off into dark green vegetation.

There was a sudden crashing in the bush. I had upset something large that I didn't think I wanted to meet. I noticed a metallic glint in the foliage. I could just make out a camera lens.

Of course they're watching you. Whatever they throw at you—stay in character. Stick to the role, live it, believe it, internalize it. You're here, wherever here is, because you said the magic words. Someone wants the deal. Omar the fucking oil man is here.

Suddenly I was startled by a flash of white above me. I froze. A giant bird dove at me from the top of the green canopy with a deafening screech. Its wings opened to at least a seven-foot wingspan just as it was about to hit the ground. It gripped a large lizard in talons longer than a grizzly bear's claws.

All this happened within ten feet of me. The bird's wide amber eyes glared at me in defiance; white feathers on its head fanned into an angry crest. With another piercing screech it took off toward the top of the trees carrying its still writhing prey, its wings pounding the air loudly.

"Exquisite creature, isn't she?" said a soft woman's voice behind me.

I turned with a start. The woman standing in front of me was at least as tall as I was with short-cropped wavy blond hair combed back from her high forehead, accentuating an aquiline nose. Her skin was tanned honey brown and peeling from too much sun. She wore white loose-fitting cotton slacks and a man's white linen shirt with the sleeves rolled to her elbows. Her demeanor seemed warm, almost friendly, except for her sharp ice-green eyes. I had seen those cold eyes somewhere before.

"Harpy eagles are named after the predatory monsters of Greek mythology—half woman, half vulture." She spoke Spanish with a French accent.

"You startled me," I said, meeting her icy gaze, my mind groping for a memory that seemed just out of reach.

She moved slowly closer.

"Did you know that these birds are almost extinct?"

"No, I've never even seen one before."

"You've never been to the Amazon?"

"Only on business. I don't usually see much."

"Too bad."

She turned and walked a few feet into the foliage, stopped and reached an arm up. I was stunned to see about six feet of emerald-green snake as thick as a man's arm slither onto her shoulders.

"I didn't introduce myself," I called. "My name is Omar Legassi. I'm supposed to meet Mario Razouk here."

"I know who you are."

In a stomach-wrenching flash, I remembered who *she* was.

It was almost twenty years ago, during the trial of Auguste Ricord in the Southern District Federal Court in Manhattan. I was in a witness room sequestered with a dozen other agents, waiting, not knowing whether or not I would be called to testify.

Jean Boulad, the French-born case agent, stuck his head in the door. "Half-hour recess," he said.

I moved, along with the others, toward the elevators and the cafeteria. The hallway outside the courtroom was jammed with attorneys, spectators, spies, and reporters from all over the world, as it had been from the beginning—a sea of faces. One face stood out.

A young woman, an unusual beauty with blond hair and green eyes, stood alone, almost hidden in the courtroom vestibule, staring in our direction as if willing us dead on the spot. The times in my life that I have looked into the eyes of rabid hatred are unforgettable—this was one of them.

"Who the fuck is that?" someone had asked Boulad as the elevator doors closed her from our view.

"Nadia Ricord. Auguste Ricord's daughter."

"I thought she was only thirteen."

"That's the legal one. He had this one with his Paraguayan mistress, then took her away from the mother. Educated her in France. Brought her up like she was his son."

"Ma-rone, you see the body on her? Definitely ain't no son."

"Don't think she wouldn't cut the fucking heart out of every man in this elevator, if she could. She's devoted to that fucking Nazi."

"If looks could kill," said someone, *"this elevator'd be a hole in the basement by now."*

"You look frightened to death—Señor Omar Legassi."

"I've never been this close to a big green snake before."

She laughed softly and stroked the large green head. The serpent seemed to stretch the way a cat would, emitting an audible hiss. "I assure you, you are a lot more dangerous to him than he is to you."

If she was Nadia Ricord, she would have recognized me by now.

"Have his fangs been removed or something?" I asked.

"Have yours?" she said. "He's an emerald tree boa—neither poisonous nor dangerous."

She gently removed the big snake from her shoulders, handling its weight easily, lowering it to the foot of a tree. It immediately glided upward, like magic, becoming invisible in the foliage.

"Legassi. What an odd name. What is its origin?"

"I was born in Morocco."

"One would think that a Moroccan would be a little more accustomed to heat," she said, removing a handkerchief from her pocket. "Please," she said, handing it to me.

"I come from desert people," I said, wiping my forehead. The handkerchief had a musky scent. "What is this place?"

"This place?" Her thoughts seemed to drift for a moment. Her eyes glanced upward. "Let's just say it's a home for endangered animals."

"Does it have a name?"

"Yes, the Amazon Wildlife Federation, but you won't find it in the phone book. The name is only for the purpose of linking us to other like-minded organizations around the world. The security of our effort depends on anonymity."

"I've never seen anything like it. Señorita, where can I find Señor Razouk?" I asked.

"Call me Nadia," she said, the name a stomach-sinking confirmation of my fears. "He'll meet you at the residence. In the meantime take advantage of your visit here. You'll see some of the rarest wildlife on earth. You never know, you may not get another chance."

I had to be in Paraguay. And this must be Auguste Ricord's famous compound. His daughter must still live here.

She moved past me toward a stand of tall trees, making a kissing sound with her lips. One of the furry bald-headed monkeys swung down from high up in the trees. Its face, if not for the fiery red color, was amazingly human in its expression. It moved across the open ground and up into her strong arms, nuzzling her like a child.

"Hello, Juanito," she murmured, nuzzling it back. "Here, my *papito*," she said, fishing a small piece of something from her shirt pocket, which the monkey examined carefully and then ate in a dainty manner.

"Juanito is an uakari monkey, Señor Legassi, a peaceful, gentle creature that needs rain forest to roam. All he wants to do is eat fruit and make love—true, *papito*?"

She kissed the creature gently on its forehead, her eyes fixed on mine. "Uakaris are now so rare that even Amazonian Indians rarely see them, yet man continues to hunt him."

"It's a shame," I said, at the moment a lot more worried about myself than Juanito. "Omar. Please."

"Yes, a terrible shame," she said. She lowered the monkey to the ground. It loped off toward the trees. She straightened and faced me again.

"Do I look familiar to you, Omar?"

"No," I said. "If I had ever seen you before, I would never have forgotten it."

"It's odd," she said slowly, her eyes studying my face. "The way you look at me, as if you know me."

"People often misread me," I said.

"And I can see why. You have an actor's face—a face that can easily change its appearance."

Suddenly she was looking past me. "Turn slowly, Omar," she said, "Not too fast, you'll frighten it."

I turned and saw a little animal that looked like a teddy bear with a long upturned nose, standing perfectly still, staring intently into the foliage.

"It's a coati," she whispered. "A baby." She was standing close behind me. "Can you see what it sees, what has it mesmerized?"

I saw nothing but masses of tangled shades of green.

Then I saw it.

At first I thought it was a large rust-colored insect fluttering against the field of green. The coati looked as if it was about to pounce.

Suddenly the vegetation exploded outward. There was a flash of pale green and a snake had the little animal by its nose, hissing. Its tail was a bright rust color that it had used to lure the coati close enough for the strike. The poor little animal's legs were convulsing as the snake began to swallow it, headfirst.

Instinctively, I moved to save it.

"No!" she said sharply, her fist pressing on my chest with a strength that surprised me. "Leave it alone!" She stared enraptured as the little animal, jerking spasmodically, was slowly swallowed by the snake.

"A palm viper," she said. "In nature many things are not what they seem. We see our own dark side and it makes us uncomfortable. But this is the way it was meant to be.

"You've had a long trip, Omar. You'd probably like to freshen up. I'll take you to your room." She started toward the glass doors.

I followed Nadia out of the dome and through long hallways, passing people in white laboratory coats and armed men in khaki uniforms, all of whom nodded and lowered their eyes. She remained cool and aloof, nodding slightly at each, never uttering a word.

We left the rear of the building and she led me along a landscaped path to the oyster-shaped building. We entered through glass doors into a large main salon, with two staircases spiraling upward in different directions.

"This is the residence," she said, leading me up the staircase. When we reached the top, her hand pressed the small of my back to guide me down the first hallway. The floor was tiled in a large diamond pattern. I found myself unconsciously placing my right foot in every other diamond.

I needed all the help I could get.

I fought an inner battle to relax and live my role. I told myself that if she had recognized me, I would be dead already. How could I possibly think she would remember me? Only a glimpse among a dozen agents as elevator doors closed—thirty or forty pounds heavier, clean-shaven, and twenty years younger.

Then I thought of Baldie and his computer. He had my fingerprints and all my identification—how well was my cover going to hold up? And in my mind's eye I saw the lonely house on the Pampas, the black writhing trail of maggots, feeding and breeding in what was left of René.

Nadia opened a door and led me into a spacious suite with a large double bed and sliding glass doors that opened onto a balcony overlooking the jungle. A terry cloth robe lay on the bed.

"You can freshen up and take a shower. I'll have someone pick up your clothes. They'll be cleaned and returned within the hour."

"I hadn't planned on staying," I said.

"Do you want to leave, Omar?"

"I came to have lunch with Señor Razouk."

"He'll be along shortly," she said, taking a step closer to me. "Perhaps you're afraid of me, Omar."

"Should I be?" I asked, a sharp reminder that a deep cover identity is only an elaborate illusion, like the russet tail of the palm viper; that to confuse illusion with reality is fatal. Perhaps René made that crucial mistake.

I moved away from her, tearing off my wet shirt, taking the opportunity to show her the dragon tattoo—one of my Omar Legassi certificates of authenticity.

She moved near me again, her fingertip tracing Omar's dragon.

"Does it signify something special?"

"Yes . . . that I too am an animal lover."

"That speaks well of you, Omar," she said, her hand lingering on my arm.

As she left the room I again thought of the palm viper. And it occurred to me that I had played the viper's role for twenty years, as had René, and that sooner or later I was going to lure something bigger than I could handle, and I was going to end up dinner.

25

It was well after nightfall and still no Razouk. Since Nadia left I hadn't seen a soul. *Not a good sign.* There was a phone in the suite, but who could I call?

I slipped outside onto the balcony to check out any possible escape routes. The area around the residence was well lit and patrolled by armed men handling ferocious black dogs—a breed that looked like a cross between a rottweiler and a wolf. I was about thirty feet above the ground. Below the balcony one of these beasts snarled furiously, spun at the end of his chain, and jerked upward. A bright light shone up at me. I shielded my eyes. A guard praised him softly.

I retreated back inside and lay down on the bed in the darkness, adrenaline coursing through me—flight or fight. I could do neither. I had to get myself under control or it would be my doom. I kept telling myself that there wasn't even a hint that she'd recognized me or that my cover was blown.

Stay in character. Stick to the role that got you here.

I wondered for the umpteenth time in my career what it was that possessed seemingly normal people to become deep cover agents: to dive deep with no lifeline into a world where a slight flaw in your act or your cover meant death. Why did I have to come as close to death as I dared, like a bullfighter who let the horns come closer at every pass until they drew blood? Did I have something to prove? Did René?

What I knew for certain was that the high of it all was addictive. It was a drug no different than the White Queen—an incredible high followed by an intolerable low, followed by the need to experience the high again.

I calmed myself as I often did with the words of an old South Bronx pool hustler, "The Great Gubi," a mentor of my nasty youth, who said: *The bad news about death is that we're all gonna die; the good news is that you're the last to know.*

Finally, after five hours of waiting, there was a light knock at the door. An Amazonian Indian woman speaking in badly garbled Spanish brought my freshly cleaned and pressed clothing and asked me to follow her.

I quickly dressed, zipped the Mossad billfold shut, activating the recorder, and slid it into my inside jacket pocket. The woman led me through a series of empty, silent hallways to a set of large double doors of carved mahogany that opened into an elegant dining room.

At the head of a long rectangular table sat Mario Razouk. On either side of him sat two elderly men, who turned to stare at me. Around the edge of the room in shadows were a half-dozen lean, well-dressed young men. Bruno stood directly behind Razouk.

"Omar," said Razouk without getting to his feet. "A thousand greetings and *salaamas*. Please, take a seat."

How should Omar react? Angry? Furious? Curious?

"What's going on?" I said, taking the one available seat at the middle of the table.

Razouk signaled and a procession of servants filed into the room carrying trays of food and selections of wine and champagne. A rolling tray was brought in on which lay a thick-bodied fish, which looked about five feet long, lavishly garnished with exotic vegetables and fruit.

"Please, please Omar," said Razouk raising his hand, "Have you ever eaten pirarucu, my brother? The most delicious fish in the Amazon. I promise, you taste it you won't want to talk." In Arabic he added, "I ordered it especially for you."

The glow in his eyes was that of a man who was looking forward to a lot more than just the pleasure of a meal. At least an apology was due, yet there wasn't anything apologetic in his words or manner—he hadn't even introduced me to his companions.

Food was placed in front of me. I had to eat like a man who had no reason to fear anything. *Omar Legassi would be under con-*

trol. The dryness of my mouth and throat made it difficult to swallow. I gulped a morsel of fish down with wine.

"Good, no?" said Razouk, his mouth full.

For the next half hour we ate silently. I could feel them studying me. Looking at myself through their eyes and seeing every flaw in my act was frightening, at first. I was convinced I would never leave that room alive. But gradually, as always happened during twenty years of undercover work, it was as though DEA Special Agent Michael Levine vanished, sunk deep into a corner of my mind where he couldn't get in the way, and I *was* Omar Legassi.

I looked at the men around me through Omar's eyes, with Omar's point of view. I wanted to make a few million dollars, these men were my opportunity to do that. I actually began to enjoy the remaining part of the meal. The pirarucu wasn't bad.

After coffee, pastries, and liqueurs were served, Razouk broke the silence.

"The reason you are here, Omar, is that we are giving your proposition serious consideration."

I sensed a tone of suspicion in his voice and decided that it was time for Omar to go on the offensive. *Only an undercover agent would take this much shit without blowing his stack.*

"I don't know where *here* is," I said curtly. "I thought *here* was supposed to be Montevideo, eight hours ago. And I came to do business, not to be fed, fingerprinted, and photographed."

"The gentleman is correct—we have been extremely rude," said the man on my right with a thick German accent. He was a slight man in his early seventies, with thick white hair and pale blue eyes that at the moment seemed mildly amused.

"We haven't even introduced ourselves. I am Dr. Carlos Hess."

The other man opposite me, a pasty-faced, balding man with a pencil mustache, in his late sixties, scowled at the others. "I think we have wasted enough time." He spoke with a French accent. "The fact that we have put you through some inconvenience for security purposes, Señor Legassi, shouldn't surprise you. The burning question—before business can be discussed—is whether or not your offer is real."

I took out my four-inch gold cigarette holder and slowly fitted a cigarette, lit it, and took a deep drag before answering. "Listen, whatever-your-name-is, who the hell said I wanted to do any business with *you?*"

"Omar," began Razouk apologetically.

The Frenchman interrupted sharply. "Where have you been for the past two years, Señor Legassi? You suddenly disappear and then reappear in the oil business?"

"If your question is, *where* have I been? the answer is, none of your fucking business. And the fact that you don't know everything about me should indicate that perhaps I'm a little smarter than you are."

"You told Monsieur Razouk you had been working recently with the Colombian cartels. Our sources say it is a lie," persisted the Frenchman.

"Excuse me," I said. "I don't believe I caught your name."

"Sarti."

Quick looks told me that there was no love lost between Sarti and the others. *Something to exploit.*

"Look, Sarti," I said. "I can give you names, dates, and times of my last transaction, but *if* I did—and you were smart—you would have nothing to do with me. The fact that I did a deal with them and your sources could find nothing should be reassuring to you."

"Somehow it is not, Monsieur."

"Let's cut out the bullshit!" I snapped. "You say your name is Sarti; he says his name is Hess . . . I don't know if those are your real names, nor do I give a *fuck*. My only concern—*if* we do business—is, can *you* deliver? The way *I* set up a transaction there will be no way that you will be exposed to any risk whatsoever. So I don't see what difference it makes what you know about me . . . unless you want to fucking marry me."

Razouk's laughter boomed.

"The more you talk, the more difference it makes to me," snapped Sarti angrily.

"Calm down, Jean," said the German, his pale blue eyes twinkling. "I'm interested in hearing what Omar has to say. How *would* you arrange such a transaction?"

You can never go wrong tweaking a Frenchman in front of a German and vice versa.

I blew smoke across the table in the direction of Sarti before answering.

"Let's speak hypothetically," I said. "Let's say I do have access to several million barrels of oil. . . . But before I go any further, do I understand that I'm speaking to people with access to co-caine base, or is this entire trip bullshit?" I directed the last at Sarti.

"Hypothetically we have as much as you could ever want," said Hess, enjoying himself.

"Señor Razouk asked if I could prove I had the oil. I can. Can you do the same?"

"Of course," said Hess.

"This is idiotic," fumed Sarti.

It was time to wiggle the russet-colored tail of the viper.

I ran down the details of the trade: black gold for white; oil for cocaine base, emphasizing that by retrading the oil for arms, not only would they make as much as five and six times the money that an ordinary sale of cocaine base would yield, but the money trail would vanish into thin air.

"Is this not *precisely* what we need?" said Razouk.

"But you still did not answer my question," insisted Sarti. "How can we do this transaction without being exposed to risk?"

"That depends on whether or not you trade the oil for arms instead of just selling it. By trading it for arms with oil-poor countries like North Korea and then selling the arms back to the Middle East, you can make six and seven times your profit. All that is up to you, your connections and your ingenuity."

"You *still* haven't answered my question," said Sarti.

"It is so simple," I said, "by now I thought you'd have under-stood without me having to explain." Sarti fumed; Omar Legassi grinned.

"All parties to the transaction meet at an isolated location that is mutually agreeable," I continued. "Whatever money is to be transferred is brought to that location. The oil, cocaine, and arms are delivered to locations far from us—*with* our authorization—but we touch nothing illegal.

"As far as your part of the deal goes, the only thing an investi-gation could ever prove is that you sold some oil. And even proving that would take a major miracle. The variables are en-tirely up to your imagination, gentlemen, but I think you'll agree: The idea is foolproof."

There was a long silence. Sarti was fuming. I had made the whole affair something personal, between him and me. The friction worked for me, keeping me on edge, sharp, thinking clearly.

"And what would stop us from cutting you out, Monsieur Legassi, and going directly to the oil source ourselves?" said Sarti.

"It would be extremely stupid," I said, "for some very obvious reasons. First of all, if you don't already have the identity of my source, just trying to find him would alert Interpol and another dozen police and Intelligence agencies to your activities. Second, the oil dealers don't want to touch cocaine, not to mention cocaine base—they're not drug dealers. I am.

"My bargain with them is to convert the coca base to finished cocaine and then sell it in the U.S. or Europe, out of which I take part of my commission. In other words, for *my* money, I run *all* the risks—which is what you gentlemen are trying to avoid. Am I correct?"

Razouk beamed. He looked around the table as if to say, *Did I tell you? The man is a fucking genius.* "Excellent presentation, Omar," he said. "We owe you an apology."

"Forget the apology. I'm being pressured for time. Do I have your authorization to tell my contacts in the Middle East that the deal is confirmed?"

"Just a moment," said Sarti. "Perhaps your presentation was a little too excellent for a man of your background, Monsieur Legassi."

He was a very clever man. He'd just hit the major flaw in my cover. I had no choice but to attack, to back him up against a wall, or he would corner me with some logical questions to which I had no answer.

"Then tell me you're not interested!" I snapped, locking eyes with Sarti. "No problem. Just stop wasting my *fucking* time." It was time to throw my Sunday punch. I rose to my feet. "None of you even has the authority to turn me down, do you?" I said, looking at each of them.

Razouk flamed with embarrassment.

"We are a very large organization, Omar," he said. "There are complicated lines of authority, branches of distribution in many different countries. It is not that simple."

"If you can't say no, you certainly can't say yes, can you?"

They were silent.

I took another look around at each of them. Whoever had ordered René's death was not in this room. If these men didn't have the authority to approve this deal, they certainly wouldn't have the authority to order the murder of a DEA agent, which would theoretically unleash the whole might of the U.S. government against them. *Theoretically.*

"I'm afraid this has been a colossal waste of time," I said. I turned away from the others and faced Razouk. "I'm way behind schedule, I'd like to be flown back to Buenos Aires immediately."

Razouk hesitated. He glanced around at the others and got to his feet.

"Bruno!" he snapped. "Make arrangements to get Omar to my plane."

"Come, Omar," said Razouk, his hand on my elbow, leading me toward the door.

Razouk waited until we'd passed through a double set of doors and into the next corridor before he stopped. When he spoke, his voice was just above a whisper. "Omar, forgive me. It was impossible to make the situation clear to you before they decided to invite you. It was a surprise to me too."

I could not alienate Razouk. He was the hook holding me on to the mountain.

"Of course not," I said. "Because we don't do business does not mean we can't be friends." It was a line I had used a thousand times before—it had never failed.

He grinned and put his thick arm over my shoulder.

"Son-of-a-bitching camel trader. I think I love you."

"I don't kiss on the first date."

His laugh boomed down the long hallway.

"Listen to me, my brother," he said. "Don't act in haste. The reason a decision is difficult is that this organization is much larger than you can imagine, involving many people in many countries."

"So what do I have to do—wait for a stockholders' meeting? I told you, Mario, the Moroccans are pressuring me. They won't wait."

"The plan will be presented to the head of the organization in the morning," he said. "I'm with you. I think Hess feels the same way. Fuck the French pissant. I've known him twenty-five years and have never felt a second of warmth for him."

"I don't know what to think anymore, Mario."

"Don't think, Omar—wait. With us you will lack nothing for as long as you live. I want you to join us."

"This boss of yours," I said. "Why wasn't he here?"

"I don't want to lie to you. You may never meet him, Omar. Don't ask me to explain."

26

A TALL MAN WITH WRAPAROUND SUNGLASSES HAD STAYED BEHIND ME through two turns. I was halfway to the office of Aguirre Imports when I made him. Even hanging a block behind me on the crowded streets of downtown Buenos Aires, the guy was a little too tall to go unnoticed.

Bruno had dropped me off at my apartment building a couple of hours earlier at dawn. After a nap, shower, and shave, I had decided to play hare and hounds by window-shopping my way along the mile or so between my apartment and the office, using the shop windows as mirrors to check myself for a tail. If Razouk's people were as serious as I thought, they'd make every move in the book to insure that Omar Legassi was who he said he was. And sure enough, they didn't disappoint me—the hounds were out there waiting.

Hare and hounds is a game used to train undercover officers in the art of surveillance. The first and most important lesson is when you detect surveillance, you try to identify the hounds without revealing that you're aware of their presence. If they're pros and think that you've burned them, they'll drop off and be replaced with other hounds that you don't know. At least knowing who the watchers are may give you a moment's warning when they finally make their move.

A few blocks before the office I turned a corner, crossed the street, and stopped in front of a shoe store window. In the reflection I saw him make the turn and continue past me on the other side of the street.

I dodged traffic, quick-limping across the street and got behind him at the same time noticing in window reflections that two other men had fallen in behind me. I'd seen both before. Definite hounds, their eyes on me, their movements uncertain as they tried to guess mine.

That's three. There might be more.

I matched the casual speed of the man with the sunglasses, conscious of the comforting weight of the French automatic wrapped in the morning newspaper under my arm. He was at least six feet four, with light brown closely cropped hair. His neck was heavily pockmarked—the remnants of a bad case of acne or disease. The lightweight business suit was custom-tailored to a lean, powerful V-shaped torso. He wore soft-soled shoes; a little too casual for the suit.

A *karateka* sizes up a potential opponent by the fluidity and strength of his body movement. The old masters would meet an enemy on a road, and often, instead of doing battle, each would perform a *kata*, the martial arts dance that shows off the depth of their knowledge and technique. The performance always included a hint of secret and especially deadly moves reserved for real combat—should it happen. The real threat. More often than not they would end the encounter without ever having said an angry word, by bowing to each other, each already knowing who the winner would have been by the grace, strength, and precision of the dance.

The young man in front of me walked with the graceful, long-legged gait of a lean jungle cat. My forty-plus body moved with the pain of its years and a hundred injuries. Had I been confronted by him on a road in ancient, feudal Japan I probably would have bowed and just walked away.

As I reached my destination, he paused and looked across the street. I got a quick glimpse of his profile—a large hooked nose and a severely pockmarked face. Easy enough to remember.

Shoshanna was waiting in the outer office, her face even more drawn and taut than when I left her. She took my hand and led me into my office. The blinds were drawn tight. She leaned over the desk and turned up the volume on the radio.

"I was afraid for you," she said, her voice just above a whisper.

"I didn't know you cared," I said playfully.

"We have business to discuss."

There was a tense silence between us. I saw more than weariness in her eyes. I saw fear. I felt ashamed of myself. She was no different than me. Our jobs had become what we were—not what we did.

"You haven't slept, have you?"

"It doesn't matter," she said. "We have been under intense surveillance since yesterday."

"A big man with a pockmarked face?"

"He is the one in charge. I've identified at least seven others. They are also tapping the office phone and the phone at your apartment."

"That's a good sign," I said. I gave her a quick summary of what had happened at the jungle compound.

"No mention of the White Queen?" she asked.

"No deal yet. But you just gave me an idea how to make them move quickly."

"How?"

"Come home with me and you'll see," I said. "If they're listening to my phone, I'll give them an earful. Besides, I'm starting to worry that I'm living too much like an undercover agent—not a normal criminal's life. A date with my secretary is normal."

Her smile was at first reluctant and then a brilliant flash of the Shoshanna I had met in the Negev.

"Give me your wallet," she said, opening a desk drawer and laying an exact duplicate of my Mossad recorder-wallet on the desk. "This one has fresh batteries and tape. Our people will want to hear the recordings—particularly the German. We have a library of voiceprints of escaped Nazis." She saw the look on my face. "You agreed to this."

"When does this get delivered?" I asked, emptying my wallet.

"The diplomatic pouch leaves tonight."

"I was promised copies," I said, handing it to her.

"Don't worry about that now. You have other problems. Our Intelligence just discovered that Omar Legassi is a suspect in a murder in the United States. Four years ago in New Orleans—the execution of a man and woman. A matter involving drugs."

"What does that mean?"

"Omar was never officially charged, we missed the incident. It could be serious trouble for you."

"Is there an arrest warrant?"

"No, but the French Secret Service has the information as of this morning. We only received it minutes before they did."

"But that wouldn't blow my cover. All they know is I'm suspected of murder. That's a recommendation, not a problem."

"We don't know if they have a photo of the real Omar Legassi."

"If the Mossad couldn't get one, why think the French could?"

"Anything is possible—you must be aware of the danger."

"Meet me tonight," I said.

"I don't think that is a good idea."

"If I'm never seen with a woman," I said quickly, "they're going to think I'm gay or a CIA agent—or both." Her face softened. "You're my partner—I need you."

She smiled her beautiful desert smile.

"Do you know the Rond Point *confitería*?" I said.

"Yes."

"Meet me there tonight at ten."

"Shall I wear anything in particular?"

"Something you would wear if you were going out to have a good time with a big-time drug dealer."

"I understand." She laughed.

———

I walked the mile from downtown Buenos Aires to my apartment, again checking carefully for a tail. This time I saw nothing, which made me more nervous than before. The moment I hit the apartment I went straight to the phone. The Triangle of Death was about to learn the price of listening into the private conversations of a mind-fucker.

My first call was to Tito Garza's pager in the U.S. I tore my clothing off, lay down on the bed, and waited for him to call back. I fell into a deep sleep. The ringing of the phone woke me. The digital clock said 7:00 p.m.

"*¡Hable!*"

"You paged me?" said Garza's voice, perplexed.

"Yes. It's me, Omar," I said, confident that he would immediately recognize my voice. "This is *importantísimo*," I said, using our old telephone code that meant: *Someone is listening—play along!*

"I met those people last night. Phony bastards. A waste of

time. Call our friends in Medellín for me—we have to take a chance. We can't risk losing the Moroccans."

Garza reacted quickly. "Where the fuck have you been? They've been waiting for your call."

There was no one in the world I could count on to turn on a dime the way Garza could. His anger was real; it worked.

"When we're together I'll tell you everything."

"You have people upset, *Omar*. I need to talk to you. There's shit happening you should know about."

"Now is not the time."

"When will I see you?"

"I'll know when I get to Medellín. Tell them to be at the airport day after tomorrow. Twelve noon flight. Same as last time. I just want to move fast. There is an enormous amount riding on this."

"I understand, but I don't think *you* do. I *gotta* talk to you."

"You have my pager number?"

"Yes."

"Remember the codes?" I asked. We had a simple coding system that we had used to communicate with each other via pager.

"What the fuck do you think?"

When I hung up, I lay back on the bed.

If the Triangle of Death wanted the deal as much as I hoped, they'd move quickly now, so quickly that they'd be in chains in the belly of a Huey chopper on the first leg of a one-way trip to a U.S. prison before they knew what hit them.

It was five minutes to ten when I hit the street in front of my building. Rond Point was three blocks north along Libertador—a one-way boulevard eight lanes wide, an ocean of bright lights racing toward me. There could be an army watching me. I would see nothing.

Rond Point, one of the more chic *confiterías* of Buenos Aires, was a large, well-lit, spacious Art Deco combination coffeehouse and bar. It was, as usual, filled with trendy Argentines decked out in the latest European fashions. The men with gold Dupont lighters on the bar or table before them announcing their status; the women dressed in leather chic from Le Fauve with large rocks on their long-taloned fingers, Rolex watches on their wrists, and wild theatrical hairdos forming loops, pillars, and fans on their heads. It was a place where show business rubbed elbows with the underworld while slick hungry-eyed *chantas* worked the room like vultures looking for easy prey or leftovers.

At ten o'clock the place was nowhere near as crowded as it would get after midnight. There were a couple of tables available. Two muscular, well-dressed men who had entered behind me took the next table. I ordered a coffee and a Rémy Martin, lit a cigarette in my gold holder, and settled back. I glanced over at them and caught one eyeing me. He quickly looked away.

When Shoshanna arrived she caused an immediate stir. She wore pale blue harem pants of a filmy material and a matching blouse that exposed her midriff. The color highlighted her dark features and the flashing white of her teeth, and contrasted with the darker blue of the intricate designs tattooed on her hands and high cheekbones. In this gathering place for exotic birds, at that moment she was the most exotic of them all. I got up and moved toward the door to meet her.

"Omar," she said, smiling radiantly.

I kissed her cheek *porteño*-style and whispered, "Table next to ours."

"I know," she said.

At the table, after Shoshanna ordered a Perrier and a Scotch, I took her hand in mine. It was cold and tense.

"I just had to see you before I left," I said, loud enough for our neighbors to hear.

"I'm glad," she said, her eyes looking in my direction but taking in the whole room.

I kissed her hand.

"I should tell you something," she said too softly for anyone but me to hear.

"Sounds ominous."

"My husband's name was David," she said, leaning close to me. "He was killed less than a year ago."

"You must have loved him very much."

"He was my *bishert*—my soul mate. My soul died with him. He is buried somewhere in the Negev. I don't even have a grave to visit."

I wanted to say I was sorry, but the words seemed so foolish and inadequate. "At least you found love," I said. "I don't even know what it feels like."

Her eyes focused on me for a long moment. Her face seemed to soften. Then she looked beyond me and her eyes narrowed with fear.

"Quickly, turn on the recorder and let's go," she said.

This was no time to question her. I took out the wallet, withdrew a hundred-dollar bill and left it on the table, then activated the recorder.

We went out the door, arms around each other, acting like two people in a rush to devour each other. I noticed the two men behind us getting to their feet in a hurry.

The street ahead was bathed in bright lights and dark moving shadows from the torrent of traffic.

"They are all around us," said Shoshanna.

I held my arm around her shoulder and felt her as tense as coiled steel.

"So, what else is new?" I said.

"Too many," she said breathlessly. "Too close. Something has changed."

I felt her begin to tremble. I didn't question her.

I wish I had.

We continued in silence. We were a block from my building in the shadows of a clump of trees and a parked truck, when they struck.

They appeared like ghosts from the shadows. Car doors opened and slammed. Guns were shoved in our faces. We were surrounded.

I raised my arms. "My watch is worth twenty-thousand dollars," I said. "There is six thousand in my wallet. Just take it."

"Good evening—Señor Legassi, isn't it?"

The tall man standing before me spoke with a French accent. Passing headlights flashed on a face as pockmarked as the surface of the moon, a thin-lipped smile, and dead little eyes. He was the man who had followed me earlier that morning.

Hands frisked me quickly and professionally—they found my automatic in the small of my back. A purse Shoshanna was carrying was taken from her.

We were shoved into the front seat of a Ford Falcon parked at the curb. Moon Face and two others got in behind us. Guns were placed at the backs of our necks.

"Drive," ordered Moon Face.

"She has nothing to do with this," I said.

"Please do not speak until spoken to—I will direct you."

I was ordered to follow another Ford Falcon through dark side streets, then onto Libertador, where traffic became two-way. There were at least two other cars following us. We drove northbound passing El Hipódromo, the racetrack, River Stadium, then La Quinta, the presidential residence, going farther and farther out of Buenos Aires.

Out of the corner of my eye I saw Shoshanna's hand moving slowly toward her midriff, where she carried her little gun. I felt sick and helpless. We were a trigger-pull from death. I wanted to stop her. I wanted to tell her to stay cool; that this must be some kind of test or we would be dead already. But I could say nothing.

We had gone about a half-hour north of Tigre and out into the country, when the car in front of me slowed to a crawl. He turned into a narrow path in the grass. I followed. There were two sets of headlights behind me.

"Turn off the headlights!" ordered Moon Face.

The cars behind me also turned theirs off. The lead car left his on. I followed him for several hundred yards over a rough terrain until we came to the edge of the Paraná River at a place where I could see the lights of a lone house on the other side, in Uruguay.

The headlights flicked off plunging us into darkness.

I could feel the cold steel of the gun pressed into the base of my neck.

"Your papers say you are Claudia Cezanni, a Moroccan," said Moon Face.

"Yes," said Shoshanna.

"How well do you know Señor Legassi?"

"I am his secretary. I met him in Morocco. He offered me a job."

"Do you love him?"

"Don't be ridiculous."

"And you, Señor Omar Legassi—do you love this woman?"

"The woman works for me."

"Please answer my question."

"Of course not."

There was a long silence.

"Why is it that I think you are an impostor, Señor Legassi?" breathed Moon Face.

"Is that what this is all about?" I said. "Who sent you, Sarti?"

"I will give you ten seconds to tell us who you really are or I'm afraid we will have to kill this beautiful creature."

"Wait a second." I wanted to scream that I was Michael Levine and to forget the whole thing. But I couldn't. They would kill us on the spot.

"I'm waiting."

"I *am* Omar Legassi, and there is no need for this. If you have any problems—they're with me. She knows nothing about my business."

"How about you, Señorita—is he telling the truth?"

"How would I know?" said Shoshanna coolly. "I met him just a few weeks ago. He could be anyone."

I felt the gun click behind my ear.

"Anyone? Well then, this should be no problem for the Omar Legassi we know—only a little inconvenience."

The blast of the gun in the enclosed little space blinded and deafened me. I felt Shoshanna's hand twitching on my lap. Then it went still.

The world around me suddenly got hazy and started to move in slow motion, sound became distorted. A feeling of numbness settled over me. I knew that Shoshanna had just been murdered; that it was my fault. But something was blocking all feelings about it. In the next moment I expected to die and welcomed the relief.

The car door was pulled open. I was ordered out. I don't remember moving. The next thing I knew, I was standing there in the darkness. Car engines kicked to life. Headlights clicked on. Moon Face was suddenly in front of me, a silhouette in the headlights.

"Nothing personal, Señor Legassi. A shame. She was quite lovely. A lot of people in the *confitería* will remember the two of you. We used your gun, by the way. It has your prints on it and— I'd wager—also on all the remaining bullets. Her body and the gun will be left where no one will find it, unless we want them to. An insurance policy of sorts, no?"

He disappeared. I heard a car door slam. I didn't move. I couldn't move.

"We left you a car," said Moon Face's voice. "Drive carefully."

27

I WATCHED THEIR TAILLIGHTS GROW SMALLER AND DISAPPEAR, THE sound of the gun blast still ringing in my ears. I started walking, following them mindlessly. One foot in front of the other. The numbness spread through my body as if my brain had been injected with Novocain. I had no feeling of my feet hitting the road, no consciousness of direction, only the sensation of movement.

I must have walked for many hours that way. Something protective of my sanity would not allow me a clear thought. The sky was a pale slate color when I reached the outskirts of Buenos Aires.

My thoughts began in short painful spurts, like electricity trying to bridge broken wire. Sparks of images shot deep into my brain: Shoshanna entering Rond Point smiling, her voice whispering about the death of her soul, her hand twitching in the throes of death. The darkness had spared me the visual image of her death, but the sound, feel, and smell of it would never leave me.

A car drove up alongside me, its horn blasting. The morning rush hour was beginning. I suddenly realized that I was walking down the center of Avenida del Libertador screaming at the top of my lungs. The driver made circles at his temple with a finger and sped off. People at a bus stop gawked at me. My right side was covered with blood, Shoshanna's blood.

Several quick thoughts struck me: If I didn't get off the street I would be arrested—I'd rather die than be alone with myself in a cage—any notion of vengeance would be over—revenge was all that would keep me sane.

Get off the street. Get a cab. Get yourself together.

When I arrived at my apartment the telephone message light was blinking. Razouk had called three times. *Please don't leave until we speak, Omar* was his final message.

I'd been one slick undercover, hadn't I? I'd baited my trap so cleverly. An offer they couldn't refuse. A deal that they'd want badly enough to make me pass the ultimate test—the murder of Shoshanna.

I showered, watching the water pooling at my feet pink with her blood. I wanted to cry, to scream, to pull my hair out—but I could do nothing. My mind was doing what it had done for two decades—pulling me deeper into my role.

I would give them their deal.

I turned the water off. The phone was ringing. I moved dripping wet across the bedroom. It kept ringing. I had a tape recorder wired to it. I pushed the Record button and picked it up.

"¡Hable!"

"Omar," said Mario Razouk excitedly. "I've received an order from the top. They want to move as quickly as possible."

Could it be that he doesn't know?

I waited a long moment before answering.

"I changed my mind," I said. "No deal." I hung up the phone.

An hour later I was fully dressed and had finished off a quarter-bottle of cognac when it rang again.

"Listen to me, Omar, my brother," said Razouk, speaking in a subdued tone. "I was just told of the unauthorized excesses."

"I've already made other arrangements," I said.

"I counsel you to think carefully before going into this with the Colombians, my brother. In Kahlil's words, 'suffer not the barren-handed . . . who would sell their words for your labour.' There is great regret about the woman, but there is nothing that can be done. Death is the fate of all men, nations, the moon and the stars."

"I don't need Gibran to tell me that," I said. "I've made up my mind."

"I urge you to reconsider—you will not regret it."

"I already regret it."

"Omar, listen to me carefully. There is a product that the gringos are hungry for—we are the only ones who have it. It is impossible to obtain anywhere else. It is worth many times the price of what you are about to settle for. Do you understand what I'm talking about?"

"No," I said, praying he would spell it out clearly for the tape recorder.

"The White Queen," he said.

I double-checked the tape recorder to insure that it was picking up everything.

"Is that a personal guarantee, Mario?"

"Absolutely, my brother," he said quickly. "If you agree, I'll have my car pick you up—you will see it with your own eyes."

"How could I possibly say no?" said Omar Legassi.

28

"YOU ARE EXPECTED IN THE LIBRARY, SEÑOR," SAID A UNIFORMED butler.

I had arrived at the jungle compound only minutes earlier, brought directly from the landing strip by Henri and Mr. AK-47 to the same suite I had stayed in during my first visit.

"I'll be right with you," I said, ducking into the bathroom to activate the recorder-wallet.

Two days had passed since Razouk's phone call. He had explained that the delay was necessary in order to expedite the deal. Preparations were being made. Members of the organization in other countries were being alerted.

I had waited alone, speaking to no one, never leaving my Buenos Aires apartment. The Mossad, DEA headquarters, and Garza paged me incessantly. I didn't return the calls. Perhaps only another deep cover agent could understand my reasons: I was wired into my role, delicately balanced, still too fragile to talk about Shoshanna or to hear about how the DEA suits were gunning for me. I couldn't risk being drawn back into the world of Michael Levine without risking a breakdown, a total loss of control.

The butler led me down a long corridor to the library, a large room with windows covered by bamboo blinds. Narrow strips of light fell across the dark mahogany and leather furniture. In the center of the room sat a radiant Nadia Ricord in a white caftan, curled up in the corner of a low-slung couch watching me.

"Please, come in, Omar," she said, motioning for me to take a seat beside her. "You look surprised to see me."

"I am," I said, stepping into the room. "I was told I was coming here for business."

A deep-throated growl froze me in my tracks. Lying beside her, almost invisible in the shadows, was one of the strange black dogs I'd seen from the balcony. His eyes were locked on mine like radar, the whites gleaming. His lips curled back to reveal an impressive set of fangs.

"*Shhh,*" she said. "Notice the way he studies your eyes. He uses senses, long lost to man, to judge your intentions."

"What do you call him—Jaws?" said Omar Legassi.

She made a soft clucking sound and the beast suddenly turned puppy, nuzzling her with his big head in her lap. She laughed wildly, took the head in both her hands and kissed the dog on the nose.

"My Indio is a Beauceron—an ancient French breed. One of the few that man's so-called selective breeding hasn't ruined. He's primordial. Isn't he beautiful?"

"Very impressive, but I don't have time to chat."

"You aren't wasting time, Omar. This is your first step." She patted the seat beside her. "Come, sit with me."

"Another time, Nadia. Señor Razouk must be waiting for me. I've been given certain promises . . . guarantees."

Suddenly her stark beauty transformed into something dark. She got to her feet and began to pace the room. The dog stood, its head lowered toward me.

"You've been given no promises, Omar," she said, stopping in front of me. We were eye to eye. She stood at least six feet tall. "You were told that we have certain merchandise and that we would *like* to accept your offer. Those were *my* orders."

"*Your* orders?"

"Yes," she said casually. "I was under the impression you wanted to move quickly."

How could I have missed it? Nadia Ricord has taken over the Triangle of Death from her father.

I had witnessed too many inexplicable events in my life, from the fulfillment of Santeria and voodoo curses to sudden premonitions that had saved my life, to doubt what I was feeling. I sensed the presence of a terrible evil.

"Mario said you have *La Reina Blanca*," I said.

"What do you know about it?"

"That a lot of people are looking for it."

"Yes," she said, her green eyes locked on mine. "A lot of people."

"That's why I'm here."

"You're an Arab, Omar," she said. The dog moved to her side, his thick shoulders reaching just below her hip. "You've had business in the Middle East—some arms trafficking?"

The tension slowly crept up my spine. My testing was far from over.

"So you've done some checking on me."

"That shouldn't surprise you."

"No, it doesn't." I held her gaze.

"Part of your plan, as I understand it, involves the retrade of oil for arms and then the sale of the arms to the Middle East."

"I'm sure I don't have to tell you, Nadia: the world is a seller's market. Arms-producing nations are hungry for oil; oil-producing nations are hungry for arms. Everyone wants drugs."

"From your experience, who would you recommend we deal with—Iran or Iraq?"

"Either. But Saddam Hussein is easier to deal with and now he's more desperate for arms than ever."

"You've dealt directly with him?"

"People close to him."

"And if someone should tell us he represents Iraq, are there some simple questions we might ask that would detect an impostor?"

It was as if Shoshanna had come personally to my rescue. I could hear her words, see her face.

"Yes. Ask him what clan he belongs to. If he says he is anything but Tikriti, he's a liar."

She studied me for a moment and then said, "Give me your hand."

I reached my hand out. She took it in both of hers, turned it over and studied my palm. The dog growled, a low rumble that I could feel in my groin. "Indio doesn't seem to trust you. Caution is never a waste of time, Omar."

"Then you'll understand *my* caution. You say you have *La Reina Blanca*. I've met others who make the same claim—how do I know you're telling me the truth?"

"What others?" She pulled her hands away sharply.

"Colombians. Important Colombians."

"They say they have *La Reina Blanca*?"

"They say they *will* have it. Very soon."

"Who?"

"What difference does a name make?"

"In this instance a big difference," she said.

"*El Búfalo*, for one."

The effect of his name was immediate. Her face went taut with fury. "You know him?"

"We've done business."

"He is a liar!" She began to pace the room.

"Why should I believe you and not him?"

"I will instruct Dr. Hess to show you our laboratory this afternoon."

"Fine, then there's nothing more to talk about. As you know, I want to move quickly. Do you?"

"A lot faster than you may be ready for," she said.

She turned and strode across the wide room toward the door. The dog moved in tandem with her, his right shoulder pressed to her hip. As she walked the split in her caftan revealed a long, silky bronze thigh. Her feet were bare. The door closed behind her.

"Most of the facility is buried underground," explained the man who called himself Dr. Hess, seated beside me in the rear of the Range Rover. We were being driven along a flat jungle track, heading due east of the main compound. Hess, who had on a white laboratory coat, had a little extra twinkle in his blue eyes.

"Is it far?" I said, wanting his answer on the recording. René had disappeared without a trace. I was going to leave every kind of track I could. If I didn't survive and the recorder-wallet did, our conversation would make the location of the lab evident.

"About ten kilometers," said Hess. "We travel slowly to limit the amount of engine noise. The jungle here is full of advanced personnel detectors."

He spoke a rapid German to our driver, a young guy with short jet-black hair, in a khaki uniform, who simply nodded.

"A lot of German-speaking people here," I noted.

"Many of us have settled here after the war," he said. "Too many have lost the old traditions. But in Paraguay and Argentina are some of the direct descendants of the officer corps, like Friedrich here." The young man glanced into the rearview. "Only from these I accept personnel."

"You recruit your own people?"

"I have a certain amount of autonomy." He changed the subject abruptly. "What do you know about the processing of cocaine, Omar?"

"Give me a coca leaf, I can turn it into cocaine for you."

"Excellent. Excellent. This will save me much explanation. Be patient with an old man who gets little opportunity to boast. Nadia wants you to fully appreciate the immense opportunity you are about to have with *La Reina Blanca.*

"The hunt for a drug to control the mind has been going on for more than half a century—the Third Reich, the CIA, the KGB, the Chinese, the whole world looking for chemicals to control large masses of people.

"In 1951, Dr. James Olds, an American scientist, discovered that by stimulating the pleasure centers of rats' brains he could control them—the fundamental basis of drug addiction. The more intensely pleasurable the effect of a drug, the more addictive, the more controlled the subject becomes to the point that they only live to experience the chemical's effect. If you promise people pleasure, you can make them do anything, from murder to the prostituting of their young children.

"And what experience is more pleasurable than sex? It controls us doesn't it, Omar?"

I showed him my gold-toothed smile.

"During the war, doctors of the Third Reich noticed that soldiers paralyzed from the neck down were able to achieve the experience of sexual orgasm in their dreams. We immediately began a program of experimentation with chemicals that would achieve the same effect. I managed to rescue all the research when I left Germany. It was not until recent years that this research became invaluable. The advances in genetics resulted in our ability to clone discrete amounts of DNA from one plant into the molecular structure of others.

"I began experimenting with the genetic structure of the coca leaf and its variants, introducing DNA from other types of Amazonian vegetation with certain neurological properties into the chromosomal structure of each of the two hundred variants of the coca leaf."

"So you created a new coca leaf," I said.

"Exactly," said Dr. Hess, beaming. "One that is completely undetectable from the ordinary coca leaf, unless you identify the specific gene it was cloned from. The *La Reina* variation, I call it."

"And the new leaf is converted to cocaine by the ordinary process?"

"Precisely," said Doctor Hess. "The difference is that *La Reina* cocaine is the most addictive substance man has ever known. It is also the most seductive."

The Range Rover broke out into a vast cleared area. A half-dozen huge, glass enclosures, each about the size of a football field, were lined up side by side.

"Greenhouses in the jungle?" I asked.

"The problem with the new leaf has been its fragility," said Hess.

We left the Range Rover and Hess led the way into the first greenhouse. It was comfortably cool inside. Rows of small coca plants extended the full length and width of the enclosure. Hess turned down a ramp that led to an underground entrance and a heavy steel door. He punched numbers into a computer lock. The door clicked open. Ahead of us lay a long downward-sloping corridor painted a hospital white.

At first I couldn't believe my ears. A recording of Billie Holiday singing "My Man" was playing over a speaker system.

"You like the blues?" asked Hess switching to English. "They are my favorite." He started off down another hallway.

"Where did you learn English?" I asked.

"A prisoner-of-war camp in the American South."

At the end of the hallway he led me through double doors and into a large, well-lit laboratory. Three women in white lab coats wearing surgical masks moved among rows of large glass vats. The smell of ether and acetone was powerful. Crystallized cocaine was spread out on rows of flat tables, drying beneath special heat lamps.

I was inside the largest, best-equipped cocaine laboratory I had ever seen.

"My man, I love him so . . ." sang Billie Holiday.

He led the way through the lab, walking quickly, into a small refrigerated room. The walls were lined with wide metal shelves on which lay flat, rectangular-shaped aluminum foil–wrapped packages, each about an inch in width.

"Each weighs a kilo," said Hess. "You'll find there are two hundred—the world's total existing supply of *La Reina Blanca*."

"Why so little, Dr. Hess? The Medellín cartel is producing thousands of kilos a day to meet the American and European demand. *La Reina Blanca* should be stealing the whole market."

"Right now we can only grow it in a carefully controlled environment. The leaf is fragile. But we are on the verge of a major breakthrough; a variation that will flourish in almost any environment. Soon we will be able to produce as much as two thousand kilos a day."

"How soon?"

"Within a month or two."

"And why the odd-shaped packages?"

"At present our shipping method is to conceal the substance inside the walls of cages used for rare animal shipments," said Hess, his blue eyes twinkling with humor. "The Amazon Wildlife Federation is a highly respected, nonprofit organization. Besides, no Customs officer in his right mind wants to climb inside a cage with a jaguar, or handle a snake whose bite can kill you within seconds."

"So that's what this whole place is," said Omar Legassi in amazement, "a front."

"Oh no," said Hess. "For Nadia the federation is most important. But it all works out quite nicely, doesn't it?"

"What bothers me about the whole thing, Doctor, is if this stuff is as undetectable as you say—how can I prove to a customer that it's the real thing, without a doctor of genetic engineering and some kind of supermicroscope?"

He laughed. "Ah! The question of a drug dealer. Come, Omar, select one of the packages and I will show you."

I picked up one of the packages, about the size and shape of small Sicilian pizza pie. Hess then led me to a small office where all the traditional cocaine-testing implements—a heat thermometer, a cobalt reagent tester, a beaker of water, a beaker of Clorox, and a microscope—had already been laid out neatly on a metal table. There was also a large bottle of Inisitol, a powder used to "cut"—dilute—cocaine, a sensitive gram scale, a strainer, several razor blades, and other implements used for the cutting process.

Hess watched me closely as I performed all the tests a professional drug trafficker would to verify the purity of his merchandise. The results were conclusive.

237

"One hundred percent pure cocaine," I said. "But still not *La Reina.*"

Hess smiled enigmatically. "Take a gram of this substance and dilute it."

"How many times?"

"Try thirty," said Hess.

I measured out one gram of *La Reina Blanca* on the scale.

"Be careful," warned Hess. "You don't want to breathe that in."

Very carefully, using the strainer and a razor blade, I mixed one gram of *La Reina* with twenty-nine grams of Inisitol. There was now enough powder to fill the bottom of a plastic Baggie.

"I see you've done that a few times before," laughed Hess.

He led me down another maze of corridors, deeper into the earth, to a hallway that led between large observation windows. Behind each window was a room with four youngsters in hospital pajamas. Color television sets mounted high on the wall showed cartoons as the kids, ranging in age from about ten to eighteen, sat on beds staring listlessly into space, or on floors rocking back and forth. A cacophony of Spanish-speaking cartoon character voices filled the hallway.

"They cannot see us," said Hess, pausing at one of the windows.

One kid with Indian features sat in a corner tearing at bloody scabs on his arms and neck. All of them had severe burns and blisters on their hands and around their nostrils.

"They are *basuqueros,* street urchins from Rio, São Paulo, and Bogotá already heavily addicted to smoking cocaine base—what is also called crack. On the street they steal, they sell their sisters, spread disease. The police shoot them for sport, like water rats. At least here they serve science."

A woman in a lab coat appeared through a door at the end of the corridor. She and the doctor spoke briefly in German.

"Give her your sample, Omar," said Hess.

I handed the woman the plastic Baggie. In a moment she reappeared on the other side of the glass. *"Miren lo que tengo aquí,"* said her voice coming from a hidden speaker. She dangled the Baggie half full of white powder over her head.

The four kids alerted like hungry dogs. They stared bug-eyed, straining toward her, moaning, babbling and whining, but not moving. One emaciated kid with black Indian hair began to spin around on his knees, in small circles getting close to her. The woman raised what looked like a short cattle prod. The kid flung himself into a corner, shrieking like a frightened baboon.

"Watch this," said Hess.

The woman poured the thirty grams of diluted White Queen into a glass-funnel apparatus on the wall. A red bulb was mounted above it. The funnel emptied into four long plastic tubes. At the end of each was a metallic straw about four inches in length.

The moment the woman left, the kids scrambled toward the tubes, squealing, whining, and making feints at the metal straws with their hands but seeming afraid to touch them.

"There is nothing they won't do for this stuff," said Hess.

"What are they afraid of?"

"If they touch the tube before the red bulb is lit, they usually get an electric shock," said Hess. "A powerful one . . . But sometimes we leave the current off to see how far they'll go."

As he spoke, the Indian kid made a pass at the metal tube. Then he grabbed and held on. For a split second his black hair stood straight up on end like a cartoon character's. He flew backward, bouncing off our window and falling to the ground in convulsions.

"They will risk anything," said Hess, mesmerized. "We have complete control of them."

The red bulb suddenly glowed.

"Watch this," said Hess.

The other three kids leapt for the metal straws. Each shoved one deep into his nostril and began inhaling. Clouds of white powder rushed down the tubes and up their noses. A few seconds of frantic snorting and each slumped to the ground sucking air loudly and holding his groin with both hands. The pulse in their necks bounced violently; their eyes squeezed shut, their mouths gaped wide showing rotted teeth and bleeding gums.

"At this moment," said Hess, "they are experiencing a prolonged orgasm, more intense than anything they could achieve through normal sex. One or two experiences with *La Reina* is usually enough for complete and irrevocable addiction.

"In answer to your question—how can you tell if it is *La Reina Blanca*?—I doubt that prospective buyers will find any lack of volunteers to test it. And within a short time you will see the beginning of mass production."

The Indian boy's convulsions ceased. His eyes froze open.

"And a whole new world," added Omar Legassi. I looked away so that he wouldn't see the horror that I feared might show in my eyes.

Hess paused and thought about the words. He smiled.

"In 1944 I never thought I would live to see this, Omar. But, yes—a whole new world. You could say that our Nadia is a visionary."

I prayed that the Mossad recorder was everything they said it was.

Later, in my room, alone, I fell exhausted into a large Jacuzzi bath. I tried to put the pieces of the puzzle together. It was unheard for a woman—even Auguste Ricord's daughter—to control a multinational criminal organization. Especially one whose home base was in South America. If she had the power to authorize this deal, she had the power to authorize the murders of René and Shoshanna. But I needed proof.

I thought of Marita's words, that René had fallen for a woman—someone special.

I lay back, the hot water rushing around me, closed my eyes, and reminded myself that—unauthorized mission or not—I was still an American DEA agent, not Omar Legassi, a murderer who could take out a gun and get instant revenge. I visualized my undercover scenario, how I would continue to gain her confidence, lure her into a trap, gather the evidence I'd need for a trial, and then cage her and the rest of those bastards for the rest of their lives.

At the moment the American justice system seemed far too kind.

29

"*MAR-HA-BA!* WELCOME, OMAR," SAID RAZOUK AS I ENTERED THE main dining room. "I'm afraid there is going to be a slight delay. Nadia was pulled away on some urgent business."

"That's okay," I said. "I'm getting used to sitting around and waiting for you people to get together."

I took a seat at the center of the long table. Razouk, the Frenchman Sarti, and Dr. Hess were already seated opposite me. Along the edges of the room were a half-dozen lean, well-dressed bodyguards. Bruno, as usual, was a few steps behind Razouk's chair. Dr. Hess smiled a greeting. Sarti never looked in my direction.

"It is different this time, my brother," said Razouk solemnly.

Dinner was served Brazilian-style, a fish stew with a salad of vegetables I couldn't even recognize. They ate in tense silence. I was acting relaxed and aloof—as Omar Legassi should have been. It was their turn to show *me*.

I was drinking an after-dinner coffee when Nadia finally arrived.

She breezed into the room once again dressed all in white, her face flushed, the sleek black dog loping at her side. She was followed closely by a tall, thick-necked angular man in a muddied khaki uniform. I recognized the pockmarked face and black rodent eyes immediately—Moon Face.

"Indio. *Puerta!*" she said. The dog slid smoothly into a prone Sphinx-like position beside the door. "Forgive my lateness. Foundation business that I couldn't postpone."

Moon Face held Nadia's chair for her at the head of the table. He wore an automatic pistol and a large Bowie knife in a shoulder sling. *"Merci,* Jacques," she said, her eyes seeking mine.

So Moon Face had a name—Jacques.

"Do you know what *Garrimpeiros* are, Omar?"

"No," I said, noticing bloodstains on Jacques's pants as he backed to the side of the room. His eyes met mine. If I'd had a gun at that moment, the case—and my life—would have ended right then and there. I averted my gaze.

"They are free-lance miners," she said. "They burn the rain forest, pollute the rivers with mercury, slaughter anything they can sell for a few cruzeiros. Forgive me, Omar, I could go on all night. And they are just one of many cancers that must be eradicated if the Amazon is to survive."

"Problems this time, Jacques?" asked Hess.

"No," said Jacques, his eyes still on me. "Not this time."

"Your accommodations, Omar," said Nadia, "have you been made comfortable enough?"

"I'm not here for comfort," I said, aware that I was running the risk of antagonizing her. But time was my enemy. I had no idea how long my cover would hold up. I couldn't allow the momentum to slow.

"Who the hell does this . . . African think he is?" exploded Sarti in French.

"If you can keep your mouth shut, Jean, we'll find out," said Nadia.

"Need I remind you, Nadia," Sarti said sternly. "Your father never would have allowed this. Our people in Germany and Italy have sided with me in strong opposition to your so-called deal." His arm waved toward me. "I don't trust this low-life."

"You've made that perfectly clear, Jean," said Nadia.

"If there's still doubt about me," I interrupted, "why the hell am I here?"

She stared at me coolly. "Omar, in this business one is always proving himself. A friend and lover one day is a deceiver and traitor the next. We will take all the precautions necessary to insure that you're neither a fraud nor a danger. Do you have an objection to this?"

"Only impatience."

"Were you satisfied by what you saw today?"

"The distribution of *La Reina* is an extremely risky business," I said. "You have to use people to test it. People die."

"Do I sense a change of heart, Omar?" said Nadia.

"No, just bargaining," I said. "Sooner or later we'll discuss price. I was pointing out why you shouldn't overvalue your product and undervalue my risks."

Razouk laughed. "I told you this was a Moroccan camel trader."

"Are you, Omar?" asked Nadia.

"A Moroccan, or a camel trader?" I said.

"Why be flip, Monsieur?" snapped the Frenchman. "Why not just answer the question?"

"I thought the question was flip," I said. "I'm obviously not a camel trader. You all seem to know I was born in Morocco, isn't that good enough for you?"

"Can we continue?" said Nadia.

"Where does that leave us?" I asked, looking around the room.

"Let's begin with an agreement of value," said Razouk. "The price of *La Reina Blanca* must be factored at roughly fifty times that of cocaine. Are you in agreement, Omar?"

"In principle, yes," I said.

"Fine," said Nadia. "We leave for Morocco tomorrow, then."

"I'd love to," I said. "But we haven't decided prices, amounts, logistics."

"Once I see proof that you can deliver on your words, we'll settle the rest of the details."

"But I've made no preparations," I protested.

My mind raced. I hadn't spoken to the oil dealer, Belkassami, since I left Morocco. I had assumed I'd have time to make sure things were still the same: that he wasn't back with Fatima and wondering who the hell I was.

"None are necessary," said Nadia. "Arrangements have already been made. We leave on the foundation plane in the morning. If your position is as you describe it, there should be no problem. You gave us the impression you were in a rush to get started."

Undercover agents have died for hesitating when they should have reacted naturally and with confidence; and for reacting naturally and with confidence when they should have hesitated.

"There may be a serious problem," I said. "The people I deal with are old-world Arabs. A woman is out of place on a business deal."

"Maybe it's time they were educated," said Nadia.

"Omar is right, Nadia," said Razouk. "Unless you were his wife or his woman, your presence could be a cause for concern. It could ruin the entire deal."

I could have kissed him.

"You won't mind if I travel as your woman, would you, Omar?"

"But aren't you exposing yourself to unnecessary danger? I'm being paid to take those risks."

"Isn't that the fun of it, Omar?"

"Nadia," interrupted Sarti. "None of this was discussed—"

Before Nadia could answer, I said, "Fine. Let's do it."

Sarti was about to speak again but the sudden thumping of Latin drums and a bass guitar vibrating through the walls of the dining room interrupted him.

Nadia twisted angrily in her seat. "Julio! Go talk to him, Jacques!"

Moon Face moved toward the door, just as a tall, bare-chested young man of about eighteen, his waist-length black hair tied in a ponytail, barged past him into the room bringing with him the sound of a New York street voice chanting, *"Mete la semilla la maraca, pa'que suene . . . Ka ku cha, baby, ka ku cha."* It was a hard-driving disco-salsa number that I used to punch the heavy bag and do *kata* to—"El Barrio."

"Julio," snapped Nadia. "Shut that noise off!"

"Mete la semilla la maraca pa'que suene. . . ."

Julio disappeared into the next room. The music stopped. He returned smiling and moved to her side. He was barefoot and wearing black ghee pants—the bottom half of a karate uniform—with a black belt tied around his waist. His smooth chest was damp with perspiration. He kissed the side of her neck.

"Didn't you promise, Julio?" she said.

"But I'm bored, Mother," he said, his intense brown eyes roving the table, something crazed about them. It was either *kata* or cocaine, I guessed.

Nadia's anger melted to a rosy blush. "You should be studying, *mi amor.*"

This kid definitely touched a nerve in her. His eyes found me. He was an extraordinary-looking young man with fine-chiseled features.

"The mysterious Señor Legassi," he said, pointing a finger at me as if it were a pistol. His knuckles were swollen and callused.

"Mysterious?" I said.

"I have no secrets from my son," said Nadia, her hand absently stroking his forearms draped around her neck. "If by some miracle he is admitted to a good university in the U.S.—without studying"—she pinched him—"he will be taking over some of our business interests."

Her hand continued to stroke his forearm. I was witnessing her soft underbelly exposed. The art of undercover work is like rock climbing; every vulnerability is a crevice, a potential handhold, leverage. She was definitely vulnerable to Julio. If I could, I'd make him vulnerable to me.

"I thought we settled on UCLA," he said, still eyeing me curiously.

"I don't want to discuss this now," she said.

"He doesn't look so dangerous to me," said Julio, eyeing me as he straddled a chair alongside his mother.

"Was I supposed to be dangerous?" I laughed.

"You're a suspect in a homicide, aren't you?" said Julio.

"Before I answer that," I said, "let's agree. I'll show you mine; you show me yours?"

"But Omar," she said, smiling coolly, "I *am* showing you mine."

Both mother and son had their eyes fixed on me as if concentrating on a game board—I saw no family resemblance. Were it not for his fine features and height, he might have been just a handsome Latino kid from the ghettos of Bogotá or the Bronx.

"Okay, what do you want to know?" I asked.

"What does it feel like to kill a man?" challenged Julio.

"What do you imagine it feels like?"

"Don't you patronize me!" he roared suddenly, the veins in his neck billowing out like ropes. "How do you know I haven't killed a hundred motherfuckers like you?"

"*Tranquilo*, Julio," said Nadia.

Abruptly he was calm again. "Can you answer my question, or can't you?"

"Do you study martial arts?" I asked.

245

"Is there a reason you won't answer me?" he insisted. I detected a hint of a Colombian accent.

"I'm trying to find out if you'll understand my answer. Do you understand the concept of *Ai Uchi*?"

Julio stared at me as if through a lens that had just changed focus.

"Your hands," he said. "Show me!"

"What is it, Julio?" said Nadia.

"Quiet, Mother." He was out of his chair moving around the table toward me, his movements as lithe and quick as a panther's; the confident glide of a *karateka*. I hoped he was as well versed in the philosophy.

I held my hands up for him to examine. He looked into my eyes as he felt the hard calluses and bone growths on the two punching knuckles of each hand, then the ridge of calluses across my palms from the grinding tightness of my fists during the countless hours of *kata* and karate training of the past twenty years; then the thick calluses on the edges and heels of my hands. To a martial artist my hands were a dead giveaway.

"What style?" he asked.

"Mostly *goju*. And you?"

"*Shoto-kai*."

"Funakoshi's style. I know it well. Were you doing *kata* to the music?" I asked, fishing for a route to connect with him.

"You didn't answer my question!"

"I am trying to teach you how to ask the question," I said. "*Ai Uchi*—the ultimate in timing. You understand the concept?"

"Why don't you explain it?" insisted Julio.

Behind him I noticed Sarti watching us intently and had the feeling that he understood exactly what I was trying to do.

"It is to slice your opponent with a sword at the precise moment he slices you. To achieve it, a Zen warrior would say, requires the total absence of anger; to throw away fear; to abandon your life. It is to invite your enemy into your house as an honored guest."

"This is nonsense," said Sarti.

"What is he talking about, Julio?" said Nadia.

"*A Book of Five Rings*," said Julio without taking his eyes off me.

"Did you read it?" I asked.

"Only quotes from it—my *sensei* recommended it."

"Your *sensei* must be a good one."

"I couldn't find a copy of it in South America."

"If you like I'll have my English copy translated into Spanish for you."

"I speak English," he said. "You still didn't answer my question."

"Your question was too general and too important to be asked or answered frivolously. I've never killed anyone, but there have been people who died at my hand. Do you understand the difference?"

I saw pain and confusion in his eyes. "Yes, I do," he said.

"Well I don't," said Sarti getting to his feet. "I'm fed up with this idiocy." He waved his arm toward Julio and me. "You are making a terrible mistake with this man. And you're blind not to see it."

Sarti started toward the door. One of the bodyguards, a tall, rawboned man with close-cropped military-style hair, moved quickly to his side.

"*Ojo!*" snapped Nadia over her shoulder.

The massive black dog rushed snarling at Sarti. It stopped, its bared fangs inches from the old man's groin. The bodyguard took a step back. His hand moved in a blur of speed. His gun was aimed at the dog's head. I heard a metallic click.

Moon Face's reaction was just a blink of an eye quicker. The Bowie knife slashed in a lightning arc. For a millisecond the bodyguard stared in shock at the stump of a hand gushing a geyser of blood all over Sarti. He fell to his knees. The dog pounced on the hand, still wrapped tightly around the gun, tearing at it as if it were a living thing. The bodyguard writhed in pain, his mouth moving but no words coming out, the geyser of blood now reaching the ceiling.

Julio tore the black karate belt from around his middle and was wrapping a tourniquet on the man's arm before anyone else reacted.

"Dr. Hess!" he shouted. "Help me!"

The white-haired German looked at Nadia.

"Quickly!" Julio screamed. He had slowed the blood flow to a trickle. "Haven't you had enough blood yet, Mother?" he added bitterly.

The security men stood by watching with what seemed like amused interest. Bruno was intent on Razouk, waiting for instructions. Jacques, the bloody knife gripped in his fist, was eyeing Sarti and Nadia, the whites of his eyes glowing like an attack dog's, waiting for her order.

The man fainted. Julio gently supported his head as he held the tourniquet. "He'll die, Doctor."

"Go ahead and help him," said Nadia, finally.

"Get him to the infirmary," ordered Hess, standing. Two of the other bodyguards lifted the man as Julio kept tension on the tourniquet. They carried him outside.

"Should I try to save the hand?" asked Hess, pausing and indicating the gory chew toy still being gnawed at by the dog.

"*Basta!*" ordered Nadia. The dog dropped the hand on the bloodstained Persian rug. "*Venga!*" The animal moved to her side.

Hess stooped and picked up the hand with a handkerchief.

"Stay with Julio, Doctor. I don't like to see him upset. But I doubt that a dead man will have much need for his hand," she said as she stroked the dog's head.

Hess nodded and slowly left the room.

"Please have a seat, Jean," said Nadia, switching to French. Sarti, his face a ghostly pale, was halfway to the door. He moved shakily back to his seat. "Where did you think you were going to go, back to Paris?"

"Must this be public, Nadia?" he said. "Before an outsider."

"It was you who made it public," she said, her voice ominously composed. "What do you think would happen if I decide, out of respect for my father and for past loyalties, to allow you to live and instead make a phone call to our associates in Paris?"

Sarti lowered his eyes.

"I will tell you, *mon amour*. You are an old man. You are a risk. It is one thing to disagree, another to disrespect."

"Please, Nadia," he said, his voice almost a whisper.

Jacques moved behind him.

"Don't you see, Jean? You show what a danger you are by your foolishness here at my table," she said as if explaining something obvious to a child. "If you can indulge in a temper tantrum here, just think what you might do elsewhere."

Razouk, across from me, shifted uncomfortably in his chair. He was unable to look at Sarti and unable to avoid it.

Sarti's eyes suddenly glistened. "I was only thinking of the security of the organization."

"Disrespect me, disrespect my son, in our home, and this is for the good of the organization?" she said, sounding hurt.

"Please, Nadia," he said.

"Jean, Jean, Jean," she said, shaking her head sadly. She abruptly smiled. "You are the same age as my father, no?"

Sarti blinked as if the sun were suddenly too bright. "He was older, Nadia," he said, his voice tight and coming from high in his throat. "As children, he was a few years ahead of me in school."

Nadia nodded as if acknowledging a shared intimacy.

If she gave Moon Face a signal, I missed it. His strike was a blur of speed and efficiency. He drove the length of the thick-bladed Bowie knife into Sarti's back to the hilt, withdrew and sheathed it before Sarti's head, his eyes wide in death, hit the table. No blood spurted from the wound. The blade had stopped his heart cold. It was a move that only a highly trained martial artist could accomplish.

Razouk shook his head sadly and looked down at the table.

"Hurry," said Nadia, clapping her hands and glancing back at the door. "Get him out of here."

Two security men under Bruno's command lugged Sarti's body toward the door.

"Don't let Julio see," said Nadia. "I want him to know nothing of this."

"Of course, madam," said Bruno, as they wrestled the body outside.

Nadia turned and looked at me. Her eyes were ringed in red. She seemed on the verge of tears. I was an outsider, a witness, an unknown commodity.

"Come," she said, patting the seat beside her. "Sit here, Omar."

Running or fighting did not seem to be options.

I sat beside Nadia and met her gaze. She leaned close and took one of my hands in hers.

"My son seems to have taken a liking to you, Omar," she said.

"And I to him."

"There is something about you. I'm not sure what it is, but you remind me of someone."

"How so?"

"It's not a physical resemblance. It has to do with your presence; how you look out at the world."

"Was he someone you cared about?"
"I didn't say it was a *he*, did I?"
"No, you didn't."
"Omar, please don't disappoint me."

30

THE TRIP TO MOROCCO BEGAN JUST AFTER DAWN WITH A DRIVE THROUGH the jungle in a caravan of Range Rovers loaded with teams of armed men and equipment. I rode alone with Razouk. He was uncharacteristically quiet.

"Where's Nadia?" I asked.

"She decided at the last minute that she wants Julio to come," he said. "They'll be right behind us."

When we arrived at the airfield, the camouflage covering of the runway was being rolled back by a crew of Indians. The foundation plane was a pale green Boeing 727 with a red, green, and gold insignia on its tail—an impressionistic version of a harpy eagle in flight.

The interior of the 150-foot-long jet looked like a luxurious ocean liner from the 1930s decorated in monochromatic colors. We entered through the aft ladder into a living room with a large U-shaped leather couch and several overstuffed velvet easy chairs that inclined into beds. The windows were covered with wooden venetian blinds. A dozen people could sleep, eat, and travel quite comfortably in the aft compartment alone.

The security men unloaded their gear and started to settle in. A wall cabinet was opened and I glimpsed a row of Uzis hung on pegs and an assortment of handguns.

The entire plane was covered with thick off-white carpeting that seemed to swallow my feet. The passageway connecting the fore and aft sections was wood-paneled with built-in picture frames featuring *National Geographic*–type photos of endangered animals. The forward cabin was a large living room/office area furnished with leather sectional couches, recliner chairs, and a desk with a computer, fax, and phone.

Razouk and I waited alone in the forward lounge. He looked troubled.

"I'm glad I have a chance to talk to you alone, my brother," he said.

"I'd say we've got about fifteen or twenty hours to talk."

"No. We make a stop at Ezeiza. Bruno and I will be leaving."

"That's too bad."

"Be careful, my friend," he said, his voice low, his eyes on the passageway.

"What's wrong?"

"I've known Nadia since she was a child. I loved her father . . ." His voice trailed off. He wagged his head.

"What are you trying to say, Mario?"

"You have seen a lot. And she does not trust you."

"Do you?"

"All men have secrets, Omar. Gibran said, '. . . there are those who have the truth within them but they tell it not in words.' When I remember those words, I think of you."

"You didn't answer me."

"Last night she questioned me in great detail about how well I know you, how we met. I lied to her," he said, lowering his voice even further. "I said I knew others who had done business with you in the Middle East. I made myself responsible for you."

"Why?"

"You would now be with Allah if I told the truth."

We were both silent.

"If there is something wrong, something you are hiding . . . I am a dead man," said Razouk. "If there *is* something wrong, Omar, don't even tell me. You will have opportunities in Morocco to just walk away. I beg you—just do it."

His black-olive eyes bore into mine like thousands before him, trying to see a truth hidden behind twenty years of carefully constructed mirrors.

"If you were in doubt, why did you bring me?" I asked.

"I have no doubts about you, Omar. I feel your affection. You would not knowingly hurt me. It's Nadia. Things have changed . . ."

He stopped talking and looked up. Nadia, Moon Face, and Julio had entered the cabin. Nadia, dressed in a bone-white tailored suit and dark wraparound sunglasses that hid her eyes, looked like a glamorous business executive. She beckoned impatiently for Razouk to follow her into the other cabin.

"Mind some company?" said Julio, flopping into a lounge chair across from me.

"Great."

Julio was curious about me; I had to play the kid carefully, to bond with him in any way that I could. He seemed to be the only key to Nadia's human side. Bushido—the Zen warrior philosophy—was his passion of the moment.

For more than two decades I had lived and breathed martial arts; I had even been a member of the U.S. karate team selected to fight in the first South American Caribbean championships in Panama in 1974. I used to bore people stiff with the aphorisms and legends of Bushido. Agents ran when they saw me coming. Behind my back Garza used to call it "Bullshito." And now I had an audience of one who could not get enough of it.

Julio told me that one of the best *senseis* in Buenos Aires was flown to the compound twice a week for private karate lessons, but that the man was Japanese with a poor grasp of Spanish and had great difficulty communicating the philosophy in a way he could understand.

"What about Jacques?" I asked. "I'd guess he's a master *karateka*—you ever talk to him about it?"

Julio laughed. "Jacques? I might as well talk to Indio the dog."

"Well, what is it about Bushido philosophy that appeals to you?"

"I don't know . . . there's just something about it that's so cool. Like a nobility. My mom thinks it's stupid; she thinks only animals have nobility."

His sensitive eyes—like his mother's—constantly searched mine for reaction. I used to teach ghetto kids martial arts and was always struck by the sadness and hunger I saw in their eyes; the same look I saw in Julio's.

"I have to disagree with your mother," I said, taking a risk. "I've seen great nobility in all kinds of people. What you did last night to save that man showed nobility."

"That's funny," he said ironically. "She called it weakness. He was gonna shoot Indio. She wouldn't trade the life of her dog for a thousand men." He shrugged his shoulders and looked out the window. "The guy died anyway."

"And what do you think?" I asked, wondering whether he was aware of Sarti's fate as well.

"What do I think? I think I'm just along for the ride."

He didn't say another word to me for the entire flight.

31

CASABLANCA

I STOOD IN THE DARKNESS OF THE BALCONY OVERLOOKING THE ENTRANCE to the Riad Salam hotel and the Mediterranean Sea. The night was balmy, yet sweat beaded on my brow and ran off me in rivulets. Moroccan drum and flute music drifting through the air on a breeze that smelled of oil and sea mingled with the sounds of waves, punctuated now and then with shouts and laughter.

It was almost 3:00 a.m. and this was about the tenth time I had wandered out here to peer down at the deserted street five stories below me and then out at the distant lights of passing ships dotting the darkness. The fear I felt twisting in my gut was like bare live wires, jolting me onto my feet every time I tried to sleep.

The next couple of hours would be the most crucial. Belkassami would be coming in the morning to take us to Libya, where his oil was stored. I had to have my wits about me—at least two or three hours of sleep. Yet the sense that something was about to happen had the hairs on the back of my neck standing on end.

Nadia and Julio were in the two-room suite next door. I looked over at their balcony; the French doors were closed. Only darkness inside. Not a sound. True to her word, Jacques and her army of watchers had been invisible since our arrival.

I wondered why Belkassami had insisted we stay here in a small isolated hotel when we had reservations at the Hyatt, which was located downtown and only blocks from his office. I could have protested, but everything was going so smoothly—perhaps, too smoothly.

We had quickly agreed to three million barrels of oil for two hundred kilos of *La Reina*—which I guaranteed would gross Belkassami a minimum of $120 million—more than double what he would have grossed by simply selling the oil. My commission would be approximately $10 million.

He also seemed to buy the story that Nadia was my woman. What reason would I have had to object to staying at any hotel he recommended? We were on his turf; he had everything to protect, everything to be paranoid about. It seemed like a harmless request at the time. I couldn't take the chance of refusing and letting him think I had something to hide.

Nadia never said a word—only those laser eyes watching every nuance of the interaction between us. She went overboard in performing the role of my woman, hanging on my arm, stroking my hands, even kissing my ear.

The sound of a car engine jolted me back out onto the balcony. An old Chevrolet rolled slowly by the front of the hotel, its engine tapping loudly. It passed beneath a streetlight. Four or five people in it.

Something is wrong. Moving too slowly. If it's Belkassami checking on us, Nadia and I should be in a room together or the whole fucking thing collapses.

I started to climb over my balcony to jump the three or four feet to Nadia's. I stopped. I heard the engine growing louder again and ducked. I could see three cars racing toward the hotel, their headlights out. They stopped below my balcony.

I peeked over the edge. Doors opened. The interior lights of one car illuminated. Belkassami was in the passenger seat. A dozen men moved quickly into the hotel.

I leapt the short distance to Nadia's balcony. I tapped hard on the window. *Nothing.* I tried the French doors. With a shove they opened. I stepped through drawn curtains into darkness.

"Nadia!" I whispered. "Julio!"

Shadows moved. I could make out the shape of a large bed. Lights came on. The bed was empty, the covers and sheets a tangled mess.

"What the hell are you doing in here?" It sounded more a hiss than a voice. I turned. Nadia, her face contorted with rage, held a blunt little gun, the barrel inches from my face. She was naked. Beside her, also naked, was Julio, his face crimson, the look in his eyes that of a trapped animal. It was a second before I realized that I had caught them in bed together.

"No time! Belkassami's here with an army. I'm supposed to be in this room with you! Julio, get in my room—quick, use the balcony!"

There was noise in the hallway. Julio looked at his mother.

Nadia lowered the gun. "Go!" she ordered.

Julio moved quickly out the balcony door.

Nadia switched off the light and slipped into bed. "Don't you think you'd better get in?" she whispered, holding the sheet up for me.

I slid into bed beside her.

"You're sweating . . . and you're trembling," she said.

Her breath on my face smelled of marijuana. I felt the length of her body against mine, and a growing knot of terror in my stomach.

More muffled noises from outside.

"*Shit!* They're going to break in," I said.

"Of course," she whispered, her mouth brushing my ear. "He knows you about as well as I do. Don't worry, *mon amour,* if he wanted to kill you, he wouldn't go to all this trouble."

A key scraped in the lock. The door clicked open quietly.

"Shhh," whispered Nadia, her lips against my ear. "I'm your woman, remember." She moved her body onto mine, her leg covering me. She slid the cold gun down my belly and snuggled it between my legs.

Shadows slipped into the room. The light came on. Belkassami was smiling down at us; a half-dozen men flanked him around the bed, some had their heads and faces wrapped PLO style. They all had guns.

"What the fuck is going on?" I demanded.

"Omar, my friend," he said, his toupee riding back and forth like a hobby horse. "I hope you will forgive this intrusion. But my clients, whom I hope you will meet, have insisted on assurances." He shrugged his shoulders. "They think there is a possibility that you are a CIA agent, or worse—that you are working for OPEC."

The door opened and another group of men ushered in Julio, wrapped in a bedsheet. He couldn't meet my gaze.

"And who is the young man?" asked Belkassami.

"My son," said Nadia.

"My apologies. Madam Ricord, is it not?"

"Madam Ricord it is," she said.

"I know that name," he said, studying her.

"It's a common name in France." She smiled; her eyes bore into his. Belkassami's smile disappeared; there was a hint of uncertainty.

"Unfortunately the presence of you and your son includes you in this . . . inconvenience," he said, switching to French. "But I'm certain that brother Omar will clear everything up."

"And I'm certain, Monsieur, that a gentleman like yourself, won't make this inconvenience too unpleasant," said Nadia.

"Why don't you get to the point," I said.

"The point is, my friend, the people I represent want assurances that you are who you say you are, and that—as you promised—you already have a customer for the cocaine."

"And what kind of assurance is that supposed to be?"

"A million-dollar advance."

"That was not part of our agreement."

Belkassami's rotten teeth peeked out at me. "Neither was your unannounced appearance, my friend."

I looked at Nadia. She was studying me closely, hugging her body to me as if afraid, but there wasn't a hint of fear in her eyes.

"If you don't trust me, Hassan, let's forget the whole deal."

"I'm afraid it is too late for that, Omar."

———

It was dawn when we drove inside the walls of an isolated seafront villa. It was very still. Julio looked dazed as we were led from the cars into a large, unkempt house that looked uninhabited. Nadia was cool and composed.

The kidnapping had been carried out in as businesslike and gentlemanly fashion as possible. Nadia had been allowed to dress privately. We were comfortably seated in the rear of a Mercedes sedan equipped with window blinds.

"Just a business precaution," Belkassami had assured me a dozen times. "If you were in my client's position you would do the same."

We were all seated around a large living room full of decrepit overstuffed furniture. The mood was tense. Belkassami's men kept their faces masked. A speaker phone was on a table before me.

I punched in Tito Garza's pager number in the U.S., signaling him to call the phone number given me by Belkassami. He returned the call within the hour. Belkassami pressed the speaker phone so that everyone in the room could hear the conversation.

"Somebody call me?" said Garza's voice, echoing in the large room.

"It's me, Omar," I said. *"Muy importantísimo."*

Adding the word *muy* meant that not only was the call being monitored but that I had a gun to my head.

"Where the fuck is 212 area code?"

"Casablanca, Morocco."

"You're shitting me! It's the same as New York."

"Listen up, will you—I have *La Reina.*"

"You sure?" said Garza. I could hear the excitement in his voice. His question was also a code, requiring a specific response.

"Yes," I answered. If I was lying for any reason I would have said *positive,* or *affirmative.* "I have two hundred white silk shirts. Is that Italian gentleman still interested?"

"You fucking kidding, or what," said Garza.

"They want it bad enough to put up front money?"

"Not without a sample," he said.

Nadia gave me an almost imperceptible nod.

"You got it," I said.

"When?"

"I'll have to get back to you on that."

"I understand. How much front money are we talking about?"

"A million."

"Jesus."

"Tell the people that each of the two hundred will take a thirty hit."

Garza whistled.

"And they'll have a worldwide exclusive," I added.

"The sample better fucking speak for itself," said Garza. "If it don't you're hanging me out to fucking dry. I'm going direct to the people."

"I understand," I said.

Direct to the people meant that Garza was going undercover, direct to the Mafia, without notifying DEA.

"Lemme know as soon as you arrange for the sample," said Garza.

"Where are you?"

"Miami, but I'm gonna have to go to the people in New York."

"Okay. I'll get back to you."

Garza hung up. I turned to Belkassami.

"You heard enough," I said coolly. "I need at least twenty-four hours."

"Of course." He grinned. "I am in no rush."

"But I am," I said. "Take us back to the hotel, right now, so that I can make the arrangements in private—or no deal."

His eyes bulged. The toupee looked as if it was about to do a pancake flip. Now the shoe was on the other foot. For $120 million he wasn't going to fuck with me.

"Brother Omar," he said, "you will never be sorry."

"I hope not."

———

The moment we returned to the waterfront hotel, Nadia made a local call. Speaking in French, she gave some brief coded instructions along with Garza's pager number to someone. When she hung up, she said, "Your man will be contacted for the delivery of a sample."

I paged Garza. When he returned the call I told him he would be contacted and gave him Belkassami's Swiss bank account number for the million-dollar transfer. There was nothing left to do but wait.

If Nadia was disturbed by being kidnapped, or by being caught naked in bed with her son, she concealed it pretty well. She sat on the still-rumpled bed, her back against the headboard, smoking a joint, watching me with hooded eyes and a vague smile. She had unbuttoned the top three buttons of her white blouse and pulled her skirt up above the middle of her thighs. An ancient ceiling fan churned hot air above us. I was slumped in an easy chair against the far wall, my sleep-deprived brain functioning like sand-clogged gears: too tired to move, too charged to sleep. Julio sat on the balcony. He had not said a word, or even looked at me, since I barged into the room that morning.

"Here," said Nadia, offering me the marijuana joint.

"What happened to Jacques and your men?" I asked, waving it away.

"They are close," she said enigmatically. "If I had given a signal you would have seen them."

"Why didn't you?"

"I want you to be successful, Omar. I've made some far-reaching arrangements based on your word. I'm getting exactly what I needed as well—assurances."

"You still don't trust me."

"Don't look upset, *mon amour*. As I told you, I want you to be successful. Julio and I are actually growing quite fond of you." She took a deep toke off the joint and patted the bed beside her. "Come here, I'm feeling lonely," she said sleepily. "Talk to me. Let's show Julio that we're still friends." I looked out the balcony door at Julio, just visible through the curtain, seated with his back to the door. "I'm not his birth mother, you know. Without me, he has nobody."

Julio suddenly appeared from the balcony and headed toward the door.

"Where are you going?" she asked.

"Next door, to sleep," he mumbled.

"No, no," I said, getting to my feet. "I'm a lot older than you, I need the sleep more." I patted his shoulder and felt him stiffen.

He started toward the door ahead of me.

"Julio!" she called. "You're not going anywhere."

He paused, then turned slowly. Mother and son locked eyes in a struggle I wanted no part of.

I quietly let myself out of the room.

32

NEW YORK CITY

TITO GARZA SAT HUNCHED OVER A BEER WATCHING THE DOORWAY AND the faces of the crowd passing by on Sixth Avenue. His patience was running out. This was his third beer and the delivery man was a half-hour late. He had no idea what the fuck he was looking for. The guy who had called spoke Spanish with a French accent. Tito for some reason got the impression that the guy was a little twerp. His voice was soft; maybe he was a *maricón*. Maybe that's why he chose the No Name bar to deliver the sample.

It was a typical transient joint in the bustling heart of Greenwich Village, near West 8th. And this was a typical Friday night crowd—the place was packed with tourists, teenagers from New Jersey looking for adventure, drag queens eyeing the teenagers, neighborhood crones, hustlers, grifters, and derelicts.

The music blasting from the jukebox was an ancient jazz number called "Night Rider," featuring Stan Getz on tenor sax. *A bad omen.* Ever since Levine let that sax player take a walk Garza couldn't listen to him play a fucking note without remembering.

I hate this fucking city, thought Garza, downing his beer and getting to his feet. Levine was in trouble, but what else could he do? How long was he supposed to wait? Half an hour was long enough with Vinnie and Georgie sitting out there covering him, and all of them working off-the-books—without the suits knowing a fucking thing. What did Levine expect—deep cover in Casablanca without telling anyone? He'd finally gone *chiflado*, off his rocker. *La Reina Blanca.* Bullshit. Nobody had it, at least not in fucking Morocco.

I'm outta here. Garza got to his feet, pulling money from his pocket. He felt a light tap on his shoulder. The man was about his height but powerfully built with even features and alert dark eyes.

"You are Cortez?" he asked.

Garza recognized the voice immediately. He flicked a toe switch in his boot activating an alarm in Vinnie's and Georgie's cars.

"You been watching me all this time?" asked Garza.

The man ignored the question. "I have something for you."

"Lemme buy you a drink," offered Garza, taking the stool again, trying to memorize the "scrip"—dark, straight hair, clean-shaven, thirty-five years of age, green corduroy suit, tiny gold ring in left ear. Frenchie had managed to observe Garza for half an hour without being noticed. Definitely a pro.

The Frenchman took a pack of Marlboro cigarettes from his pocket and placed it on the bar. "She is in the cigarettes," he said softly. "I'm going to the john." He moved easily through the crowded bar just as Georgie entered the front door, his eyes searching the darkness.

Garza picked up the cigarette box and slipped it into his leather coat, noting its weight—a good OZ. The jukebox exploded into a salsa tune. Celia Cruz, *La Cubanísima*, was singing with Johnny Pacheco *y su Tumbao.* It was one of Garza's favorites, "Toro Mata." *A good omen.* He sang along, tapping out the conga beat on the bar.

Georgie drifted over trying to get the bartender's attention, at the same time shooting Garza an inquisitive look.

"Got the thing," whispered Garza. *"El tipo está en el baño.* Corduroy suit, gold earring."

Georgie ordered a bottle of beer with no glass and moved off toward the john.

No class, thought Garza, tapping to the music, suddenly feeling good—better than good. Fucking high. The whole puñeta, pinche *fucking government is looking for* La Reina Blanca *and I got her in my pocket.* With any luck Georgie and Vinnie would follow this fucking frog back to his stash.

After about five minutes Garza started getting nervous. He peered into the crowded darkness waiting to see either Georgie or the Frenchman reappear. Something was wrong. Garza was stunned when Georgie, looking flushed and wide-eyed, walked in through the front door again.

"*El tipo habrá cogido brisa*," said Georgie breathlessly. "Through the window in the john, *ese*. When I went in there it was wide-open. The lights were out. I went out and followed the alley—it leads to Carmine Street. He's in the wind."

"Cool it, cool it," said Garza beneath his breath. "That's why he chose this place. Somebody could have an eyeball on us right now. Split! Grab Vinnie and meet me at the MD."

A half-hour later the three agents sat in a rear booth at the Market Diner on 43rd Street. Garza opened the Marlboro box. A glassine bag was stuffed inside, full of glistening white powder.

"You're cold meat, unless we get a Sicilian undercover to do this," said O'Brien. "Gianotti's crew despises anything not Sicilian—they don't even trust Italians. And there ain't nuthin' they hate more than blacks."

"I look black to you?" snapped Garza.

"You know what I mean. To them it's all the same."

"I got something they want bad," said Garza, patting the Marlboro box. "Besides, it's almost midnight; Gianotti himself is expecting me. What are we gonna do, call headquarters and tell 'em we've been working off the books, send us a Sicilian undercover agent, quick?"

"Tito, Tito, Tito," said O'Brien, shaking his head. "You know what you're playing with here? Gianotti's had guys fucking burned alive cause he's in a bad mood. And he's the guy they call 'Gentleman.' "

"And how you so sure that shit is *La Reina*, *ese*?" said Georgie.

"Levine said it is."

"How's Levine know—he here to check it?"

"Yeah," said Georgie, looking worried. "Even the lab hasn't figured out how to test the stuff."

"And what if they make you take it?" said Vinnie.

"I think you gotta consider sending me in," said Georgie. "I can pass for Italian."

"What are you, fucking kidding?" said Garza. "You look like Pancho Villa's butler. Those wiseguys'll think you're a fucking pop-up target in Coney Island. Besides, Levine was *my* partner. I'm the one who's going in."

Garza parked on Prince Street just off the corner of Mulberry in New York's Little Italy. The Sons of Sicily Social and Athletic Club, the storefront headquarters of the most powerful Mafia family in the U.S., was around the corner in the middle of the block. He locked the car and hunched into the cold wind. His hand closed over the Marlboro box in the pocket of his black leather coat. He didn't know where Georgie and O'Brien had set up, and he didn't want to know. He couldn't afford to even think about them during his act.

All the ID in his pockets said he was Tony Cortez, a midlevel cocaine dealer. Anyone checking official records would learn that Tony Cortez was born in Cuba and arrived in the U.S. as a result of the infamous Mariel boat invasion, or "Castro's Gift to America." The Miami and New York police departments, and the FBI, all had records of Tony Cortez being arrested and convicted of drug sales.

As Garza turned onto Mulberry Street the wind battered him hard. He gritted his chattering teeth and strode toward the darkened storefront. As he drew closer he saw faint cracks of light showing from around the heavily curtained window. This was it. *Show time!* as Levine used to say. He skipped up the two steps and tried the door—locked. He rapped on the glass.

A curtain parted. A wide face appeared, studied him a moment, then disappeared. He heard the click of locks. The door swung inward. He stepped inside and found himself in what looked like an old-world coffee shop, with a half-dozen wrought-iron tables and a marble counter. One of the tables was occupied by two big men in suits with gleaming white shirts and ties.

The door closed behind him. He heard the locks click again.

He recognized John "The Gentleman" Gianotti immediately. Garza had only seen him in newspapers and magazines; the media had made "the Dapper Capo" as recognizable as any celebrity, although somehow none of the photos captured how ominous the man was in person.

"Cortez?" said Gianotti.

The man seated beside him had one hooded little eye that seemed locked in a perpetual stare, while the other was wide and unblinking, and wandered crazily. It was Phil "Evil Eye" Caglioti, who was also called "Crazy Phil"—a common nickname for those in the mob who had beaten murder raps claiming insanity. In Phil's case, as a teenager he had stabbed his older brother to death using an ice pick. As Garza recalled, there were more than a hundred stab wounds.

"Yeah," said Garza, stepping closer to the table.

"You bring whatchu said?"

"Yeah, I brought it."

"Ya ain't too fuckin' talkative, are you?"

"There ain't much to talk about," said Garza. "I got it. The word on the street says you offered a hundred grand for the connection."

Garza was suddenly frisked from behind. Hands patted around his ankles and worked upward around his legs. "Raise your arms," said a soft voice behind him. Garza did as ordered. The hands worked expertly, under his leather coat, up into the armpits. They found the Marlboro box in the coat pocket. In one quick motion it was fished out and tossed on the table in front of Gianotti, quickly followed by Garza's wallet full of false ID and a flash roll of about ten thousand dollars in hundreds. The hands turned Garza around and he found himself facing another familiar face.

Pascuale "Pat the Cat" Gallo was not a face that Garza would forget. The lanky, smooth-talking, immaculately pompadoured wiseguy with the amazing resemblance to Mickey Rourke the actor, had once been one of the most successful undercover detectives on the NYPD.

A DEA–FBI task force had arrested Gallo along with a dozen other corrupt cops on murder, drug, and racketeering charges. Eight years earlier, he had sold the names of DEA informants to the mob, about a dozen of whom ended up dying slow and ugly deaths. Gallo had been sentenced to more than three hundred years in jail, but five years into his sentence the DEA agent in charge of the case was himself arrested and charged with selling information to the mob. Among his admissions was an illegal wiretap, which resulted in Gallo's going free. His mob nickname evolved, first, from the remarkable number of "rats" he'd sent to their maker, then, later, for the return of some three hundred years of his own life.

"I know you, don't I?" said Gallo.

"I dunno," answered Garza, playing with the toe button. "Do you?"

"You look familiar."

"Yeah, you too," said Garza.

"This it?" said Crazy Phil, doing his best to focus his wandering eye on the bag of white powder. Gianotti had on eyeglasses and was going through Garza's ID.

"Yeah," said Garza.

"Pat, call dat guy downtown and check dis guy out," ordered Gianotti. "Let's get downstairs wit dis shit!" He handed Garza's wallet to the ex-cop and got to his feet.

Another mobster in a suit stepped out of a rear door and held it open. "Let's go," said Crazy Phil, indicating that Garza should precede them into the basement.

"Why there?" asked Garza.

" 'Cause it's fucking soundproof and barricaded," said Crazy Phil. "You got sumthin' to be scared of?"

Garza sucked up his fear and headed toward the fabled "dungeon" where, according to mob informants, more than fifty murders had been committed. There was no turning back now.

He started down a dank stairway, lit by a dim yellow bulb. He made a mental note that once Levine's case went down, they would run a check on all law enforcement computer systems to see who had run the name Antonio Cortez this morning—they would have Gianotti's "guy downtown" by the balls.

"And bring me one a them fucking yam crackheads from uptown," ordered Gianotti.

Crazy Phil led the way through two dark rooms filled with debris, each with double-weighted steel doors at either end. Finally they reached a windowless concrete bunker illuminated by a yellow lightbulb hanging by a bare wire over a heavy wooden table. A half-dozen straight-backed wooden chairs were scattered around the room.

"Why dontchu take a seat, Mr. Cortez," said Gianotti, pulling a chair up to the table. Garza sat opposite him. Crazy Phil, examining the white powder in the light, sat to his right. Behind him, in shadow, were at least two others.

"Talk to me," said Gianotti.

"That's an ounce of White Queen," said Garza. "It takes up to thirty hits and can still knock the dick off a crackhead."

There was laughter behind Garza, which buoyed him a bit. "That means you could make that one ounce thirty tomorrow and sell each for whatever the market will bear. And right now,

267

what you got in your hands, is the only supply available. A conservative estimate, if you zee it out, is six to ten thousand bucks an ounce."

"We don't do zees, spic," said Crazy Phil.

"Shut the fuck up!" snapped Gianotti. "So what's the bottom line, Mr. Cortez?"

"I plug you right into the connection for two hundred kilos of what you got in your hand. You got an exclusive, the only supply in the fucking world. Two hundred keys cut thirty times is six thousand keys. You know the market, I don't have to tell you. If the first thing works out, you get every shipment that follows."

Gianotti took the bag of white powder from Crazy Phil's hand and held it up to the light. He opened it and put his nose near the opening.

"I'd be careful, Mr. Gianotti," said Garza. "That's pure."

"You'll try it, right, Phillie boy?" said Gianotti, holding the bag out toward Crazy Phil, who just stared at it, slack-jawed. His roaming eye seemed to roll up into his skull for a moment the way a shark's does, leaving an eerie white blob. "From what I hear you'll die a happy muthafucka."

Garza heard more nasty laughter from behind him.

"So Cortez, you still didn't gimme the bottom line," said Gianotti.

Garza took a deep breath. "You want the contract, you gotta put up a million bucks out front."

Gianotti stared blankly. "You gotta be fucking kidding," he said.

"You muthafucking spic," said Crazy Phil, starting to his feet.

Gianotti's move was a blur. He backhanded Crazy Phil hard across the mouth. Blood spurted and Phil bounced back in his seat. "You keep dat fucking trap shut!" screamed Gentleman John.

Garza had heard his temper was violent and unpredictable and that as a young buttonman he had been one of the most feared street fighters in the mob. Crazy Phil tried to stop the blood flow with a handkerchief; it soaked through and trickled down onto his suit and tie.

Garza shrugged his shoulders.

"Mr. Gianotti, I'm just a messenger boy. I suggested your name to the connection because I thought I could make an extra hundred grand. If you don't wanna do it, sir, that's fine with me. You can keep the sample as a gift for your troubles."

"Where's your connection at?" said Gianotti.

"Outside the country, sir."

"You don' have to fucking *sir* me. When they want their money?"

"Today, or the deal's off. The Swiss bank account number is on a slip of paper in my wallet."

"And suppose I hang you upside down and cut your fucking dick off and shove it in your mouth—then what?"

"It wouldn't mean shit to them," said Garza. "I'd be dead tonight instead of tomorrow or next year and you'd lose a chance to make four hundred million bucks in one move. End of story."

Gianotti stared at Garza. Then his face cracked into the Godfather smile made famous on the front page of every newspaper and half the magazines in the world.

"I like you, Cortez," he said. "Let's see if everything checks out; then we talk."

———

It was an hour before Pat the Cat returned with a skinny black kid in tow who looked as if he'd been sleeping in the street. He wore a torn, stained overcoat two sizes two large and had duct tape wrapped around his sneakers. He had the unmistakable crazed look of a crackhead. His smell was overpowering, yet it didn't seem to be noticed by anyone but Garza.

"What's the word?" said Gianotti.

"Cortez checks out," said Pat the Cat. "A Marielito."

"You're a fucking Cuban," said Gianotti, smiling. "I like Cubans. I did a lotta business with Mariel people. Good people. Phillie, you oughta apologize to Mr. Cortez for callin' him a spic. He's a Mariel Cubano."

Crazy Phil just dabbed his mouth and stared around cockeyed. Garza smiled. *What could you say to a compliment like that?*

"Okay," said Gianotti, rubbing his hands together and leaning across the table as if about to dig into a good meal. "Let's give the *moolinyam* some a that toot an' see what happens."

Garza experienced a sudden sinking sensation. They were going to give uncut *La Reina Blanca* to the crackhead.

"You might wanna cut that a couple of times," he reminded Gianotti. "The shit is pure."

Gianotti glared at Garza. "You already fucking tol' me that. Now I wanna see for myself. You better fucking pray that shit is pure, my Cuban friend. If it ain't, I'm gonna have Crazy Phil here inject it right into your brain through your eyeball." He turned to Pat the Cat. "Proceed with the testing please, Doctor."

Pat the Cat spilled some of *La Reina Blanca* on the table top, drawing it down into a long, thick white line. The kid stared at it hungrily.

"How would you like to test some shit for us, kid?" he said, pulling out a roll and extracting a hundred-dollar bill off the top.

"Whatchu got, man?"

"Cumbomb," said Gianotti. "If it's good shit, you get a gram *and* the hundred." As he spoke Gallo rolled the hundred-dollar bill into a tube and handed it to the kid.

"The man say it be pure shit, man," said the kid, staring at the strip of white powder glowing dully under the naked bulb.

"That's what you're gonna tell us, right, kid?" said Gianotti.

"Muthafuck it all," said the kid, inserting the rolled bill deep into his nostril, bending and inhaling hard. The powder vanished with a whoosh. The kid stood up bolt-straight, as if he'd been struck by lightning.

"Like a fucking Hoover," laughed one of the buttonmen.

"Nah, an Electrolux," said another.

The kid's eyes bugged out. "Ohhh man," he said. "Oooh. Ooooh." He grabbed his groin with both hands. He started to tremble. "Ahhh," he said as the trembling became convulsions. Suddenly he fell forward, slamming his head against the table, then bounced off onto the concrete floor. Foam and blood gushed from his mouth. His chest heaved violently.

"How you feelin' kid, pretty good?" said Crazy Phil, cackling and spraying blood.

"He's gonna die," said Garza.

"Yeah," said Crazy Phil, looking at Garza. "Then you pass two tests, fucko. The shit is righteous and so are you. 'Cause this makes you a fucking accessory. You dig, Pedro?"

"Unnnh," the kid grunted, his face twisted into a grotesque mask. The grunt turned to a death rattle. In a moment he was still. His eyes wide-open. Foam and blood fizzed at his mouth.

"Open his fucking pants!" Gianotti ordered Crazy Phil.

"What for?"

"Check his fucking johnson you *svatcheem*. See if he came."

33

Belkassami didn't have to say a word. The shit-eating grin on his face as he waited with his squad of goons to greet us at the front of our hotel told me he was a million dollars richer. Once again Garza had come through for me. With a flourish Belkassami presented Nadia with a little gift that turned out to be an antique tiara of twenty-two-carat gold openwork, set with emeralds.

"This is worn by our Fasi brides," he said. "Very old."

She accepted it without a word, inscrutable behind dark glasses.

Next we were whisked to an airport about ten miles outside of Casablanca, in a Mercedes sedan. A Dassault Mystère-Falcon executive jet with a Libyan flag on its tail was waiting in front of a small hangar, ready to take off. A Libyan military officer watched from the gangway as the Mercedes pulled to a dust-billowing stop.

I stepped out into the desert heat. Nadia in her white suit took my arm. Her hand felt cool on my skin. Julio followed sullenly, still avoiding eye contact with me. He had wanted to stay at the hotel, but after a private little conference with his mother he had had a change of heart.

I felt bad for the kid, but there was nothing an Arab drug dealer could do for him.

"Omar Legassi, my good friend," said Belkassami, grasping my hand. "I present you Major al-Megrahi of the Libyan Air Force."

Nadia was not introduced. She seemed to accept her new nonperson status—at least for the time being.

I shook hands with the major, a stocky man with a handlebar mustache. Julio suddenly stepped forward. The major looked at him curiously. "Who is the boy?"

"The son of my woman," I said. "He doesn't speak Arabic."

"Do you speak English, young man?" said the major.

"Yes," said Julio, brightening and extending his hand.

Nadia hovered close behind.

"Excellent," said the major, shaking Julio's hand and holding it a little too long. "I love the opportunity to practice my English."

During the two-hour flight Major al-Megrahi—whose face twitched at the mention of the United States or Israel, much the same way Belkassami's did at the mention of Fatima—said that he had been one of the officers who had taken control of the Libyan government in 1969, along with Colonel Qadhafi.

"The notion of my country's oil being converted to poison in the veins of imperialist and Zionist dogs is a delicious one," he said, eyeing Julio. "Colonel Qadhafi has instructed me to oversee the entire operation from our side. He said to convey his welcome and his wishes that this be a long and fruitful arrangement."

Before I could answer, Julio spoke up: "I'd love to meet the colonel."

The major beamed. "On your next visit, it is my promise."

Julio glanced over at Nadia. I didn't miss it. She had obviously coached him. Since women can't maneuver in the Arab business world, I was certain that she had instructed Julio to make the appropriate connections for her. Belkassami didn't know it yet, but he and I were being squeezed out of the picture. The only direct connection she lacked now was with the Mafia buyers. Once she had that, Omar Legassi would be expendable.

———

Sidra, Libya, is an immense oil depot. Supertankers lined the harbor waiting to fill their holds with the purest burning oil in the world.

"Three million barrels will require two supertankers," said Belkassami, reasserting his role as middleman.

"I have a surprise for you, Omar," announced the major, smiling impishly as we returned to the plane. "We are going to make a little stop in Tripoli. Someone is very anxious to see you."

"Who is that?" I said, forcing a curious smile.

Nadia was honed into my reactions like a human polygraph.

"An old friend of yours—a Palestinian."

"I know a lot of Palestinians," I said, my heart racing.

"This one is a very good friend," he laughed. "The Bear himself."

The name clicked immediately with Omar Legassi's Interpol record.

Yasir Haithem, a/k/a "The Bear." Commander of a Fatah terrorist group. Believed to have purchased arms shipments from Legassi.

"Yasir," I said, trying to sound mildly amused.

The major clapped his hands in delight. "He can hardly wait to see you."

"Well I'd love to see him, too," I said, as calmly as I could. "But we're anxious to return to South America to make final arrangements. Please apologize for me, Major."

I was nauseous from the rush of adrenaline. I kept my hands moving to hide their trembling.

"Ohhh," said the major, crestfallen. "He will be disappointed. He has traveled a considerable distance to see you in Tripoli."

Suddenly I felt Nadia's cool hand on my arm. "But, *mi amor,*" she said; her dark glasses were off, her ice-green eyes boring into mine. "Julio and I were so looking forward to meeting all your old friends. It won't take long will it, Major?"

"Not at all, madam," he said brightening. "It is en route to Casablanca."

"I insist," said Nadia, her hand squeezing my arm tightly.

Everyone was watching me now. Even Belkassami had a curious look on his face.

"Fine," I heard myself say.

———

Two hours later our plane touched down in Tripoli in the middle of a desert wind storm. As we taxied toward a weathered hangar in the middle of a patch of desert a half-mile beyond the main terminal, four cars were waiting for us, so dented and rusted, they appeared to be held together with wire and tin cans.

The eight men watching our approach were as rough and weatherbeaten as their cars. They leaned into the wind, dark and ominous in ragged, flapping combinations of military uniforms and red-and-black-checkered Palestinian kaffiyehs that some used to cover their faces. All were heavily armed with pistols and Chinese-made 56-1 assault rifles.

It was not shaping up to be one of my better days.

Nadia's eyes were on me as the door was opened and the stepladder lowered. She had sat beside me during the flight. I remember her speaking to me, but had had a difficult time concentrating on her words. My mind groped frantically for a plan. I had none. My fate was in free fall again.

"Legassi?" shouted an olive-skinned young man in a worn military uniform, waiting at the bottom of the ladder. He had bushy black hair and a scraggly mustache. All his front teeth were missing.

"Yes," I said, stepping down to meet him. Nadia followed right behind me, shielding her face from the wind.

"Follow me," he said in a rapid, saliva-spewing Arabic. The rest of what he said was difficult for me to follow, but I got the gist of it. The Bear could not come to the airport. They were bringing me to him.

I leaned over to Nadia and shouted into the wind: "He's going to take me to him. Why don't you wait here for me, it shouldn't take too long."

"No! I want to meet your friend," she shouted back. She didn't hide the suspicion in her voice.

The major shouted from the doorway of the plane to the young Fatah soldier, "Where is he?"

"At the house."

"Omar, I will take Julio and follow," called the major, his hand on Julio's shoulder. "I want him to see some of my country."

The soldiers led us to the cars. Nadia and I were seated in the rear of what was once a Mercedes taxi—the lead of a four-car caravan. The major, Julio, and Belkassami in the second car; the remaining Fatah men hustled into the follow-up cars. Engines roared and we were off, racing across windswept desert roads, horns blowing, swerving around slower cars. Donkeys, camels, and people hustled out of our way.

Suddenly we were out of the windstorm and I was aware of the approaching skyline of Tripoli dominated by an immense fortress.

"What is that place?" asked Nadia in French.

"*Al-Saraya Al-Hamra*, the old castle. It has been there since the time of the Romans," answered the young Palestinian as he swerved around a slow-moving car. Horns blared behind us as the others followed.

"How interesting. Isn't that interesting, Omar?"

"Yes, very interesting," I said, wiping the sweat from my brow.

We passed palm-lined boulevards along an avenue called Sirah al-Fatah, then a strip of oceanfront, finally a mad zigzag dash into a catacomb of ancient narrow streets that seemed to have been laid out helter-skelter, without any plan.

Our driver wheeled sharply into a walled courtyard and skidded to a dusty halt. Car doors opened and slammed. Nadia got out first.

I looked up at a broad, blue sky and took a deep breath. *Any day is a good day to die* is an old Arab saying. *This is it*, I thought.

A large ramshackle adobe building with a columned facade dominated the fortress-like surroundings. Men in a hodgepodge of military uniforms and Arab headgear appeared at the front door, all armed to the teeth.

A bearded man about the size and build of a heavyweight professional wrestler, strode out the door and stopped, arms on his hips, glaring down at me. He wore his kaffiyeh in the style of Yasir Arafat. A pistol belt weighted down by a heavy automatic girded his thick middle. Our eyes met. I felt my heart stop beating.

"Omar, you motherless desert snake," he said in Arabic. He grinned a mouthful of gold teeth. He walked toward me, his heavy arms outstretched. He switched to English: "The moment I heard it was you, I came."

For a moment I thought I'd faint. Then he caught me in his arms and kissed me on the mouth Arab-style. It took a moment for the voice to register. It was the voice from that night in the desert; the same deep, raspy voice that was urging me to be killed—the voice of a Mossad agent.

"Yasir," I managed. "It's been a long time."

Nadia laughed out loud with surprise. She clapped her hands.

"Two years since Jerusalem. Much too long my friend. Come." His thick arm was around my shoulder; ignoring the others, he walked me through his armed entourage into the building. I could feel his tension. "We have much to talk about," he said. "I want to hear about everything you've been up to."

My head spun dizzily as he ushered me through what once must have been a large elegant foyer, now piled with weapons and military gear, through a rear door and into a dimly lit hallway.

"Be careful," he whispered, putting his finger to his lips.

At the end of the hallway was a heavy wooden door that led to a cluttered office. A framed photo of Arafat stared at me from the wall. Voices chattered dully from a military radio atop a console.

The moment the door was closed The Bear said, "Do not raise your voice any higher than I am speaking right now."

He turned on a portable radio on his desk. Middle Eastern drums and flutes wailed across the room beneath a woman's shrill voice singing in Arabic.

"Give me the wallet," he ordered. "Quickly."

He retrieved a duplicate of my recorder-wallet from inside his shirt and handed it to me with trembling hands. I took mine from my inside jacket pocket and, trying unsuccessfully to hide my own tremors, removed my money and documents then handed it to him.

"Why did you do this?" I said as I replaced everything in the new wallet. "You took about ten years off my life."

"We had to. Your Nadia was searching all over Europe and the Middle East for someone who knew Omar personally."

"Nadia set this up?"

"You're lucky I was in a position to intercede. Or you would be dead . . . like Shoshanna."

"You know."

"Yes. What we don't know is how?"

"It's on the tape," I said. "I'm sorry."

"So am I, but now is not the time to grieve. I have some information for you."

There was a loud noise from the hallway. The Bear's arms were a blur of movement. His gun was aimed at the door. Some voices arguing in Arabic. They moved away.

"We don't have much time," he said. "Our intelligence learned that Nadia has negotiated to trade the oil for arms with North Korea. The weapons then go to Saddam Hussein."

"I already figured something like that."

"We must know exactly how you plan to wrap this up."

"I'm going to try and get all the parties to this deal—Nadia, the Mafia, and the Libyans—in one location, as soon as possible. They think they're meeting to coordinate deliveries and make payments. The Koreans and Hussein's people will have to be there too. It will be a trap. American DEA agents and military will arrest all of them for murder, drug- and arms-trafficking, and bring them back to the States for trial." I patted the Mossad wallet. "I've got enough evidence here to put them away forever *and* expose the Triangle of Death."

"And what about the drug?"

"I hope this wallet thing works—it's all in here. The lab where they're manufacturing it is ten kilometers northeast of the main compound. We'll hit it at the same time we close the trap."

He stood facing me. I noticed that his heavy beard tried unsuccessfully to hide a white rope of a scar that ran from his jawline to his eyebrow. His nose was a pulpy mess that looked like it had been smashed with a baseball bat. One side of his neck was scarred and discolored from burns.

"There is something else we wanted you to know," he said. "We made a voiceprint comparison of your recording of Dr. Hess. His true name is Franz Weir. He was an assistant to Mengele. His laboratory was in the subbasement of Building Ten in Auschwitz. According to those who survived the camp, no one sent to Weir ever returned."

"From what I can tell there are a whole bunch of these Nazis working with this organization."

"But this one is special," said The Bear. "Did you know that your mother had a first cousin named Kayla? The same name as your mother."

"No. My mother never talks about Europe."

"Ask Avi. They are both named after your great-grandmother."

"So, you and Avi know my family history better than I do."

"Kayla was one of those sent to Hess."

He studied me. I thought I understood the purpose of him telling me this family story: The Mossad wanted to insure the total destruction of the organization *and* the drug, and feared that I might stop once I had René's killers. I didn't show the sense of rage that I suppose he expected to see. Nothing was going to bring back René or Shoshanna. I felt ashamed. The rest of my feelings were blocked out so that I could play my role.

"What do you want me to do?" I said finally.

His broad face cracked in a sudden gold-studded grin. "You and I have a quick drink," he said, turning and heading to his desk. "What else would two old friends like Omar and Yasir do?"

He pulled out a bottle of Rémy Martin cognac from a drawer and two dirty glasses, which he wiped with the tail of his shirt. He filled each tumbler half full and handed me one.

"*In sha' Allah*," he said, and gulped some down.

I downed the contents in one swallow. The trembling of my hands eased for the first time.

"What are you going to do?" I asked.

"If your plan works, there won't be anything left to do. Besides," he said, suddenly laughing. "We're a tiny country; South America is half a world away—what could we possibly do?"

"And that's it?"

"We must know when and where your grand finale will be."

"Why is that?"

"I should think that would be obvious to you. Once they know who you are—if I'm still here, I'm exposed. And I'm in no rush to die."

"What about the real Omar? What are the odds that he is going to pop up somewhere?"

"Zero. Two years ago he sold arms to the PLO; the wrong PLO. Me." He held his thick right hand up. "This hand closed his eyes."

"But what if someone else blows my cover, ten minutes from now?"

"This is one Jew who won't die alone," he said, patting the gun on his hip. "I already know who I'm taking with me. Do you?"

34

"Bravo, Omar," said Nadia, leaning back in her seat, her eyes again hidden behind the dark glasses.

The Mercedes lurched and swerved its way through the maze of streets surrounding the Bear's stronghold. Horns blared around us. We were alone again in the rear seat.

"There's no time left for bravos." I said. "I've got a customer in New York who's advanced me a million dollars. By the time we get back to Casablanca I'd like to have something to tell him."

For the moment Nadia trusted me, but my cover was held together by spit, thread, and tissue. I pushed her for all I was worth to set a date, time, and place for the final summit meeting of all the parties to the transaction. The trap.

"I already have a location in mind," she said.

"Where?"

"Mario is making the arrangements, all the parties will be advised in plenty of time. You can tell your friend Señor Belkassami to go ahead and ship three million barrels of oil to the China Sea as soon as he can. Once the shipment reaches Okinawa, he'll be given further instructions."

I allowed myself a slow smile. She had taken the bait. Now, getting DEA and my government behind me was my only remaining obstacle. *Or so I thought.*

Later that night while Nadia made preparations for our return to South America, I rushed to Belkassami's Casablanca office, where he and the major were waiting for me. I rigged a speakerphone conversation with Garza and Mafia capo Gentleman John Gianotti in New York City, so that Belkassami and the major could listen.

Speaking in code through Garza, Gianotti confirmed his agreement—to pay $120 million for two hundred kilos of pure *La Reina Blanca* delivered to the U.S.—less the $1 million already on deposit in Belkassami's Swiss account. Gianotti would personally bring the cash to a designated meeting spot outside the U.S., where he would turn it over to Belkassami and the major once receipt of the drugs had been confirmed.

Belkassami and the major were flushed and teary-eyed with excitement. It was all real now. They pounded me on the back and toasted each other quietly as I spoke on the phone.

The deal, less Omar Legassi's commission of $10 million, would gross them $110 million. They would more than double the current OPEC price and poison the children of the Great Satan, all in one move. And this, they thought, was just the beginning.

Before hanging up, Garza had asked that I call him to "settle that other thing"—code indicating that he had to speak to me urgently. I read enormous stress in his voice. At this point the last thing in the world I needed was for him to remind me of how much trouble I was in with Stratton and the DEA suits. Whatever it was, it could wait until I put the finishing touches to the trap— when it would be impossible for the suits to do anything but back me up.

From the meeting I rushed to the airport, where Nadia and her crew had taken over a private lounge belonging to Air France while the foundation plane was being preflighted for the long trip back to South America.

When I arrived, Nadia was in the midst of an angry phone call. "I don't care what you have to do," I heard her say. "I hold you responsible for every hectare that burns—did you hear me? . . . Did you hear me *clearly*? I want a full report within the next ten minutes . . ."

Later I would learn that an area of the Amazon, roughly the size of New York State, was being cleared by fire and that from satellites circling high above the earth it seemed that the whole jungle was burning.

I felt a touch on my shoulder and looked up to see Julio peering down at me nervously.

"Can I sit with you for a moment?" he said tentatively, looking as if he was about to bolt.

"Of course."

He quickly glanced across the room at his mother, busy on another animated telephone conversation, and took a seat on an overstuffed chair beside mine. A small table and lamp separated us. He had placed himself so that I blocked Nadia's view of him.

"There's something I've got to tell you," he said softly, without making eye contact. His left hand unconsciously did a karate exercise called the "tight fist"—clenching rock-hard, relaxing, then clenching again.

"I'm glad you're finally speaking to me," I said.

"What happened that night . . . I didn't want you to get the wrong idea."

"I didn't get any ideas, Julio—wrong or right."

"I guess I love my mother . . . but maybe some things are wrong. Some things . . . you just can't do anything about."

I was on very thin ice. I really liked the kid and wished there was some way that I could help him, but he was still Nadia's son. The case was still a long way from over.

"I told you I studied *goju* karate, right?"

"Yeah," he said, his eyes again flicking anxiously toward Nadia.

"Your *sensei* ever explain what *goju* meant?"

He looked at me uncertainly. "It means hard-soft, doesn't it?"

"Right," I said, leaning in close to him. "Hard-soft, the combination you've got to be to survive. In hand-to-hand combat if you attack hard every time, against every opponent, you're not going to live too long, Julio. Sooner or later you come up against a guy who's bigger and harder than you. The last thing you want to do is attack hard. You'll get your own dick jammed down your throat."

Julio smiled. "The yin and the yang."

"Right," I said. "You want to be soft, supple, evasive—let him attack. Wait for him to fuck up, to go after you so hard that he's off balance. That's your opening. At that moment you turn as hard as a fucking bayonet and attack for all you're worth. But to get to that moment you've got to be soft, relaxed, go with the flow."

"Cool," he said.

Just a kid.

"The Japanese look at everything in life as war—from business to sex—one man competing with others for every fucking thing life gives you. War, from the cradle to the grave. War can be anything, any situation you find yourself in. A bad teacher. A bad relationship. Any situation you feel trapped in. That's the time to get soft, Julio. To recognize, right now there's nothing I can do but go with the flow. But nothing stays the same forever. Shit happens and happens fast, and suddenly your opening is there and you get hard."

"There's something you should know, Omar . . ." he began, and then suddenly stopped talking. He was looking past me. I turned. Nadia was off the phone and glaring at us.

Julio sprang to his feet and headed across the room toward the john. Nadia's eyes followed him. He passed the reception desk where a ground stewardess had just delivered a stack of newspapers—the international edition of the *Herald Tribune* in English. The headlines caught my eye. CIA CONFIRMS VILLARINO DIED HUNTING CARTEL SUPERDRUG.

I picked up a newspaper and brought it back to my seat. The article was based on an Associated Press news release:

AP—U.S. Government sources today indicated that the Central Intelligence Agency has obtained "extremely reliable information" proving that the Medellín cartel had ordered the torture death of undercover DEA agent René Villarino because he was "close to revealing that the Cartel had developed a new and more potent form of cocaine known on the streets as 'The White Queen' . . ."

I put the paper down. I had to get to a phone, to call Stratton. I looked at my watch. There was an hour left before Nadia's plane would be ready.

I glanced up at Nadia. She and Julio were locked head-to-head in an intense conversation. Moon Face was on the phone surrounded by a couple of his security men. I might not get another chance. I got to my feet and walked casually toward the door.

The telephone center was at the far end of the terminal, about a two-block walk. I hustled toward it. *Omar Legassi has business to take care of. There should be nothing unusual about him making a last-minute private phone call.* Something heavy was going down at headquarters; I had heard it in Garza's voice and there it was on the front page of the *Herald Tribune.*

I listened to clicks on the line as the call was put through to Alexandria, Virginia, Stratton's home phone. He'd be awake getting ready to go to work.

The phone was answered on the first ring. "Yeah."

"It's me," I said. "I'm a long way from you and in no position to talk. I saw the headlines."

"My fucking hero," he said.

For a second I thought I had the wrong number. "Do you know who you're talking to?"

"You jiving me, or what? It's over. Case closed, and you're the guy who did it. Everybody in the office is calling you a bona fide, muthafucking genius. Whitfield himself is talking about giving you a medal. You ever think you'd live to see that, Levine? The Agency got the skinny on the cartel. If you had busted *El Búfalo* when everybody wanted you to, the whole thing would've been burnt. You saved the day, you dinky-dau son of a bitch."

"It can't be true," I said.

"It's true!" said Stratton. "The spooks have turned over tape-recorded conversations and informant statements. It's the cartel, we just don't know exactly who did what, yet—but we will. We're about ready to drop a fucking hammer on them. We're gonna take down every Colombian who ever spit on an American sidewalk. It's lucky you called. Main Justice is overseeing the indictments; they want Mister Buffalo, bad, and you're the only guy that puts him in the trick bag." Stratton laughed, a wry, barking sound.

"After all your conniving and all the suits' bullshit about prosecuting you, you're gonna end up a fucking hero. You better get your heroic ass on the next plane to D.C."

"Whoa, whoa, where'd all this supposedly true bullshit come from?" I asked, trying to keep myself calm.

"The station chief in B.A."

"Forrest Gregg? I can't fucking believe this! Someone is using him, Bobby! You know the spooks aren't that bright when it comes to the drug business. It's a red herring. Someone's trying to throw us off the track."

"Gregg's no fool! And neither are the people working for him."

"The Argentines? They're snakes. They're for sale to the highest bidder."

"If they're putting a red herring over on us, they're doing a pretty convincing job of it," said Stratton.

"For an American buck they'll do anything for anyone—even DEA. And the people I'm into already have half the Argentine government in their pockets."

"Who's that?"

The question hung there between us for a moment like the six thousand miles of transatlantic cable connecting us. *How much could I tell Stratton?* I just couldn't take the chance. In a couple of days I'd lay the case on the suits in a way that they couldn't turn me down.

"I can't talk on the phone."

"Then come in and tell me."

"I will, just get me another couple of days."

"*You* can't? *I* can't! I don't care where you are, you've got twenty-four hours to get here. That's an order!"

I clicked the phone a few times trying to fake a bad connection.

"I know what you're trying to pull, Levine . . ." shouted Stratton as I hung up.

I sat there in the booth partition wondering about myself. What did I really know about Nadia's power and influence? Forrest Gregg's information might be at least partially accurate. I didn't know whom Nadia had sold *La Reina* to in the past— maybe it was the cartel. Maybe René *had* gotten mixed up with them. *No! El Búfalo* told me that he, too, was looking for the connection. He had no reason to lie to me. And René's last known contact in this world was with Mario Razouk.

I looked at my watch; I'd been gone too long. As I hustled out of the telephone center I came face-to-face with Moon Face and one of his goons. He was smiling a lipless grimace, his tiny dark eyes narrowed almost to invisibility. I thought of Shoshanna and knew I had to get away from him before I tried to jam his nose bone back into his brain with the palm of my hand and blow the whole case. I moved past him and down the long hallway. The two men fell into step behind me.

Finally, on board the plane as we taxied for takeoff, I sat isolated in the front cabin. I closed my eyes and laid my head back. I was exhausted. There was nothing more I could do. I felt sleep pulling me down and didn't resist.

My first conscious awareness, coming out of a deep sleep, was the frightening feeling that I was being watched. Then I smelled Nadia's perfume. I opened my eyes. Nadia was standing over me.

"May I join you?"

"Of course," I said, momentarily unnerved by her closeness. I could see suspicion in her too-intense green eyes. I glanced around the dimly lit cabin and saw Moon Face and two of the goons I recognized from the night of Shoshanna's murder lounging in seats near the rear. I had reserved a special place for them in my memory. Big blond storm trooper types. The thinner of the two had a GI brush cut; the other was a skinhead with platinum eyebrows and a weight lifter's body. But at the moment it didn't matter how many goons she had in the cabin. The plane was a five-mile-high prison cell moving at almost six hundred miles an hour and I wasn't going anywhere.

"I need to talk with you," she said, taking a seat beside me.

"I must have slept through takeoff," I croaked, not liking the defensive sound of my voice. *Why should Omar feel defensive when everything was going perfectly well?*

"That was four hours ago,"

"I guess I'm not as young as I thought," I said, aware that the technique of waking someone out of a sound sleep was a good one for jarring well-constructed defenses.

"I have a few questions."

"Questions?"

"Why did you leave the First Class lounge to call the United States?" Her voice was neither accusatory nor suspicious; it was a direct probe. "You could have used the phone in the lounge, couldn't you?"

"No offense," I said, holding her gaze. "But that's my business."

She didn't blink; she continued evenly: "Omar Legassi disappears two years ago in the Middle East. He reappears in Buenos Aires."

"What are you getting at?"

"The Palestinian happens to say he has not seen you in two years. Precisely two years, and loud enough for everyone present to hear."

"What does that mean?"

"By itself? Perhaps nothing, although the identity of people who vanish or die does make for an excellent false identity."

"What are you accusing me of?"

"Nothing," she said, unperturbed. "I'm listing facts. You pick up a newspaper an hour before our flight and you run to make a phone call."

"I didn't *run* anywhere."

"We found nothing in Omar Legassi's background to indicate even an interest in Japanese philosophy. On the contrary, his record is that of a man just a step above the gutter; not a very thoughtful or meditative man."

"If Jesus hadn't been a carpenter and an ex-convict, I'd be flattered," I wisecracked, and was immediately sorry.

"Even more important than these inconsistencies . . . I have a feeling about you; I've seen you someplace before. It's somewhere at the edge of my mind. My instinct seems to warn me about you."

"I wish your instinct had spoken up before I committed myself."

"So you understand then."

"Understand what?"

"Why I have decided to cancel our arrangement."

She sat very close to me, her eyes continuing their probe.

Mike Levine the undercover agent, way out on a limb, would try to reason with her, cajole her, convince her that she was jumping to rash, illogical conclusions. Omar Legassi, gangster, drug dealer, the sleazebag described in the criminal records—watching ten million bucks slip away from him—would have done exactly the same thing, even pleaded, or ranted and raved. Both reactions, I thought, would have failed.

"That's too bad," I said, laying my head back against the seat and closing my eyes. *Give in to the superior strength of an opponent; go with it. Never try to meet it head on—my advice to Julio.*

"You're taking this remarkably well."

"Do I have a choice?" I said slowly, easily, sleepily, closing my eyes.

"Yes," she said. I opened my eyes. Her face was still very close to mine, studying me. "Kill for me," she said, "and there will be no doubt."

"I'm not a murderer."

"Omar Legassi has killed many times before."

"People who deserved to die."

"Few deserve it more than this man."

"Who?"

"*El Búfalo.*"

"The man has an army of killers. I couldn't get near him."

"If you did business with him you've been near him."

"I don't want to commit suicide. I would need time—a couple of weeks to set it up. I'd have to finesse him into a vulnerable position."

"He will be vulnerable for forty-eight hours beginning tomorrow afternoon when his boat anchors off the coast of Cartagena."

"That doesn't leave me much time, does it?"

"Perhaps the Italians who advanced the money will want to help," she said cagily.

"Perhaps," I said. "I'm curious. You obviously have the power—why don't you do it yourself?"

She smiled for the first time.

"Because I don't have to. Because I don't want to be wrong about you. Because I'm happy to give you an opportunity to truly be with me."

She put her hand over mine.

"I want three million for the hit," I said.

If Omar did it, he wouldn't do it for free.

She blinked and then smiled. "Then you agree?"

"You haven't answered me. Three million, cash."

"Fine," she said. "That will be the final payment, after the oil is transferred."

"Agreed," I said.

"And one more thing," she said.

"What's that?"

"I want to be there to watch."

"Aren't you afraid the cartel will learn you're behind this?"

"Oh, I want them to know," she said. "*El Búfalo* broadcast all over the world that he was looking for *La Reina Blanca*. I want the world to know he found her."

35

I WAITED IN THE SHADOWS ACROSS THE ROAD FROM THE BRIGHTLY LIT entrance of the Cartagena Hilton, watching the street. It was after three in the morning. People flowed in and out of the hotel, which had one of the most popular gambling casinos on the Caribbean coast. Cabbies congregated along the hotel's circular driveway, talking loud and drinking beer. It was tourist season and the late night streets surrounding the hotel were alive with activity.

For a moment the possibility that Nadia wouldn't show up for the *El Búfalo* hit lifted my spirits. There was still a chance to call it off—ten more minutes until the point of no return when my carefully planned operation, a step I had never even contemplated before, moved into high gear and there would be no stopping it. I had more plates spinning now than I'd ever had in my twenty-year career. The odds of the whole thing blowing up in my face were a lot higher than of it succeeding.

I checked my watch every few seconds, trying to push the second hand around quicker. Nadia's not showing would give me the excuse to cancel, but, I wondered, do I really want that? What happens then?

A black Buick sedan approached and slowed. I saw a flash of white in the rear seat and knew it was her. I stepped out of the shadows letting the light shine on my face. The car bore a Panamanian diplomatic license plate, 714126-CD. I was afraid to repeat the number for the Mossad recorder; afraid she'd see my lips move, so I memorized it using an old trick, changing the numbers to form letters and the word *GLAZ* (*G* being the seventh letter, etc.). The CD stood for *Cuerpo Diplomático*.

The car came to a stop beside me. Nadia was alone in the backseat. Moon Face watched me from the passenger seat. The door lock clicked. *Here goes nothing.* I slipped into the velveteen softness beside her.

"I'm glad you could make it," I said.

"So am I."

"Now what?" said Jacques impatiently.

"My people are already in place," I said. "Do you have the boat?"

"Everything is as you instructed," he said, his little eyes glittering.

"Let's go then. There's not much time."

The car moved slowly at first through narrow congested streets, then picked up speed as we hit a main drag that took us past the walls of the enormous colonial fortress that is the center of Cartagena. Music drifted back from the stereo, a classical choral piece. After about ten minutes of driving, I noted that we were on the outskirts of Cartagena heading east on the coast road toward Barranquilla.

"Where's your boat?" I asked.

"La Boguilla," said Jacques.

"That's not too bright, is it? You're right on top of him." I said, unable to resist sticking it to the moon-faced motherfucker in front of his boss lady. I saw him stiffen and it felt good.

"It won't be there long," said Nadia.

I knew La Boguilla. It was a little fishing village famous for its wild weekend parties. I had done an undercover deal there more than ten years earlier—a freighter-load of marijuana. It occurred to me that most of the places I had been and the memories tied to them were undercover deals. Michael Levine, civilian tourist, had never been anywhere.

"What about radio equipment?" I asked.

"It is already tuned to the frequency you designated," said Jacques. "We've heard nothing."

Ten minutes later we swung into the parking lot of a dimly lit marina. Docked at the pier immediately ahead was a Hatteras yacht flying a Panamanian flag.

"That's it," said Jacques.

The Hatteras is a medium sized, fast-moving yacht with a short rear deck and a high cabin. A three-man crew wearing striped polo shirts and white ducks watched as we boarded. They could have been an America's Cup yacht-racing team, except for the captain, a tall, angular man with heavily tattooed arms. He greeted Nadia in French.

"Everything is as you ordered, Mademoiselle."

Jacques took off his suit jacket and tossed it onto a bench. He wore the heavy Bowie knife in a shoulder sling. The square butt of an automatic protruded from his belt.

"Has there been any contact on that frequency?" asked Nadia.

"None," said the captain.

All eyes were on me.

"They're waiting for my signal," I said.

"*La Rebelde*, is she here?" asked Nadia.

"Yes," said the captain. He handed Nadia and me each a pair of night-vision field glasses. "About five hundred meters off starboard."

"I think we'd better move," I said.

Nadia nodded her head. The captain signaled with a wave of his hand. The powerful engine rumbled to life under my feet. The running lights flicked on. The boat was fast and surprisingly quiet as it cut smoothly through the small chopping waves. Nadia put the glasses to her eyes and stared out into the darkness.

"Where's the radio?" I asked.

"This way," said the captain, leading me inside the large double-decked cabin. The boat was equipped with state-of-the-art radar and radio equipment. He handed me a mike. "It is tuned as was directed."

"Take us close enough to see them with the glasses," I said. "But not too close."

The captain repeated my order to the man at the wheel, I felt the boat change course slightly. I said a silent prayer as I pressed the piece of cloth hacked from René's burial suit in one hand and the mike button with the other.

"This is Snake One," I said.

Silence.

I looked around. Nadia had entered the cabin and was watching me. I pressed the mike again. "This is Snake One."

Static. A voice crackled: "*Snake Two and Three.*"

"How is the party?"

"Is that you . . . coming out from the marina?" said the voice.

"Affirmative."

"Not too close. We're waiting for the Indian."

"What does that mean?" asked Nadia, her eyes wide with excitement.

"El Búfalo is the Indian—he's not on board yet."

"Where are your people?"

"They're professionals. They know what they're doing."

"Too close!" squawked the radio voice.

I could see dim lights shining from the cabin of a large yacht at anchor, about two hundred yards ahead. The captain responded immediately by ordering a change of course. After a moment the radio voice said, *"Better."*

"Can you see?" I asked Nadia.

Nadia raised the night-vision glasses. "I can see his boat; I can even see the name—*La Rebelde*—his pride and joy. Perfect."

"Cut engine!" ordered the captain, speaking softly. Voices carried a long way over water at night. "Weigh anchor!"

Small waves lapped at the boat as it rode gently at anchor. Other than a mild creaking sound everything was quiet. It seemed that hours passed. The sky began to streak with light. Jacques sat in a corner of the cabin watching me.

I heard the faint sound of a distant motor.

I picked up the glasses and scanned the area. A light moved out from the direction of the marina. I focused on it. It was an open dinghy with three or four men in it. One of them had an unmistakable silhouette—a huge head.

"It's him," said Nadia beside me, her eyes glued to the glasses.

"Snake One," squawked the radio voice.

I pressed the mike. "Snake One."

"Indian," said the voice.

"Go!" I ordered. I dropped the mike, feeling sick.

The sound of the dinghy grew louder. I picked up the night-vision glasses and focused them. It was still dark, yet I could see everything brightly illuminated in an eerie green glow.

The dinghy tied up to *La Rebelde.* Two men clambered on board. They reached down and helped *El Búfalo* climb onto the deck. He appeared close enough to touch. The three men staggered a bit on deck. They were met there by two others. Voices and laughter wafted across the water—they sounded drunk or stoned.

"Pendejito de mierda!" cursed *El Búfalo,* his voice sounding as clear and distinct as it did the night he sat beside me in the limo in Fort Lauderdale.

"Yes," breathed Nadia. "Yes."

El Búfalo and his crew staggered into a doorway and disappeared below deck.

A faint rumble erupted from the distant shore line. Two white wakes knifed swiftly across the water toward *La Rebelde.* They moved with incredible speed and little sound. Two high-speed cigarette boats skimmed the water, each with several hooded men on board. I glimpsed short-barreled automatic weapons with bulky silencers. They faced forward as still as statues. As they approached the yacht their engines suddenly cut. Two men in each paddled quickly and silently to close the remaining distance.

As the black-clad silhouettes climbed silently up the side of *La Rebelde,* I could hardly breathe. One, two, five, eight men were on deck crouching together as if in a football huddle. They suddenly separated and vanished below deck.

"Magnifique," breathed Nadia beside me.

A blinding flash lit up the interior of *La Rebelde,* followed by a dull boom. A series of flashes inside the cabins was followed closely by the *pftt-pftt-pftt* of silenced automatic weapons. More flashes lit up *La Rebelde,* followed by the *brrrack, brrrack* of an Ingram submachine gun. Now there were shouts. A scream of pain. A sudden bright flash from the deck lit up the water, followed by a loud boom. A cloud of black smoke mushroomed outward, obscuring the scene.

Something has gone terribly wrong!

The sound of sirens erupted from the direction of Cartagena. My insides were twisting. I could hardly breathe. *Omar Legassi would feel no anguish; it would be like watching the exciting finish to a horse race for him.* I let Mike Levine slip away, deep inside me.

Flames leapt above the black cloud of smoke. Engines roared; the sleek cigarette boats streaked out from beneath the spreading cloud. The sky was getting brighter above the eastern horizon.

"I want to see him dead," said Nadia, lowering the glasses. "That was the agreement."

"Some things are out of my hands," I said, noticing that one of the cigarette boats had veered around in a short arc and was heading toward us.

"What is this?" said Jacques, the automatic in his hand.

"Put that away, these are my people!" I shouted, moving to the port side to watch the speeding boat approach.

"Put it away!" ordered Nadia.

The cigarette boat pulled alongside. Four black-hooded men were on board; they were blood-spattered. One lay on his back bleeding badly from chest wounds.

"For Omar!" shouted one of them, tossing a small canvas bag onto the deck. I recognized the voice. The engine roared and the speedboat streaked for the shoreline.

The sound of sirens from shore grew louder. The sun peeked up over the horizon. *La Rebelde* was engulfed in flames and listing onto its side. The engine rumbled beneath my feet. We moved swiftly toward shore.

Jacques opened the canvas bag and retrieved a bloody paper package. He slowly unwrapped it with Nadia looking on. It was an enormous jade and gold serpent ring with two large emerald eyes—*El Búfalo*'s fabled *iman*. It was wedged tightly in folds of fat on its original mounting: *El Búfalo*'s finger.

Nadia reached out and took the ring and finger in her hands turning it over and examining it. She looked directly into my eyes.

"I don't know whether you're Omar Legassi or not—but whoever you are, we have a deal."

36

"YOU FUCKING GET HERE," SCREAMED GARZA THE MOMENT HE HEARD my voice.

"There was no way I could call you," I said as I watched the crowd around me for listeners.

I was on a public phone in Ezeiza International Airport in Buenos Aires, on my way to DEA Headquarters in Washington. It had been a mistake to call Garza. I should have waited until I arrived in the States. But I just had to know what happened in Cartagena.

"I don't care about any of your fucking bullshit!" he screamed. "You got us into this fucking mess, now you're gonna get us out, or go down the fucking tubes with us. You better get your ass to the Miami safe house, like yesterday, or I swear to God I'll be the first to testify against you."

"Just calm down, Tito."

"Calm down? You *are* fucking nuts! I'm gonna hang up on you in another second and just call Stratton."

The hit on *El Búfalo* had been botched. None of our people were supposed to die, but I didn't know the full extent of the disaster, and Garza wasn't talking.

The newspapers had described the gun battle and sinking of *La Rebelde* as part of a turf war between Colombian drug cartels. Five bodies had been found, burned too badly to be identified.

"Just tell me what happened," I pleaded. I had never heard him lose it like this. I felt like screaming myself. I hunched over the phone, turning my back on the crowded terminal, feeling my head swim.

"You'll see it in the fucking headlines in the morning, asshole. I'll let you sweat like you did us."

"Tito, I need to know."

"You motherfucker! I know you—you coulda found a way to call. Leaving us hanging out here. Gianotti's people think I ripped 'em off for a million bucks—we gotta hide from them *and* DEA. Just be here in the morning!" He slammed the phone down.

Once again Michael Levine, rogue agent, was in a chin-deep pit of shit. My actions—once the suits got wind of them—would be called criminal, even accessory to homicide.

My new status as the suits' hero had not lasted long.

On the other hand, Omar Legassi, drug dealer, was about to close the biggest deal of his criminal life. In eight days time, he would be $13 million richer—including payment for the murder of *El Búfalo*—and he had been invited to join one of the most powerful criminal organizations in history as a top-level member. The audience for this performance, only inches away, would expect to see success in his voice, his eyes, his walk—not a man coming apart at the seams.

Nadia had been finally won over. She had not questioned me when I told her that I needed to go to the States to make the final arrangements with the Gianotti family and that I had to bring a sample of *La Reina* with me—chosen at random from the two-hundred-kilo shipment—so that I could give Gianotti my guarantee that I had checked the shipment personally before it left.

She had even arranged for me to witness the drug being expertly built into the walls and bottoms of the animal cages that would carry a shipment of jaguars into Miami. Once the animals were removed, the cages would be held in a warehouse belonging to the Amazon Wildlife Federation and released to Gianotti's people at the moment of payment.

The final meet had been arranged just as I had conceived it. The Gianotti family would pay $120 million in cash to Belkassami the oil dealer. The Libyan major would then authorize via shortwave radio that the oil shipment be delivered to North Korea, whose representative would then release the arms shipment to Iraq. The biggest winner of all would be Nadia, who would receive approximately $300 million in gold and U.S. dollars from the Iraqis—and this was just the first transaction.

All the parties to the deal—Belkassami and the Libyan major, the Gianotti family, Korean government agents, and Saddam Hussein's people—would meet in eight days time at an isolated jungle hotel on the Argentine border with Brazil, at a place where the Iguazú River suddenly dives shrieking and thundering into a massive chasm called *La Garganta del Diablo*—the Devil's Throat.

"Iguazú is one of the last strongholds for the harpy eagle," she told me, as if this fact would give her some special aid from the gods.

All final preparations concerning the Iguazú meeting were made right from the jungle compound, except for those with the Gianotti Mafia family, which I insisted I'd have to do in person. It was my hole card, my only excuse to get to DEA headquarters.

Nadia seemed wild with enthusiasm, more careless than I'd ever seen her. Her organization would become the fulcrum of a huge criminal enterprise, giving her as much subterranean power as any nation on earth. Julio told me that a big part of the money would be going toward long-term lease/purchase agreements of enormous tracts of rain forest in the name of the foundation. I thought it ironic that her passion to preserve the Amazon at the expense of mankind had her charging right into my trap.

For one brief moment the biggest, deadliest criminals on earth would be in one location. My trap was now set; all it lacked were the crushing jaws that the combined military and law enforcement might of the U.S. government would provide. Then and only then could Michael Levine, deep cover DEA agent, surface and perform his final task—the destruction of all Omar Legassi's work.

But I might have a lot more explaining to do than I thought, before anybody in headquarters was going to listen to me.

———

The ten-hour overnight flight to the U.S. was a sleepless, stomach-twisting nightmare. I felt the walls of the plane closing in on me. We touched down in Miami at exactly 8:00 a.m. I had reservations on a connecting flight to Washington, D.C., that I wasn't going to make.

I used my diplomatic passport to breeze quickly through Immigration and Customs, carrying an ounce of *La Reina Blanca* in my pocket. I hurried to the main terminal and headed to a newspaper stand—the only way I could ever find out what was really going on in headquarters.

The headline of *The Miami Herald* screamed the news: EL BUFALO FINGERED IN TORTURE DEATH OF VILLARINO.

AP—Reliable government sources indicated today that the U.S. Drug Enforcement Administration has the man directly responsible for the torture murder of DEA undercover agent René Villarino as notorious Medellín cartel boss Felix *El Búfalo* Restrepo. The sources indicate that the CIA has supplied DEA with at least one witness to the murder who fingers Restrepo.

In the meantime a DEA investigation continues in Colombia to identify the badly burned remains of five men killed in a high-seas shoot-out off the coast of Medellín, Colombia, involving a luxury yacht, *La Rebelde,* belonging to *El Búfalo.* The infamous Medellín cartel boss was last seen heading toward his yacht, only minutes before the shoot-out and fiery explosion, and has been listed as missing and presumed dead . . .

I crumpled the newspaper under my arm and ran for the taxi stand in front of the terminal. DEA and CIA's publicly singling out *El Búfalo* as René's killer not only had my head swimming but was about to destroy my entire plan.

The safe house was on Southwest 10th Street in Little Havana, about a half-hour cab ride from the airport. The taxi dropped me off in front of a decaying pink stucco house, on a quiet block with a dozen similar houses on both sides of the street, each with a palm tree in its small square front yard; each surrounded by a chain link fence. A suburban slum.

As I opened the outside gate, the front door opened. Garza stood back in the doorway glaring at me. He looked disheveled in a sweaty T-shirt, he hadn't shaved in days, and there were deep hollows around his eyes.

"What's going on?" I said as I reached the door.

"Follow me," he ordered, shutting the door behind us and charging off into the house. He led the way through a small, sparsely furnished living room to a basement door. The curtains were drawn on all the windows. There was no air-conditioning, and the house reeked of sweat and body odor. I followed Garza down a narrow stairway to the basement.

Instinctively I flicked on a mini tape recorder that I carried in my pants pocket. Before leaving Argentina I had closed my deal with the Mossad by leaving my final recorder-wallet at the Aguirre Imports office. I didn't know what I was walking into, and twenty-five paranoid years of undercover work had taught me, *when in doubt tape yourself.*

Vinnie O'Brien, in shorts and a T-shirt, was near the foot of the stairs watching me. The square black handle of a Glock automatic jutted out from under his thick arm.

"Vinnie," I said. He eyed me suspiciously without responding. The scene at the bottom of the stairs stunned me speechless.

El Búfalo in stained shorts and sweat-soaked T-shirt occupied most of a sagging couch against the far wall. His right hand was heavily wrapped in bloodstained bandages. The long room looked like the bottom of a Dumpster. The remains of a couple dozen fast-food meals and assorted garbage littered every flat surface. He obviously favored Big Macs. A large population of well-fed roaches and palmetto bugs promenaded casually up and down the walls.

Beside him, sitting on the edge of an overstuffed chair, a tanned, well-dressed, bullnecked man with a clean-shaven head watched me. Bruce Fisher was one of the top criminal attorneys in the country. Prosecutors called him "the Junkyard Dog" for his gutter tactics in and out of the courtroom. *No blow too low* was the saying that followed his name.

"Tell him whatchu told me!" snapped Garza.

"Somebody mind telling me what happened?" I said.

"Hijo de puta," said *El Búfalo* with a laugh, shaking his huge head. "It's Money Man. You really fooled me. I made you for anything but a cop."

"Don't say anything, Felix," warned Fisher.

"Okay, you wanted Levine—he's here!" screamed Garza, moving toward Fisher. "Now tell him what you told me."

"The deal is off," said Fisher. "I'm advising my client to turn himself into DEA today. As far as I'm concerned you've reneged on the deal."

"I didn't renege on anything," I said. "The deal was—he plays dead and I do everything I can to get him out."

"Your deal, you son of a bitch," said Garza, his face jutting into mine, "got Georgie in the hospital with a bullet in his gut."

"Is he all right?" For a moment I felt dizzy.

"Fuck you!" shouted Garza. "Fuck you! *Now* all of a sudden you care."

"Chill," said O'Brien, glancing nervously at the lawyer.

"I saw the boat go up in flames," I said. "Somebody in a hood hands me a bag with his ring, finger still attached. That's all I know."

"If you had fucking called me like you was supposed to, you'd know, wouldn't you?" snapped Garza.

"I don't have time to listen to a civil servant squabble," said Fisher, getting to his feet. "My client was kidnapped and mutilated by U.S. government agents. Four of his employees were murdered. I'm telling the newspapers he's alive and well. We'll see you in court." He got up to leave.

"You piece of shit lawyer," screamed Garza diving across the room, grabbing Fisher by his tie and jamming his gun into the lawyer's nostril. "How you gonna do in court with a hole through the middle of your motherfucking *chupasangre* face."

"Yo, yo, yo, Tito," said O'Brien, his hand over Garza's gun. "Easy man, easy. This is Levine's show."

Fisher's Miami tan had vanished, replaced by Bela Lugosi white.

"You're fucking dead!" said Garza. "You bald dickhead."

"I don't have to take this," said Fisher, moving toward the stairs.

"Shut up!" I screamed at the top of my lungs. For a moment it was quiet. "You agreed to play dead—right?" I asked Restrepo.

"Sure, wouldn't you? They invade my boat with guns pointing at me. The little *Cubano* over there"—he jerked his head toward Garza—"says DEA's got me on a hand-to-hand sale with you, the Money Man, who's really a cop, and they're going to lock me up forever anyway—so what do I have to lose? He promised if I play dead you'll cut me a break.

"But now they stick me with a murder of a DEA agent in Argentina—that's not part of the deal. I've never even been to Argentina."

"That's enough," ordered Fisher. "Don't say another word, Felix."

"I'm gonna kill that motherfucker," said Garza, moving toward Fisher.

O'Brien blocked his path.

"You want to know who hired me to kill you?" I said. The room suddenly got quiet. "If they can send me out to hit you on your own boat, don't you think they can get you anytime they want? And you, Counselor, you're a dead man too." I suddenly had Fisher's undivided attention.

"What are you getting at?"

"These people want him dead so bad that they'll kill you on general principle. And you can't stop them—but I can."

"Who?" asked *El Búfalo.*

"El Triángulo de la Muerte," I said. "The Triangle of Death."

The huge man stared at me, the whites of his eyes showing around dull black pupils.

"They've got *La Reina Blanca,*" I said. "You're hunting it—they want you out of the way. You're lucky they hired me to do the hit, or you'd already be history."

"That's a lie," said *El Búfalo,* his massive body folding into itself like a thick spring compressing. "Everybody's looking for *La Reina*—that's no reason to hit me. Give me a name."

"Nadia Ricord," I said.

El Búfalo blinked rapidly, his chest rising and falling. It was like the instant of dead calm after a detonator had been pushed.

"That fucking whore!" he roared. His bandaged hand came around in a short arc and smashed the coffee table in front of him to splinters. He lurched to his feet bellowing like a wounded bull. "That fucking perverted whore!"

The couch bounced off the wall and rolled onto its side.

Garza raised his gun. O'Brien drew his.

"Felix, they'll kill you!" shouted Fisher as he ducked for cover behind a chair.

"Go ahead, kill me!" roared *El Búfalo.* "I should have known that snake bitch was behind all of this." Blood soaked through his bandaged right hand; he didn't seem to notice.

"As your lawyer," shouted Fisher from behind the chair, "I advise you to stop talking immediately."

"You want to get even?" I said, standing in front of him.

"Get out of the fucking way, Levine!" shouted Garza, on one knee, his gun aimed at *El Búfalo.*

"How?" he said.

"I need a week. Stay dead a week, and Nadia gets busted, along with her top people."

"And if we don't buy the deal?" said Fisher, peeking up from behind the chair.

BLAM! Garza fired his gun. Plaster splintered above Fisher's head.

"That's attempted homicide," said a muffled voice from beneath the chair.

"You shut your fucking lawyer hole," screamed Garza.

"You don't buy the deal," I said, "Nadia Ricord wins! *El Búfalo's* hung with the murder of a DEA agent. He goes to the chair—or she kills him. They offered me three million dollars to take you out. How long you think you're gonna last on the outside with that kind of money on your head? You're dead either way. I'm the only chance you've got left."

"She still wears white, like a virgin?" hissed *El Búfalo*.

"Yes," I said. "You know her well?"

"Better than she wants to remember, *esa hija de puta*." He shook his head balefully. "She should wear black, like a black widow. Anybody comes too close ends up dead, and she is three places removed. *Más víbora que el terciopelo*"—more snake than a fer-de-lance.

"You help me," I said. "I help you."

"How can you help him?" said Fisher, standing behind the chair. "You going to give him back his finger?"

"Let him talk, Brucie," said *El Búfalo*.

"How did that happen?" I said, indicating the finger.

Restrepo shrugged. "One of your people try to get the ring off, when it gets stuck, he cut the whole thing off."

I looked at O'Brien for an explanation.

"We hired some mercenaries," said Vinnie. "They went nuts. One minute everything's under control; Twinkie over here was agreein' to everything. Then one of his boys draws a gun and all hell breaks loose. Four of his guys and one mercenary turn crispie critters. Georgie caught a bullet in the gut, and Twinkie here was minus one finger."

"Real nice," said Fisher. "They teach this at the DEA academy?"

"Shhh, Brucie," said *El Búfalo*, putting a sausage finger to his lips. "I'll take it from here."

"What about my fee?" said Fisher. "I've already put in a full week on this. I had to literally shut down my practice."

"You keep your mouth shut, I'll guarantee your fee," I said.

"She still got her pretty little boy with her?" said *El Búfalo*.

"Her son, Julio?" I asked.

He laughed. "That what she calls him—her son?"

"Yes, that's what she calls him."

"I know why that filthy bitch wants me dead," he said. "How old is the kid now, seventeen, eighteen?"

"Yeah."

"A pretty little kid he was—big brown eyes, right?"

"Right."

"Now he must be getting ready to go out in the world where he might hear some things," said *El Búfalo*.

"What kind of things?" I asked.

He looked at me for a long moment, his huge chest still heaving. "*¿Me das imunidad, total?*" he asked.

"I can't be your attorney," said Fisher, "if you speak in a language I don't understand."

"Whatever I tell you," continued *El Búfalo*, ignoring him, "you can't use against me."

"You've got it," I said.

"Your personal word of honor?"

"Mr. Fisher, I just gave your client my word that what he's about to tell me is off the record."

"This is crazy," said Fisher. "You all belong in a madhouse."

"Go ahead," I said.

"I knew Julio's father, ten years ago. Negron was the family name. They were associated with the Medellín cartel. In those years the cartel was a group of individual families doing their own thing, each helping the other and pooling their resources on big transactions, or to take care of problems."

"How did Nadia fit in?"

"She ran errands for her father, Auguste Ricord. He had powerful connections everywhere. I never met him, but he was very respected. Everyone thought she worked for him; that he gave the orders from the gringo jail. So when we found out strange things about her, we thought, 'Well, this is her business.'"

"What kind of strange things?"

"She likes to play with young boys—you know—to bring them in her bed. She likes the street kids from Bogotá, from

Asunción, from Rio. She picks them up and then *poof*, they disappear."

"What do you mean *disappear*?"

El Búfalo shrugged his massive shoulders. "Ask her what happens to them."

"Julio was a street kid?"

"No, Julio was special. Nadia did business with Julio's father. Every time she came from Paraguay to Medellín she stayed in the family villa. She got very close to the whole family—even the mother. The kids called her *Tía* Nadia, Aunt Nadia. Then rumors started that Julio's father was fucking her, that he was in love with her. And then began the problem with Miami."

"What problem?"

"Nadia controlled her father's cocaine sources in Bolivia. Sometimes the Negrons buy from her wholesale and then ship to their customers in Miami. One day comes a very big order from Miami. Other members of the cartel put money in with the Negrons for a couple hundred kilos of coke, I don't remember the exact amount, maybe five hundred.

"What was supposed to happen is that Nadia would deliver the coke to the Miami customer and then bring the money— about sixteen million—to Negron, who would then distribute it to the cartel. Now the coke disappears and there's no money. Nadia claims she delivered the coke; that Negron got paid and stole the money. Negron says it's not true—he never got paid."

"And you believed her."

"Nobody believes anything. The cartel sent me to Miami to talk to the customer. He says he paid Negron himself. The sentence for stealing from the cartel, of course, is death. People are sent to do this."

"What do you mean people?" I asked.

"You want to know the story, you let me tell it my way," said *El Búfalo*. "All I tell you is that this one I don't do personally."

"You killed the whole family?"

"This was the early days; they want to send a message—you don't fuck with Medellín. And the way they think—even now—if you let children live, you will always have an enemy."

"How many children?"

"Three," said Restrepo. "Nadia pleaded with great big tears to save the youngest—Julio. What a fucking act." He shook his buffalo's head in wonder. "Everybody fell for it. Finally, she convinced Escobar to give her little Julio."

"How were the others killed?"

"They shot them; they took the little boy out, then they burned the house. Then they bring me little Julio; I delivered him to Nadia."

"And that's why she wants to kill you?"

"No. Later, I did business with this same customer in Miami, and I learned the truth. Nadia made the delivery. She told the customer that if he lied and said he paid all the money to Negron, he could pay her half price and have the whole load. It turned out she was fucking both this guy and Julio's father. The cartel never knew that she was the one who had stolen the money, not Negron."

"So she conned you into killing the whole Negron family."

"Not me," said Restrepo. "The members. In those years I was just a collector."

"And what happened to the customer?"

"He had a problem with me."

"He's dead?"

"Nobody lives forever."

"Did you tell Medellín what you learned?"

"I didn't say nothing; she's part of something very big, very secret. I didn't know how much power she had. I wanted my own business, so I think, 'Someday this will be useful.' Then, maybe two, three months ago, I hear *La Reina Blanca* is coming from the Triangle. So I sent word; maybe she can help me with this White Queen thing; that I have some information she might not want people to know."

"You tried to blackmail her?"

"Yes," said *El Búfalo*. "And she told me, 'No problem,' she's going to open up a line through my group; she always had respect for me, an' all that bullshit, then she sends you to hit me."

"How do I know this isn't all bullshit?"

He laughed. "I could tell you whatever, *'mano*. You asking me to do you a favor. What do I got to lose?"

"You're doing yourself the favor. If she can get to you inside the cartel, she can get to you in the federal jail."

"So I die." He laughed. "You know how long you gonna live, *'mano*?"

He turned, and set the couch back on its legs as if he were

turning a blanket. Then he plunked his massive weight down on it. There was a dull crack; it sagged and held. "I don't think I'm going to live too much longer, no matter what I do. I can prove what I say."

"How?"

"When the Negron thing happened, the members wanted everything valuable from the house, to pay what he owed. Negron had a big gold medal of Santa Barbara; on the back are the names of two daughters and little Julio, with the dates of their birth. I still have it."

"Where?"

"In a safety deposit box, here in Miami."

"We're going to get it," I said.

"No problem."

Minutes later I followed Garza upstairs to the darkened living room.

"Now what?" said Garza, speaking softly so that we couldn't be heard below.

"I lay the whole thing in headquarters's lap, and we set up for the big bust in Iguazú."

"What you want me and Vinnie to do in the meantime?"

"Take him to his safety deposit box for the Negron medallion ASAP. Have it messengered to me at headquarters."

"We're broke. We blew the whole forty thousand on that fucking debacle. We gave whatever was left to the family of the guy who went ten-seven."

"They know who you are?"

"No. Anonymous."

"That's fine," I said, opening my attaché case. I handed Garza two packets of hundreds. "That's twenty thousand dollars. Don't give Fisher more than half. Then get out of this dump. Get a room at the Sheraton River House. It has all kinds of back and side entrances."

"Can I ask you something?"

"What?"

"Where'd you get all this bread?"

"I won it in a card game."

"Bullshit!"

"Don't start with me, Garza."

"I know you ain't a thief . . ."

"I said, don't start with me Garza!" He was silent. "The most important thing you gotta do is get ahold of Gianotti."

"Get ahold of him? He's got a fucking hit contract out on me; he thinks I split with his money."

"Well he's gonna be happy to know his shipment's on the way to the Port of Miami." I took out a folded piece of paper and handed it to Garza. "That's the details—where and when he's got to be, with the money. Iguazú. Call me in headquarters if there's a problem."

"He's crazed. All the other families invested; they're gonna have a fucking Mafia army with that money. Gianotti's put himself way out front."

"The more the merrier," I said. "We got our own army, don't we?"

"That's what they tell us."

"Well, by tonight there's either going to be a squad of DEA agents down here working for you, or we're going to have to hire our own defense attorneys. I'm firing every gun I have."

I started for the door.

"Hey, Levine," called Garza.

I turned. He was grinning.

"You're still a *pendejo* asshole."

37

WASHINGTON, D.C.

I STOOD STARING UP AT A GRAY, NONDESCRIPT TWELVE-STORY OFFICE building. DEA headquarters. I fished my official DEA credentials out of my inside pocket; it was the first time I'd opened them in almost three months. The large blue letters, *DEA*, were emblazoned over the words THIS IS TO CERTIFY THAT MICHAEL LEVINE WHOSE SIGNATURE AND PHOTO APPEARS BELOW, IS DULY APPOINTED A SPECIAL AGENT IN THE UNITED STATES DRUG ENFORCEMENT ADMINISTRATION, UNITED STATES DEPARTMENT OF JUSTICE . . .

I stared at my photo; a sudden feeling of doubt crept up my spine. Who was I? Why was I here? It was on the edge of my memory, too vague. I had not slept in forty-eight hours. It felt like years. When I flashed the credentials at the security desk would alarms go off? Would they know who I am? Would I be arrested? I felt the weight of the automatic on my hip. *They'd find the gun on me! Who are you? What's your business here?*

The panic slowly dissipated. How fragile the mind is to be playing such games. How desperately at that moment I wished there was someone I could talk to. I'd had several episodes like this during my career, they were growing more frequent during the last few weeks.

The uniformed security guard at the front desk looked at my credentials and then at me. I held my breath. He handed me a clip-on security badge with a big blue *E* emblazoned across it—*Employee.*

I was DEA Special Agent Michael Levine again.

I got to Stratton's office by going up to the ninth floor, a level with mostly administrative functions where few knew me, and down a back staircase to the fourth floor where the door to the stairwell opened beside his office. Two paces through a beige-carpeted, antiseptic hallway filled with the sound of braying printers and murmuring voices and I was at his door.

Stratton, a telephone jammed between his shoulder and his ear, had his broad, football player's back to me and his feet up on a credenza as I slowly opened the door. He glanced over his shoulder. The telex slid from his hands. His eyes glowed white against his coffee-colored skin and locked on to mine like missile radar.

"I have to call you back," he said into the phone as he swiveled slowly around in his chair to face me.

"Before you say a word," I said. "This is *La Reina Blanca.*" I tossed the glassine bag of white powder onto his desk. "I just came from the source; the same people who killed René. I'm ready to tell you everything now."

———

By early evening I had told my story three times, from beginning to end, instinctively leaving out my involvement with the Mossad. The final telling was in a closed-door recorded session in the War Room, with Administrator Whitfield and Myles Bydon, chief of Internal Security. As far as I was concerned it was three times too many. My cover had to last one more week, when Nadia had set the final meeting at Iguazú.

The DEA laboratory, following my suggestion, had begun to check the chromosomal structure of the sample of the White Queen.

The Psychological and Scientific Testing Division had a frightening forecast: If the two hundred kilos of undiluted White Queen were distributed on U.S. streets, the death toll would reach as high as three million within four years—not counting deaths from violent acts. More than seventy-five percent of the victims would be fifteen to twenty-nine years of age. The costs to the economy would be in the trillions; the cost to our civilization, incalculable. And this, if we didn't stop Nadia, would be just the beginning.

I could feel the entire massive bureaucracy changing gears as I spoke and silently marveled at how efficient it could work when you pushed the right buttons. A squad of agents had already been dispatched to Miami to relieve Garza and O'Brien in their baby-sitting duties for *El Búfalo;* Georgie Mendoza was en route, via medevac, from a Colombian hospital to Walter Reed; DEA combat troops and Special Forces soldiers, already assigned to various jungle outposts in Bolivia, Peru, and Colombia, were quietly placed on full alert and sent to a jungle base in Brazil where they would be within striking distance of both Nadia's jungle compound and Iguazú, where the grand finale of the Triangle of Death would take place.

Ten million dollars were immediately transferred into a special secret funding account to finance the operation. Additional funding was promised by an unnamed senator, a friend of DEA, in exchange for the senator's taking part in the initial press conference and receiving media credit for his secret support. The DIA was placed on alert status to coordinate the seizures of the weapons and oil shipments on the high seas. All of this would key off my signal from the jungle meeting at Iguazú.

In a matter of days my own status in the agency had gone from rogue agent to hero and back again to criminal-rogue-agent, and now to superhero. The buzz was flying that I would be credited with the most important law enforcement sting in the decade if not the century. At least that was the phrase Whitfield had used when he summoned his PIO to take part in the meeting. He had direct contacts, private lines, and faxes to all the major network news shows. He had Larry King's home phone number.

By 10:00 p.m. that evening, one problem remained, the most sensitive of all: The information coming from CIA Station Chief Forrest Gregg had been clearly wrong. Whitfield brought it up before I had the chance.

"We have to notify CIA that there's a problem with their sources." he said.

"No sir!" I said. "We can't take the chance."

"That's bullshit!" fumed Bydon.

"Forrest Gregg's sources are his Argentine assets," I said. "You can't trust them." I wanted to say, *How can you trust any government that commits mass murder of its own people?* But I knew that some of those in the room sympathized with that government. Instead I said, "The Triangle owns them; they must have used them to stage tape-recorded confessions and anything else they had to do to con the spooks into buying into the story and throwing us off the track."

"Then we should make Gregg aware of what we know," said Whitfield.

"We can't risk the Argentines detecting a change in his attitude," I insisted.

"I don't like it!" snapped Bydon. "Forrest Gregg is a dedicated, fine officer; he's worked around the clock for weeks trying to help us. Embarrassing the CIA is the ultimate betrayal for their efforts."

"I fully agree with Myles," said Whitfield, his rubbery lips flapping with emotion.

"I don't want to embarrass anyone," I said. "When everyone's in a cage, we tell him quietly. We hit him with this now and he might act differently. The Argentines are pros; they're gonna know something's up."

"I think we can trust Forrest Gregg to keep it quiet," said Whitfield. "So he misjudged the Argentines—the best of us slip up sometimes."

"I'd say agent Villarino was a case in point," added Bydon.

I felt my face flame. My hands began to tremble.

"The only reason we're here is because René led the way," I said. "I don't know too many people who have the balls to be the first at anything. I only followed his footsteps. And maybe, after this goes down, we'll find out that he didn't slip up—somebody else did."

Whitfield and Bydon glared at me. I had cornered them. If my cover was blown and I survived, they knew I'd make it public. The only weapon the suits respected.

"Okay," said Whitfield reluctantly. "CIA is frozen out. We'll wait until the Iguazú operation is over before we notify them."

———

Stratton led the way into his office. It was late, close to midnight.

"Looks like everybody's happy now, right, Bobby?" I said. "When this hits, Whitfield'll do *Larry King Live*, write a book about how to win the fucking drug war, and run for the Senate. Congress'll up our budget again."

"Don't get too starry-eyed," he said.

"Why not?"

"Number one, this bust is a major military op. Number two, if you survive that, you got even bigger problems."

"Oh yeah?"

"The suits are gonna do you," he said softly.

"I thought it was my turn in the hero barrel," I said.

"You really gone dinky-dau, haven't you? You had your hero shot—you blew it. You sit up there and tell a story three times—once, they even tape-recorded you—admitting you lied to me; you lied on a leave slip; you left your post on false pretenses; you used OG funds for gambling; you disobeyed direct orders from people who throw darts at your fucking photo every day—and you think they're gonna forget it? You know what Section 1001, false official statement, is? They've got you on twenty counts of that without even lifting a finger. And that's just for starters.

"Shit! I don't know why I bother," said Stratton, "you never trusted me."

"If I had told you everything from the beginning, what would you have done?"

"I would have told you to get with the program," he snapped. "Villarino's dead. I saw a lot of guys die for bullshit. Nothing you can fucking do to bring anyone back." Veins were taut in his neck; he leaned across the desk, spraying spittle. "I would have told you that no drug case is worth your life, your liberty, or your family." His eyes were molten with fury. I didn't think it was directed at me.

"Can I ask you something?" I said.

He shook his head. "I don't think you heard a fucking word I said."

"Why'd you quit the Agency?"

He stared at me, blinking. "None of your fucking business. It ain't gonna help you."

Outside his window snowflakes began to drift.

"It's snowing, Bobby," I said. "You better get going, you want to make it home."

"Won't be the first time I slept on this couch . . . or the last. You got any on-the-job injuries?"

"Like everyone, a couple. Why?" I already knew the answer.

"Soon as this thing comes down, go sick, Mike. Shoot for a disability."

"How much time do I have?"

"They're already drawing up charges on you. They'll wait a

couple of months after it all goes down. You're gonna be arrested right here in headquarters. You'll be front-page stuff.

"You got twenty years of undercover—claim stress trauma. With your record no one's gonna argue."

The snow was falling heavily now.

"Thanks, Bobby," I said, extending my hand.

He stared at it. "For what?"

"You didn't have to say anything."

"I think you're a concrete-headed motherfucker—but you don't deserve this. Oh yeah, this came for you," he said, tossing me a small paper-wrapped box off his desk.

I read the return address: *Garza. Sheraton River House, Miami.* It was Julio's father's medallion. *El Búfalo* had come through.

Stratton looked at it for an indecisive moment. "Good luck!" he said finally. I guess he didn't want to know anything else.

38

BUENOS AIRES

FORREST GREGG, CIA STATION CHIEF, DROVE SLOWLY ALONG AVENIDA del Libertador. It was a few minutes past midnight and the rain came down in solid sheets that battered the car like shrapnel; the kind of tropical downpour that periodically turned Buenos Aires with its ancient sewer system into a chaos of rushing water, up-ended cars, and half-submerged buildings. His thoughts came as swirling and chaotic as the weather.

It occurred to him that the night of his supposedly chance first meeting with Nadia, a little more than three years ago, was the same kind of stormy night.

The Sheraton loomed ahead—a solitary modern tower facing the ancient Retiro Plaza, a vast empty space, its back to the Río de la Plata waterfront. It was the only building constructed in the area since the turn of the century. Gregg liked to call it "the Monolith" after the image in Kubrick's 2001.

He knew the place intimately, its luxury suites had been wired for sound and video for scores of secret meetings and operations that the world would never hear about; events that had altered the course of history.

He turned up a small hill and drove past the hotel's entrance to the rear parking lot, finding a spot near the basement entrance. The skies unloaded again. Drops of rain the size of grapes hammered the metal roof, roaring in his ears. In the penthouse suite the sound would be distant, muffled and soothing, as it was that first night.

Minutes later, drenched and breathless from hobbling as fast as he could with his cane through the downpour, he stepped out of the elevator into a darkened hallway. The door slid closed behind him. Blackness.

"Stand still!" said a man's voice behind him. Lights came on. Big hands with scarred knuckles patted him down from behind.

"Turn around," said the voice.

"How are you, Jacques?" he said turning to look into eyes that looked like wet watermelon seeds. Jacques stepped aside.

Nadia, wearing a white terry cloth robe, watched him from the doorway of the suite at the end of the hall. The sight was like a blow to his heart. She would always be the loveliest thing he had ever seen. His drug. *His poison.*

"Come," she said softly, and stepped inside. Her feet were bare.

He closed the door behind him. The room had not changed at all. Gilt-edged French provincial furniture. A wet bar. Through the double door would be a large round bed.

She faced him.

"You don't look well, Forrest."

"I don't feel very well," he said, his voice a hoarse whisper. "Why did you want to see me?"

She moved closer to him. "Would you like to make love to me again?" Her hands reached out slowly and unbuttoned his wet shirt. Her robe fell open. She was naked beneath it.

He wanted to jerk away, but he couldn't move. Her hands lay flat on his chest, the long nails scratching lightly, burning through his skin. Her eyes bore into his.

"Your heart is beating like a frightened bird's. I know what that feels like."

"Why are you doing this, Nadia?" The words came out strangled.

"I need a small favor."

"No more favors."

She abruptly moved away from him, closing her robe.

"Weren't you ever curious why I chose you, *mi amor*?"

"It no longer interests me."

"Considering your line of work, I should think you'd be very interested. I studied everything about you—your school and medical histories, even the testimony during your divorce trial. How many people do you think know about your obscenely little hands and feet and your chest . . . with its blue veins and skin like old parchment?"

"You're a bloody whore," he said, his voice just above a whisper.

"A disease . . . Gottron's syndrome, isn't it? Would you like to know what else I learned about you before I arranged our first meeting? The file is right here. An overweight, balding, myopic man, a man of average intelligence and low self-esteem, with the might of the most powerful nation on earth at his disposal. You were perfect, Forrest."

She continued talking, her magenta lips moving, but he could no longer understand the words. He could only stand there frozen. Useless. Impotent.

"You have several million dollars hidden away that you've stolen from your government. I could add several more to that number before you retire."

"You made your point, Nadia. You've already gotten all you're ever going to get from me."

"Even if you care so little about yourself, you must care about your daughter. Jennifer is in her first year at Princeton, correct? So beautiful and so very proud of her long family history of service to your country. A grandfather, two uncles, and a father who served their nation with honor.

"Refuse me the small favor I'm about to ask of you, Forrest, and I promise—I will insure that all your dirt is made public. Your family name will be reviled for as long as there is a history of your country. But one consolation: Your little Jennifer won't be around to hear it."

He heard the rain, distant and soft as it was that first night.

"I need a drink," he said. His voice croaked painfully. A glass of whiskey was handed to him. He gulped from it. Felt his brain begin to numb.

"Tell me what you want," he said, his head bowed, his eyes unfocused.

"Is the name Omar Legassi familiar to you?" she asked.

"No. Not at all."

He downed the rest of the glass. It was taken from his hands and replaced with a manila file, thick with documents.

"I have become vulnerable to this man which means you are too, Forrest. Several years of his life are unaccounted for. Our investigation has eliminated every possibility but one . . ."

Gregg felt his jacket pocket for eyeglasses. He opened the file. The first page was an Interpol Criminal Record Report on a Moroccan-born Argentine named Omar Legassi. The list of arrests swam before his eyes.

"The only possibility remaining," said Nadia, "is that he is an American agent. I don't think I have to explain what this means for you. On the next page are some recent photographs we took of the man who claims to be Omar Legassi. Do you know this man?"

Forrest Gregg turned the page. The file fell from his hand.

39

IGUAZÚ

THIS IS IT—THE DAY OF THE RIP, AS UNDERCOVER AGENTS CALL IT. THE day the trap is slammed shut. In this storybook game that is the undercover life, every story ends with a "rip-off." Days, weeks, months of scheming, conning, and maneuvering end in one explosive moment of muscle and firepower.

Sometimes, the moment you drop your false identity and reveal that you're an undercover agent, your target might lose control of his bodily functions, go into convulsions from the shock; heart attacks are common, as are leaps from high windows and reckless car chases. Sometimes they die, often they wish they had. If they have guns, they will use them. No one who plays this game remains unchanged, unaffected.

And then, when it's over and I think I can't handle another one without losing my mind, it begins all over again, and like the addict I've become, I'm back on the needle. But this one, I swear, is my last.

The endless expanse of green draws steadily closer as we descend. The loudspeaker announces the imminent landing of Aerolíneas Argentina Flight 1053, nonstop from Buenos Aires into Iguazú.

Suddenly an enormous expanse of rushing blue water appears below my window. We glide above its surface. At the far side, like a luxury carpet of green, is the jungle. We skim even lower.

The passengers gasp as they watch the wide body of water suddenly dive into an enormous chasm, sending up mighty clouds of mist and dozens of sparkling, brightly hued rainbows. Its visual force is such that I imagine I can hear the roar that gave it its name—*La Garganta del Diablo*—the Devil's Throat. It's one of the most spectacular natural sights on earth, the falls at Iguazú.

The Spanish *conquistadores* heard its gargantuan roar long before they saw it. They named it as they approached through the jungles in fearful wonder. I had been to this spot once before—as in all my life's travel, working a deep cover assignment. The details of the case had been long forgotten, but the memory of standing on a rickety walkway at the edge of the massive falls and feeling overcome by the enormity and beauty of it would always be clear.

Nadia had chosen the spot well. The Hotel International sat in a jungle clearing a thousand yards from the edge of the falls. Its only road led to a well-maintained jungle airstrip and then farther along the Paraná River to the tiny town of Puerto Iguazú. The only other sign of civilization in the area was a brightly colored hotel on the other side of the falls in Brazil. It was the perfect location for a conference of an organization called the International Association of Investors and Venture Capitalists.

The plane was about to touch down when I retrieved my new attaché case from beneath the seat in front of me. I didn't want to take a chance on its being jarred during the landing. It probably wouldn't make a difference, but a cloud of paranoia had hovered over me for the past week and the electronic device concealed in this case would transmit a radio signal keying off the biggest rip in law enforcement since the first action against the Triangle of Death more than twenty years ago.

Yesterday, we had held the preraid briefing for more than 450 combat-ready men—DEA agents and Army Special Forces—in a wilderness clearing near the jungle town of Cascavel, Brazil.

The location was chosen as the staging area for the operation by a Green Beret general because it was a half-hour helicopter flight east of Nadia's compound and Hess's laboratory, and ten minutes north of the Hotel International at Iguazú. The ideal place from which to launch a five-point strike.

First, a low-flying helicopter squadron would swoop onto the hotel grounds. All parties to the deal, including Nadia, would be arrested. Two other squadrons would launch simultaneous strikes on Nadia's compound and laboratory on the other side of the border in the Paraguayan jungle. Two C-130 cargo jets would be waiting in São Paulo to transport all prisoners taken in Paraguay and Argentina, directly to the U.S.

In the U.S., forty Mafia buttonmen, representatives of all the five families controlling American organized crime—all of whom had now invested in the venture—had arrived in Miami in cars with specially built, hidden compartments, to receive the load of two hundred kilos of *La Reina Blanca*. Tito Garza was with them, still in his undercover role as Tony Cortez. At that moment they were under massive surveillance by DEA, the FBI, and Florida State law enforcement officers.

Wiretaps along with information from Garza revealed plans to transport portions of the superdrug to New York City, Los Angeles, New Orleans, Atlanta, Chicago, Las Vegas, Detroit, Dallas, Toronto, and Montreal, to open up new markets. The single shipment of *La Reina Blanca* would net the Mafia many times the total amount of money they'd grossed during all the years of Prohibition combined.

On the high seas both the arms shipment, now hours off the coast of Iraq, and the oil shipment, well on its way to North Korea, were under satellite surveillance. U.S. Navy battle cruisers and aircraft carriers were circling for the kill.

No one but Nadia knew exactly where the jaguar cages filled with *La Reina Blanca* were. My signal to spring this massive worldwide trap would come when Nadia made one telephone call from the hotel announcing the pickup location of the drug shipment in Miami. I would then turn a key locking my new attaché case, which would send a radio alert signal that would begin the entire operation now designated "Operation Eagle."

"You're part of a team now," Stratton had told me at the briefing. "Just turn the key and leave the driving to us."

The attaché case, made of black ostrich skin, rested on my lap as we skimmed the jungle canopy. The lock gleamed in an eighteen-carat-gold setting. The key was on a gold chain around my neck behind a medallion inscribed, *El que se arrepiente, paga dos veces*—He who repents, pays twice.

The plane taxied along a red clay landing strip between impenetrable walls of green and came to a halt alongside a clearing where a small bus and a jeep were waiting. The humidity and smell of jungle rot seeped into the fuselage.

Mario Razouk in beige slacks and a white guayabera shirt stood alone at the edge of the runway shielding his eyes against the blazing morning sun. The only structures in sight were a hangar with a corrugated tin roof and a small terminal. The last time I'd been here, there was nothing.

The engine of the Boeing 727 shut down with a whine. The handful of passengers—European tourists and Argentine vacationers, all going to the hotel—gathered their things from the overhead racks. I grabbed my two-suiter and squeezed past them. Razouk was at the bottom of the stairway, arms wide, as I stepped out of the plane.

"Omar, my friend," said the great bear of a man as he hugged me. His hair seemed to have gotten grayer. There was a weariness around his eyes. He smelled of hashish and whiskey.

"I missed you, you Moroccan son-of-a-bitching camel trader," he said fondly to the man who would soon steal his remaining years. There was a tone in his voice and a haunted look in his eyes that had me immediately wary.

"I missed you too, my friend. How are things going?"

He put his arm over my shoulder and guided me toward the jeep. "All our venture capitalists have arrived." He laughed at his joke. "More than a few are anxious to talk to you."

He got into the driver's seat.

"No driver?" I said tossing the two-suiter on the backseat and getting in. I rested the ostrich-skin case on my lap.

"I wanted to talk with you," he said. A flatness of tone and a quick, wary glance around confirmed that something was wrong. For a few minutes he drove silently over the red clay road that snaked ahead tunneling through dense subtropical forest. His massive body was wedged uncomfortably behind the wheel. I waited uneasily for him to speak.

"Reading Gibran is like reading the Koran, Omar," he began, glancing from me to the road and back again. "Allah chose poets as messengers. You search the *suras* for your own truth in their verses. The words of that Lebanese son of a bitch have always rung a bell in my soul."

He fell silent as he steered around a sharp curve. The road ahead was muddy. He pushed a button and the four-wheel-drive kicked in with a whine.

"Gibran describes Death as a woman of unearthly beauty, dressed in garments as white as snow. Did you know that, Omar?"

"No," I answered.

"When I see Nadia, I cannot get those words from my mind. Omar, I was in Morocco before you were born, arranging petrol shipments to General Rommel. You've heard of him?"

"A German general."

"Good man. Doomed by his own sense of honor, his loyalty to beasts with no honor of their own. We are what we are."

"What's wrong, Mario?"

"I'm tired, Omar. I suppose I've lived a little too long. When you get your money today, leave immediately and never look back."

The words, said so casually, took a moment to be absorbed.

"What are you saying?"

"I'm afraid that Nadia is your 'woman in white,' Omar. I have been instructed to meet the key parties to the transaction and to make you unnecessary for all future transactions."

"And have you already done this?"

"With the exception of the Italian, Mr. Gianotti, who has asked to speak to you personally. After today, you have laid the groundwork for her to establish her own ties."

"When does she arrive?"

"This afternoon at five."

"Will I have a chance to collect my money and leave?"

"I think so. But she is never obvious." He shrugged. "Sometimes I think all mankind is her enemy. She takes from men what is useful to her and destroys the donor. She's either a devil or a god."

"Why are you telling me this?"

"I'm a merchant, Omar. I buy and sell. Not a thief. Not a killer. Not a traitor. I brought you into this."

"Thank you, my friend," I said, wishing that I could give him the same warning he gave me. Omar Legassi would do it in a heartbeat, but Special Agent Michael Levine couldn't risk the collapse of the whole operation.

Razouk drove to the front of the hotel, a modern low-slung building of white concrete and glass, four stories high, facing the mighty falls.

"What's the schedule?" I asked.

"At four p.m. we have a *parrilla* at poolside for all our guests. Nadia arrives by helicopter at five to meet everyone. We adjourn to a conference room on the third floor, where special telephone lines have been prepared, along with a shortwave radio. The transaction is completed. Plans for the next one are discussed."

"Nadia's money?"

"She has made a separate deal with the Iraqis. I'm not sure of the details, but you can be sure she will be paid."

Bruno, in a pale blue linen suit and dark wraparound glasses, appeared beside the car. "We have some business," said Razouk quickly. "I'm sorry, my friend. I wish I could tell you more."

A young, smiling bellhop grabbed my two-suiter and led me to my room. "Your conference has the entire floor," he said. "Interesting group. From all over the world, aren't you?" His Spanish was Caribbean-accented, which struck me as odd.

"Yes," I answered.

He paused to unlock my door. A group of four Oriental men passed in the hallway; their eyes took a quick and thorough inventory. They nodded as one. I acknowledged with a slight dip of my head.

"Koreans," said the bellhop. He opened the door to a luxury suite—modern furniture, large bed. A glass wall with sliding doors led out to a balcony.

He closed the door behind us and reached quickly into his inside pocket.

"Andy Marquez," he said, flashing a DEA badge.

"How'd you get the bellhop job? The hotel is in on this?"

"No, I actually got hired by the hotel as a bellhop." He laughed. "A phone call from a Brazilian police chief as a reference."

"How many undercovers are here?"

"A dozen should've come in on your flight posing as tourists. Eight are already here, including me. Our UCs will be wearing something red above the waist—flower, handkerchief, hat. And white shoes or sneakers."

"Do they know I'm the guy they're *not* supposed to shoot?"

"They've all seen your photo."

"How many badguys?"

"They've got eighteen rooms on this floor. The Godfather's got four."

"Gianotti's here already?"

"He came in on an Learjet registered to the Sand Dune Palace in Vegas. We think the whole hundred-and-twenty million is on board. He's got armed guards watching it twenty-four hours."

"Great! What else?"

"The Koreans have four rooms. People from Morocco, Libya, and Iraq in six, and the rest are registered to the guy running the thing—Razouk."

"You better get going," I said. "You're already in here too long."

"Sorry," he said, moving quickly for the door. He was young and eager.

"How long you on the job?"

He paused with a hand on the doorknob. "Two years. Just got transferred to São Paulo from Detroit."

"You know about the *parrilla* this afternoon?"

"I'll be serving," he said eagerly.

"Remember, once I turn the key, our guys are about ten minutes away. We don't make our move till the choppers land," I said, wondering whether this kid had any idea how long ten minutes could be when you're waiting for your backup.

"You got it. Good luck," he said with a teenager's grin, and vanished into the hallway.

Young guys cannot imagine their own deaths. Life is a movie for them.

I lay down and stared at the ceiling. I could feel the roar of the falls. I took the dark-stained piece of René's burial suit from my pocket and held it up to the light. *This is it, buddy. This is as far as I can go.* I could see the light at the end of a very long tunnel. I forced myself to repeat a lesson I'd learned a thousand times during my career.

Near the end of an operation—the rip—the tendency is to run, to hurry to get it over with, and that is when the target is most alert, most vulnerable, and most deadly; that is when you should tread the slowest and with the most caution.

40

THE LATE AFTERNOON SUN WAS STILL HIGH WHEN I STEPPED OUT INTO the courtyard of the hotel. Nadia was due to arrive in a few minutes. My cover had to last no more than another hour or so. Superstition had kept me in my room until the last minute.

Tango music drifted up from the direction of the pool. I followed a paved walkway toward the music. A few paces and I was at the top of concrete steps leading down to an elliptical pool surrounded by a concrete patio. An area at the far end had been cordoned off. A quartet, its back to the pool, sweated over a brisk rendition of "La Cumparcita." A group of about twenty men was being served by hustling waiters.

I moved slowly down the steps, noting that Razouk stood off to the side with a group of Iraqis. He caught my eye and looked away. The Koreans were at a table with Bruno, who was speaking through an interpreter. I recognized the thick swept-back silver hair and rough, chiseled features of Gentleman John Gianotti. He, Belkassami, and the Libyan major were seated around a table shaded by a large umbrella. They stopped talking and watched my approach.

I tried to carry the ostrich attaché case as if it were the most natural thing in the world to have with me, but I was too conscious of it. It was burning a groove in my hand.

"Omar," said Belkassami, wrapping his arms around me. I turned my head to avoid kissing the mouthful of black rot. His hand barely missed the gun at the small of my back. "We have already seen our money in the Italian's plane" he said in Arabic. "You did well for us."

"Do I lie?" I said, flashing him a wide grin, moving past him.

"The famous Omar," said Gianotti, motioning me to take an empty seat beside him. He wore a fine silk sport jacket over a starched white shirt. "Your good friend Mr. Cortez says hello."

I grasped Gianotti's hand, thick, hard, and callused—a fighter's hand. I had read somewhere that he'd boxed during one of his rare stints in prison.

"A pleasure," I said, taking the seat.

Two of his men were on their feet behind us. They wore tropical sport shirts that hung to the hip. I recognized both. Crazy Phil Cagliotti and the ex-cop, Pat "the Cat" Gallo.

"I just wanted to put a face wit' ya name," said Gianotti, his eyes searching mine. "You una'stand dis ting's your responsibility."

"Of course," I said, holding his gaze.

"Would anyone care for a drink?" said a voice behind me.

DEA Agent Andy Marquez leaned over me in a white waiter's uniform. He had a bright red handkerchief stuffed in his jacket pocket. As he took drink orders I noticed a young couple strolling hand in hand along a path just above the pool. She wore a bright red straw hat; he, a red bandanna. They glanced down at us and continued toward a jungle path about fifty feet distant.

"Legassi," said Gianotti. He put his face very close to mine as he spoke and tilted it at an angle as if trying to look into my mouth. "I saw you comin' down da steps and I said to myself, *ma-rone*, I know dat fuckin' guy from someplace. Where'dju learn English?"

"I lived, on and off, for many years in America. I did time there."

"No shit!" His eyebrows arched. "Where'dju do time?"

"Lewisburg," I answered—too quickly. *A mistake.*

"Lewisburg?" He twisted excitedly in his seat. "Yo! Hey Philly!"

"Yeah, boss," said Crazy Phil, edging closer, his wandering eye rolling around in his head like a loose marble. I couldn't tell if he was looking at me or Gianotti, or both at the same time.

"You did a bit in Lewisburg, right? So'd Omar ovah heah. See if youse know each other."

"When'ju do your bit?" he said, his left eye nailing me.

I was exactly where I didn't want to be, center ring and one wrong answer from blowing my cover. I glanced over at the other group and caught Razouk's eye. "Mario," I called, getting to my feet quickly and checking my watch.

Razouk looked surprised. Gianotti gaped at me openmouthed, clouds of anger gathered in his light brown eyes.

"Guy axed you a fuckin' question!"

"Can I have a word with you?" I said, ignoring Gianotti and stepping away from the table.

"You don't ignore a fuckin' question!" Gianotti's voice rose. Others turned to look.

"Please excuse me," I muttered quickly. "There's not much time, and I want to make sure everything runs smoothly."

Gianotti, Crazy Phil, and Pat "the Cat" Gallo huddled behind me as I moved away. Gallo, the ex-cop, was doing the talking, his eyes on me. Belkassami and the major look confused.

"It's after five," I said, looking at my watch. "Where's Nadia?"

Razouk glanced at Gianotti's table then down at my attaché case.

"She'll be here any minute."

A steady thumping beat suddenly mixed with the distant thunder of the falls. It quickly grew louder and seemed to be everywhere at once. Razouk heard it. Everyone heard it. Heads craned. Eyes peered skyward. There was a sudden air of apprehension.

Andy Marquez, the young undercover agent, came toward us carrying a tray of drinks. On the rise above us, two young men in white tennis shorts and red sweatbands looked around. The young woman in the red straw hat, now halfway between the pool and the jungle, paused to watch us.

A helicopter leapt over the horizon and swung toward the hotel from the west, flying out of the sun. Two others swung into view, hovering in the distance for a moment and then disappearing below the horizon.

"There she is now," said Razouk.

Around me men got to their feet, shading their eyes. Gianotti was still watching me.

The silhouette of the chopper was familiar. It was a Huey Cobra gunship. My first thought was that there were too many choppers for it to be Nadia—the hit signal must have been given prematurely.

Peripherally I saw figures encircling us, flashes of red and white; the undercovers were thinking the same thing. But as the chopper drew closer I saw that it was painted a camouflage green with no markings. Then I remembered that I'd seen several like it parked at Nadia's compound.

Suddenly the ground around me exploded in a series of chopping little explosions, grass and dirt flying. My face was spattered hard with something wet.

Under fire!

I dove to the ground and belly-crawled a couple of yards up a small rise to a palm tree. More ground exploded around me. I shoved my face into the base of the tree. Shouts, screams, and moans came from everywhere. I peeked out.

The young DEA undercover agent in the red straw hat was blasted off her feet. She fell like a rag doll, her arms and legs splayed out and limp.

The chopper hovered above the pool, steady streams of flame leapt from its open doorway accompanied by the steady *brrrack* of automatic weapons fire. At poolside people were toppling over like bowling pins. Spent cartridges tumbled into the water. Ravaged bodies littered the concrete and grass. Blood was splattered everywhere. A man floated facedown in the pool, a cloud of red spreading around him.

A half-dozen bullets thunked into the tree trunk near my head. More tore up the ground around me. I ducked behind the tree, tore the key from my neck, jammed it into the lock, and twisted it. Backup was now ten minutes away. *I have to survive ten minutes.*

I left the case behind the tree. I saw Razouk on his back, his chest covered with blood, but he was still moving.

I drew the automatic and peeked over the rise, just enough to line the sights 'on the pilot's cabin. The chopper raised higher to get a line of fire on me. I started squeezing off rounds, one at a time, my hand trembling, trying to hold a sight picture. *Concentrate on the sights, not the target. The sights!* I heard more firing around me.

Andy Marquez, the young undercover agent, was on his belly firing, out in the open. "Take cover!" I screamed. Other agents were firing from the ridge and the tree line.

I squeezed off two more shots at the darkness of the chopper's open doorway. Gunfire from the chopper paused. Smoke streamed out from the doorway. It started to sway like a pendulum. I was on my feet running and firing, racing toward Razouk. I jammed the gun into my belt, grabbed the old man by his arms, and ran backward as hard as I could, digging in with my heels, dragging him toward a clump of palm trees.

I knelt over him. His eyes were wide, looking right into mine. His massive chest heaved; bright red blood pulsed from three large perforations. His hand grabbed my wrist in a viselike grip. He pulled himself up, his lips moving.

"It's Nadia," he gasped. "Run." His eyes burned into mine. A long, gurgling rattle began from deep in his chest. His head lolled back. I set him down gently, extricated his fingers from my wrist and closed his eyes.

Good-bye, my brother.

The air exploded above my head with the crack of bullets snapping the sound barrier. A line of men in ski masks moved out from the tree line firing automatic weapons.

The chopper moaned and veered out of control, turned on one side, and plummeted straight down. An explosion shook the ground. A ball of flame rose out of the jungle. Another unmarked chopper leapt into the air and rushed toward the pool, guns blazing.

I lay across Razouk's body, my head on his shoulder, and raised the gun to aim at a man in a ski mask tearing over the hill toward me. The air reeked of cordite and death. The slide on my automatic was locked to the rear—it was empty.

I lay motionless. The masked man continued toward me running in a combat crouch. He suddenly went down, tumbling head over heels, and lay still. Others appeared behind him in a skirmish line moving toward the pool, firing. Another Ski Mask paused to fire a bullet into a motionless body, then looked up. I could see his eyes looking straight at me. He saw that I was alive and started toward me.

I was numb with terror. My thoughts of death always used to come down to wondering what my last sight and thought would be. *Here it is* was my only thought.

Ski Mask was over me, raising his gun. I started to move. The middle of his chest suddenly went *thunk.* A geyser of blood exploded out his back. He sat down, eyes glazed over, the gun dropped in his lap. Still flat on my belly, I glanced back as a volley of lead ripped the young life from Andy Marquez. He had just saved my life and paid with his.

The firing suddenly ceased. It was quiet. The only sound was the thumping blades of the chopper hovering over the pool. I felt its wind beating at me. Ski-masked men were now moving, casually, as if they had all the time in the world.

They think everyone's dead.

Bodies were sprawled all around the pool, on the rise, in front of the hotel, and along the path toward the jungle. A Ski Mask knelt to check a dead man's face against a mug shot. I was close enough to see that it was a photo of me as Omar Legassi. All around me masked men were checking the faces of the dead against photos of my face.

I lay perfectly still, only my eyes moving, seeing, remembering. *I'm a witness, maybe the only one left.* They wore khaki fatigues like those I'd seen on the men in Nadia's compound. The image of Moon Face in his bloody khakis flashed. I was suddenly overcome with rage.

Death *is* the woman in white. I would do anything to survive; whatever it took to keep life in my body until she paid.

Footsteps moved in my direction. The dead man in the ski mask lay a foot from my outstretched gun-hand. I let the gun slip from my fingers and inched my hand toward his head, keeping my body as rigid as I could make it appear, waiting for a shout, a gunshot, and the pain of a bullet.

My fingers touched the wool of the dead man's ski mask, I slowly pinched it between thumb and forefinger. It felt hot and damp. A gentle pull and it came away revealing a baby-faced young man with tousled auburn hair.

Somebody's son.

I slid my arm back, slowly. Voices behind me spoke in German. I inched the mask closer. I slowly turned my head. A group of masked men milled around examining the dead. One picked up a guitar from the pile of instruments, chairs, and bodies that had been the tango quartet. He strummed some discordant notes. Several stood at the edge of the pool their backs to me, facing the ridge.

The chopper was now hovering directly over me.

I slipped the mask on over my head and got to my feet. The dead man's mucus and blood smeared my nose and mouth. I gagged, but quickly controlled it. I stooped for the man's weapon—an American-made M-16. Ready to fire.

I started uphill toward the top of the rise, forcing myself to walk slowly and casually, praying for enough hesitation and confusion for me to reach the jungle. I slid my hand over the grip of the M-16. If I could get over the rise about twenty feet ahead of me, I'd be out of sight of most of the men on the ground. Then there were only about fifty feet remaining to the jungle—a three- or four-second sprint on my bad knee.

A voice behind me shouted in German.

I gritted my teeth and fought the urge to bolt. *Don't run. Don't fucking run. Six more strides.* The men checking bodies at the end of the pool turned toward me.

Four, three . . .

The air cracked over my head, followed closely by a gunshot. *You never hear the one that kills you.* I exploded toward the ridge, firing the M-16 back over my shoulder toward the pool. Masked men dove for cover. I was over the rise and running as hard as I could. The tree line was about fifty feet ahead. A chopper roared and swerved above me. Bullets kicked up the ground.

My legs felt like lead but kept chugging. Suddenly a deep pain burned through my stomach. I dove at the green wall ahead of me and crashed to the ground.

I'm hit.

I tore the ski mask from my face, crawling and stumbling to my feet, and then charged forward with every ounce of energy left in me. Blood spread rapidly on my shirt and pants. There was gunfire above and behind me. Bullets zipped through foliage near my head.

I ducked behind a tree.

I'm losing blood.

I heard voices behind me. More gunfire. I aimed the M-16 at the sounds and fired a long burst, raking back and forth, until the gun was empty.

The chopper was again directly overhead. A hail of bullets zipped straight down through the treetops pounding the ground around me.

I dropped the M-16 and ran blindly, recklessly, crashing headlong through the jungle, feeling my skin torn and ripped from a thousand directions.

Terror had finally taken total control; even my breathing was a hysterical whine. Automatically I ran toward the roar of the falls. My only thought was that I wanted to live.

41

THE MEMORY OF MY ESCAPE FROM IGUAZÚ WILL ALWAYS BE AS THAT OF A nightmare: running terrified through a green tangle, Death floating after me in a white gown, falling a long way, crashing through brush and foliage into fast-moving water, choking, flailing for my life, grabbing a floating log, the beating of a helicopter overhead, machine-gun fire, then blackness.

I woke up in a dark place smelling of earth and a wood fire, cracks of sunlight streaming in through spaces in the walls, wondering if I was dead. I lay perfectly still for a long time, listening and trying to remember. I touched my stomach. It had been bandaged with a rough cloth material. I was wearing loose-fitting cotton pants and nothing else.

There was a murmur of voices outside, children's laughter. Then I felt the heat and humidity, smelled the rotting vegetation, heard the cackle of jungle birds. I sat up, my bare feet touched a dirt floor. My bed was a rough-hewn cot made of woven vine and wood, with a folded blanket for a mattress.

My brain seemed to be running on a low battery. Thoughts would not focus. Then I remembered René, Shoshanna's wonderful smile, that both were dead and that I had something to do with it. Then reality hit me.

Nadia.

"Where am I?" I called out.

Silence.

The door swung open. Bright sunlight flooded in behind two

small figures. They moved closer, speaking to me excitedly in a language that sounded familiar. Two small Indian boys in shorts and bare feet.

"¿Dónde estoy?" I said. "¿Cuánto hace que estoy aquí?"

They looked at me blankly. A tall, bearded man in a white shirt with a high-button cleric's collar appeared in the doorway.

"They only speak Guarani," he said. He entered the room, speaking to the children in their language. They glanced at me and ran off chattering. He lowered a wall panel, flooding the room with sunlight.

"God's will," he said. "How are you feeling?" A large crucifix hung to the middle of his chest.

"Where am I?" I asked. My head ached with fever.

"A hamlet. Not far from Puerto Iguazú. I'm Father Juan Carlos."

The priest told me that a group of children had found me semiconscious and clinging to a log caught in some brush on a bank of the Iguazú, a few kilometers south of Puerto Iguazú. He and some of his parishioners had brought me back to this hut two days ago.

Flashes of memory like soundless movie clips: the feel of the wet log and mud on my cheek, the squeal of children, men carrying me, crying out in pain; lying face up on a table.

I touched the rough bandages around my stomach.

"I'm afraid I am the only medical help here," he said. "You had a bullet in your stomach. Not deep and very flat; a ricochet, I would guess. I have some experience with bullet wounds. I thought it best to remove it and clean it. Infection is very bad here."

A purple burn scar spread beneath his beard, extending from his chin to the corner of his left eye. The eye was false.

"You lost blood. I've given you all the penicillin I had left until our supplies come from the diocese in Buenos Aires."

"I'm going to get you all the penicillin you'll ever need, Father," I croaked.

"It was His will, Señor . . ."

"Levine," I said, "Michael Levine." Omar Legassi was dead. "Father, do you know what happened—how I was shot?"

His expression was suddenly guarded. "How could I know, Señor?"

"There was nothing in the news? Nothing about the Hotel International?"

"Our village is kilometers and centuries from civilization, Señor. I sometimes don't see a newspaper for months. There was a rumor of trouble. But here, we do better not to pay attention to rumors."

I got to my feet. A wave of dizziness and nausea hit me. The priest put his arm around me. "You shouldn't be on your feet."

"Father, I've got to get to a phone."

"Señor, you have fever; you've lost blood . . ."

"Did you ever see combat, Father?"

He blinked as if smacked in the face.

"I was in the Falklands."

"If God wanted me to survive, Father, it's for what I've got to do right now. Please help me!"

Late in the afternoon on the riverbank, dizzy with fever, I said good-bye to Father Juan Carlos. I wore sandals and a clerical shirt that he had given me. A group of barefoot Indian kids watched with wide brown eyes that didn't blink. Two of his parishioners, barrel-chested Indians in dirty T-shirts and shorts, were going to take me ten kilometers down river to Puerto Iguazú, in an old motorboat.

The priest handed me a package wrapped in brown paper. "These are the things you had in your pockets. We dried them as best we could."

The package contained about $4,500 in U.S. and Argentine currency, which had been dried and somewhat faded in the sun, and the passport of Omar Legassi—everything I had in my pants pockets when I left my room.

I took about three hundred out of the money, shoved it into my pocket, and handed the rest to the priest. "Please," I said.

He accepted the money without a word.

I looked at the passport. The ink had run, it was faded and moldy, but my photo and the name Omar Legassi were still recognizable. I handed it to the priest.

"Would you burn that, and maybe say a little prayer for me?"

"As you wish," he said.

I looked at the kids. *"Gracias, mis hijos,"* I said. *"Los adoro. Los quiero mucho."* They grinned and shuffled nervously. "Do they understand?"

"I'll explain," said the priest.

We shook hands. I eased myself into the middle of the boat. Pain radiated out from my stomach wound.

"You will need penicillin soon," said the priest.

The small outboard coughed then kicked over. I raised my hand as we chugged off toward the center of the muddy river, greasy black smoke trailing from the little motor. The priest nodded, his eyes following me. The kids watched, silent and unmoving.

I have met a few extraordinary people in my life who have stories to tell that the world should hear; stories that remain hidden in jungles or tenement basements waiting for someone to come along and uncover them. I told myself I would do something for him; I didn't know what.

A turn in the river and they were gone.

Three hours later I was alone, walking on the main street of Puerto Iguazú, a steamy, subtropical river town that was trying hard to be a tourist trap. Souvenir shops and street vendors hawking "Devil's Throat" photos, posters, T-shirts, and native craft lined both sides of the street. I was stunned, wondering what had happened to the sleepy little outpost to nowhere that I remembered.

Posters of the actor Robert De Niro dressed in the garb of a Jesuit missionary stared at me from every storefront; advertisements for a movie called *The Mission*, which had been filmed at Iguazú years earlier. The Hollywood hype must have offered hope to the town fathers that Puerto Iguazú would henceforth be on the map of world tourism. From the few tourists evident on the street, I guessed that the town was doing a lot worse than the movie did.

On a street corner, a shifty-eyed mestizo vendor was selling Indian dolls, macumba potions, and movie posters that he claimed were autographed by De Niro and Jeremy Irons—Irons posters were a buck cheaper. I asked him where the best hotel was.

"I think you're bleeding, Señor," he said, pointing out the stain coming through my shirt.

"Thank you. I apparently cut myself shaving," I answered, wondering once again whether I was delirious or if my final words on earth would be a wisecrack.

Without batting an eye he directed me to a place two blocks

down the street, then stood there watching me until I reached the entrance.

The hotel was small, neat, and clean. The lobby was empty, with the exception of an elderly Dutch couple complaining in broken English to a grinning but uncomprehending desk clerk. There was a lobby newsstand selling day-old editions of *Clarín*. I froze in my tracks, staring at the front page—it was an enlargement of my passport photo. The caption read: DIPLOMAT MISSING, ANOTHER VICTIM OF IGUAZÚ MASSACRE?

Two hundred fifty U.S. dollars later I was in an air-conditioned room waiting for my phone to ring. A hundred bucks for the thirty-five-dollar room, fifty to register without ID, fifty for an unlabeled bottle of what the desk clerk said was bourbon and a dirty envelope full of codeine and penicillin tablets, and fifty to put through a priority collect telephone call to Bobby Stratton.

I gulped down four penicillin and two codeine tablets with a couple of swallows of what tasted like homemade corn whiskey, and reread the AP articles that supposedly covered what I had just lived through. Like most news coverage of the drug war, it had nothing to do with reality. But this report broke all records.

The report called it the "Iguazú Massacre," describing it as "a shoot-out between rival Colombian drug gangs, DEA, and the American Mafia over a gigantic drug deal." Ten American DEA agents had been listed as killed, ten wounded, and one missing— me! The only survivors listed were Gentleman John Gianotti and Pat "the Cat" Gallo. Gianotti had been wounded in the shoulder and hip. Pat the Cat had escaped without a scratch.

Tourists taking cover on the jungle paths near the falls had described me as "fleeing wildly toward the falls," pursued by a "gang of masked assassins" and "bleeding profusely." I was believed to have drowned. However, a massive search, now headed by Colonel Adolfo Martenz of the *Gendarmería Nacional*, "a personal friend of the missing diplomat," was still under way.

Some two-dozen tourists from far-flung places like South Korea and the Middle East were described as "innocent victims of the crossfire." Names had been withheld from the press.

I gulped more whiskey and tore through the paper again, rereading related articles about the drug war, the Mafia, and the cartels that speculated about Argentina's growing involvement in the drug trade. There was no mention of *La Reina Blanca*, Nadia Ricord, or the Triangle of Death; no mention of drugs seized in

Miami; no mention of arms or oil shipments; not a hint of what had really happened.

A euphemism for drunk is "feeling no pain." When the phone rang I was feeling a lot less pain.

"Is it you?" said Stratton's voice.

"Who'd you think it was calling collect from Argentina?"

"I can't fucking believe this." He spoke softly as if not wanting to be overheard. "You okay?"

"No. As a matter of fact I'm pretty fucked up."

"I'll have people pick you up within a couple of hours. Just sit tight."

"What happened?"

"What d'ya mean?"

"Reality. What happened to reality, Bobby? That was no fucking Colombian–Mafia shootout."

Stratton was silent for a long moment. Too long.

"When you get here you'll know everything."

"I only wanna know one fucking thing," I said, unable to keep from slurring my words. "Did we take her down? Did we get Nadia?"

Another silence that told me the answer.

"Why the fuck not?"

"Don't you scream at me!" said Stratton.

"Scream at you? Do you know what I just lived through?"

Silence.

Suddenly I was out of control, blubbering like a baby. "How do you live with it, Bobby? Killed. Murdered. Our own people. How, Bobby? Why?"

"Not over the phone. We're coming for you."

"She's getting a walk on this, isn't she?"

"I can't."

"Who does she know? What, is she fucking the president?"

"I can't, you dinky-dau son of a bitch," he said, his voice softening. "I had no part in it. It's above top secret now."

"Above top secret? Murder American agents, *above* top secret? Bobby, please." I hated the drunken whine in my voice. "Just tell me one thing, is she getting a pass on this?"

"I can't talk."

"No! . . . Please . . . Don't say that. All I wanna know . . . is she getting a walk?"

Silence.

"I am losing my fucking mind."

"Give me your word you're coming in," he said softly.

"You have it," I said.

"She's untouchable."

The word kept repeating in my head. *Untouchable.* I started to say something stupid like, *Elliot Ness.* Then clips of my career flashed in my mind's eye. *Passes, Byes, Walks, Get-out-of-jail-free cards—politicians, friends of politicians, CIA assets, DIA assets, diplomats. Cases dropped, charges dropped, investigations blocked, look the other way. Our government has other priorities. YOU DON'T KNOW THE BIG PICTURE!* Each time was a chunk out of my heart.

I felt weak, tired, impotent, hurting all over, unable to speak. I felt like crying, screaming, pulling my hair out, but my body was too numb to react. All I could do was stare at the phone. *Close to death* were the words that went through my brain.

"There's nothing I can do, Mike." He sounded tired, whipped. "Not even the administrator . . . They dropped the cone of silence . . . But if it means anything, I was assured that she had absolutely nothing to do with René . . .

"Mike? Are you there? . . ."

I hung up the phone, took a couple of codeine pills, guzzled down some more booze, and fell back on the bed.

Gichin Funakoshi was a Japanese many credit with being the father of modern karate. He wrote of the training and philosophy of physical combat as metaphors for how a man should live his life. He said that in a fight when you discover your opponent's weakness and see the opening, the blow you strike should *always* be a deadly one; that a man who lives his life thinking there will always be another opportunity will always fail.

I imagined old man Funakoshi sitting at the foot of my bed in his black ghee. *If you were me, what would you do, dude?* said my dimming brain.

He smiled and bowed his head.

Oos!

When I opened my eyes my room was full of men in olive-drab military uniforms, standing over me. I lay there staring as they blended together to form three. One of them was Colonel Adolfo Martenz.

"How'd you find me?" I croaked. Pain knifed from my stomach through my groin and down my legs.

"Examine him, Doctor!" ordered Martenz.

One of the men took a pair of scissors out of a black medical bag and began to cut through my rough bandage, now caked with drying blood.

"To find you was easier than getting you to return a phone call," said Martenz. "I left a dozen urgent messages for you at the embassy."

"Indisposed. I need you, Adolfo." I was slurring my words.

"Need me?" He looked surprised.

I felt searing pain as the bandage was pulled from my wound.

"Left a nice hole," said the doctor. "It looks like you're going to have two belly buttons."

"I know who killed René. I want to fucking kill her. Help me and our debt is settled."

"Debt?" he said.

I wanted to say, *Please Adolfo, understand, I've been through hell; I'm drunk and in pain.* But those words didn't come out.

"You going to help me or not?" I demanded.

"This is going to hurt," said the doctor as he sprinkled my wound with a powder. Burning pain exploded from my stomach to the tips of my hair. I screamed for a long time. Hands held me down. When it subsided I felt ninety percent more sober.

"Did you say *her*?" asked Martenz.

"Yes," I gasped.

"Lay-vee-nay," he said. "I have your friend's murderer. It's not a woman."

42

EARLY THE NEXT MORNING MARTENZ PICKED ME UP AT THE *Gendarmería* infirmary where I'd spent the night being stitched, bandaged, and pumped full of antibiotics. He was tense, almost energized, and, oddly, in the best mood I had ever seen him. Wherever he was taking me I knew, without his saying a word, that the debt was about to be paid off.

Martenz drove to a prison compound, a gray, low-slung concrete bunker on the outskirts of B.A., and parked in an underground garage. As we got out of the car, two soldiers with FAL submachine guns slung over their shoulders, snapped to attention. The click of their boot heels echoed across the cavernous garage.

"*¡Abrelo!*" ordered Martenz.

"*¡Sí, mi comandante!*" snapped one of the men. He leapt to a heavy steel door, barked a command into a speaker. A loud click followed and the door slid open.

I followed Martenz down a long corridor. On both sides we passed one-way mirrors that viewed windowless cells each with a plain metal cot, a sink, and a toilet bowl. At the far end of the corridor a door opened and another uniformed soldier snapped to attention and saluted Martenz. A half-dozen metal chairs were lined up facing a one-way mirror, behind which was a desk and several chairs—an interrogation room.

"Wait here, Lay-vee-nay," said Martenz. He disappeared through another door.

I waited. Sounds came from hidden speakers: a muffled clang of metal, the murmur of voices, a distant, angry shout. A metallic click came from somewhere overhead.

A door in the next room opened. Martenz entered followed by a shirtless, barefoot prisoner in hand and leg irons who shambled forward in an exaggerated bowlegged shuffle. He was followed by a man in a white laboratory coat. He had a shaved head and a stethoscope hung round his neck. His sleeves were rolled halfway up muscular forearms. An object was slung over his shoulder by a leather strap. When he turned I saw that it was a battery-powered cattle prod.

The prisoner's face was swollen and unshaven, his hair matted and filthy. He gripped soiled, loose-fitting pajama bottoms with iron-manacled hands to keep them from falling to his knees.

"Sit!" ordered the doctor, his voice a deep baritone.

The prisoner, his eyes white with fear, followed the order hesitantly, jerkily, like a frightened dog. I suddenly recognized the man and felt a sickening dip of my stomach. It was Comandante Borsalino—Snakeface—the secret policeman and CIA asset. The last time I had seen him was in the CIA office when Forrest Gregg gave me the Bolivian lead.

The doctor shackled Snakeface's arms and legs to the chair with handcuffs and leg irons. Then, with one violent motion, he jerked the loose-fitting pajama pants down to mid-thigh, exposing burned and swollen genitals.

"*Mi comandante*," said the doctor with exaggerated courtesy as he took a seat on the edge of the table, above and slightly behind Snakeface. He rested the business end of the cattle prod on the skin of Snakeface's thigh. "I would like you to repeat your story for the colonel."

I'd heard tapes of drug traffickers being tortured by the Argentine secret police. They were in the files of the Buenos Aires DEA office when I took over. The torturers all seemed to be soft-spoken, reasonable men who questioned their subjects as if they wanted to help them. There was no need for anger or threats. The technique, combined with excruciating pain, was brutal and effective. One of the reasons I had fired Snakeface from the DEA payroll was that his voice was prominent on many of those tapes. For a moment I had the feeling that the son of a bitch deserved to have the tables turned—but I still wanted no fucking part of it.

"Martenz!" I called out. "If this is for me—I don't want it!"

341

There was no reaction inside the room. Martenz had his back to me, facing Snakeface.

"Please," whimpered Snakeface. His eyes searched their faces for pity.

I pounded on the window. It felt as hard and thick as the wall of a bomb shelter.

"Martenz!"

"It is very important," said the doctor, tapping the cattle prod on Snakeface's thigh, "that you leave nothing out."

"Sometimes my memory . . . the details escape me," whined Snakeface.

"Come now," said the doctor's voice over the speaker. "You torture an American DEA agent to death and you expect the colonel to believe you don't remember?"

The words hit me like a punch in the middle of my forehead. I sat down heavily, my mind numbed by shock.

"I'll tell you everything," whimpered Snakeface.

"That's much better," said the doctor gently. "Now, I want you to begin at the beginning."

"A call from the embassy comes . . . I'm told a drug trafficker is in a room at the Sheraton . . ."

"Tch, tch, tch." The doctor wagged his head. *"Which* embassy? *Who* called you? Why did he call *you*? I don't want to have to remind you again, *Comandante*. You are a professional, you know better."

"Señor Gregg called me from the American embassy," said Snakeface quickly. "I do work for him . . . for the CIA."

"The colonel doesn't understand what *work* means; he thought you worked for Argentina—*nuestra patria*."

"I betrayed my country," he sobbed.

The doctor slammed the metal rod on the table. Snakeface's body jerked spasmodically. "Why?" shouted the doctor.

"For the money." Snakeface's voice quavered. "I was paid a salary. Monthly."

"I am losing patience, *mi comandante. Who* paid you? *What* did they pay you for? The colonel has no idea what you're talking about."

"For the CIA . . . my unit did jobs for them."

"For exactly *who* in the American embassy did you do these jobs?"

"Señor Gregg . . . the CIA."

The doctor got to his feet and strode around behind Snakeface, tapping the cattle prod into his cupped palm.

"Did you report your *employment* for the gringos to your superiors?"

"No . . . sir."

"You are still on the CIA payroll?"

Snakeface closed his eyes. "Yes . . . sir."

"What kinds of *jobs* did you do for the gringos? Explain to the colonel."

Snakeface glanced up at Martenz. Whatever he saw left a look of utter desolation on his face. He lowered his eyes quickly.

"We would . . . capture . . . people. Suspects. Drug traffickers. Question them. Sometimes a fugitive . . . we deliver him where they say."

"What else? What other . . . *jobs* did you do?"

"Intercept telephone conversations . . ."

"What else?" snapped the doctor impatiently. "I warn you . . ."

"K-k-kill. We killed."

"The Americans paid you to kill?" he said with mock surprise, the cattle prod going *tap, tap, tap* into the palm of his hand.

"Please," begged Snakeface. "Please don't . . ."

"Did you get permission from your superiors to *kill*?"

Snakeface began to sob, his face screwed up like a child's. The doctor reached over and touched his swollen, inflamed genitals lightly with the tip of the metal rod. It sparked with a sharp, air-rending snap. Snakeface's body jerked bolt-upright. He screamed for a long time; it gradually turned into a low, keening moan. His head slumped onto his chest. Drool ran from his mouth. I couldn't hear Snakeface's pain, all I could hear was René's.

"The colonel is waiting," said the doctor softly.

"Noooo," he moaned. "Please . . . no more. We only killed drug dealers . . . and Leftists."

Martenz strode to the other side of Snakeface and peered directly at me before asking the next question.

"How do I know you are telling me the truth?"

"It is on the recordings, sir."

"You tape-recorded *all* your conversations with the CIA?"

"Yes, sir."

"And these are among the tape cassettes we recovered from your home and your office?"

"Yes, *mi coronel*," sobbed Snakeface.

Martenz nodded at the doctor.

"Now, *mi comandante*," said the doctor, "I want you to tell us again—and I don't want you to leave out any details—how you and your men kidnapped and tortured the American DEA agent Villarino."

"I didn't know he was an American agent," pleaded Snakeface. "Señor Gregg told us that he was a drug dealer. I swear on the souls of my children—"

"I'm not interested in what you were told," said the doctor. "Only what you did."

"Señor Gregg called . . . in the middle of the night. He told me that, in the penthouse of the Sheraton, there was a drug dealer—an Italian. That he is with a woman. He wanted us to . . . interrogate this man. To identify his contacts. And that once we were satisfied that he had told us everything, he should become a . . . *desaparecido*."

"Who was the woman?" asked the doctor.

"Señor Gregg told us not to speak with her, to forget we saw her."

"Why?"

"I don't know. . . . We go to the door of the penthouse . . . tap three times. She opens it. The man is in bed, nude . . . drugged."

"What did she look like?"

"Beautiful. Tall. Green eyes . . . very short blond hair . . . she . . . she wore white."

The doctor led Snakeface through a description of how they stuffed the unconscious René into a sea trunk and put him in the rear of a panel truck. I felt my heart tearing itself to shreds when he described how Villarino had withstood the torture longer than anyone he could remember, and that finally, when René pleaded that he had two sons and claimed that he was an undercover DEA agent, they didn't believe him, but that it no longer mattered—by that time his condition was so poor, he would not have survived anyway.

I could not think clearly about what I had just heard. I was incapable of putting the information together in a way that made sense. I just wanted to go to some cool, dark place and lie down for a while. I suddenly realized that Snakeface was being helped gently from the room. It was over.

An hour later I was sitting across Martenz's desk from him, at *Gendarmería* headquarters, a bottle of cognac between us. After half the bottle had disappeared, he said: "What happened today, never happened."

"Not you too," I said.

He downed half the drink. "My loyalty is to Argentina," he said. He stared out his window at the Buenos Aires waterfront. "Always Argentina. We're a democracy now—haven't you heard?"

"What are you saying—I'm supposed to forget today and keep my mouth shut about who tortured my friend to death?" I shoved the phone across his desk toward him. "Call René's sons for me. Tell *them* to forget it!"

"Lay-vee-nay. Your government wants human rights," he said with drunken sarcasm. "You spend millions to corrupt us, to train us; you pay us to murder and torture, and now you're unhappy. As far as Argentina is concerned—we know nothing about René Villarino."

"I can't let that happen," I said.

Martenz interrupted me with a bitter laugh.

"You? Miguel Lay-vee-nay? The man whose government tries to bury him in Positos?" He laughed bitterly. "Argentina cannot risk being blamed by public opinion in your country. We need your money. In any case, these are my orders. I've already violated them by telling you anything."

"What happens to Borsalino and the others—the men who killed René?"

"What would you like to happen?"

"I want them dead!" I blurted.

Martenz devoured me with his eyes, as if he were about to lay down a straight flush to my four of a kind. He poured cognac into both our glasses. He raised his glass in a toast.

"You already have your wish, Lay-vee-nay," he said slowly, his eyes never leaving mine. "There were four others with Borsalino. You knew them all. All had wives and children. Men who only followed orders. They were executed as we drove here." He gulped down his drink.

"What about Forrest Gregg?" I asked.

"Not an Argentine problem."

"Are you doing me a favor, or are you trying to torture *me* to death—how do I prove anything against him?"

Martenz leaned forward, opened a desk drawer and withdrew a Sony mini-recorder. He placed it on the desk, facing me.

"Your good friend *Comandante* Borsalino was well trained by his gringo handlers. He recorded everything. This one he kept in a safety deposit box." He shoved the recorder across the desk to me. "Keep it; your government paid for it. I will deny knowing anything about it."

I picked it up and turned it over in my hands.

"What good is a tape recording going to do me?" I said. "I need proof of who Borsalino is, his relationship to Gregg."

"The recording is self-explanatory."

"Not for the American justice system. I need Borsalino's full confession; the details of how you got the recording, or any two-bit attorney in the country will get Gregg off."

"The American justice system," mused Martenz with a wry smile. "Not an Argentine problem."

He poured another drink. I watched him gulp it down.

"Colonel," I said. "One more favor, and I'll never ask another. Forrest Gregg has an Argentine bodyguard detail. Tonight, they've got to be called away."

"Done," he said quickly. "There's one more thing, Lay-vee-nay. Your embassy has asked the Federal Police to arrest you."

"Why? On what charges?"

"There is an international warrant of arrest. I never saw you. This day never happened. That's as far as I can go, my friend," said Martenz. "Our account is balanced."

43

I FLICKED OFF MY HEADLIGHTS AS I REACHED THE HIGH, IVY-COVERED stone wall that surrounded Forrest Gregg's estate. I coasted past the wrought-iron gate and glimpsed the large old fieldstone house set back about a hundred feet from the street in a clump of trees.

It was well past midnight. A dim light was visible on the ground floor. I tried to picture the layout of the interior. The effort brought with it an image of our two little girls, Jen and Niki, in Jennifer's playroom, heads together, giggling, whispering their secrets, as close as twelve-year-old classmates could be. I forced it from my mind.

That was someone else—the man inside that house was a stranger.

The first thing I had to do was get my Camaro with its diplomatic plates out of sight. I parked on a hilltop about six blocks from Gregg's house, facing the river.

My plan was simple, I'd done it a thousand times before. I would arrest Forrest Gregg for conspiracy to murder René. I'd flip him the way I had flipped thousands of scumbags like him. I'd get him talking. He'd tell me everything. If I was good at anything in life it was at flipping mutts and low-lifes, and turning them into stool pigeons. This button-pushing spook was no different. He'd fold like a bad poker hand. He'd fill in the blanks. Testify in court.

The snippet of tape Martenz had given me, the Mossad tapes,

my testimony, and Gregg's statement would be overwhelming evidence. Whatever protection Nadia had would vanish the way it had from other criminals who thought they were protected—the two of them would end up in the can together.

I took a deep breath and felt a sting from my newly stitched wound. I checked the rearview for headlights. I was getting careless—I had not even checked myself for a tail.

I pulled the Glock nine-millimeter from my ankle holster and checked it. It was fully loaded with fifteen hollow-point bullets that would expand on impact, ripping a hole the size of a silver dollar through flesh and bone. I slipped the gun into a side pocket of my leather shoulder bag, next to the two Sony minirecorders—mine and the one Martenz had given me.

There was nothing left to do but *do* it.

Ten minutes later I was at the gate. I pressed the iron handle gently. The lock clicked. *Martenz had lived up to his promise.* The gate slid open with a dull squeak that seemed to carry far into the night. I slipped into the shadows along the path that led to a side entrance.

The door opened easily. I stepped inside a dark hallway. I paused for a moment, listening, waiting for my eyes to accustom themselves to the darkness. A dull sound of voices came from upstairs, sounding like a television or radio. The sound of a man's cough off to my right.

I slipped my hand inside the front pocket of the shoulder bag, pressed the On button of the recorder, and started forward on the balls of my feet. The old wooden floor creaked under my weight.

A silver thread of light shone from beneath a double sliding door—the door to Gregg's study. I inched my way toward it until my face was against the cool, hard wood.

More coughing inside.

With both my hands resting flat on the wood I gently slid the doors apart, just a crack. Forrest Gregg, in a flannel robe, sat behind a wide antique mahogany desk staring straight at me as if he could see through the door. Smoke drifted across his face from an ashtray full of cigarette butts, several still smoldering.

I dropped my right hand into the rear flap of the bag—it hung almost to my hip—and gripped the handle of the Glock. With my left hand I pulled the sliding door open.

Gregg stared right through me, as if he were stoned or in a trance. His big face was so pale in the gloom that he looked like an apparition. An open bottle of Jack Daniel's was on the desk in front of him alongside an old leather-bound Holy Bible that he once told me had been in his family for two hundred years.

"Michael me boy," he said, his tone flat. "Reports of your death were apparently exaggerated."

"You expecting me?" I said. I stood across the desk from him. The only light in the room was a shaded desk lamp that cast shadows on walls lined with well-stocked bookshelves.

"You?" He considered the thought. "Not necessarily. But someone. My bodyguard detail is suddenly called away . . ." He shrugged.

"You don't seem curious about me being here."

His eyes focused on me for a moment. There was a look of deep resignation in them.

"I suppose you'll tell me when you're ready. Have a seat."

I sat across from him, My hand stayed inside the bag on the gun. He didn't seem to notice. I tried to think of some psychological tack to open him up. He had ordered an American DEA agent's death. *Why? What was his involvement with Nadia? Iguazú? Why was Nadia protected from arrest?* He was the end of the line for me. My tape recorder was rolling for the last time.

"I'm placing you under arrest, Forrest," I said. "For the torture-murder of a DEA agent. My friend René Villarino."

"Shouldn't you read me my Miranda warnings, Michael?" The attempt was at sarcasm, but he was trembling.

"Good idea. Before I ask you any questions it is my duty to advise you that you have a right to an attorney," I said, beginning a statement I had repeated so many times that I could reel it off in my sleep. "If you don't want to speak without your attorney present—"

"What makes you think *I* killed him?" he interrupted. He reached for the bottle, his hand trembled violently. I thought about stopping him and decided not to—I wanted him talking more than I wanted him sober.

I placed the recorder Martenz had given me on top of his desk. His eyes followed it as if it could bite. I pressed the Play button. Gregg's tape-recorded voice echoed in the silence:

"Why the hell are you calling at this hour?"

"That man . . . in the Sheraton with the woman. There's a problem," said Snakeface's voice.

"Son of a bitch! What the . . ." said Gregg.

"He says he's undercover . . . for the DEA . . ."

"Jesus . . ."

The sound was garbled as both Gregg and Snakeface spoke at once.

"He says his name is Villarino."

"He's lying, you bloody fool!"

"I don't think so. He knows Señor Lay-vee-nay. Knows his children's names . . . Listen."

A click was heard. Snakeface must have placed a cassette player to the phone. René Villarino's voice was heard pleading:

"No more . . . (Panting for breath) *I can't . . .* (Cry of pain. Moan.) *Please . . . My sons."*

"Do you think of your sons when you sell drugs?" said Snakeface softly.

"I beg you . . . (moaning in pain) *. . . Call DEA . . .* (gasping for breath). *My real name . . . René . . . Villarino. Dear God . . . I'm dying . . ."* (gasping, moaning).

"I'm losing patience with you," said Snakeface.

"Mother of God," said René's voice.

The tape ended.

"You trained him pretty fucking good," I said, my finger pressing lightly on the trigger. I was close to losing it. "Too bad you didn't train him not to turn rat. Borsalino taped every conversation he ever had with you. I've got them all," I bluffed.

Gregg's eyes darted wildly. He picked up the bottle but was unable to control his trembling hand, and put it down. He would never be weaker. It was the time to hammer him with everything I had and pray for an avalanche of words.

"There's something else I want you to see," I said.

I took my hand off my gun and reached inside the bag for another item Martenz had given me. I slowly removed a manila envelope, watching his eyes. They were focused on the envelope, the pupils dilated. I took my time removing three eight-by-ten black-and-white photos. They were clear depictions of the gore that remained of René, complete with maggot trail.

I laid them on the desk before Gregg.

"That's what was left of my friend when I saw him," I said.

People can do some horrible things and then find ways in their own minds to justify it, but for some those defenses crumble like a house of cards when they are confronted with a visual image of what they've done.

"That's what you did to an American agent, the father of two boys," I said. *"You* did that."

"I didn't know," insisted Gregg. "I was led to believe he was a drug dealer. By the time Borsalino called, it was too late—he never would have made it."

I wanted to drive a *seiken* two-knuckle front punch into the center of his lying face with all the focus and concentration of twenty-five years of training. But I also wanted him to keep talking.

"I always thought you were a good man," I said, offering him a carrot. If you want to make a guy talk after you hit him with a hammer, you offer him a carrot. "Our kids used to play together . . ."

"She lied, Michael," he pleaded, all too aware that I would know who he was talking about. "She had René's Interpol record—money laundering, drug trafficking, homicide. His arrest photos. Everything said Fabrizio Calvi, Italian drug dealer. I knew the cartels were after it. She said Calvi wanted *La Reina Blanca* for himself or he would expose us. I believed her."

As he spoke he leaned forward, his tormented eyes imploring me. I should have noticed his right arm, but he always kept his small hands out of sight and all I was conscious of at the moment was the rolling tape recorder in my bag.

Keep talking, motherfucker.

"Who? Expose *what?"* I said.

"No need to play games. You already know her—Nadia."

"Then it *was* you who blew the Iguazú operation," I accused.

"It wasn't supposed to happen that way. She promised she simply would not show up to the meeting."

"Did you blow René's cover too?"

"Never! Do you have any idea of the power this woman has? I swear on my children, Michael—on Jennifer. René blew his own cover. He told her that he was an Italian. She videotaped him making love to her. He got so carried away, he used an expression that only a native Corsican would use. She sent her people over there and his cover began to unravel."

"How do you know this?"

"She showed me the videotape. A bloody shame Villarino fell for her. The way I fell. The way you fell, Michael. Did you go to bed with her?"

"We're not talking about me."

His face contorted into a bizarre grin.

"Of course you did. Didn't she tell you that you belonged together? The way she told me . . . the way she told René as he mounted her . . ."

He swigged from the bottle and began coughing again, a dry, hacking sound. "Bloody bitch," he gasped. "I'm glad you're here, Michael. Thank God it's over.

"You think I'm trying to save myself, don't you—that I'm lying to you?"

"The thought occurred to me."

"You have no idea of the danger you're in."

"I'm listening."

"Do you read the Bible?" His left hand came to rest on the large leather-bound book. "Revelations describes beasts who donned white robes to disguise themselves as angels in order to steal men's souls. One is described as having the aspect of an eagle, Michael. Isn't that interesting?"

"Whatever she is, you are," I said.

He laughed, a crazed bark. "What do you think you know about her?"

"That you and she murdered people I cared about; that she runs an organization that's trying to inject our country with terminal cancer; and that you lied and murdered to protect her."

His mouth was moving before the words came out. "You haven't an inkling."

"I told you. I'm listening."

"Do you know where she is right now?"

"No idea."

"On her way to the Hotel de Paris in Monte Carlo to accept one of the world's most prestigious awards for saving endangered wildlife. Isn't that rich?" He laughed. "DEA headquarters knows what she's done and exactly where she's going yet they're doing nothing to arrest her. Why do you think that is?"

"Go ahead."

"She has developed what our country has sought for almost four decades, Michael—the ultimate chemical weapon."

"*La Reina*," I said.

"Make *La Reina Blanca* available in a country and within weeks a significant and predictable portion of the population is turned into murderous, uncontrollable zombies doomed to a slow, expensive death. You destroy that nation's economy, its faith in its government. The nation implodes on itself. You win a war and you never fire a shot.

"Look at what heroin and cocaine have already done—La Reina makes those drugs look like powdered sugar."

"You're not telling me anything I don't know," I said. "What I don't understand is how the fuck you, a so-called American, can put that shit on our streets."

"The drug was not supposed to hit the street, yet—Nadia betrayed us. Oh my God, Michael." He wagged his head. "How can you be so good at what you do and have so little understanding of what really pulls your strings? Don't you realize that there are factions in your government that want this to happen—an emergency situation too hot for a constitutional government to handle."

"To what end?" I asked.

"A suspension of the Constitution, of course. The legislation is already in place. All perfectly legal. Check it out yourself. It's called FEMA, Federal Emergency Management Agency. 'Turn in your guns, you bloody bastards, from here on out, we're watching you, you antigovernment rabble rousers.' And who would be king, Michael?"

"CIA," I said.

"Whether you believe me or not, I'm not one of those. But I'm a realist. And I suspect that you're anything but."

"Nadia works for the CIA?"

"Nadia works for no one! At this moment she is perhaps the most powerful, most protected person on earth. The Triangle of Death bridges three continents, and now—thanks to you—she has extended her influence to North Korea and the Middle East."

"Thanks to me?"

"Thanks to your ingenious deal. The arms and oil trade went through, quite smoothly, I might add. Of course it took a little work on the part of your friends at the Mossad."

I felt the blood drain from my face. He didn't miss it.

"Michael, don't look so crestfallen. Don't you know by now that in this business you can trust no one. Twists and turns, double agents, triple agents. National interests are always multiple, transient, and duplicitous. Arabs, Jews, and Nazis all work together where their interests are common. Actually, you've done us all an unexpected favor by putting Nadia into the arms business. Right now we need to quietly arm Saddam Hussein again. Iraq is our only military hammer against Iran."

"She got her money?"

"Of course she was paid. We made sure of that. The people she killed meant nothing to their governments—they're as much bloody pawns as you and I. The Iraqis transferred in the neighborhood of three hundred million into one of her accounts. Not bad for a day's work."

"Why are we protecting her?"

"In a bloody word: *La Reina Blanca*, the White Queen. We helped her perfect it. Yes, she attempted to betray us, but we're quite willing to forgive her because she still controls it, and now that she's back in line and more useful than ever, we're getting just what we wanted."

"What's that?"

"Wherever the drug turns up, the DEA and the CIA claim it's the Medellín cartel behind it, or some other cartel, or the Russian mafia. When Nadia is no longer useful I suppose we'll turn on her too."

"You're telling me that while DEA was going after the source of the White Queen, the CIA was backing its development?"

"I cannot believe that shocks you, Michael."

"You sound proud of yourself," I said.

"No! Realistic." He took another swig and winced. "Reality beat me into submission. As it should have you, when DEA destroyed you for complaining about CIA protection of the Bolivian cocaine cartels."

"*Tried* to destroy me."

"You *are* destroyed and don't know it yet. But you may come to look upon this evening as the luckiest of your life."

"You said we helped her develop *La Reina*—can you prove that?"

"Not exactly, but there's a long history associated with this project. Some of it is public record."

"What project is that?"

"Right after World War II the Agency obtained some of the materials from Hitler's search for the ultimate mind-control weapon. The first CIA program to continue that research began during the Eisenhower administration, under the direction of DCI Allen Dulles. Under this program, the Agency literally financed the development of LSD for its potential as a warfare weapon. The program was code-named MK–Delta. Later it was called MK–Ultra."

"Whoa, whoa. Now you're telling me the CIA developed LSD also?"

"That's the least of it, Michael. Later, during the Kennedy administration, under DCI Richard Helms, the whole thing was continued under a program called MK–Search.

"If you don't believe this is all true, Michael, you can look it up in your local public library. I read the entire case file when I was assigned to work with Nadia. I know it by heart."

"You were *assigned* to work with Nadia?"

"I thought I was, but later I learned that she had manipulated that too. She has bloody contacts in all the covert agencies. She set her sights on me. But I'm getting ahead of myself.

"Now we come to Dr. Franz Weir. Nadia's Dr. Hess. You've met him. I already know, Michael. Weir was the best man the Nazis had. The Agency found him in a POW camp in Alabama and put him back to work.

"Just as Weir's research started to look promising the whole program was blown out of the water. The Agency had administered LSD and other hallucinogenic substances to unsuspecting U.S. soldiers, to patients in mental hospitals, to unsuspecting scientists, and even to Agency personnel. We used agents from your old bureau, FBN, to set up houses of prostitution where the johns were slipped LSD by the hookers, with their reactions measured and filmed through one-way mirrors. All paid for by the U.S. taxpayer for God and country.

"We'll never know how many lives were destroyed. National Security put the lid on that embarrassing information.

"You see what a snakepit this whole thing is, Michael? I want you to understand why I did what I did, how big, deep, and dark this whole thing is. Arresting me won't accomplish a thing."

"What does all this have to do with Nadia Ricord?"

"I'm getting to that. When the whole mess was about to hit the newspapers, with revelations that should have blasted the CIA to kingdom come, the Agency spin doctors took over. Files were destroyed, burned and shredded. People disappeared. Weir and others like him were told to disappear.

"Our man Weir next runs to South America, where he's welcomed into the Triangle of Death with open arms. He does wonders for the improvement of heroin and cocaine production. He stays up-to-date on advances in biogenetic engineering that open up possibilities for superpotent designer drugs that defy the imagination. He convinces Auguste Ricord to contact his old mentor, CIA, to retrieve his research and to cut a deal for Agency backing and protection.

"Ricord, as you must know, was no stranger to covert deals with government agencies—assassination, use of drug money to fund covert operations—the whole panoply of dirty business. He had made himself so useful to the French Secret Service that France—in spite of sentencing him to death in absentia—didn't pursue his extradition. But he learned as all of us eventually do, that all security is only an illusion. He was finally arrested by your alma mater, the DEA, before the deal was cut.

"By this time little Nadia is well trained to take over daddy's business interests, following daddy's directions from federal prison. She makes contact with the Agency and makes herself useful. You must have noticed, she has her own little army."

"Is that who hit us in Iguazú?"

"Of course she was behind it, but she's much too clever to send people who can be traced directly to her. I would suggest that she conned one of the Colombian cartels into doing it for her. I think you'll find that the hundred and twenty million in Mafia money sitting on the tarmac at Iguazú has vanished. I guarantee you, no one will ever know who did it. As a matter of fact, the last news I heard was that certain Italian gentlemen think it was a man named Omar, who happens to look just like you, who stole their money."

He saw in my eyes that I believed him. And more: that his words frightened me. This seemed to encourage him.

"At Dr. Weir's urging, Nadia gets approval from her father in jail, to approach the Agency with the possibility of resuming research into a superdrug. She's got Dr. Weir. She's got first-class international connections. She's hooked directly into the ex-Nazi circuit. She has a large organization. All she needs from CIA is access to the latest classified research and equipment in botanical genetics and some of Weir's old research under MK–Ultra. An offer we couldn't refuse. Then she asks, specifically, for me to be her case officer."

"Why you?"

Gregg seemed to sink inside himself. The picture of a man lost in terminal self-pity. I had seen the same picture in my mirror enough to recognize it easily. He took another swallow of whiskey.

"Nadia has the instinct of a lioness in recognizing weakness in her prey. She made a study of me. I guess I was ripe to break the rules. She knew it. She wanted absolute control over *La Reina* from the beginning. She also wanted the Agency's support and protection. The only way to get it all was to find a weak link."

"You."

"She gave me all her mumbo-jumbo about the rain forest, the endangered wildlife, her prized harpy eagle and the jaguar going extinct. She needed the money to lease a million acres of Amazon from Brazil and Paraguay. Then we'd sail off into the sunset, two people in blissful love." He laughed bitterly. He should have been drunk, but he wasn't. His eyes glowed with an eerie intensity.

"Sounds bloody naive, doesn't it—twenty years in this business and falling for that line?"

"Naive is not the word I'd use," I said.

"The irony is, Michael, that you beat her at her own game and didn't even know it. And the ultimate irony is that she's turned the tables again . . . Unless . . ." He stopped talking.

"Unless what?"

He took another swig of whiskey and made a decision. He slid his left hand beneath the desk. It was the first time I really noticed how unnaturally still he held his right arm. But I was immediately distracted by a loud click in the shadows behind me.

"I'm not well, Michael," he said. "The bookcase to the right of the door is unhinged. Just pull it toward you."

I eased out of my chair and half backed away from Gregg, keeping him in view. A light tug and the bookshelf swung open revealing a small room. On the floor sat two Samsonite suitcases.

"Open them," said Gregg.

I got behind one of the bags and turned it onto its side, keeping an eye on Gregg. I smelled the money before I saw it. The case was stuffed with neat rubber-band-wrapped stacks of hundred-dollar bills.

"Rainy-day money," said Gregg. "A day like today. There's a million and a half in each. Take it all. Run as far as you can. It's all I have on hand. If you don't already have one, open a numbered account in Switzerland; I'll transfer another ten million into it within two months. I can arrange a change of identity for you and leave Michael Levine listed as dead."

I moved back toward his desk. He read the look on my face. Or he thought he did. He started talking fast and furious.

"I'm not bribing you, Michael," he pleaded. "I'm offering you a chance to save yourself. You think charging me with René's murder will hurt her? She'll love it. You'll be disturbing a hornets' nest the size of Langley, Virginia. The Agency media specialists will cut a spin that'll make you think you've crossed into another dimension. You've made it easy for them. You're already on record as an agent with integrity problems. By now they know you've been working with the Mossad. You'll be arrested as a thief, a spy, a turncoat, and they will happily lump me in with you.

"And while you are reeling around wondering how the world could have turned on you, trying to raise money for attorneys who most likely will sell you out for the Agency, your last thought will be of your own security. That's when it will happen.

"One night you will park on a dark street. A stranger will slip out of the shadows. Perhaps a woman. The weapon most likely a twenty-two-caliber short. A classic professional hit. With your history there won't be any shortage of suspects. And that will be your history, Michael Levine."

"Also, the history of the Gregg family name, right Forrest?" I said.

He blinked rapidly. "It doesn't have to be, Michael. What will your boy Keith think—he's a police officer isn't he?"

He eyed me like a man who'd bet everything he owned on a full house and was waiting to see my cards. I knew that everything he said was probably true; that I probably ought to take the money and just fucking run.

"What about the money?" I asked. "They'll just forget about it?"

He brightened. I'd given him hope.

"When did you ever hear of a CIA agent being indicted for stealing money? Think of the hundreds of billions in drug cash floating through banks that *we* control; the billions in Black Ops funds that even Congress doesn't know about. Use your head, Michael, please. For both of us. You're still officially listed as missing."

I toyed with the idea of picking up the money and running. Every alternative seemed hopeless.

Then I looked across the desk at the pale, bloated face of the man who killed my best friend, and rage took over. I slipped my hand back inside the bag and found the handle of the gun. This time his eyes followed.

I think we both knew at that moment it was all over. Some inner control gave way. Words that had been forming at the back of my brain since he'd begun talking came tumbling out.

"You're a lying sack of shit," I said.

His eyes gaped wide. His mouth started to form a word.

"You were in love with her. You stole millions. You were going to help her dump a couple of tons of white nightmare on your own country. Where your daughter is. Where my kids are. And you want me to believe killing René was some kind of mistake? That you had nothing to do with the massacre?"

"Friendly fire," he blurted. "People are accidentally killed in all wars—"

"Bullshit!" I shouted. I couldn't listen to another word. "You knew he was DEA, you son of a bitch. Nadia told you. René found out about you because he was cleverer and smarter than you *and* he was fucking your woman. It drove you nuts!"

"I swear to God—"

"*Shut up!* Watching them *fuck* on that video was too much for you, wasn't it? René nailed her pretty good, didn't he? She must have fallen for him too. Then she found out he was DEA and went nuts. But she was too smart to kill a DEA agent herself, so she got you, a fucking jealous, low-life spook agent to do it. This was personal. You couldn't hurt René enough, could you?

"You were right about one thing, Forrest—you motherfuckers *think* you're above the law."

Gregg pushed back from his desk. I saw the short, ugly barrel of a shotgun in his hands. A High Standard, a special police model that fired twelve shotgun shells as fast as you could pull the trigger. It was pointed at my chest. His hand was no longer trembling. His face was like a wax mask.

"Kill me, it won't make a difference," I said, thinking of firing the Glock through the bag. I was about eight feet from him, a long way to fire a handgun from the hip, and through a bag. He could cut me in half with that cannon with his eyes closed.

"The tapes are already in my lawyer's hands," I said. "Along with a declaration of what I was going to do tonight. They'll charge you with my murder *and* René's." As I spoke I realized that that was probably what I should have done.

"She's killed us both," he said as he turned the barrel into his right temple, the thumb of his tiny white hand on the trigger.

"No!" My shout was drowned in a mighty blast. His head disintegrated in a cloud of pink and gray.

I stood there, my ears ringing, staring down at Forrest Gregg's torso slumped over the armrest of his chair. The top third of his head had been blasted all over the room, though the area from just above his cheek to his open and still moving mouth remained untouched. Blood pulsed from where the brain had been. His heart was still beating. The absurd notion to try to save him propelled me a step forward.

Outside an alarm was wailing.

I was suddenly struck with the crystal-clear image of what I had to do now and the urgency of how fast I had better move. There was still one remaining battle to be fought and it would take money.

Inside the room behind the bookcase I scooped ten packages of hundreds into my leather bag. If $100,000 wasn't enough, a billion wouldn't do it, and money would be my last worry.

44

RIO DE JANEIRO, BRAZIL

IT WAS NOT QUITE TWENTY-FOUR HOURS SINCE GREGG HAD BLOWN HIS brains all over his study, yet it felt as if light-years had passed. I'd been waiting for the past three hours at a greasy little coffee counter in the in-transit section of Rio's International Airport, watching the flow of people spewing out of arrival doors.

I was wired from too much coffee and too little sleep. The flood of people around me started to look like a river of multicolored, multilingual talking heads. All four flights due from the U.S. had already arrived. Tito Garza was a no-show. I had tried paging him a half-dozen times. No answer.

My plan with Garza backing me up was pretty risky. A bookie might give me ten to one—against. Attempting it alone might be called suicide.

Gregg had been right about one thing—the suits were coming after me with a vengeance. I had risked a phone call to the embassy to try and get a reading as to where I stood with DEA. Jackie, my secretary, immediately recognized my voice and performed her final act of loyalty.

"You must have a wrong number," she said, her voice distant and as tight as a truck spring. She hung up quickly.

There was probably a trace on the call. She had taken a hell of a chance for me.

After that call, I knew I couldn't risk calling my kids. If there was a trace on the embassy phone, they'd have one on my kids' phones too. If I was under indictment it was not beyond the suits' imagination or morality to arrest one of my children for aiding and abetting an escaping felon. They were very creative when it came to fucking up the lives of the men and women under their command.

More spinning plates had begun to wobble, but I had no time to worry about them. Earlier that morning, I had gone to the Aguirre office in Buenos Aires to pass the word to the Mossad that I needed copies of the tapes I'd given them as soon as possible. The office was vacant and spotless, as if it had never existed. I telephoned the Mossad number in Tel Aviv and was told it was "not a working number," and that my cousin Avi's number was "temporarily out of service."

Once again Gregg's words about the Mossad haunted me. None of this could change my plan; if it failed, not even the God of Abraham, Isaac, and Jacob would be able to help me.

I picked up my leather shoulder bag, within which was my blue U.S. tourist passport, approximately $104,000 in cash, the gold medallion taken from the body of Julio's father and *El Búfalo*'s recorded description of the murder of Julio's family—all the weapons I had, except for my cowboy boots, handcrafted in Texas with aluminum-reinforced, sharply pointed toes that could kick a hole in a forehead. I felt like a ninja cowboy.

The loudspeaker announced the boarding of my Air France flight to Paris in Spanish, Portuguese, English, and French. There was no turning back.

People started moving toward the gate. I looked at the tickets. Two first-class round-trip tickets in our true names—Tito Garza and Michael Levine—paid for in cash. The last thing the suits would expect is that I'd be dumb enough to use my true name. It would take about twenty-four to thirty-six hours, I guessed, before the lookout systems in France notified them, and by that time I'd have had my last shot at Nadia.

I joined the flow of people heading along the concourse toward my gate, keeping my head down, trying to blend in. I was conscious of the tightness of the skin around my stomach wound but was not in pain. My right knee was as stiff as usual but in good enough condition for one more round—and since it was probably my last, I was ready to let it all hang out.

I had told Julio all about the *goju* karate philosophy of waiting until your opponent was off balance and unsuspecting, to "get hard"—to attack. If there was ever a time to get hard, this was it.

"You gonna fucking leave without me?" called a familiar voice.

I turned. Garza ran up behind me, out of breath. His eyes were bloodshot, he needed a shave. He was wearing tan linen slacks and an electric-blue Miami blazer with large gold buttons that looked as if it had been slept in.

"I watched all four flights come in," I said. "I figured you were a no-show. I didn't think you'd be coming dressed like Howdy Doody."

"Fuck you! Go fuck yourself!" He jabbed his index finger into my shoulder. "You fuck up my life, destroy Vinnie and Georgie—an' you're gonna fucking leave without me?"

People glanced at us. I kept moving toward the gate. Garza, fuming, was ready to stop and fight it out.

"Can you keep it down?" I said. "Mr. Undercover. I'm glad you dressed to blend in with the crowd. Does that jacket glow in the dark?"

"*Te odio*, motherfucker."

"I told you we *had* to catch this flight, Tito. What'd you expect?"

"Me, Georgie, and Vinnie were suspended without fucking pay. They made us turn in our guns and badges—grand jury, fucking subpoenaed. 'Cause of *you*."

"I didn't know."

"Fuck you, you didn't know. Whatchu think, I could just walk up to the *chingado* fucking airline counter, pick up my fucking ticket and get on the fucking plane without attracting attention? It's a good thing for you my ex works for the airlines. I had to beg her to pick up my tickets and transfer them to Aerolíneas."

"But I didn't know—"

"Fuck you!—you didn't know. And what happens? The three of us been standing up for you. We refused to testify and you— you're gonna just fucking leave! ¡Qué come-mierda más grande!"

We reached the end of a long line queuing up to the flight gate. A growing number of people were noticing us. The line toward the boarding gate edged forward slowly. It was about a block long. The plane would be packed.

"Here," I said, handing him his ticket.

"If I had any way outta this, *Judío*," he said, "I swear on my mother's grave, I'd tear this up and spit in your fucking face!"

We edged toward the door, silently. Garza was in a sullen

funk. I felt ashamed of myself for ragging him. But I knew that an apology would set him off again, and we had already attracted too much attention.

The Air France flight attendant, an attractive blonde whose little brass name plate read *Janine,* smiled at Garza as she took his ticket. I watched his face perform a lightning transformation.

"I see you did not check in, *Monsieur* Garza," Janine said, her blue eyes wilting him further. "I must see your passport, please."

"Sure, baby," he said, pulling his tourist's blue passport from the inside pocket of his blazer and handing it to her with a flourish, as if it were a rare book of poetry.

"Voo lay voo coo-shay avec moi?" he said while I looked for a hole to crawl into.

"Pardon?" she said, the sudden arch of her eyebrows the only break in her cool.

"It's a song," he said, with what could only be described as an innocent leer. "It's the only French I know, *mamita.*"

"I see," she said, examining his passport and ticket.

"You working this flight, sweetheart?" Garza cocked his head at an angle and looked her up and down. I looked away. He was the only man I knew who I'd bet capable of making love an hour before his own execution. She looked into his eyes again. He grinned like the village idiot.

"Yes, but as you are in First Class, *Monsieur,* I probably won't have the pleasure of serving you," she said with more than a hint of sarcasm, a quality entirely wasted on Garza when coming from a pretty woman. She tore the ticket and returned the passport along with the stub.

I tugged him along the corridor with me. He glanced back, his hand cupped on his groin. "What a *mamita.* You see the look she gave me?" He paused and made a kissing sound with his lips.

"Amazing self-control," I muttered, tugging him along by an elbow and feeling the urge to both laugh and cry at the same time.

He jerked his arm away. "Fuck you!"

In general I handle flying a lot better when I'm under a lot of outside stress. I have this feeling that The Big Guy usually zaps you when things are going really well. I noticed Geraldo Rivera among the passengers.

The Big Guy just wouldn't dare.

Garza sat sullenly beside me, downing champagne cocktails.

He hadn't said a word since *Fuck you.* I knew him well enough to know that it would be best to wait for him to speak first. I gulped down a couple of codeine tablets that the *Gendarmería* had given me for pain.

"What are you, a fucking junkie now?" said Garza, glaring at me.

"I got shot at Iguazú."

He wagged his head. "Yeah. It's a fucking miracle I didn't get my head cut off in Miami."

"What happened?"

"I'm in a suite at the Fontainebleau. Buttonmen from all the five families are there. When you didn't call like you was supposed to, they start panicking. These guineas invested twenty-four million a family in this deal and now it's a fucking *jodienda.* Phone calls start coming in from all over the country. 'What's going on?' 'Where's the shit?'

"First thing they think of is: Gentleman John beat them for the bread. These guineas don't trust their own mothers. A call comes in from some *capo di tutti frutti,* who says we should call the hotel at Iguazú direct and find out what the fuck is going on. I don't like the look I see on these guys' faces. Hands are going inside coats. So while the call's going through and no one's lookin' at me, I slip into the bathroom then out the door.

"And it's a good thing I did, because later I hear that somebody in Iguazú picked up the phone screaming that there's shooting and soldiers running around. So the wiseguys in the hotel figured that they were getting ripped off and they ice Gianotti's guys right on the spot. Made three of them lay in the Jacuzzi together and filled the tub with lead from three Uzis. There was plenty a room in that tub for four. It was all over the Miami papers."

"What about the dope?" I asked.

"The task force stormed every fucking warehouse in Miami; tore apart every kind of animal cage we could find—even fucking parakeets. No dope. Not a gram. Next thing happens is everybody's ordered into Miami headquarters—about a hundred-fifty of us crowded into the meeting hall like fucking sardines. They lock the doors. Bydon's there with a dozen *maricón* shooflies and a couple of spooks. They make us sign a nondisclosure form. If we say a word about what happened, we get thirty years for violation of some secrecy act."

"You signed it?"

"What, are you fucking kidding? Of course I signed it. Bydon said he's personally gonna take the gun and badge off any man who refuses. Good-bye job. Good-bye pension. *Pa'carajo!*

"If you was there, you woulda signed it too!

"It didn't matter anyway. Next thing happens is they drag me and Vinnie to that *pendejo maricón* Bydon's office in Washington. Three shooflies on each of us; stick us in separate little rooms. They take our guns and badges, read us our fucking rights. In the meantime, they're doing the same thing to Georgie in the fucking hospital. And what do you think they wanna talk about? *You,* Levine. Unless we testify against *you,* they're gonna charge *us* with about fifty fucking felonies—everything from kidnapping to homicide."

"And what did you say?"

"They did a pretty good job of scaring the shit out of us—too good. That fucking zombie Bydon wanted to record statements on the spot. We said 'Nooo fucking way' and asked for attorneys. They gave us a week. That's when I get the call from you. And you say '*Venga!*' Just come! No fucking who, what, why. *Nada más.* But I figure you destroyed my fucking life anyway, I might as well die with you.

"Then I finally get to Rio, and you're fucking leaving!"

"Right, Tito," I said, laying my head back. All I could think about were Gregg's words. The Agency spin doctors were already hard at work. Would they anticipate my final play?

Garza was watching me. "*¿Y qué?* You gonna tell me what I got myself into, or not?"

It took me about an hour and a half to fill Garza in on everything he didn't know. You don't ask a man to die with you and keep anything back.

"Hey, why'd this Nadia bitch have to off *everybody?*" said Garza.

"You know anything about the first Triangle of Death case—Operation Springboard?"

"Gimme a break—I was in fucking high school."

"It got the name when the prosecutor marked a map of the world with a black dot for each murder related to their operation. A couple of hundred on three continents formed a rough black triangle. I think it was *Time* magazine, or one of them, that named them."

"Coño!"

"The name caught on so good that even the badguys started calling themselves Triangle of Death. Like when the press named the Medellín cartel.

"Old man Ricord was a believer in eliminating problems before they happened. Let's say he was in a deal with ten people and he found out one was a *chota*—all ten had to die. No witnesses. No chance of any kind of testimony linking him in a conspiracy."

"Cold muthafucka."

"Right! Nadia learned from the master."

"Fucking *Judío*," said Garza, shaking his head. "Only you."

He laid his head back on the seat next to mine. The in-flight movie was playing. The screen showed a bunch of near-naked teenagers running around and destroying property in suburban L.A.

"You got any other questions?" I asked.

Two teenagers on the screen were making out as a maniac in a ski mask moved toward them through dense woods carrying a bloody ax.

"Yeah, there's something I always wanted to ask you," he said. "That time in New York with that *Monguín* shit—did you set me up?"

"Is that what you've been thinking, all these years?"

"If I'm gonna fucking die with you, I just gotta know. Nothing's gonna change anything. I just gotta know the truth."

"Tito, you're a Cuban, it's a Cuban expression, and you didn't know what it meant—how the fuck would I know it means 'the guy who can't raise a hard-on'? When O'Grady asked you, why didn't you just tell him you didn't know? You knew the guy hated you; he was looking to make an ass out of you."

"I didn't think the dumb Mick was smart enough."

"Well that dumb Mick knew that you were a guy with an answer for everything," I said. "And of all the things in the world, why did you have to say it meant 'the wise one'? And whether you believe me or not, I'm probably the only guy in New York who never called you *Monguín* behind your back."

Garza was quiet for a long moment, "You know what, Levine—I believe you."

The arrival in Paris went smoothly. French Customs and Immigration didn't give us a second glance. So far, so good. Next we had to catch a flight to Nice. I bought two tickets and then telephoned René's brother Paolo. He picked up the phone on the first ring.

"We arrive where I told you at three," I said.

"Everything is ready, *Mighe*."

On the flight to Nice I began to carefully rehearse Garza for what might be our last UC bit together. After we'd gone over the plan the first time, Garza sat there shaking his head.

"What's wrong?" I said.

"What's wrong? You think you and me are gonna just go in there like *pendejo* Batman and *maricón* fucking Robin and arrest that psycho bitch?"

"Not *we*," I said. "*Me!* You just do what I tell you. Follow the plan or you'll fuck us both up."

Garza laid his head back, wagging it from side to side. "And then we're gonna fly her to *chingado* Israel?"

"Tito, this is our only shot," I said. "We don't *have* a choice."

"*Chingado*. What a fucking mess, Levine . . ."

———

Paolo was waiting for us at the airport in Nice.

"He's like lookin' at a fucking double of Villarino," muttered Garza.

Paolo hugged us both tightly. He looked at me, wide-eyed and breathless with anticipation. He was hungry for *vendetta*.

I had told him almost nothing when I called him, just the arrangements I needed him to make. I could hear his frustration, but he was an experienced cop; he knew that anything said on an international telephone conversation might as well be broadcast on the front pages of *The New York Times*.

Paolo's eyes scanned ahead and then behind us as he led us toward the airport exit. Within a few breathless minutes Garza and I were seated comfortably in a late model Peugeot and speeding toward the center of Nice. Run-down old buildings and streets drifted by; I was surprised at how big and sprawling the city was. It wasn't how I'd pictured the French Riviera.

"Everything is arranged, *Mighe*," said Paolo at the wheel. "Precisely as you wanted."

"Is Julio with her?"

"Yes."

"What kind of security does she have?"

"She has registered with an entourage of twelve and the place is crawling with French Secret Service. They might just as well be working for her."

Garza looked at me and rolled his eyes toward the heavens.

"You have her rooms and the hotel layout?" I asked.

"Absolutely."

"What time is the ceremony?"

"At ten p.m."

"How long will it take us to get there?"

"Route 8A, even with traffic, is no more than an hour."

I looked at my watch. It was 3:30 p.m.

Fifteen minutes later Paolo opened the door to a sparsely furnished room with two single beds, frayed carpets, and a mini-bar. We were in the Hotel La Mer, a nondescript little joint on Place Messéna, right in the center of downtown Nice.

"I hope this will do," said Paolo. "It is cash, no questions."

Garza slumped onto one of the beds. "I could sleep for a fucking month! Wake me up when this is over."

"Perfect," I said, sitting on the other bed. "We're out of here by seven p.m."

I noticed two tuxedos, with shirts, suspenders, and black bow ties, hanging in the open closet.

"If the fit is wrong, there is still time," said Paolo.

The tuxedos fit reasonably well, considering Paolo had rented them by estimating our sizes. Garza's was slightly big, but the looseness served to conceal his eight-inch-long MAB automatic pistol, loaded with fifteen hollow-point bullets. Paolo had brought one for each of us.

"*Qué cañóne, más hermoso,*" said Garza, brightening. He loved guns almost as much as women. He hefted it and slid it into his waistband. "Beautiful."

Paolo had also prepared forged invitations to the awards ceremony on fine linen paper with gold-embossed letters and blue silk ribbons. They wouldn't fool the sponsors of the event, but they'd get us past hotel security. They were addressed to Señores Agustín San Remo and Martin Soslayo, Argentinean consular officers.

Garza examined his and wagged his head. "Fucking Levine. We're goin' down in flames." He slumped back on the bed in his tuxedo.

"What about shoes?" I asked.

Paolo had forgotten. My black snakeskin boots would pass, but Garza was wearing two-tone Miami pimp shoes that went with a tux like an olive in a milkshake. I gave Paolo five hundred dollars. He would take one of Garza's shoes along for size and find a suitable replacement pair before he picked us up.

Paolo explained that the plane he had arranged to fly us direct to Tel Aviv with Nadia was an execu-jet registered to a French bank, which was already standing by at the airport. The bank's pilot wanted $50,000 cash to make the run—half the money out front.

I counted out the $25,000, then added another $5,000 to cover Paolo's expenses. He tried to refuse the expense money.

"It's U.S. government money, Paolo," I said. "They owe your family a lot more."

"This woman killed my brother, *Mighe*?" said Paolo softly.

I thought about how to begin my answer. I wanted René's family to know everything so that they could close the door on his murder.

"A lot of people killed René. Most are already dead. She is the last."

Over the next half hour, with Garza snoring in the other bed, I told Paolo how René had died and why. When I finished there were tears in his eyes.

"*Mighe*," said Paolo. "Tonight I want to be there."

"No!" I snapped. This was one of the things I was afraid of. I'd lose my mind if I caused his death and I survived.

"You're staying out of this."

"He was my brother,"

"Listen to me, Paolo," I said. "The place is crawling with French Secret Service and Nadia's security. If we fail, and you go down with us, there's no one left for *vendetta*. She wins again. Don't you get it?

"If we die, you kill her. They won't be expecting you. They don't know who you are. If you die with us tonight, it's all over. We're out of the game."

Garza had his eyes closed, but I knew he was listening. Paolo searched my eyes for a reason to protest. There was none.

"I think you fucked up," said Garza after Paolo had left. "We need every bit of help we can get tonight. Besides, who the fuck you think you are with this *vendetta* shit—Zorba the Greek?"

He lay back and closed his eyes.

45

MONTE CARLO

"No wonder they call these fucking people frogs," announced Garza, disgusted. He was changing stations on the car radio incessantly, the way he did when we were partners. It used to drive me nuts, but at the moment I was more concerned with getting stopped by a police patrol. We were driving slowly along the shore road from Nice to Monte Carlo in a black Renault sedan that Paolo had "borrowed" from a long-term parking lot.

Garza flicked the radio off. "No fucking salsa music. Can you believe that shit?"

The moon was low over the Mediterranean. Luxury yachts dotted the bay. In the distance, just off Avenue d'Ostende, yards from the edge of Monte Carlo's waterfront, sat the Hotel de Paris, looking like a glittering jewel in a deep blue setting.

I parked about a hundred yards short of the hotel's broad driveway lined with Rolls-Royces, Jaguars, and stretch limos. The entrance reminded me a little of the Plaza Hotel in New York, with golden awnings, floral displays, and brass banisters leading up a wide marble staircase. Elegant women in gowns and men in tuxedos flowed up the stairway like an incoming tide. Valets in short blue jackets with gold trim hustled back and forth. Above the entrance were four floors of balconied rooms with wrought-iron railings separated by gold leaf columns. The top floor where the luxury apartments were located had sculptures of naked nymphs decorating the balconies. One of these suites was Nadia's.

"Jesus," said Garza, gawking beside me.

"Incredible, isn't it?" I said struck by the sheer garishness of the sight.

"Yeah, you see the ass on that *mamita*. She just gave me a fucking look like you wouldn't believe."

A platinum blonde with a deep bronze tan, wearing a tight, strapless mini dress walked toward the hotel on the arm of a guy in a top hat. They were about a hundred feet from us. She would have needed field glasses to see Garza.

"You don't get your mind on the job, you're out of the *mamita* business for good."

I handed him an envelope containing the mini-recorder and the gold medallion *El Búfalo* had taken from the body of Julio's father.

"Remember, after I point out Julio, you wait till after the ceremony. Look for a chance to pull his coattail and get him away from her. Tell him Omar sent you. The recorder is set to go right on *El Búfalo* describing how the kid's family was murdered. Just press Play. *Don't* fuck around with it."

Garza shook his head.

"What is it now?"

"*Estás más chiflado que nunca.* This whole thing's nutty."

"We've already been through this a hundred times," I said, starting to feel butterflies. "Just make sure the kid knows exactly what the recording is. Hand him the medallion. Do your thing. Then go like hell for the car."

"Suppose the kid don't wanna come?"

"I'm betting everything he will. I just don't want him hurt. You got that?"

I pulled out the map of the hotel's layout and pointed out the service entrance at the rear. "You have the car waiting, motor running, where you can see that door. You hear a commotion, police coming, you wait as long as you can then split.

"If I don't make it, the money's in the trunk. You and the kid head to the plane. Call my cousin Avi when you get to Israel."

"And suppose she calls your bluff—'Go ahead, off me, motherfucker, I don't believe you're gonna pull that trigger,' and she starts screamin' her lungs out?"

"I'll worry about it when it happens. Just do your thing."

"You oughta let me handle the bitch. Push comes to shove, I don't think you got the *cojones* to do her. I'll just hide under her fucking bed, when it gets real quiet I wrap this cannon with blankets and pop her right through the mattress, then we party in *Judío*-land. I hear the babes in Israel got *tetas* that don't end, man."

"And then we go home to a hero's welcome, right? Wrong! We go right to jail. Just do what I told you."

"Well why do we have to split up? Why don't I go with you?"

"If they make me before I get to her, there won't be a fucking thing you can do to help me. You'll just go down with me."

"It's lame."

"That's what you said about every scam I ever laid out."

"I wish I could bet on this one."

"How much?" I said.

"How much you got?"

"After we pay the pilot there's about fifty thousand dollars left in my bag."

"Yeah, but you lose, you ain't gonna be there to pay. And I don't get to see your fucking face."

"You'll manage."

Garza and I, in our ill-fitting tuxedos, joined a wave of people moving up the stairway into the entrance chattering in half a dozen languages. I noticed security agents in tuxedos were everywhere, carrying walkie-talkies or talking into lapel mikes, scanning in every direction but ours. I had shaved Omar Legassi's beard and removed the fake gold caps from my teeth. It was the best I could do.

"See you at Point A," I whispered as we entered the lobby and separated.

Point A was the last of a row of glass doors leading from the La Salle Empire, the room where the award dinner was already under way, to the terrace outside. It was there I would point out Julio and Nadia's bodyguards to Garza. I had to be certain he knew exactly who the cast of players was. There was no margin for error. From that point on we were both on our own until I brought Nadia to the car.

The lobby was a vast, ornately carved marble hall with a giant glass-domed ceiling. Huge crystal chandeliers hung from high ceiling arches. A string quartet played from someplace, lost in the middle of the glitzy crowd.

As I started slowly up a wide stairway toward the mezzanine level, I saw Garza talking to the blonde in the mini dress. *You try to foresee the flaw in every scam, but sometimes you just overlook the obvious.* He saw me and grinned. Just at that moment the woman's escort appeared. Relieved, I continued up the stairs.

On the fourth level, I passed the closed doors of the La Salle Empire, where a group of security men were having a heated conversation about their overtime pay. I strolled by casually. They never even glanced up.

I turned the corner at the end of the hallway and slipped outside the first glass door onto the terrace. The night air was cool and smelled of the ocean. I moved the length of the terrace as quickly as I could, staying just beyond the reach of the lights coming from the banquet hall. I could see clearly inside.

The huge hall was jammed with as many people as it could handle, all seated at large round tables. Gold and crystal chandeliers hung suspended from the high ceiling, casting the vast room in a warm glow. A large wall at the end of the room was a baroque mural depicting naked nymphs and children dancing in a pastoral setting.

The lights suddenly dimmed. A podium on a small stage directly across from me was spotlighted. Next to it stood a large cage. Inside on a perch was a huge harpy eagle. For a moment it opened its wings and the crowd gasped. A patrician-looking white-haired man stepped up to the podium. His voice was muffled through the double-thick glass.

I reached Point A, the last glass door. I was partially shielded from the inside by heavy velvet drapes. If the diagram Paolo had made for me was accurate, through this door I would find the kitchen about twenty feet to my right.

I scanned the crowd for Nadia's table. All I could see was the backs of heads—a whole roomful. The white-haired man was now going on at great length. I checked my watch; it was 9:45 p.m. If this was the awards ceremony, it had begun fifteen minutes early.

A flash of bright light attracted my eye. A door opened at the end of the hall to my left. A thin man with his hair cut in a military brush style entered quickly and moved between the tables. He passed in front of the spotlight and I recognized him. It was Brush Cut, one of Jacques's storm troopers from the night of Shoshanna's murder. He leaned over and spoke to someone seated near the podium. In a moment a tall, angular figure rose to his feet. It was Jacques. The two moved quickly toward the exit.

I should have been alerted that something was up, and that that *something* might be me. But I was totally focused on the spot they had left. Nadia was in there somewhere.

I saw a flash of white and my attention was focused on a table near the podium. A man's ponytail was silhouetted in the spotlight. Suddenly there was a long round of applause. The entire audience rose for a standing ovation. When they finally sat, it was like a curtain dropping.

There on the stage in a white slip sheath was Nadia. She seemed to glow as if she were radioactive. Her green eyes moved across the crowd like a searchlight, for an instant resting on me. She couldn't possibly see me in the darkness but I ducked reflexively, flashing on that day in the courthouse when her eyes had first met mine.

The white-haired man held a large inscribed globe, which I guessed, by its pinkish hue, was pure gold. He was about to hand it to Nadia. She would get another standing ovation and that would be my cue; my only chance to move into the room undetected.

Where the fuck is Garza?

I glanced along the balcony. Not a sign of him. He had a good description of Julio, but could he find him in this crowd?

I pulled out my pen and a packet of blue Post-its and scribbled a rectangle for the podium, a circle for Nadia's table, and finally an arrow pointing at the table. I posted it on the edge of the glass door and prayed.

The applause began. People rose to their feet.

I slipped inside quickly and moved along the edge of the room. At the kitchen door a cluster of cooks and waiters gawked at the podium. I glanced back. Julio was on his feet, the only one not applauding. Nadia smiled down with that special smile she had reserved only for him.

I pushed through the swinging doors into the kitchen, past steaming ovens and piles of dirty dishes, moving casually with the attitude of a security man on a routine check. A couple of the dishwashers looked at me. I nodded, glancing into corners, under counters.

Paolo's map was excellent. The service door was exactly where it was supposed to be. In a moment I was through it and moving quickly through a bare hallway toward a green metal door at the far end, noting the service elevator I would use to bring Nadia down to the car.

I opened the door a crack. Not a sound. I stepped out into a dimly lit hallway feeling soft carpeting beneath my feet. I was facing the beige-and-gold double doors of Nadia's suite. The lock, as Paolo had said, was a conventional wafer-tumbler lock. I could open it with a rake and a tension bar.

Before I could even begin, I heard footsteps behind me.

A large, bald man in a tuxedo, who seemed to fill the hallway, walked toward me quickly. His head was down and at an angle. He watched me through the tops of his eyes like a wary bulldog. He wore a hotel security pin and carried a walkie-talkie.

I smiled and nodded at him, as he came.

"Que faites-vous?" he said when he was about twenty feet from me.

I answered in Spanish. "Security for Señorita Ricord—do you speak Spanish?"

He kept coming. His eyes raked me up and down. He was a confident man. Too confident for his own good. Before he could reach for his gun or radio, I drew the automatic and pushed it into his cheek. He looked beyond it into my eyes. This was a man who had faced guns before.

"You have a gun?"

He nodded, his face expressionless.

I held the heavy French automatic back against my hip with my right hand aimed at his middle. I opened his jacket with my left. He was carrying a Beretta nine-millimeter automatic in an upside-down shoulder holster. I jerked it free and shoved it into my belt. I noticed a ring of keys fastened to his belt on a retractable ring.

I pointed the gun at the walkie-talkie.

"Tell them all is clear. You're taking a break."

He followed my instructions to the letter. After his base station acknowledged his transmission, I took the radio away from him, turned it off and clipped it onto my belt.

"Open the door," I ordered.

He hesitated. He was considering lying about the keys.

I raised the gun to his head. "It's not worth it, my friend."

He opened the door. I followed him inside, my gun pressed to his spine. He was in his late fifties, I guessed. Probably retired police or military. Just a guy doing his job, the way René was, the way I was. I didn't want to hurt him.

We were inside of a large living room area in a darkness relieved only by a shaft of light coming from a bedroom. I could hear water dripping from a small bathroom off to my right. I still had my gun pressed to his spine. He was relaxed. A professional.

"What's your name?" I asked in a low voice, almost a whisper.

His answer was no louder. "Reiu-Sicart. Georges Reiu-Sicart."

"You retired police or military, Georges?"

"*Sûreté.*"

I decided to level with him.

"Georges. I'm a cop, like you. From the U.S. This woman killed one of ours. I'm taking her back. I'm going to tie you up and gag you. If you force me to kill you, I'll feel like shit for the rest of my life—understand?"

"Yes."

The lights suddenly came on, glaring and bright.

"There are guns pointed at you from three directions," said a familiar voice behind me. "Very carefully, lay your gun on the ground."

The barrel of an Uzi with a silencer was aimed at me from inside the bathroom doorway, and just the eye, hand, and a portion of forehead of the man aiming it.

I crouched slowly and laid the gun at my feet. I straightened up right into the path of a ham-hock hand bashing my head like a Ping-Pong slam, delivered by my new friend Georges. I saw white flashes. Both my ears rang. The side of my face began to swell, the eye already half closed.

"I am grateful to you gentlemen," said Georges, turning to meet his rescuers.

Jacques's angular body appeared in the doorway of the bedroom. I could see the bone handle of his Bowie knife and the butt of his automatic. His tiny black eyes moved from me to Georges and back again.

"How nice that you found us, Omar, we've been looking all over for you. By the way—you are standing in a perfect crossfire. I wouldn't move a hair."

"He has my gun and radio," said Georges.

The man with the Uzi stepped out of the bathroom. It was Skinhead, the guy with the platinum eyebrows and Arnold Schwarzenegger's body, Brush Cut's partner.

I felt a gun barrel at the back of my head. Brush Cut frisked me, snatching the gun and radio from my belt.

"Please. May I have them?" said Georges, extending his hand.

"Of course," said Jacques.

His movement was lightning quick. The Bowie knife was out of its sheath and buried in Georges's chest in one fluid thrust. Jacques ended the thrust with a *kiai*—a sharp exhalation of air exploding from the bottom of the gut, timed perfectly with the thrust. Masters of the martial arts say that the *kiai* causes a momentary tightening of the muscles adding as much as ten percent to the power of the thrust.

He danced backward with the grace of a bullfighter, leaving the blade buried to the hilt.

Georges stood gaping at the handle protruding from his chest. No blood came from the wound. His body suddenly went ragdoll, crumpling first onto his butt, then flopping backward.

"You know a little about karate—perfect technique, no?" said Jacques mockingly. He moved around me, keeping his distance. "Not a drop of blood. His heart stops before the brain. I even gave him a moment to consider his mistakes."

I studied Jacques. I saw my own death in his eyes. My mind flitted, like a frightened fly, from thought to thought. René. Shoshanna. Garza. Paolo. Cousin Avi. My son Keith. I tried to think of something to say, a bluff, a con. I was out of material. Out of time.

Jacques circled, coming to a stop in front of me, keeping about two paces between us, his hand on the butt of his automatic.

"In a few minutes the authorities will find you and our surprised-looking friend here, dead. The local police will have an easy case. A crazed American undercover agent, a black belt, hunted by his own government, breaks into the hotel room of a wealthy woman, where he is followed by the chief of hotel security. The desperate American stabs the security man, but he is able to fire a bullet as he dies. *Voilà!* What a tragedy."

"Too clever for you," I said. "You're nothing but one of Nadia's dogs."

He launched himself, spinning in the air. The wheel kick caught me high on the cheekbone. He was quick, but not that quick. I saw it coming and could have blocked it, but this was no *kumite* match. I let the sole of his shoe connect, rolled my head with it, and went down like I was hit by a truck.

I felt wetness beneath the bandages. The dive had opened my stitches. I lay there and groaned for a moment, looking at three pairs of black patent leather shoes surrounding me. Blood trickled from my cheek onto the pink-and-gray diamond-patterned carpet.

"You're fucking up, Jock-O," I said, struggling to a sitting position. "Bruises and cuts on my face? I stab him, and he shoots me? The police won't believe any of it."

Jacques looked down at me as if I was a turkey he was getting ready to carve for Thanksgiving. His two storm troopers were by his side, smiling.

"The words of a man afraid to die," said Skinhead.

I met his gaze with my good eye; my left eye was almost swollen shut. I had spent my whole life preparing for this moment. Fighting for your life stood you a better chance of survival than begging for it.

Enrage your opponent, were Sensei's words. If he loses his temper, he loses control.

"You're going to kill me?" I heard myself say. "I thought that you guys only killed unarmed women and old men, when you weren't fucking Nadia's monkeys."

Skinhead raised his right foot to kick me, for an instant balanced only on his left. I snapped a round kick off with my good left knee, the aluminum toe of my boot driving into the soft bones of his ankle. I felt it crunch.

He dropped to the ground with a crash. His head bounced. I ducked under the swinging butt of an Uzi and snapped a *sokuto geri*—sword foot—into Skinhead's face, driving the knife edge of my boot into his nose extending the kick a foot beyond his head. Blood exploded everywhere.

I scrambled on the ground, focused on Skinhead's Uzi laying beside him. I had it in my hand and was rolling over when my head exploded with a blinding, painful flash and everything fell into darkness.

———

"Very clever, Jacques," said a soft, familiar voice. "How are you going to explain this lovely mess to the police?"

I opened my eyes. Nadia was just a few feet from me. I closed them again. *Shit!* My jaw felt stiff and sore; probably broken. I couldn't move. My hands had been tied tightly behind me and my legs were bound together.

"We'll put some bruises on the Frenchman," said Jacques. "It will look like they fought."

"There's only one problem with that, my little genius," she fumed. "One does not bruise after death. And what about him?" she said, indicating Skinhead, who was sprawled on the couch holding a bloody towel to his face. His Uzi was on the floor at his feet.

"His nose and ankle are broken," said Jacques.

"He must be out of here before we call security. All his blood cleaned up."

"Of course!"

"There's no time," she snapped. "This one is already dead too long."

I opened my good eye.

"Nadia Ricord," I said. "I am placing you under arrest for the murder of DEA agent René Villarino."

Nadia just stared at me. Then she laughed in disbelief.

"I'm so glad you are awake, Omar, or whatever your name is."

"I just wanted to make it official," I said. "It's been a long trip."

Her smile vanished. "You know, I didn't enjoy killing Fabrizio—oh I forgot, his name was René—but killing you will be a pleasure. Get Omar on his feet."

I felt powerful hands grip me beneath my arms and lift me to a standing position.

"Stand him exactly where you were when you stabbed the other one," she ordered. "At least the ballistics must be precise."

I was dragged a few feet and held upright. Jacques moved directly in front of me with Nadia, leaving Brush Cut beside me. He had the cop's Beretta in his hand.

"Now, Jacques!"

I heard the door creak open.

Garza. Thank you God.

I felt Brush Cut grip my arm and the back of my shirt.

"Let me do it," said a voice.

I turned to see Julio entering the room, moving toward Jacques. The jacket of his tux flapped open, his blazing white shirt was open at the collar.

"Where did you disappear to, Julio?" said Nadia.

"He betrayed me," he said, holding his hand out for the gun. His face was flushed. His chest was heaving mightily. "This motherfucker made me think he was my friend to get to you, Mother. He used me. Give it to me, Jacques!"

"He doesn't even know how to use a gun," protested Jacques.

"See, Jacques doubts that I have what it takes to be your son. They all doubt it."

"Go ahead and give him the gun," said Nadia.

"Are you ready to live up to your bullshit, Omar? The way of the warrior?" said Julio, facing me, trembling with fury.

"The safety is still on," laughed Jacques, handing Julio the gun.

"This?" said Julio, feeling for the safety lever with his thumb.

"Exactly," said Nadia, whose green eyes fastened on mine. "Aim for the middle of his chest."

Julio aimed the gun at me.

"Make sure you hit the heart, not the ceiling," laughed Jacques. "The heart is in the middle of his chest."

"Like this, Jacques?" he said, turning and firing the gun point-blank into Jacques's ear. His head burst like a watermelon.

"Julio!" screamed Nadia.

I slammed my forehead into the side of Brush Cut's face as he turned his gun on Julio. Brush Cut went down, the silenced Uzi firing wildly, *pfft-pfft-pfft*. Bullets exploded plaster and glass, and ricocheted wildly around the room.

Julio fired again, hitting Nadia above the hip. Her white dress blossomed red. She sat down on the ground, staring up at him as if seeing a ghost.

Skinhead, screaming like a stuck pig, had dropped his bloody towel and was raising the Uzi.

"Julio, behind you!" I screamed.

The door exploded open and Garza dove through. For a moment he seemed to hang suspended in midair, the whites of his eyes shining and focused. The gun bucked in his hand, flame leapt from the barrel. Skinhead's head snapped back with the impact; he tumbled backward over the couch, his hands reaching for the pulpy mass that had been his face.

Brush Cut on the ground beside me tried to raise his gun again. Garza, rolling on the ground, fired three more rapid shots. I heard the impacts on Brush Cut's chest, *thump, thump, thump*. He sighed and laid his head down on his arm as if going to sleep.

Julio stood over Nadia, his gun pointed down at her. She stared up into his eyes. I noticed the gold of his father's medallion against his chest.

"Drop it, kid!" shouted Garza.

"Why, my precious son?" she breathed.

Tears welled in Julio's eyes. "I'm not your son."

"Julio, *no!*" I shouted.

He fired. A bullet tore into her other hip. "This is for my real mother and father." He fired again. Her shoulder blossomed red and she moaned, but her eyes stared up at him unblinking.

"For my brothers and sisters that you killed while they slept in their beds. For every time you put your filthy hands on me." He fired twice. *Blam! Blam!* The middle of her chest bounced with the impacts. Her body arched and then relaxed. Her eyes remained open.

I watched the startling green irises of a bird of prey turn flat and opaque.

Nadia Ricord was no more.

46

EPILOGUE

THE YEAR THAT FOLLOWED "THE NIGHT WE HIT THE JACKPOT AT MONTE Carlo," as Garza would call it, turned out as unexpected and unprecedented as a truthful politician. It was the year I learned how to barter my silence.

It was the year that would seal shut the true events surrounding the murders of René Villarino, a Mossad agent whom I only knew as Shoshanna, and ten DEA agents who died at Iguazú, along with the existence of a drug that could send civilization as we know it into extinction. It was a year that would end with DEA's sending me on my final deep cover assignment, Operation Trifecta, the case that would push me over the line and into breaking my silence with my first book, *Deep Cover*, and into vowing that before I died, I would tell everything I knew.

Armed soldiers had surrounded our plane the moment we landed in Tel Aviv. An Israeli army colonel informed us that the United States had issued international arrest warrants for both me and Garza. We were fugitives from justice. We were to be transferred to a TWA flight going to New York. We would not be allowed anything that even resembled an officially sanctioned entry into Israel, and therefore—with the exception of the French bank's pilot, who was removed for questioning—we would be confined in the plane that we had arrived in. I was not even allowed to make a phone call.

Two soldiers were posted on the plane with us but were prohibited from speaking to us. We were fed and doctors were sent to attend my wounds. My cousin's name meant nothing to anyone, nor did any of the other names I mentioned.

Julio, who had tried to commit suicide on the way out of the hotel (we had to wrestle the gun out of his hand), had not spoken a word since killing Nadia. He sat in the rear seat and stared at his hands. I was worried that his next attempt would be successful.

Garza, who had been chattering away for most of the flight about the *mamitas* in Israel and the *mamitas* he would meet in Hollywood once we had sold the movie rights to the case, stared at me with disbelief after the colonel left us.

"Some *jodienda* plan this was, Levine," he said. "You got me to jump out of the fucking plane with you, only you forgot our parachutes."

It was after midnight of our first day of Israeli captivity that a familiar figure appeared in the doorway. It was The Bear, the Mossad deep cover agent whose real name I never knew. He hugged me warmly and then got right to the point.

Israel was going to deny all official knowledge of me. If the U.S. government could prove that any Israelis helped me, the Israeli government would prosecute them for corruption, implying that I had bribed them; which meant that by my trying to involve the Israeli government in what The Bear called American business, I would expose my cousin to arrest and a long prison sentence.

"Why?" I asked.

"It seems," he began, his wide bearded face cracking to a wry smile, "that a military operation has occurred in the Paraguayan jungle. Two hundred kilos of a certain drug, a certain German doctor who created it, and all his research papers have all apparently perished in a very powerful explosion.

"Your government, for reasons we cannot fathom—along with the Paraguayan government—have filed a protest with my government. They seem to think our little country had something to do with an illegal military incursion into Paraguayan territories, and damages to a U.S.-funded wildlife refuge. Of course, we have denied any knowledge whatsoever of this event."

"Of course," I agreed. "And, I suppose, it would be dumb of me to even ask for the tapes I gave you."

He shrugged, wagging his head apologetically.

"And suppose I go to the media with the story anyway?" I said.

The Bear looked uncomfortable. "It could backfire on you, my friend. There is already one American Jew spending his life in jail, charged with spying for us. We wouldn't want another Jonathan Pollard."

I looked around the plane. Julio sat on the floor at the rear, his head between his knees. Garza was bundled on the floor in a sleeping bag the Israeli army had supplied. I realized that The Bear hadn't come to me out of courtesy, love, or brotherhood. Spies just don't think that way. They wanted something and the only thing I had to offer was my silence.

"Are you open for a deal or is that Israel's final position?"

"I can tell certain people what you have to say."

My deal was simple, it was as much as I thought I could get. Israel was the only place in the world that had more doctors and psychiatrists per square yard than Manhattan. If Israel would grant asylum and treatment to Julio, I'd keep my mouth shut about them.

Just before dawn Julio was taken off the plane. I gave The Bear my final $50,000. Forty thousand was to go for Julio's care, five thousand was to go to a certain priest in a jungle hamlet near Puerto Iguazú, and five thousand was to go to the World Wildlife Fund.

Julio ended up marrying an Israeli girl. He is now in his last year of studies for a Ph.D. in Jungian psychology in Zurich. I see them whenever I can, although as the years pass I think he is growing more and more uncomfortable with me. He's moved on and I'm a reminder of things he'd rather forget.

Paolo, René's brother, went back to Corsica and married Marita Salazar. They own a small cabaret in Calvi and write me from time to time.

———

Garza and I were handcuffed and escorted by four Israeli policemen to a TWA 747 jumbo jet, for our final First Class ride together. The Israelis were excited, it would be the first trip to the U.S. for them. All they wanted to talk about was Disneyland and the Hard Rock Café.

On the plane Garza and his two escorts were seated in the first three center seats of First Class; we were right behind. The flight attendant gave out newspapers and magazines. I was feeling no fear of flying, but in no mood to read. It was another one of those times when I was certain that the plane would be just fine.

The Big Guy simply doesn't zap you when you're this miserable.

Garza suddenly bopped me on the head from behind and thrust a newspaper over the seat at me.

"What's that?"

"Just fucking read!"

It was a day-old *Herald Tribune.* A small story on the front page began with the headline MEDELLÍN CARTEL CHIEF FOUND DEAD IN JAIL CELL. My hands shook as I read the report that began:

> Felix Restrepo, Medellín cartel terror chief, better known as *El Búfalo,* the man reputed to be the real power behind big name cartel chiefs like Pablo Escobar, Carlos Lehder, and Jorge Ochoa, and the man who ordered the torture death of under-cover DEA agent René Villarino, was found dead this morning in his top-security jail cell in Atlanta Federal Penitentiary, where he was awaiting trial. Preliminary tests indicate that he died of cardiac arrest . . .

The plane began to taxi. I put the paper down, unable to read any more.

"We are fucking dead," hissed Garza.

———

In Washington, D.C., Internal Security inspectors took us into custody. We were brought to their headquarters, the tenth floor of an ancient office building on 13th and K streets, and separated.

It didn't take much of an interrogation to get a story out of me. I told them everything that had happened, leaving out the Israeli part of the deal as I had promised. An accord must have been reached between the two governments, because I was not questioned about what should have been a glaring fluff job. At least that's the only logical explanation.

When my interrogators wanted to know what evidence I had, I noted the tension in the room. I directed them to a closet in my home in Buenos Aires, where I had stored copies of Forrest Gregg's tape-recorded confession and suicide.

I guess I wasn't really surprised when they told me they already had them. They wanted to know if I had any other copies.

"Sure," I said, "but you're not getting them."

They didn't seem very surprised by my answer either.

I knew I had a chance to survive when, after twenty-four hours of interrogation, Garza, Vinnie O'Brien, Georgie, and I were put in an Alexandria, Virginia, motel instead of jail to await DEA's, and our government's, decision on how to handle us, and not a word was mentioned in the media. Our pay never stopped coming and we were allowed to call our families, as long as we did not discuss the case.

It all ended on a cold March day in Bobby Stratton's office. I was the last to arrive. Garza, Georgie, and Vinnie were already there in suits and ties, sitting opposite his desk looking like high school kids who'd been caught vandalizing the school. Enter the ringleader, the guy who got them jammed up, so we could all hear the verdict together.

"Sit," ordered Stratton, sliding a cable across the desk to me.

It had a red jacket clipped to it that said TOP SECRET. I picked it up and took a seat alongside Vinnie O'Brien. I noticed the others were holding copies of the same cable. I'd seen it before. It was the NIACT IMMEDIATE cable about *La Reina Blanca*, sent back in December.

"For starters," said Stratton, "the four of you violated national security and the Classified Documents Act by spilling that cable to a foreign power."

Garza flushed and slumped back in his seat.

"The cable's just starters," continued Stratton. "You all violated every DEA reg in the book—overseas without headquarters permission, undercover without written authorization, misuse and unauthorized use of government funds and equipment, illegal arrests without authority. Then there's accessory to homicide, and a few dozen others that ain't gonna take too much creativity to tack on . . ." He peered around at all of us.

"So we're criminals," I said.

"Yeah, you're criminals. If it were up to me I'd give the four of you fucking medals—but it's not up to me. Let's get this straight. I'm not here to hurt you bastards. I don't even wanna be here. But I'm glad I am."

He looked directly at me. I saw his pain, and felt a terrible premonition of things to come. I looked out the window.

"Listen up, Levine. You got a chance to slide, to walk out of here with your jobs intact. You're luckier than you know. Right now, the CIA's reeling from bad press. Your big mouth got you into this, it just might get you out. They're leery of handling you and that Forrest Gregg tape recording—but don't push your luck."

Stratton went on at length about there being nothing left to prove; that everyone who had anything to do with René's death was dead; that *La Reina Blanca* had been destroyed and that by trying to embarrass the government with Gregg's tape recording I'd only be hurting myself and Gregg's family, and, of course, destroying the careers of Vinnie, Georgie, and Garza.

As he spoke my attention wandered out the window to the filthy gray little park across the street. A two-block square patch of dying trees, rotting benches, and campsites for the homeless.

A crackhead lurked by a tree. You can't miss these guys. The desperation in their eyes glows like a cat's when its trapped in headlights; their movements are jumpy, quick, erratic. He was either waiting to cop dope or to take someone off. I find crackheads fascinating to watch. Like a glimpse of the end of the world.

"You listening to me?" snapped Stratton.

"I heard every word," I said. "What do they want?"

"You each sign a nondisclosure agreement; that the events of the Villarino–*La Reina Blanca* investigation are top secret; that you recognize that their disclosure could be damaging to the nation's security, and that you will never reveal those events, under penalty requirements set down in the secrecy acts."

"That's it? That's fucking it?" said Garza.

"You're back in the real world," said Stratton. "DEA's version of it."

"I go back to Argentina?" I asked, watching a man in a black leather coat approaching the crackhead warily.

"No way," said Stratton. "You go from here to a desk job in New York."

The drug deal in the park went down almost invisibly; drugs and money changed hands with a speed and sleight-of-hand that would have made Harry Houdini envious. *The end of the world.*

I looked at Stratton and the others. "And if I don't sign?"

"All four of you sign, or no deal. You walk outta here without a job. Within a week you're indicted for everything they can think of. Do your worst. Them's not my words, but you can bank 'em."

"Hey, yo, Levine . . ." said Vinnie, pale and visibly shaken.

"Come on, *ese,* this ain't no game," said Georgie. "I got a family."

"You don't fucking sign," said Garza, the veins in his forehead popping, "this time I'll kill you, you motherfucker. I swear on the Virgin."

"Shut the fuck up!" said Stratton.

"I gotta say what I gotta say," said Garza. "Muthafuckin' Levine, you owe me!"

All four stared at me.

"Where do I sign?" I said.

Garza was right. I did owe him. It's one thing to send yourself down the tubes, it's another to drag along people who tried to help you.

Vinnie and Georgie smiled slowly.

"You my bro', man," said Vinnie.

Stratton shoved a document across the desk at me. I found the dotted line, signed my name slowly and clearly, dated it, and handed it across to him.

It was quiet as the others signed. Then we all sat there staring at each other for a long time without saying a word.

I guess the closest way to describe how I felt at that moment was that it was as if I had just fought ten bloody, bruising rounds with a son of a bitch I hated enough to beat up his grandma, and the judges ruled it a draw. All I'd proved was that I could survive.

But I did get my breakfast.

I got to my feet. I had nothing else to say and I wanted to see my kids. I started for the door.

"No hard feelings, GI," said Stratton.

"Fuck no," I said, opening the door. "That paper didn't say anything about writing fiction did it?"

GLOSSARY

Agency, the	CIA
ASAC	Assistant Special Agent in Charge
asshole	anyone not a DEA agent
basuca	(Sp.) cocaine base; the raw material used to make cocaine (base), which is sometimes smoked like crack, having a similar effect
basuquero	someone addicted to smoking cocaine base
batfuckers	Bureau of Alcohol Tobacco and Firearms
BNDD	Bureau of Narcotics and Dangerous Drugs
bug	a hidden microphone
burn	to be recognized as an undercover agent or surveillance agent
burnbag	bag used to store classified material before destroyed by burning; an extremely ugly woman
buttonman	Mafia soldier
buy/bust	an undercover operation wherein the undercover agent baits a drug dealer into making a sale, during which he or she is arrested
CA	Country Attaché, DEA's chief officer at foreign posts
cabrón	(Sp.) schmuck

capo	(Ital.) Mafia supervisory position
chiflado	(Sp.) crazy
chingado	(Sp.) all verb, noun, adverb, and adjective forms of *fuck*
chota	(Sp.) stool pigeon, informant
chupasangre	(Sp.) bloodsucker
CI	confidential informant
CIA	Central Intelligence Agency, or (in halls of DEA) Cocaine Import Agency
cojones	(Sp.) balls, guts, courage
come-mierda	(Sp.) shit-eater, interchangeable with *asshole*
Company, the	the CIA
contract	assassination order, or an offer of money for a murder
CONUS	continental U.S.
cover	undercover identity or role; surveil; act as bodyguard or backup
crackhead	a crack addict
cut	dilute; or substance used to dilute drugs
dando y dando	(Sp.) cash on delivery
DCI	Director of Central Intelligence
DEA	Drug Enforcement Administration, or (in halls of both CIA and DEA) Don't Expect Anything
deep cover	the adopting of a complete new identity over an extended period of time and cutting all official ties to the government or agency that employs you
desaparecido	(Sp.) disappeared, dead
DIA	Defense Intelligence Agency
dinky-dau	crazy (Vietnam)
do	kill, screw, mess up
FBN	Federal Bureau of Narcotics
Five Families	Italian organized crime in the U.S. is believed by law enforcement authorities to be dominated by five Mafia families
flash	the act of the undercover agent showing money as a means of enticement
flash roll	a large amount of cash used as bait

FLEOA	Federal Law Enforcement Officers' Association
flip	turn a criminal into an informant
Glock	Austrian-made 9mm semiautomatic pistol, made primarily of hard plastic; favored weapon of DEA agents
G/S	DEA group supervisor
GTR	Government Travel Request
hand-to-hand	an undercover purchase of drugs
hinky	suspicious
HQ	headquarters
HQCO	"cablese" for Headquarters Coordinating Officer
IMMEDIATE	"cablese" for "Immediate action *must* be taken by addressee of cable"
In sha' Allah	(Arab.) If God is willing, so be it, maybe, perhaps, etc.
in-the-wind	fled; became a fugitive
jammed up	in trouble
jodienda	(Sp.) a complete fucking mess
Judío	(Sp.) Jew
kata	(Jap.) dancelike martial arts training forms
key	kilo
kilo	2.2 pounds
knock-off	a raid or an arrest
kumite	(Jap.) karate, controlled sparring match
lapel mike	tiny walkie-talkie disguised as a lapel pin, used by undercover agents for close-in surveillance
made/make	recognized someone as an undercover agent; observed surveillance
mae geri	(Jap.) karate front kick
maricón	(Sp.) homosexual
milico	Argentine slang for military or police
MK-DELTA; MK-SEARCH; MK-ULTRA	Secret CIA programs to develop mind control drugs
monguín	Cuban slang for "he who can't raise it"—an impotent man

moolinyam; yam	Italian for eggplant, used on the street as pejorative for blacks
mule	drug or money courier used for smuggling. In South America prostitutes are commonly used
mutt	species of human having one or more ancestors who barked and howled at the moon
NADDIS	Narcotics and Dangerous Drugs Information System
NARCOR	State Department Narcotics Coordinator
NIACT	"cablese" for Night Action. Recipient of cable at foreign embassy—teletype operator or Marine duty officer—must awaken addressee of cable at any hour received
NOFORN	"cablese" for "No foreign eyes are to see contents of cable." This includes non–U.S. citizen clerical help, foreign police, and/ or Intelligence counterparts. Generally sold by disaffected CIA agents at garage sales
NSA	National Security Agency
NWG	nerd with gun; CIA agent
OD	overdose
off	kill
OG	official government, as in OGF "official government funds," etc.
OP	observation post
Operation Phoenix	Vietnam operation whereby U.S. snipers were sent into Cambodia to off village leaders designated as "communist sympathizers" by Harvard graduate CIA agents
Operation Springboard	DEA designation for operation that was alleged to have destroyed August Ricord and the Triangle of Death in 1970s.
OZ	ounce
P and G	pack and go
pa'carajo	(Sp.) go to hell
pendejo	(Sp.) schmuck, (Yid.) putz

PIO	Public Information Officer
POL R	CIA foreign station designator
RAC	Resident Agent in Charge; medieval torture device
rat	informer
ripoff, rip	a robbery of any kind; also a raid or an arrest
rubber-gun squad	where DEA puts its bed wetters, misfits, and psychos before loosing them on the general public
SAC	Special Agent in Charge
SCPD	Scientific and Psychological Division
script	description
seiken	(Jap.) karate two-knuckle front punch
sensei	(Jap.) teacher
set, the set	the place where an undercover scenario takes place
shoofly	Internal Affairs investigator
skate	get away with something
sokuto geri	(Jap.) karate, sword-foot kick, or side kick using knife edge of foot
spook	CIA agent
stool	stool pigeon, informant
suit	law enforcement management or administrative type
SWAT	Special Weapons Assault Team
ten-eight	radio code indicating "on duty"
ten-one-thousand	radio code indicating "agent/officer in trouble, needs assistance"
ten-seven	radio code for "going off duty," also used to indicate death
ten-twenty	radio code for "What is your location?"
throwaway	an extra weapon carried by corrupt law enforcement officers, to be used to plant on dead body to justify a shooting
twenty	location
TOP SECRET	security classification used *only* on matters affecting U.S. national security

Triangle of Death	a criminal organization begun by Auguste Ricord, thought destroyed during the Nixon administration. Its name was derived from the number of murders it was believed to be involved in on three continents
UC	undercover
UC bit	an undercover role
UC buy	an undercover purchase of drugs
UC phone	an unregistered, untraceable undercover phone, usually in a DEA office or in a front business
uncle	radio code for "undercover agent," or "undercover," or your mother's brother
undercover	assuming another identity or pose for any length of time
War Room	the planning and strategy room at DEA headquarters
wired	wearing a concealed microphone; stoned on stimulants
yoko geri	(Jap.) karate roundhouse kick
zee; zee it out	ounce; sell drugs an ounce at a time